Death of an Officer's Lady

by

Lexie Conyngham

A Murray of Letho Mystery

Lexie Conyngham

First published in 2015 by The Kellas Cat Press, Aberdeen.

Copyright Alexandra Conyngham, 2015

The right of the author to be identified as the author of this work as been asserted by her in accordance with the Copyright, Designs and Patent Act, 1988.

ISBN: 9780993192777

Cover design by ellieillustrates.co.uk

DEDICATION

To the staff of the National War Museum of Scotland, Edinburgh Castle – it was a fantastic job to have, and the best view from a ladies' loo anywhere in the Civil Service!

Dramatis Personae

At Letho
Charles Murray of Letho
Lady Agostinella Murray
Henry Robbins, butler
Mrs. Mack, cook
Walter Fenwick, a very junior servant

In Edinburgh and its environs
Alicia Argo and her son, awaiting the return of her husband from Belgium
Sangster, a master baker
Mrs. Sangster, his wife
Findlay, a watchmaker, and his family
Willie Jack Dundas, old friend of Charles Murray
Letitia, his wife, who has at her disposal an aunt and uncle, the latter of diminutive stature
Mrs. Brotherstone, a caring neighbour
Bessie Cordiner, a neighbour who cares for some things
Mr. Malcolm, a neighbour who cares mostly for interesting corpses
William Campbell, furnished lodgings keeper
Matt Chisholm, the same
Eppy, approximately the same, with her family
Miss Smillie, kept in a furnished lodging
Lauder and Jemima, servants
Johnnie Norrie, lately a quarryman
Ebb, also involved in quarrying
Mrs. and Miss Brown, a couple of weighty characters
Sergeant George Home, a police officer
Sergeant Clyne, likewise, and newly promoted

In Brussels
George Murray, brother of Charles
Lieutenant James Argo, fairly new to the soldiery game
General Fry, his wife and mother-in-law
Esther Fry

Carolina Fry

Sir Alexander Gordon, aide-de-camp to His Grace the Duke of Wellington (and like His Grace, an historical figure)

Major Saddler

Captain Gunn

Sergeant Lamb

Private Farrie, George's batman

Private Liddell, a soldier with a healthy appetite

James Graham, a drummer boy with a limited sense of rhythm but a good running pace

Chapter One

I

Edinburgh

She was careful to leave the rent money for the landlord: she did not want anyone to think she had flitted because she could not pay. The candle flame swerved and plunged as she spun quickly in the empty room, making sure that the money was all that was left. No trace: good. No way of following her.

She snipped out the candle with a pinch, pulled her shawl over her bonnet and hauled one of their bundles under her arm.

'Let's go,' she whispered.

They never made a sound on the stone stair. But as they vanished through the street door into the night, one of the flat doors they had passed opened silently. There was a breath a little like a laugh, but she was too far away to hear it.

II

Belgium

'We should never have stuck him on Elba: we should have locked him in the Tower of London and thrown away the key.'

'Ken what he was doing on Elba? He raised an army and a navy. What kind of exile's that?'

'Och, the wee mannie canna help himself. Put him in a nunnery and he'd raise three regiments.'

'That's what I mean. Tower of London, that's what I say.'

'Now, the only way to stop the likes of him is that guillotine thing they had in the Revolution. Best way to deal wi' a Frenchie with notions.'

George Murray turned away to hide a grin as he passed the soldiers. They had found an edge of grass to make themselves a little teashop, with a fire, a saucepan, and tin cups, though the tea smelled as if it had been used a few too many times. He did not expect them to salute: there were far too many officers on the streets of Brussels at present for all to be recognised, and the soldiers had a way of building a little room for themselves out of no walls and barely a ceiling, as if they were cut off from the people passing by.

Besides, he was inclined to agree with them about Napoleon Bonaparte. Elba was no safe prison for a man like that, and now he was out and in Paris and raising who knew what force against them. Well, Wellington would know. Wellington had brought them here, to overfill Brussels with red coats and bonnets and kilts and boots, shakoes and rifles and bayonets on every corner. Wellington in his grand house on the Park, and the French Royal family in their chateau, and every soldier in uniform, all on tenterhooks to hear the first movement from Paris. Would he fight or would he run, the little Corsican? Or would he stay in Paris and bluff, luring Wellington ever further south, through the part of France least friendly to the Allies, nibbling away at his army until the final confrontation on the Seine?

Well, it was no immediate concern to George: he was off to meet a fellow officer in a coffee house for the latest gossip and a bowl of fine soup. There was no harm being quartered in a civilised place and taking a rest before the final confrontation with Bonaparte. It had to be the final confrontation, for Wellington had had enough of his boldness, and where Wellington led, George would cheerfully follow.

III

Letho, Fife

If he squinted up at the sky through the May-green branches, listening to the birdsong, he could almost believe that everything was all right with the world.

And it was, here and now: the air was mild, though it had been chilly; his horse mumbled contentedly at the grass under the tree; the dogs lay and panted, pretending to be restful. No one, as far as he knew, was around: no one would notice that their dignified laird and master, all of thirty-two years old and highly respectable, was lounging on his back up a tree, contemplating the emptiness of the Fife sky and scuffing his boots on the branch above his long legs.

'Mr. Murray, sir?'

The voice, when it came, was sudden enough to cause a painful shock – painful because of his position on the branch. Sharp points he had been carefully avoiding jabbed his legs and back. His hat, cradled on his chest, tumbled to the ground. Otherwise, the voice was unalarming: stolid, a little cautious, not quite sure yet if it were intending tenor or bass.

Charles Murray of Letho wriggled round so that he could look at the ground instead of the sky, and blinked to rid his eyes of the bright images of leaves.

'Who's there?'

'Um …'

'Come along, speak up! Who is it?' He felt himself start to slither on the powdery lichen of the branch, scrambled for purchase and then jumped. His cuff caught and ripped just before he hit the ground, but he was otherwise quite pleased with his landing – upright, at least. He brushed some of the green dust off his differently green coat, picked up his hat, and looked around. A boy of about eleven was regarding him solemnly.

'Walter,' said Murray with a sigh. 'What are you doing here?'

'I'm taking a basket to my grandpa, sir,' said Walter, his hands clasped seriously behind his back, a servant in the making. Anyone less likely to laugh at his master falling out of a tree would be hard to find, certainly amongst eleven-year-old boys.

'This is hardly the most direct path between the kitchens and your grandfather's cottage, Walter,' said Murray, attempting to resume some dignity. 'And besides, where is the basket?'

'That would be the problem, sir. You see, I've lost it.'

'Lost it?'

'I set it down somewhere – it was *somewhere*, sir,' he emphasised, as though baskets were prone to slipping out of reality, 'and now it's away.'

'You think someone stole it?' A basketful of Mrs. Mack's cooking would certainly be worth stealing, but Murray was surprised that someone would have been bold enough in broad daylight so near the path.

'Ah, no, sir, I wouldn't go so far as to say that.' Walter's brow wrinkled, though it was a little hard to see: his shining brown hair sat round on his head as if someone had clapped him into a ripe horse chestnut. 'It's more a matter of me forgetting where I was when I set it down.'

'I see. And do you remember if you were on this path at all?'

'Do you know, I don't think I was, sir?' Walter looked pleasantly surprised at this revelation.

'Well, then, I doubt the basket is, either. They don't tend to move of their own volition. Here,' said Murray, untying his horse as the dogs sprang to their feet, 'let us go to the path near your grandfather's cottage, through here, and work our way back.'

Walter was reunited with his uninjured basket, concealed in long grass, in a matter of ten minutes or so. He gently removed one or two adventurous snails from its sides, and set off to his grandfather's cottage – Mr. Fenwick had been the butler at Letho for many years and merited supplies from the kitchens. Murray, with a sigh, pulled himself up on to his horse, and set it to meander, not too fast, back to Letho House. He knew he sighed far too much these days.

His manservant, Robbins, met him in the hall, and was too well-trained to comment on the state of his coat.

'A letter for you, sir,' he said with a slight bow. Since they had returned from India Robbins had resumed a little of the distance between man and master that they had lost abroad.

'Thank you, Robbins. Where is my wife?'

'Lady Agostinella is in her parlour, sir.'

'I'll be in the library.'

'Sir.'

Safe at his desk in the library, Murray pushed aside an advertisement for Aberdeenshire turnip seeds and a copy of the *Edinburgh Quarterly*, and looked at the letter with pleasure. It was from his brother George, an officer in the Royal Scots. Murray knew they were currently in Belgium, waiting to see whether the British Government would opt for peace or war. The latter seemed all too necessary.

Brussels,
12th. May, 1815

My Dear Brother,

As you can see we're still in Brussels, which is no bad thing as you know I like the city. I'm not sure I should like it so much in the ordinary way but it is so full of soldiery that there is a pleasant hum about the place and it is busy and business-like, and nearly everyone speaks English. On an ordinary day when war is not expected at every turn, it is a city probably much more to your liking than to mine – old buildings, and parks, and so on.

As to the war there is little news. Bonaparte is still in Paris, unless he has left in the last few days. We hear that Murat is in a bad way, and losing battles left, right and centre, and also that support for the Bourbons is growing. We're mostly all here, though Blucher's headquarters is at Namur and Wellington's is at Mons, much nearer the French border, though Namur was held by the French for years. Mind you, Brussels has been going back and forth between the French and the Austrians for long enough. How anyone can live in such a place where the very country you belong to changes from week to week, it seems, is beyond me!

Now, here is a reason for writing: I am to ask you a favour. Only if it suits your turn of mind, though, for I thought it might be something that would be of interest to you if you are still in Edinburgh. If you have already gone to Letho and this catches up with you there, then no matter – it is likely to be nothing.

I have a junior officer with me at the moment, a Lieutenant James Argo, a nice fellow and a little in need of looking after. Just lately he has been more anxious than usual, and I find that though he has been writing constantly to his wife in Edinburgh, he has had no reply for some weeks. Well, you know what the post is like at present, with everything going through Mons – trust Wellington to have it arranged efficiently, but it must needs take time.

Anyway, the wife, Alicia Argo (there cannot be too many of them!) lives in Potterrow, and I said I would ask if you would pop round and see if she is well and safe, or Argo will not be fit to fight for worry. Though perhaps she has abandoned him, and that would not be good news either – he seems greatly attached to her.

I shall write again, no doubt, before we leave Brussels. My best regards to the Lady Agostinella and to all who know me.

Your loving brother,
George

Murray smiled at George's delight in living in a Brussels crowded with soldiers, then frowned at the little mystery he had outlined. There were so many possible reasons, ordinary and extraordinary, for a wife not to seem to respond to her husband's letters. Letters were chancy things at the best of times: this one had travelled some distance to reach him, after all. His Queen Street house in Edinburgh was closed up for the moment, so Patie, the groom next door, must have collected the letter from the carrier and sent it on up to Fife. It would only have added a couple of days to its journey, assuming that Patie had not tried to open it first, for Patie was a martyr to voracious curiosity.

Well, he was no longer in Edinburgh, and had indeed gone to Letho for the summer. There was a great deal to do on the estate at this time of year, and after his long absence in India he felt the need to put work in, to reconnect with the state of the majestic black cattle and the experimental Cotswold sheep on his pastures, to speak to the tenants about their farms, to see the stages of crop rotation on the improved lands and in the heavy clay fields where the soil was harder to work. More to the point, he wanted to stretch his legs and stride over fields and through the loose little woodlands of Fife, to ride in the fresh air and feel the good earth under his horse's hooves, and not to see any metropolis mightier than Cupar or St. Andrews. The mere thought of Edinburgh in the summer, crowded and stinking and hot, was enough to make him feel that Lieutenant Argo's absent wife could fend for herself.

The Potterrow … the street was off Nicolson Street, in the Old Town, an area inhabited mostly by merchants and the better kind of tradesmen. His friends the Armstrongs lived nearby: it would be pleasant to see them if they were not away. But where would he stay? The Queen Street house was large, too large to open just for him and a servant or two for a few days. His dearest friends, the Blairs, who would readily have put him up for as long as he liked, were visiting family in Sussex as they usually did in the summer. There was no question of Agostinella coming with him: she had made it clear that Edinburgh held no interest for her. No, it was altogether too awkward: there was no point in going to Edinburgh.

He rang for Robbins.

'Yes, sir?'

'My brother George has sent me a little mystery to look into, but it is in Edinburgh.'

'Is it urgent, sir?' Robbins' pale, hooded eyes took on a wary expression: he had his own reasons for wanting to stay in Letho just now.

'I believe it might be. One of his officers has had no letter from his wife in some time and is worried that something might be amiss.'

'Do you intend to go, sir?'

'It makes little sense, Robbins. There is plenty to oversee here.'

'I'm sure the steward would be happy to keep an eye on things for a couple of weeks, sir. It's not as if he doesn't know his job.'

'True enough ...'

'Would you want to open the house, sir?'

'I'm trying to think who I would stay with if I didn't open the house. I don't want to take you away just now, and I wouldn't trust anyone else to open the house.'

'Thank you, sir.'

'How is Mary today?'

'She's doing well, I believe, sir. She says it will be a few days only: I pray she is right, and yet I dread it.'

'I know.'

Robbins' wife was expecting their first child, but she had lost children before by previous husbands: mothers, too, were easily lost in childbirth, but Mary was strong and calm – Murray could not imagine her submitting to any accident or illness.

'And what about Artemesia? How is she keeping?'

Like Murray himself, his first footman Daniel had married a girl from Naples. Unlike Murray, Daniel's wife had with indecent rapidity produced twin boys, a feat which was followed at a more reasonable pace with the births of two daughters. She was now expecting again, as if it was their sole aim to cram the little cottage they had been given with as many human beings as was physically possible. A good cook, Artemesia managed to fill a fair share of the cottage herself, and Daniel was plumper than he had been. It sometimes seemed to Murray that his entire household was being taken over by children, though not above stairs.

'Artemesia is said to be blooming. She always does.' Robbins managed to infuse just a little disapproval into his expression, though whether this applied to the consistency of the bloom, the frequency of the bloom, or Daniel's enthusiasm for the bloom, was not clear. It was said by some that Robbins had softened since his marriage, but if he had, then Daniel had not benefited from it.

'So I can't take you and I can't take Daniel,' Murray said thoughtfully, 'if I were to go.'

'I'm sure Daniel wouldn't mind a fortnight in Edinburgh,' Robbins remarked.

'He might not, but I'm not sure I want to encourage him,' said Murray. 'And William?'

'William's not so keen on Edinburgh, not that that should stop him if you want him, sir,' said Robbins. 'At least his wife's not expecting at the moment.'

'Ah, we're all old married men now, that's the trouble, Robbins,' sighed Murray.

'There's Walter,' said Robbins suddenly. 'You know, sir, Mr. Fenwick's grandson. He's not coming along too badly: it might be time to give him a few more tasks to himself.'

'Walter. Yes, I met him this afternoon. He seems a serious lad.'

'He is. I couldn't see him fooling around like Daniel, sir, and he has more wit about him than William, I think.'

'He's not married yet, then?' asked Murray facetiously. Robbins' mouth tweaked slightly, his version of a grin.

'Not the last I saw him, sir, no.'

'Well, sound him out, but no promises, Robbins. I'll probably not go at all.'

Robbins bowed and was about to leave, then turned back.

'Forgive me, sir, but didn't Mr. William Dundas say before you left Edinburgh that you were welcome to stay at his new flat?'

Murray frowned, remembering.

'So he did – he seemed very proud of his new set-up. In Prince's Street, wasn't it?'

'I believe so, sir – forgive me, it was something he was saying to you as he left after supper. He was not perhaps … I should not have been listening.'

'Oh, Robbins, how could you not? And yes, he was far gone on the brandy. And I'm glad you remembered. That might indeed be a solution. If I were to go. But I probably won't go at all.'

Lady Agostinella Murray, née de Palaeopolitani de Cumae, was seated in her parlour, a shady room to the north of the house. She had been offered for this purpose a number of rooms, including

Murray's late mother's own parlour on the sunny south with a pretty view, but she had declined them, saying that the air was not right. Murray found the shady room a little disturbing: Lady Agostinella was such an insubstantial creature herself, a wisp of ancient tissue, that it was hard to see whether or not she was in the room unless she moved. Even when she was definitely not there, the room still seemed dusty and a little haunted.

When she called a faint 'Entrez!' at Murray's knock, she and her maid were at their needlework. They usually were. Murray assumed the maid also helped her dress and arrange her hair, though he never saw this happen. Robbins, questioned, said the maid made only rare appearances in the servants' hall, and never spoke except to ask for things for her mistress.

'Good day, my lady,' said Murray in French, and kissed her offered hand. 'I trust you are well?'

'My throat is a little sore. I fear I have a chill coming on.'

'The air is very mild outside: perhaps a walk would help you shake it off?'

Lady Agostinella shuddered.

'I think not.'

'Very well.' He sat on a stool which had been covered in the embroidery his wife and her maid were working, in shades of ash and mud, for all he could see. His elbows slumped on to his knees, though he tried to keep upright. 'I've been out about the river fields. The flax is coming on well – it had a good start this year.'

'We never grew flax in Naples.'

'I can't imagine the climate would be right for it there, though I may be wrong. Er, the flowers are very pretty, a delightful shade of blue.'

'I may go and see it, if the weather improves.'

And Daniel may become Moderator of the General Assembly, thought Murray, but it's unlikely.

'You have spent the morning in agricultural pursuits?' she asked, almost managing to sound interested.

'Yes, yes I have.' And up a tree, he thought. 'And you: has the morning gone well?'

She shrugged.

'The firewood in my room was damp, I think, and very smoky. Then there was no more black silk for my embroidery. But aside from these it was satisfactory.'

'Oh, good, good.' He wished the maid would go away. She was always there. Agostinella had told him that the maid spoke neither English nor much French, but nevertheless Murray always had the sense that she was listening. Listening and taking notes. Not good notes, either, or at least not ones sympathetic to him.

'I've just received a letter from my brother George,' he announced, feeling that they had exhausted the delights of their respective mornings.

'The soldier.'

'That's the one.' He had just the one, but George and Agostinella had not met. 'Perhaps if all goes well with him in this coming war, I shall have the pleasure of introducing him to you soon.'

Lady Agostinella did not reply. Perhaps she was overwhelmed at the thought, though she seemed to be unpicking some unsatisfactory stitch.

'He has asked if I would go back down to Edinburgh as a favour to him.'

'Back to Edinburgh? Why?'

'One of his fellow officers is worried that something might have happened to his wife. He hasn't received a letter for some weeks.'

'Always you are drawn to deaths!' Agostinella exclaimed, making him jump.

'Deaths? There's no thought that she might have died.'

'Mysteries, then! Always you must look into this and poke into that – it has never done you any good, has it?'

Murray reflected a little unwillingly. She was quite right: mysteries had a tendency to be detrimental to his health.

'Well, indeed,' he said. 'That is a good point. Then there is the matter of where I would stay if I did go. If you were to come too –'

'I shall not be returning to Edinburgh this season.'

'No, of course not.' Edinburgh society had been excited to welcome Murray's new wife – an Italian contessa, no less! – but despite some effort on both sides, the season had ended in mutual disappointment. 'I was only saying that if you were to come too, it would make it worthwhile to open the Queen Street house, but as you aren't coming I shall – should – have to find somewhere else to stay.'

'Most of your friends, I assume, will have left the town by now. The season is all but over.'

'Most of them, yes. Willie Jack Dundas did say I could stay with him.' He did not elaborate: as Robbins had hinted, Willie Jack was well into his cups when he made the offer but fortunately had been sober enough to get Murray alone in the hallway before he had added, slurring, 'If I had a wife like that I'd want a bolthole, my friend,' pressing his fingers hard into Murray's chest for support. To be fair, he had had a struggle with the word 'bolthole'. It had been an interesting evening.

'To stay with Willie Jack Dundas? No, that is not a good idea, either. I say no. You should not go back to Edinburgh.'

IV

Letho's servants' hall was fresh and new, a bright and dry building of which the servants universally approved. Walter in particular, the latest recruit to the staff, found it dazzling, and haunted the kitchen with its glinting batterie de cuisine, its duck-egg walls, its black Carron stove and, miracle of miracles, its running water, pumped indoors from a nearby spring.

Mrs. Mack, the cook, liked Walter because he was calm and quiet, and not impudent in the common way of new boys. Daniel, for instance, when he was new – well, Daniel had never really grown out of a certain cocky aggravation which drove Mrs. Mack to want to give him laldy with a rolling pin, were he not twice her height. Thus when Robbins came into the kitchen after supper, it was not Daniel he found perched solemnly on a creepy stool by the kitchen fire listening to Mrs. Mack's stories, but Walter, which was what Robbins had hoped.

'Walter?'

'Sir?'

The boy stood smartly, and Robbins was pleased. He would do.

'Here's something new for you. You're to go with the master tomorrow. He's off to Edinburgh.'

Chapter Two

Belgium

'Damn it,' muttered George Murray to himself, as yet another carriage rumbled past below his window. He pulled the bedclothes over his head, then registered, not with the fastest mental processes of his life, that the daylight seemed quite far advanced. He sat up, clutched his head, and pulled his watch from the watch pocket on the bed head. He squinted at the thin hands. They claimed that it was ten o'clock, and he was not sure whether they or his eyes were trying to deceive him. Then, just as he was sinking back luxuriously into his pillows, he heard the great bell on St. Michael's giving the same time.

'Erf,' he remarked expressively into his pillow. What on earth had he been doing last night? He had not been particularly inebriated when he had left Captain Willis' apartment, for Captain Willis had his wife with him in Brussels and had perforce to behave himself. Then where had he gone? He remembered some friend … who? … and an inn somewhere … Well, at least he had fetched up in his own bed, or one very like it.

After some thought, eyes closed against the cracks of daylight round the curtains, he remembered that it was Friday, a Friday in late May. That was good. George stretched to his full length and pressed his toes against the foot of the bed, then made an attempt to push back the covers and sit up. It worked, after a fashion, and only a few minutes later he was standing and ringing for his batman. Private Farrie, whom he shared with James Argo, entered the room with the expression of a man who habitually feared the worst and had never yet been disappointed. He moved slowly to provide his master with hot water and a fresh shirt.

'Have you seen Lieutenant Argo today, Farrie?' asked George when he had doused his face in the water. It had a strong ameliorative effect on the state of his head.

'Lieutenant Argo breakfasted some hours ago, sir,' was Farrie's somewhat reproving reply: Farrie liked Argo. 'He has gone out.'

'Did he say where he was going?'

'No, sir.' Farrie saluted and removed himself. His 'sirs' were always more punctuation than respect. George did not point out that he had not dismissed the man: he was more than pleased to see him go.

Breakfast was ready in the dining room downstairs. The Brussels wife on whom he and Argo had been billeted fed them well, but kept her own space in the kitchens, leaving the dining room and the front bedrooms to her uninvited guests. She seemed a capable and decent woman, and George again took a moment to regret that she had no daughter at home, which would have lent the final charm to their lodgings. He breakfasted on cold ham, cold eggs (which would have been hot had he risen earlier), bread and fresh coffee, and considered he had had as much as he deserved. More, perhaps, for as he stood before his mirror back in his room, he noticed that the month in Brussels had done some damage to his figure: his buttons were less comfortably acquainted with his buttonholes than they should have been. He made a mental note to himself to fit a little more exercise into the day as he tugged his coatee straight. Crossbelt, glowing white through Farrie's grudging attentions, sash, and headgear were added, as neat as could be, for George valued a touch of style and was proud of his uniform. Then he picked up his white gloves, gave a final nod to his reflection in the mirror, and ventured out to see what the day had in mind.

Brussels in May, he acknowledged as his head cleared, had many charms for a young officer without too much responsibility. More junior than he was, and he would have had to spend more time with the soldiers, drilling and inspecting. More senior, and he would have spent his days behind one of the mountains of paperwork he had seen in his superiors' offices. It was not that Wellington was particularly keen on paperwork himself: his ideal, it seemed to George, was to create an army so efficient that there was no need for any orders at all. When the army had left the Peninsula and headed north through France, only two pages of instructions had been required for the whole operation, so well trained were they. That was only a year ago, but Wellington's army then was not Wellington's army now. A year ago they had thought it was all over: Bonaparte was in exile on Elba, there was trouble brewing in the American colonies, and the Duke had let his best troops, and best officers, go where they were most urgently needed. Now, however, that urgent need was in the north of France, and it would take three months for Wellington's most trusted staff to return to fight with him.

Mind, thought George as he took his morning constitutional – a little later than usual – under the dense foliage of the Allée Verte, at the rate Bonaparte is moving, we could still be here in three months' time. It was no harm to Wellington, for every day brought more men to the Allied armies. The worst that could happen was that the food could run out: he had heard that Wellington had a supply contract that took them to the end of May in the Low Countries, and was now hurriedly renegotiating. George had absolute faith in him for that, though – for him it was very important to fight under a man who had a proven record of making sure the supplies were there on time.

He reached the end of the Allée, turned his horse neatly and began the return journey, the sun dappling his gaze from the opposite side now. There were still plenty of other officers doing the same, or riding in open carriages with their wives. He tipped his shako to several young ladies of his acquaintance, one he had met at a ball only a few nights ago. Most delightful, he remembered, smiling. And she would be at a dinner to which he had an invitation some time next week – lovely! Oh, yes, Brussels had its charms.

With a little sigh he drew to the end of the ride and headed off to the outskirts of town. Here the going was more complicated: soldiers newly arrived marched heavy with road dust, longing for a camp site, while busy corporals hurried back and forth with dispatches or at least an air of importance. Here and there cavalry arrived, distinguished by fine horses and an air of superiority. Some of the colours of the uniforms left George blinking: the Allies included all kinds of foreign regiments.

The armies were in cantons arranged outside on the flat land of the Low Countries – George, looking round when they had arrived, had seen scarcely an acre that was not suitable for setting up tents unless it was too damp: the notion of a hill had clearly not reached

Belgium. A short journey brought him to the lines of his company of the 3rd. Battalion The Royal Scots, and a sergeant who looked old enough to have been one of Pontius Pilate's original body guard pulled himself sharply upright and saluted as George approached. George swung down from his horse.

'All well today, Lamb?'

'All well, sir. Any news of Bonaparte?'

'He hasn't written to me yet, Lamb: I daresay he'll tip us the wink when he sets out from Paris.'

'Very good, sir,' agreed Lamb. 'No doubt we'll be the first to know.'

With a grin, George led his horse on into the lines. Automatically his gaze travelled right and left as he walked, looking for any problems or faults, though he tended to be easy on those. If pressed, George would have admitted that he was extremely fond of his men, particularly those who had served under him in northern Spain. He enjoyed their dark humour, their ways of measuring a man, and their hard-won skills for making themselves comfortable wherever they stopped. The men in turn knew that he would not go hard with them unless they crossed one of several well-defined lines: insolence, for example, or a lack of pride in the regiment, or dishonesty. The salutes he acknowledged as he walked down the row of tents were therefore friendly, as were his responses. George smiled: this was his home.

He gave his horse to one of the privates at the horse lines, and returned to the tent that was used by the company as a headquarters. Here the corporal detailed to collect the post would bring it each day, and here he found Argo, as usual, hovering tight-stringed for the corporal's arrival.

'You could go to the Post Office in the town, Argo,' said George mildly – as he had said several times before.

'But that would mean asking them to break into the bag for the company. I couldn't do that,' said Argo, as he had explained each time.

'They wouldn't mind, for an officer,' said George.

'But it's against the rules. They might get into trouble. That wouldn't be fair.'

'All right, all right. Good day to you, by the way!' added George.

'And good day to you!' Argo bowed with a smile. He was a slim fair man, handsome without recognising it in himself, and in George's view the least likely soldier he had met for a while. But there, he was new to the game: there would be time, if Bonaparte came north, for the making of many soldiers.

'I hope I didn't disturb you, coming in late last night.'

'I must have been asleep. Where did you go after Captain Willis'?'

'Hm. I was hoping you might be able to tell me!' George shrugged. 'No doubt I'll find out if it's important enough. Oh, here's the corporal.'

The corporal saluted as he entered the tent, and deposited the post bag on the table.

'Not much today, then?' Argo asked anxiously, eyeing the bag.

'Plenty to be sorted,' said the corporal slightly sourly. Keeping track of the battalion's incoming post was tricky enough. The outgoing post from the ordinary soldiers, which had to be listed individually and each signed for by an officer, was nearly impossible. Sandwiched between the demands of the soldiers, the reluctance of officers, and the complaints of the Post Office when lists arrived without letters or letters without lists, the corporal had developed, George had noticed, a very healthy cynicism over the last month. The corporal stood at his table and opened the bag, reaching inside for a handful of letters and starting to divide them into heaps.

'There's one for me,' said George, and the corporal passed it to him with a grunt. 'Oh, it's from Captain Gunn. Excellent!'

'Is he to arrive soon?' asked Argo nervously.

'I hope so: I've had enough of responsibility for a while,' George joked as he slit the letter open.

'I hope I have not given you more trouble, then,' said Argo with a frown. 'I know I worry dreadfully. I am sorry.'

'Not at all, not at all … Gunn is on his way, thank goodness. Oh! He says that Major Saddler is to arrive before him – I thought they were travelling together, in Europe at least. I wonder what has delayed Gunn?'

'What are they like, Major Saddler and Captain Gunn?' asked Argo.

'Gunn is a good man,' said George. 'The very best. He has a

funny scholarly bent – you know, likes books and things - but he's a damned good officer. I shall be tremendously glad to see him, for the last time I saw him I thought would be the last, you know? It was at Nive, just before I got the ball through my own leg. Bloody awful weather, that day, and the conditions were foul. We were pushing forward – Soult thought he had us, you know – and there was a skirmish on the right wing of our lot. I looked round, thinking we were all fine, and there was Gunn with his face slashed open. The rain was washing him down, but the blood was flowing faster than it could clean him. Then bang, I was down, and I couldn't even work out why at first. Confusing things, battles,' he admitted. 'As you know, I ended up in Bath convalescing, and I thought Gunn was dead for months till finally a letter of his came through. He's a remarkable man.'

'And Major Saddler?' Argo pressed on.

'Different sort of thing altogether,' said George shortly. 'It's up to you, of course, and I expect you would anyway, but go easy with the Major. He's a damned fine soldier, damned fine, don't mistake me. I have every respect for his skills in that way of things. No sense of humour, though.'

'Is that a bad thing?' asked Argo curiously.

'It certainly is in my book!' said George. 'I find it mightily difficult to be comfortable with anyone who doesn't laugh, don't you? But there, it takes all sorts to make an army. And he's brave, I'll certainly give him that. That's certainly more useful to an officer than Gunn's bookishness, but perhaps it will come in handy one of these days – he could bore the French to death with Shakespeare, perhaps!'

Tact did not come naturally to George but he felt he had just done rather well, particularly with the corporal nearby. Though he was genuinely fond of Gunn, Saddler was another matter altogether. George was not a sensitive man himself, but he had noticed that Saddler commanded absolute obedience from the soldiers, based entirely on the fact that they were more terrified of him than they were of the French. He fiddled with one of the stacks of unsorted mail, trying to think of a new subject to turn to, but forgot all about Saddler when he found another letter with his name on.

'Ah, a letter from Charles!' he exclaimed, finding some pennies in his pocket to pay for his post. 'Now we might hear something.' He drew Argo out of the tent, away from the tantalising heaps of mail.

'My dear George …' George read aloud as he scanned through his brother's smooth writing. 'Yes, he's received my letter, but he had already left Edinburgh for Letho – that's the family place in Fife. He must have left before the end of the season. Not that surprising: he's not a town person, my brother, but I thought he might be showing off his new wife. So, if he's in Fife … oh now! He says he's off back to Edinburgh to see if he can find your lady!'

'All the way from Fife? That's more than good of him,' gasped Argo. 'I had no thought of taking advantage of his kindness to that extent!'

'Nonsense,' said George automatically as he read on. 'My sister Agostinella is to stay in Fife and he will go back to Edinburgh on his own, so he's to stay with Willie Jack Dundas.'

'One of the Dundases? Oh, my!'

'Oh, Willie Jack's only a very minor member,' said George comfortingly. 'He's the youngest son of a cousin of the late Viscount, you know.'

Argo had gone quite pale.

'I really had no idea of putting people out. I'm sure Alicia is perfectly … perfectly well …'

'Now, you know you've been worried,' said George, folding Murray's letter into his pocket. 'Charles likes a bit of a mystery even at the best of times, and I'm sure he wouldn't have popped back to Edinburgh unless it was perfectly convenient. As to Willie Jack, he's a good friend, a young bachelor, and if he's still in town at the dead end of the season no doubt he will appreciate my brother's company.'

'Well, I don't know …'

'And who's to say there isn't a letter from her in there on that table, anyway?' George added, which was all Argo needed to scuttle back into the tent and watch the corporal's sorting with an eagle eye. The corporal cast a glance across at him and rolled his eyes ever so slightly till he met George's warning frown. Neither the corporal's care nor Argo's hovering scrutiny made any difference, however: even when the post bag was picked up and shaken there was no letter there for Argo.

'Maybe tomorrow,' said George, dropping a kindly arm across Argo's shoulders and guiding him again out of the tent. 'And remember, my brother is on his way, and if for example she has broken her wrist and cannot write, he will find even that and tell us.'

'But then –' Argo began, but George was quickly scanning the rest of his brother's letter in case there was a further clue. Argo waited politely. George pursed his lips, read quickly to the end, and pocketed the letter once again. There was nothing more in it of any use to Argo.

'Well,' he said, looking about him, 'everything seems to be in order here this morning. We'd better have a spruce-up before Major Saddler arrives, but we can plan that over some food. I've found a coffee shop near the Place where they serve a splendid mutton broth,' said George comfortably. 'Shall we go?

But at that point a skinny young corporal hurried up, his green facings scuffed and worn, looking distinctly fed up and holding a fan of letters. He saluted as if he really didn't have time for such details.

'Sir. Are you by the remotest chance Lieutenant James Argo?'

'I am.'

'Praise the Lord: another one. Here you are, sir.' He handed Argo one of the letters. 'All these, sir, twenty-three letters arrived with us this morning and not one for the Inniskillings! And me sent out on my ownsome to find where they should have gone. Now, sirs, does either of yez know where the Black Watch are, being you're Scots and all?'

George pointed him in the general direction of the Black Watch's camp, and turned back to find Argo grinning from ear to ear.

'My wife!' he exclaimed, waving the letter. 'It's from Alicia! Praise Heaven – though I fear I really have sent your good brother on a wild goose chase, Murray: you must allow me to write and apologise.' He clutched the letter to him and beamed.

'Then you'll want to read it, man, not just delt it like a baby,' said George indulgently.

'Oh, may I? You don't mind?'

'Of course not: it would be cruel to stop you, after that long wait.'

Argo needed no second bidding: he slipped his thumb round the seal and carefully tore the letter open. George politely looked about him, though Argo seemed eager to share his good news with him.

'She sent it but a week ago – but this is not her address. Oh! She has moved! So not only have I sent Mr. Murray on a fruitless hunt, I have also sent him to the wrong place! Listen: "I have had perforce to move to this flat, which is not where I should choose to live but the move was done in haste. I must beg your forgiveness, dear husband, on two counts: one, that I have worried you with no letter, and two, that this will also cause you anxiety.' At this Argo paused, reading ahead, and frowned.

'Is all well, then?' asked George, beginning to catch something of Argo's feelings.

'She says she had to move, that someone had threatened her, but that she is safe now for having moved. Murray, she says that she feared for her life!'

Chapter Three

Edinburgh

I

The first day of June, 1815, saw fine weather, and also saw Charles Murray of Letho back in Edinburgh at the dogend of the season, feeling guilty at abandoning his estate, guilty at the freedom he felt at leaving his wife for a couple of weeks, pleasantly interested in the puzzle he had come to sort out, and faintly annoyed at Walter Fenwick, who had lost several things on the journey from Fife, including, once, himself.

Murray recalled sternly that Walter was only a boy and only learning, as he took the lad with him that Thursday along busy Prince's Street and up the broad ramp of the North Bridge into the Old Town. Walter, who had made no comment on the town since they had reached it, looked about him solemnly at the buildings and the crowds and the goods on sale at the Tron Market where the North Bridge met the High Street.

'What do you think, then, Walter?' Murray asked, pausing with him to survey the scene. Above them, around the severity of the Tron Kirk, tenements towered skywards, some overhanging the road with ancient wooden balconies, some newer, stonebuilt, replacing older houses destroyed by fire. Their stern walls were cluttered with brightly painted signs advertising all kinds of businesses from swordmakers to musicians, hatters to mantua makers. Further up the street could be seen the spire of St. Giles' Kirk, surrounded from this angle by the untidy, enticing luckenbooths selling every treasure or rubbish one could dream of. Coffee shops on either side sucked in busy lawyers from the lawcourts past the kirk, and spewed them out again in chatty clusters festooned with the day's working papers, scented with coffee or broth or rich red claret. Learned gentlemen in gowns from the College took their midday stroll, debating solemnly in pairs though perhaps on no subject more academic than college gossip. Walter's shiny chestnut head turned slowly one way and the other, like a loose knob on a newel post.

'I think it's all very fine, Mr. Murray, sir,' he acknowledged.

'If you went up that way as far as you could go,' said Murray, pointing up the High Street, 'you'd find yourself at the Castle. If you went the other way and down the hill, you'd find yourself at Holyroodhouse, the palace. You've seen the Castle from Prince's Street. Do you understand where you are?'

'Yes, sir.'

'And if you get lost, where do you ask for?'

'For Prince's Street, sir, and then for Mr. William Dundas' apartment.'

'Well done. You need to keep your head, Walter, it's a big town.' He refrained from pointing out that anyone who could achieve the feat of losing himself in ten minutes in South Queensferry should not have any problem here, but short of sticking a label on the boy or tying him to his own wrist with string, he was not sure what more he could do.

The route became more complex now, anyway, and he kept a careful eye on Walter's shiny head. They carried on down South Bridge, into Adam Square, where they turned right past the College towards Potterrow.

Potterrow was a long, curving street, where tenements of the modest sort mixed with older, shorter buildings and various trades were represented: grocers, smiths, the sweetly scented meal dealer and the less fragrant candlemaker, and even a silversmith. It was a respectable if humble neighbourhood, comfortable without flirting too closely with prosperity, and lively at this time of day with people going about their business. Murray was pleased to see that the houses were numbered, but George had given him no clear address. He had half-thought to send Walter one way and go the other himself, but that was before he had travelled with the boy. They had joined Potterrow about halfway along: he mentally tossed a coin, and turned right.

The grocers to the right had not heard of Mrs. Argo, nor had any gossiping tradesmen on doorsteps. Then a shoemaker at No.4 who was on the street looking out for his daughter reckoned he had mended a pair of boots for a Mrs. Argo, and that she lived in furnished lodgings at the other end of the street. Murray and Walter turned and walked back the way they had come, past the road to the College, and on to enquire again.

It turned out that several tenements at the south end of the street were given over to furnished lodgings. Mrs. Brotherstone at No.62 was the first one to be in any way helpful: she was sure it belonged to a lodger at the house of a neighbour.

'I had to turn her down myself when she first came here. She seemed a nice body, sir, there was nothing wrong with her as a lodger. But I'm full to the gills as it is. And then the next thing I ken she's marrit on a man living at Bob Campbell's.'

Mrs. Brotherstone was a respectable looking creature herself, sturdy and sensible. She would not have sent a young woman anywhere unsafe.

'And that's where she lives?'

'I havena seen her for a bit, I have to say.' Mrs. Brotherstone frowned. 'She's not – in any trouble, is she, sir?'

'Not at all, Mrs. Brotherstone: I simply have a message from her husband.'

'Lieutenant Argo, is that? Aye, I ken him well. He's out with the army in the Low Countries, isn't he, or he was? Aye, aye. She's gey proud of him, and he of her, it's plain to see. I hope there's no harm come to him, then?'

'Not as far as I know, Mrs. Brotherstone. Bob Campbell's, you say?'

'That's right, sir, at number 47. It's a funny wee door.'

'Thank you, Mrs. Brotherstone.'

It was indeed a funny wee door, and after they had knocked, Murray had to stoop considerably to fit himself inside. He would have been more comfortable on his hands and knees. A man on the same scale as the door emerged from one of the front rooms, wiping his hands on a very white cloth. Shocked ginger curls sitting high on his head glinted in the light of a fresh wax candle – not cheap tallow, Murray noticed – and his skin was very pale.

'Mr. Campbell?'

'That's right, but we've no vacancies just the now. Oh, I beg your pardon, sir!' said the man, adjusting to the dim light of the hall and realising that Murray was not likely to be seeking lodgings in his relatively humble house. He adjusted his hair with a ghostly hand, which he then wiped again on the cloth. His apron was spotless.

'I'm not looking for a room, Mr. Campbell. I was hoping to meet someone who already has a room here, a Mrs. Argo. I have a message for her from her husband,' he added again quickly, in case any imputation should fall on either Alicia Argo or indeed himself.

'That'd be her husband in the Royal Scots? Oh, aye, he lives here when he's no away. They're not long married, ken! I'd say she was missing him! He's a fine man, a fine man.' He wound his hands through the cloth again, then used it to rub along the top of the wainscoting. The place was scrupulously clean as far as could be seen: Murray would not have hesitated on those grounds to take a room here, though he had to admit that Mr. Campbell did not make him feel particularly comfortable.

'Was?' asked Murray suddenly. 'Has something happened to her?'

'Oh, she left, that's all! She said it wasna the rooms, she said she was very happy here, and so she seemed. She was very nice about it all. She was a bonny, well-mannered woman and no trouble to me, friendly and decent, and I'd have been delighted if she'd stayed. The one I have here now in her place, well, muddy bootprints up the stairs and wet marks on the wood, and the state of her bedding! *Well.* But when they pay six weeks in advance, there's very little you can do, you understand? Well, a nice gentleman like you, you wouldn't have to worry about such things as keeping *paying guests*. And there was a time in my life when maybe I thought I wouldn't have to, either: but there, it's a satisfaction to me to have the place well kept and to please my guests when they are decent folks who do the like and understand my *position*. I like to keep a clean house, sir, to the best of my ability, and I don't like to think that I'm being taken advantage of. So I miss Mrs. Argo, I do. And I was looking forward to her fine husband's return, for we should all be very proud of our redcoats! But there, it was one morning she came through to my kitchen –' he broke off, his attempts at gentility undermined by the admission that he was so familiar with his own kitchen - 'ah, apartments,' he added, after a breath, 'and she said she had to be off.'

'Did she say why?'

Campbell bowed minutely, as if acknowledging Murray's decency in not drawing attention to the slip. His hair received another little rearrangement, and his hands worried the cloth again.

'She said something about some people, unfriendly people, finding out where she lived. It seemed a bit unlikely to me, I must say. She wasna the kind to attract unfriendliness, but there you are, there are all sorts even in Edinburgh these days. Time was you'd have kenned every body walking down the street, and all their business, and you wouldn't have blinked an eye at them knowing yours, too. But times have changed. There's people now would cast all kinds of things in your face … She asked me not to say where she'd gone,' he finished abruptly, suddenly regarding them with a suspicious eye.

'That's … that's all right, Mr. Campbell,' said Murray, not wanting to make him feel he might have endangered his erstwhile lodger. After all, this might be the puzzle solved here and now: Lieutenant Argo had been writing letters here, and Mrs. Argo had not received them and had not, in the haste of moving, had time to write. Was it up to him to wonder what unfriendliness the elusive Mrs. Argo might have attracted? He was not sure. He would report to George, and see if anything further transpired. 'Thank you for your time.'

'An honour, sir, an honour,' Campbell followed them out through the awkward little doorway into the street, still clutching his snow-white cloth. As they left him he was attending to a little dust on one front window, and watching his neighbours in the reflection.

II

The day was now their own, but Murray felt a little adrift. He had said farewell to Edinburgh for this season, and now felt ghost-like, coming back to somewhere he no longer belonged. He scanned the crowd, half-hoping to see people he knew, half-hoping he would not, for he was not here to be sociable and he felt the absence of Agostinella like a wraith about him, attracting, he thought, suspicion. He considered calling on the Armstrongs in St. Patrick's Square, but it was a little late for calling, so he strolled back down slowly to South Bridge. Once in the crowds he glanced around anxiously to make sure Walter was with him, and found he was not. A moment later, though, he found him three paces back, studiously reading a notice pasted up on a wall.

'Sir, what's a whale?'

'A mighty sea creature. You know, like the one that swallowed Jonah in the Bible.'

'There really are such things?' Walter's gaze glazed in wonder. 'Big enough to swallow a whole man? Without chewing?'

'I believe so. I have seen some prodigious fish myself, on the way to the East and back.'

'But sir, there is one here in Edinburgh! A white whale,' he read, 'found in the Forth, and it has been taken to the old – ah – Lanc-ass-trine'

'Lancastrian,' Murray put in.

'Lancastrian – oh, like the English kings!'

'That's right!' said Murray in surprise. He liked his servants to be educated.

'Lancastrian School at Calton Hill. What's 'admission'?'

'Being allowed in. In this case, for a price. I should imagine it will be a few pence for children or servants.'

'I have a few pence, Mr. Murray,' said Walter seriously. 'My mother gave me some pennies when she heard I was to come to Edinburgh.'

'Well, then, perhaps we should see about making sure you go to see the whale, if you so wish. It will be an experience for you. And I see the admission is to go to charity – I wonder which one?' he added, slightly cynically. He was not particularly keen to see a dead whale himself: he imagined that the smell might be difficult to overcome.

'I may go?' Walter wanted to make sure he had not misunderstood.

'I shall try to arrange it,' said Murray. He was not yet prepared to let Walter go on his own: he might never see him again. Walter did not smile, but his eyes lit up under his heavy fringe of hair, and he gave a little nod. For the rest of the walk back to Prince's Street, he kept a strict three paces behind Murray's long legs, and caused no trouble at all.

III

Willie Jack Dundas, youngest son of a cousin of the famous late Viscount Melville, had a famous surname, some independent means, two well-married brothers, and very little else to offer the world except that a medical man might have drawn interesting scientific data from the fact that he was permanently afflicted with a runny nose. For some reason, he and Murray, who had met at school, had managed to remain good friends through the many trials of their short lives. Willie Jack had for many years lived with his widowed mother and her elderly cousin in the Canongate, but now at last he had shown an independent streak and taken an apartment at the west end of Prince's Street, nearly opposite the West Kirk with its low, ancient graveyard. He appeared to be more than happy to have Murray to stay.

Murray had arrived late the previous night from Fife, and had breakfasted early and gone out with Willie Jack that morning before his expedition to Potterrow. Now the maid let him in and informed him that Willie Jack had not yet returned home but was expected every minute. She showed him in to the parlour where a fire had been lit and the newspaper laid out, and brought him some tea, all of which Murray found unexpectedly civilised for an establishment run by Willie Jack. Nevertheless it was very welcome, and he settled down to read the paper.

The *Courant* prided itself on its up-to-date information on the campaign in the Low Countries, and the reliable analysis of its authenticity. According to the paper, hostilities had finally begun, but Murray was relieved to see that so far the fighting was at sea – unlikely to affect George who was as poor a sailor as he himself was. More alarmingly, he read that the British were being asked to leave Brussels, which had the air of an Allied retreat. According to George the town was full of officers and their families: perhaps Wellington was simply removing the women and children from harm's way, or even from the army's way. The *Courant* was happy that the Duke was still biding his time, watching his army grow. While they sat growing in Brussels, George was safe, and Murray was content.

He was about to peruse the advertisements on the front page when the parlour door opened. He glanced up, expecting Willie Jack or the maid, and sprang to his feet as a woman entered. She stopped in mild surprise, and for a moment they stared at each other.

All Murray could think about was autumn, abundant autumn. Her hair was shining red-brown, her eyes golden brown, her whole appearance seemed to cry out that all the fruits of the season had ripened at once and were there for the picking. He was speechless.

'Mr. Murray, I presume?' asked the vision in a low, rich voice. And at that moment, to Murray's relief, Willie Jack bounced up the stairs with a clatter and appeared in the parlour.

'Ah, Charles, just in time! I was going to tell you, of course. May I present Charles Murray of Letho? This lady, Charles, is my wife.'

Murray managed to retrieve his falling jaw and make his bow, while the vision curtseyed, lowering her gaze modestly and returning to embrace her husband's arm. Willie Jack looked like a man who had picked a quince only to find it was a pineapple.

'I'm afraid I had absolutely no idea. When did this happy event occur?' asked Murray, gradually recovering.

'Two weeks ago!' said Willie Jack. 'I was going to tell you, of course, but then you wrote to ask if you could stay and I thought it would be a prodigious surprise for you! Letitia, my dearest, would you fetch a glass of brandy for Mr. Murray? I think he has had quite a shock!'

'I have long hoped to see Willie Jack safely married,' Murray smiled, 'so it is at least a delightful shock. But where did you meet? How did this happen?' He thought he had better stop there: Willie Jack had a history of interest in unsuitable women, and the fact that this one had appeared out of nowhere was not, he thought, a good sign. Too many questions at this point might elicit answers he had no wish to hear.

'We met at an Assembly! Letitia – Miss Swanson, as she was then! Her family had just taken a house in Haddingtonshire, and she had come to town for the end of the season, and there was I and there was she!'

'Delightful,' said Murray again.

'Of course I knew at once that she was the one for me, and

fortunately she was disposed to agree!' Willie Jack pecked his wife on the cheek with some enthusiasm, and she emitted a rich chuckle like a ripe plum dropping to the orchard floor.

'But then I must not detain you from your honeymoon,' Murray realised suddenly. 'You must long to be away. I shall find somewhere else to stay.' Bob Campbell's lodging house flashed through his mind, and he gave a little shiver.

'Oh, no, not at all,' said Letitia Dundas cheerfully. 'We shall be away soon to my parents' house in Haddingtonshire, only that there are rumours of illness in the village nearby, and they forbade us to come just yet.'

'Illness?' asked Murray.

'Cholera,' said Willie Jack quickly. 'So you see, we are at your disposal.'

'I hope your parents will not be affected by it,' said Murray. 'That is a serious matter.'

'Oh, it is only rumours!' said Letitia. 'No doubt spread by some old gossip whose friend has a cold. But stay, do: I have longed to meet one of dear Willie Jack's friends, and now here you are!'

'Charles is very delicate about these things, dear, I must tell you,' said Willie Jack, the loving husband explaining the dear friend. 'He is not long married himself. He went away to India some time ago, and came back with a wife! He has married an Italian contessa. She is very – she is an Italian contessa.' Willie Jack floundered, going slightly pink. Murray's mouth twitched: he himself would have had some difficulty in describing Lady Agostinella politely.

'Do let us sit,' said Letitia with some poise. 'I shall call for some more tea, Mr. Murray.'

They sat, and Murray picked up the paper to fold it back on to the table.

'I see that the white whale is advertised here, too. There was a bill up for it on the street. My lad Walter is itching to spend his few pennies on a spectacle now that he is in Edinburgh for the first time.'

'Oh, where is it?' asked Willie Jack, taking the paper.

'The old Lancastrian School at Calton Hill. Walter has a bent for self-education, I suspect, though what he will learn from visiting a heap of decaying blubber I am not very sure.'

'Calton Hill? Oh, I long to go to the tea rooms at Nelson's Monument!' cried Letitia. 'They are mentioned in the paper every day. All kinds of ices and cakes. Won't you take me, Willie Jack? Won't you? For if you won't, I shall try an application to your friend Mr. Murray, for he seems to be a kindly gentleman!'

Murray looked abruptly at the floor. Willie Jack, fortunately, took his wife by the hand and assured her that should the heavens fall to earth and the waters of the Forth wash through every street in Edinburgh, it would not prevent him escorting her to the tea rooms at Nelson's Monument.

The maid reappeared with the tea and a fine selection of biscuits and tea breads, and a letter tucked into her apron pocket. She brought it out after laying the tray down.

'It'll be your parents,' said Willie Jack to Letitia, and Murray thought she turned just a little pale.

'For Mr. Murray, sir,' said the maid with a bob, and presented the letter.

'It's from my brother George,' said Murray, with a glance at the address.

'Then please open it, if you wish,' said Letitia. 'Willie Jack says he is in the army – it must be a terrible worry for you!'

'A terrible annoyance at the moment,' Murray said. 'He has sent me on a wild goose chase today. But will you excuse me? For I must find out if he knows what I discovered earlier.'

At their assent, he opened the letter and quickly perused it.

'It seems I sent you to the wrong address,' George explained, 'for Argo has just received a letter saying she has moved. He is much relieved, and sends his deepest apologies to you for such a chase, but I wonder – would you mind very much going to her new address, just so that if there is another delay in letters I can assure him that you have found her safe and well? She has made mention of someone threatening to kill her, and that has been eating away at Argo. I can see it working on him, and I would be very pleased to have him happier and settled, for Major Saddler and Captain Gunn are to return soon and I cannot think that Saddler will have much time for a new officer with thoughts only for how his wife is.'

'Oh, George,' said Murray aloud. 'It's only ever half the information I need. Either he forgets to ask it, or he cannot be bothered to write it down!'

'Is this concerning the woman you were seeking today?' asked Willie Jack.

'That's right: apparently someone has threatened to kill her. I imagine that is why she moved, but George doesn't give any more details: who is threatening to kill her? Why? Does anyone even know? And is it true, or is she a woman of flights of fancy?'

'So many of us are,' agreed Letitia, with a broad smile.

'And men, too,' Murray acknowledged. 'So now he wants me to look for her at the next address she has sent: now, where is she? Or where is she supposed to be?'

'So,' George had written, 'here is the address from which she has just written. She was there on the nineteenth of May, to judge by her letter. She has moved to Combe's Court, Dean Village.'

'I have to go to Dean Village this time,' Murray announced.

'Dean Village?' exclaimed Willie Jack, an Edinburgh man through and through. 'That's near enough leaving the country!'

Chapter Four

Belgium

I

'It'll never work,' said Sergeant Lamb gloomily, though he maintained a steadfast hold on the damp guy rope.

'It'll work all right,' said George soothingly, though he did wonder. The iron basket of wood and kindling, soaked in sticky oil, swayed at the top of the long pole and a solid line of black drops marched across the Sergeant's red wool sleeve. He grunted.

'How do we light them, though?' asked Argo. He, too, had a hand on a rope. They were all clinging on rather desperately. The beacon had already toppled once, with messy consequences across a line of tents and one soldier with a broken arm.

'A gey long spunk?' offered one of the older soldiers holding the rope with Argo.

'If this - blessed - country had anything anyone could call a hill, sir,' said the Sergeant, with a look at the soldier, 'we'd have no need for this nonsense. What if there's a strong wind?' His grip began to slip again. George took the strain until he found a surer hold.

'Well, short of building some hills in a hurry, this is probably the best we can do,' he said philosophically. 'And this will be the one we'll see from the camp. If this signal tower is lit we'll know the Frenchies are on their way, and we'll be glad enough of the warning.'

'True enough, sir,' sighed the Sergeant. 'Though at this rate we'll still be here holding it up. Liddell, get over here with them pegs! We canna hold this all day!'

Two soldiers, one with large wooden stakes trying to escape from under his arm and the other with a menacing long-handled mallet, came jogging over and began to bang in the stakes to hold the ropes. The one with the stakes wobbled as he ran: if George was growing stout, then Private Liddell had a fair lead on him. They secured Argo's rope first, and he left it to come and help George, allowing the Sergeant to give his men the closer supervision and running commentary they required. A stake fell on his toe and his language became more poetic.

'All right, there, Argo?' George asked, trying not to laugh as he felt the weight change from the Sergeant's bulk to Argo's lighter frame.

'Grand with the rope, aye,' agreed Argo shortly. Inside, George sighed heavily. After his wave of relief at receiving his wife's letter, Argo had taken to heart the little she had said about feeling her life was in danger. George had spent the last week alternately presenting a sympathetic ear and burying his head in a wine bottle to escape.

George had told his brother all he could: Alicia Argo seemed to assume that Argo would understand her cryptic allusions, and claimed not to want to commit too much information to a letter. As far as spreading panic without conveying information went, she had shown herself to be an expert.

'She'll hardly even have received your reply yet, man,' said George, knowing very well what was on Argo's mind. 'What is it, the first of June? I always reckon about a week to Edinburgh, if you catch the right boat.'

'Aye, I suppose.'

'And it'll be about the time for my brother to get my letter asking him to go to the new address and see if she's - reassure us that she's fine and in no need of help,' he changed quickly. 'And even if she does need help,' he added, and regretted it instantly, as Argo's shoulders hunched in dread and the rope sagged. 'Even if she does, my brother might not be a soldier, but he's got a bit of practice in the odd rammie. He'll look after her.'

'My poor Alicia,' murmured Argo, as if even the protection of George's brother was a cross to be borne. 'Why does she not tell me more? These hints and half-said things – and then she says she does not wish to worry me!'

'Aye, women, eh?' said George the happy bachelor.

'No! She's not like that. She's lovely …'

George was not quite sure how to respond to that, or indeed

what Alicia Argo was not like, so he let it go. He devoutly hoped Charles would find Alicia alive, well, and under no possible threat, and would quickly send word. He liked Argo, and had no wish to see him discomfited, but he was also heartily tired of Argo's moping around the place. There was enough to do in Brussels and enough to prepare in the camp without that. George wished Gunn would come back soon, for all his odd bookish ways. Gunn was calm and cool, and when George had seen him fall wounded one of his first concerns was for that steady quiet guidance that Gunn always seemed to provide. George did not want Argo to leave: he just wanted him diluted.

The crew of stakeman and malletman arrived at the end of their rope, and for a few minutes the ground beneath their boots shook rhythmically as the stake was beaten into the soft earth far enough to hold the guyline securely. Sergeant Lamb took the end of the rope and twisted it neatly into a knot, and as soon as he had kicked the stake to his satisfaction, he slipped the rope over it and tightened the knot. The rope twanged as he tested it, and he nodded, and George and Argo cautiously let go. The signal tower held, though they watched it warily for a few minutes.

'Well, I doubt that's the best we can do,' said Sergeant Lamb, and pulled a clay pipe from his pocket with the air of a man handing over responsibility. George agreed, and patted the signal post tentatively, as if he could even then knock it over.

'Back to camp, then, lads,' he said, and the soldiers smartened up and set off, followed by the Sergeant.

'What next, then?' asked Argo resignedly.

'I'd like to have Farrie give this coatee a brush,' George decided, looking at the state of his uniform. He turned to go, and nearly walked into two tall officers who were standing behind them.

'I beg your pardon, sir,' said George at once, and was about to go on when the taller man stopped him. He was a remarkably good-looking gentleman with curling dark hair, somewhat older than George but still young, and with some alarm George recognised the elaborate gold lace of a senior aide-de-camp. He reflected with remarkable speed on the content of his recent conversation, decided that he had said nothing directly critical of any senior officers, and pulled himself up smartly. He did not have to worry about Argo: Argo was always awed by any officer with more gold on his uniform than he himself had, and would be cowering behind him.

'A lieutenant in the Royal Scots, eh?' said the handsome officer. His accent was English, cultivated, confident.

'Yes, sir,' said George.

'And your battalion?'

'The third, sir.'

The handsome officer and his companion exchanged a meaningful glance. There was something about it that George instinctively did not like. He decided that his best path was to say nothing until spoken to, in case he said the wrong thing.

'Where was the battalion about a week ago?' the other officer asked politely.

About a week ago, thought George. Where had he gone after Captain Willis' dinner? Where on earth – and what had he done, more to the point? Should he lie, say they were somewhere else? But then, what if he had met them somewhere? … and they would find out soon enough if he told that scale of a lie. No, better to tell the truth.

'The battalion was here, outside Brussels, sir. Lieutenant Argo and I had already been billeted in the town.'

He found he was half-closing his eyes, as if to ward off a blow. He made himself open them properly, just in time to see another significant look pass between the officers.

'You have two officers amongst you by the names of Saddler and Gunn, I believe?'

'Yes, sir, but they have not yet joined us. They are on their way from Edinburgh, sir.'

'On their way, yes. I fear we have encountered them already,' said the handsome officer. 'Forgive me, I should introduce myself. I am Alexander Gordon, aide-de-camp to His Grace the Duke. My friend here and I were travelling last week and lodged in a village some miles from the coast, when we came across your officers in the local inn.'

George was confused. Had Saddler and Gunn so impressed Gordon that he had come to praise the battalion? It did not seem so. He suddenly remembered that this was Sir Alexander Gordon, brother of the fourth Earl of Aberdeen, a young man rumoured to have the ear of the Duke himself. What on earth had Saddler and Gunn done?

'Er … can we be of service to your honour in passing on any message when Major Saddler and Captain Gunn arrive?' George asked.

Sir Alexander smiled.

'I think I should like to convey any message personally, when the time comes,' he said smoothly. 'We were standing in the inn yard awaiting our horses when the officer called Gunn attacked me.'

'He attacked you? *Gunn* attacked you?' George was even more confused. 'But why?'

'I have no idea,' said Sir Alexander.

'In his cups,' put in his friend.

'No, no, I don't believe so,' Sir Alexander contradicted him. 'I had a good chance to examine him, though briefly, at very close quarters, and I could see nor smell no evidence of drunkenness.'

'But he attacked you?'

'Flew at me, and then challenged me to a duel,' said Sir Alexander. 'It was the most extraordinary thing. I barely had the chance to see him, let alone cause him offence, before he launched himself across the yard. I see you are equally surprised. Is this not typical behaviour for the fellow?'

'Not at all! Forgive me, your honour, but are you sure it was Gunn? Middle height, smooth skin, fairish hair, with a sword cut down one cheek?'

'The very man,' said Sir Alexander.

'Then I am dreadfully surprised,' George admitted, frowning deeply. 'Captain Gunn is the calmest of men. Unless his injury – I have not seen him in person since he received his wound, and perhaps it has changed him? I confess, your honour, this has greatly puzzled me.'

'And me, though perhaps with less information.'

'But what happened then?' asked George. 'Did you fight him?'

'I did not. I was so taken aback I did nothing for a moment, and in that moment his friend, Major Saddler, came up behind him and dragged him back. I confess, he looked as much amazed as you. Then Gunn broke away and ran back into the inn, and when we followed after some conversation with Major Saddler we discovered that he had gone.'

'Gone?'

'Yes. He had grabbed his baggage, which apparently was not great, and left, along with a young drummer boy he was escorting to Brussels. So he has not yet arrived?'

'He sent a letter last week saying that he was on his way and implying that he and Saddler were travelling separately, but he did not say why. I confess I was surprised, a little, as they had intended to arrive together.'

'Well, when he arrives I should like to have a word or two with him,' said Sir Alexander. 'Perhaps the man is unwell, but that does not entirely excuse random attacks on fellow officers.'

'Not at all, your honour,' said George hastily. 'I shall pass the message on as soon as I see him.'

'Very good, Lieutenant. And your name, sir?'

'George Murray, sir, of Fife.'

'George Murray – a good name. Are you kin to the Duke's George Murray?'

'Only very distantly, sir,' said George with a smile.

'Well, we must get along. The Duke is off to Ghent, and we must follow. Come along, then, John.'

The two officers glided across the field with all the grace of superiority, while George, feeling unusually short, fat and shabby, watched them with his mouth open. What on earth had Gunn been thinking of?

II

George left Argo moping around the post tent and rode back into Brussels, still shaking his head over what Sir Alexander had just told him. Had Gunn been changed by his injury? Otherwise what on earth could have provoked him into attacking such a senior officer? He went from one question to the other, but he could not yet know the first answer, and the second was beyond him. He rode slowly and gradually the steady motion of the horse and the small challenges of steering through the heavy traffic eased his mind. George was rarely one to worry about anything for very long. He heard some soldiers at work on their own beacon tower singing a distinctly spicy version of 'O Johnny, will you no wed me?' that he had once taught his brother Charles, and laughed to himself. Now he wanted some more domestic entertainment: he had had enough of soldiery for the day.

He took his brown mare to her stables and returned to his billet, where Farrie seemed only too delighted to have the opportunity to grumble about the state of his coatee. George unfolded his better one from the chest, brushed down his breeches, and took a cloth to his boots, not wanting to wait for Farrie's tutting. He combed his hair before the mirror and gently replaced his shako: a shako did terrible things to one's hair. Then he considered whom he might visit, and his mind travelled almost immediately to the charming girl he had seen at that ball on Wednesday, and who had then waved to him in the Allée Verte. What was her name again? Carolina, that was it: and she had a sister, too. That was good: if he were to visit on his own, he did not want it to look specifically as if he were there to see a particular girl. If Argo had come with him – but then Argo was married, and could not be assumed to have an interest in any respectable girl. The first stages of courting, beyond which George had no current wish to go, were best done in numbers, he knew from experience.

Carolina and her sister, he remembered as he completed his grooming – Esther, that was the sister's name! And a very pretty girl, too – lived with their parents somewhere off the Park. He knew the building, which was quite a fine one, though he had not visited them before. Hum … he struggled with further details. Colonel and Mrs. … or was it General? The officer in question had not been at the ball and George had not met him. A general might be a useful acquaintance, though, he remarked to himself. From Yorkshire? Somewhere northern? Fry, that was the name. Good. George put the final touches to his sash, adjusted his sword, and called farewell to Farrie, who grunted in reply. He set off for the Park.

George was welcomed into the Frys' smartly modern apartment with gratifying enthusiasm by Mrs. Fry, at least, and the maid took his cloak and shako as he ran quick fingers through his hair. Mrs. Fry was a thin, busy woman, with eyes and complexion that spoke of some nervous energy. Her own elderly mother was staying, and Mrs. Fry was much taken up with arranging the old lady's cap lace, polishing her glasses, and plying her with random beverages. Her conversation took some patience and concentration, but George was happy to be patient for the moment and well-disposed to try to concentrate, particularly as the girls, Carolina and Esther, were arranged to advantage at a table near the fireplace where their mother and grandmother sat. Or rather, their grandmother sat: their mother was rarely still for long.

'Mr. Murray, how lovely! We have expected you long since, but at last you are come and very welcome.' This caused George a little puzzlement, but he had no chance to indulge it. 'Carolina, do sit up straight, dear. Have you shown Mr. Murray your needlepoint, Esther? Now, Mother, some tea? A little tea would warm you, and at the same time you would find it refreshing, I am sure. Mr. Murray, the Royal Scots, I think? We went to North Britain once. Some very fine scenery, and the air! Quite a tonic in itself. Have you ever been to Brighton? Mother, perhaps a very small glass of brandy? Carolina, dear, do ring for some tea.'

George smiled, unable to find a space to speak, and Carolina caught his eye and giggled. Both sisters were beaming, apparently amused at the least thing. Esther, the younger, had her hair in rather charming ringlets, which bobbed against her long neck, and there was just a touch of ankle showing beneath her gown. Carolina, the elder, was pretty, like her sister, but rather fairer: her hair sat in a smooth cap untroubled by curls, natural or induced. Both were slim like their mother, with shining blue eyes. They were dressed in fashionable green, which made them look like a couple of young twigs on a branch. George found no fault with that, and thought with pleasure that there was little to choose between them. He settled down, legs extended for comfort and just very slightly for showing off, to enjoy whatever the afternoon had to offer.

'I'm sure my husband the General would be prodigiously pleased to meet you,' Mrs. Fry went on. 'He always takes an interest in promising young officers, and of course the Scottish regiments have such a reputation! Haven't they? But he is so busy just now! I declare he has so little time for his family it is a wonder we stay here at all, when we could be back in England and not fearing every alarm of the French arriving at any minute! Has the Duke of Wellington gone to Ghent, do you know? He was to go almost immediately. Such a fuss! But there, it is good to see my husband when we do see him, and I should only fret at home. And we shall all be at that dinner this week – whose is it again? - unless the French arrive first!'

'The General must have a great deal of work to do: I shall be honoured to meet him at the dinner if he is disposed to allow me to be introduced to him,' said George dutifully when a space presented itself. 'And I am sure it is a very great comfort to him to have his family near.'

'His Grace the Duke wants us to go.' Mrs. Fry made a quick face of dissatisfaction. 'He is trying to clear all the British civilians out of Brussels, which is quite terrifying. Not that I see any sign of the Duchess of Richmond departing! But there! I have the greatest faith that the Duke and my husband the General between them will keep Bonaparte from our door. Haven't I, Mother? Has he left Paris yet, do you know? My girls say that if they were in Paris they would never leave! Mother, a little port wine? I am sure you would find it restorative.'

At that point the maid arrived, and Mrs. Fry's mother, with a faint look of disappointment, was given tea like everyone else. Mrs. Fry took the opportunity to rearrange her mother's shawl. George, including the old lady in a general smile, noticed that her bonnet had slipped up over her ear on one side, and that the ear thus revealed was discreetly stuffed with cloth. Mrs. Fry's mother noticed him noticing, opened her faded blue eyes wide, and when her daughter's back was turned slipped a hand up to pull her bonnet back down before winking at him. He blinked and looked again, but she was completely absorbed in drinking her tea.

Mrs. Fry busied herself with the tea tray, and George, dismissing what had just happened, turned his attention to Carolina and Esther.

'And how do you ladies amuse yourselves here in Brussels? Apart, of course, from promenading in the Allée Verte, for of course I have seen you there, making great ornaments for the place!'

The girls simpered in unison.

'And we have seen you, Mr. Murray! What a fine horse you have!'

'Now, was it the black or the brown?' asked George, knowing full well. The brown was for work, the black for elegance.

'The black! How beautifully a black horse shows off a uniform!' said Esther. George grinned. He liked this game.

'That is my fine Lightning,' he explained proudly. 'He does bear a soldier with great valour, I agree. I shall tell him you admired him: he is a vain fellow, and enjoys the least attention. Do you ride? For you were in a fine carriage when I saw you.'

'We have no riding horses in Brussels,' said Esther quickly, and George wondered if they had riding horses at home, either.

'I'm sure you make good horsewomen, though, when the opportunity arises,' he said smoothly. 'I notice that some young ladies are affecting what looks like military dress themselves,' he went on. 'Do you ladies not wish to enlist in the same way?'

'Oh, but this green is the absolute fashion, Mr. Murray!' cried Carolina, smoothing down her acid green skirts with flicks of her thin fingers. 'How terribly ignorant men are about such things! Have you not noticed it?'

'I noticed that the Allée Verte was remarkably full of prodigiously pretty wood elves yesterday,' said George solemnly. 'All in a kind of leafy green.'

'Not leaves, Mr. Murray!' both girls exclaimed at once. 'It is Pomona green.'

'Pomona? But that is the Roman goddess of apples, is she not?' Sometimes a little learning was handy enough, he thought. 'And apples grow on trees, unless I am very much mistaken, and trees grow in woods, and so do wood elves! So you see, your argument is no argument at all.'

The girls giggled in gratifying chorus.

'Now, Mr. Murray, some cake?' asked Mrs. Fry. 'I'm sure you young officers never eat enough, and working all day just like my husband the General. Mother, some cake? A biscuit, perhaps.' Neither quite reached the old lady, as Mrs. Fry was constantly distracted by some better offer. 'Some wine? Carolina, ring the bell, dear. And sit up straight! What part of North Britain do you come from, Mr. Murray?'

'From Fife, ma'am. My brother has my late father's estate near Cupar. It is a very pleasant spot.'

'That's nice, Mr. Murray. I don't believe we ventured as far as Fife.' George could see the usual calculations in her eyes. Fife was a long way: that was a drawback. An estate: an advantage. An older brother in possession? Not so good. George could have played along, mentioning that the older brother was married but with no children yet, more advantages and drawbacks, but he was not definitely interested in either of the Fry girls yet, so he let it lie.

'Mother! I declare that shawl has a life of its own!' Mrs. Fry exclaimed, as the maid returned with several decanters and an expression of habitual confusion. Mrs. Fry bounced up to deal with the shawl and nearly tipped over the maid with all her burdens. George, beginning to feel sympathetic, returned to the girls.

'And how did you enjoy the ball at Sir John's?' he asked, referring back to the event at which he had first met them, more than a week ago.

'Oh, it was vastly amusing!' said Esther. 'We had the most delightful time.'

'And met so many charming people!' Carolina added, with only a flicker of a sideways glance at George. 'But there, we have talked all this over before, you and I!'

'Have we?' asked George. Not for the first time that day, he felt himself floundering.

'Of course we have! Don't you remember? How very ungallant of you!' she cried, though she was starting to giggle again, teasing him. 'We met a week ago. I believe you had come from a dinner – with, I believe, a Captain Willis?'

'Ah,' said George. This, he thought, drawing in his legs, was unlikely to be good.

Chapter Five

Edinburgh

I

'I can never remember which is what, anyway,' was Willie Jack's useful contribution. Breakfast was served late in his household, and he himself was leisurely over it. Murray had been up for two hours already, unable to sleep.

'I just had the general area in my head,' admitted Murray. 'Water of Leith village, Dean village – which was it? Of course, I was not expecting Walter to lose the letter.'

'I'm awful sorry, sir,' said Walter sedately. He stood by the table, his hands behind his back, having come to volunteer his crime. 'I had it put somewhere safe, I just canna rightly remember where.'

Murray opened his mouth to reply, but changed his mind. It seemed to take a serious effort to shake Walter.

'They're not big places, either of them,' said Willie Jack consolingly. 'I daresay anyone you met might know of a new person in the area. Particularly if she's not one of the bakers – or is that the other village?'

'The Water of Leith village is the baxters' place,' said Murray, unreasonably annoyed at Willie Jack's lack of knowledge or interest in his home town, 'and the Dean village is the quarrying one.' He drew breath. He knew he was becoming irritable these days: he had to try to stop himself.

'Well, is she a baxter?' asked Willie Jack.

'She's the wife of an officer, that's all I know,' said Murray shortly. 'She could be a baker's daughter or a quarrier's daughter easily enough, or even neither.'

'Are you walking or riding?' asked Willie Jack, drawing

another plate of ham towards himself and pouring more coffee. Willie Jack was not a walker or a rider. Clearly his wife was not much of a breakfaster, either: Letitia had not made an appearance yet this morning.

'I think I'll walk,' said Murray. 'It's easier to keep track of Walter when I'm on foot.'

'I'll do my best not to lose you, sir,' said Walter, unmoved.

Prince's Street was already busy by the time Murray had left the Dundas' apartment, and he nearly lost Walter straight away, but this time to accident rather than wandering. A number of carts had tangled themselves in the middle of the broad street, and another, in a hurry, swerved around them and narrowly missed Walter in the doorway. Murray snatched him from harm's way and tried to see the cart's number, but as usual other carters magically managed to obscure his view. He cursed inwardly, and pushed Walter cautiously in front of him to the west end of the street.

Prince's Street was a one-sided affair: Willie Jack's apartment building backed on to the New Town, the grid-like formation constructed only in the last forty years but already itching to expand. Murray's own town house was in Queen Street, on its northern edge – for now, but not for much longer. George's Street was the central street of the grid, leading from Charlotte Square at one end to St. Andrew's Square at the other. Prince's Street formed the southern boundary. Across from it was land unlikely to be built on as the feat of completely draining the Nor'Loch had not yet quite been accomplished, even though it had been contained, opposite Willie Jack's building, into a canal of sorts. Above the stagnant water, the Castle loomed above grassy slopes which were much steeper, Murray knew to his cost, than they looked. At the west end of this perhaps once-picturesque valley stood the West Kirk, tucked at the bottom of a meadow with its ancient graveyard about it, in a corner between Prince's Street and Kirkbraehead, the street that doubled back into the Old Town. Murray, however, turned right: Kirkbraehead was only a section of the Queensferry road, and though he had travelled along it into Edinburgh only a couple of days before, he now headed north again along it to where the road lurched and swerved to negotiate the deep ravine of the Water of Leith. There he left the road amongst tall buildings and stepped on to the well-kept cobbles of the Water of Leith village.

The New Town had not touched this little settlement: they had no real need of it. The narrow, fast-running river that had carved its ravine had for centuries powered the mills that ground the grain that gave up the flour that the Baxters of Edinburgh transformed into the loaves that fed a city. Building their prosperity on Edinburgh's necessity, they spent their money wisely: only ten years ago they had opened the mighty West Mill, at six storeys rivalling the tallest tenements of the Old Town but established on the bank of the river as solidly as if the Last Trump would scarcely shake it. On the opposite bank, rising around Murray and Walter as they walked, were other, lesser mills, sucking their power from another of the frequent weirs. The banks of the river, where they were steep, were lined with zigzagging sandstone streets, but at the top end of the village the banks on both sides shallowed and a footbridge crossed between broad slipways, not that there was much boat traffic. The splash of churning waterwheels and the grunt and clatter of machinery came from all around, and the air was misty with flour, dry with the smell of it. Walter had never seen or heard anything like it in Fife: the chestnut head turned left and right, as his boots slipped unregarded on the cobbles.

Murray did not know the village well, rarely having had reason to be here: he reckoned the last time he had visited would have been just after the West Mill was finished, a winter slither down into the valley to wonder at the huge building. Now the valley was green where industry could not climb its steep walls, and the buildings shone where the sun reached them. The narrow streets were busy: grain was arriving and flour was leaving, clerks appeared from dark offices to blink in the sunlight and mark off sacks and carts, mill workers, dusty white, scurried from building to building, one or two wealthy guildbrothers strolled about to inspect the progress of their establishments, and a number of servants Murray would not have been surprised to see in a gentleman's house went about their business, women bringing back fruit and vegetables from Edinburgh, men attending their masters or hurrying on important errands. For a moment everyone seemed so occupied that Murray hesitated before asking directions. At last he saw a man in a plain brown coat, a clerk or a servant, with a wide-brimmed hat to his head and a pair of quite decent gloves, pausing to look down at the weir at Mar's Mill. Murray approached quickly before he could escape.

'I wonder if you could help me. I'm looking for a place that offers furnished lodgings.' Or he hoped he was: it seemed likely.

'There are a few,' said the man, pulling himself away from the view of the weir reluctantly. He did not look Murray in the eye, keeping his hat brim well down. All that could be seen was a pale chin clouded with the day's black stubble.

'Could you point me in a likely direction, then?' asked Murray after a moment.

'Up there,' the man waved, indicating a narrow street up the brae. 'That would be most likely.'

'Thank you. I wonder before I go if you could tell me – I know this is a close-knit place – if you have come across a Mrs. Argo, new to the village? Alicia Argo, a youngish woman, the wife of an army officer.'

'I know of none such,' said the man, turning away. 'Try up there.' He gave a dismissive wave, and Murray gave up on him. At least they had somewhere to start.

Making sure that Walter was following him, he took the steep path upwards and found that on the upper side of the street offices quickly gave way to houses. He passed a couple that seemed more well-to-do, then selected a tenement, an old one but with a clean air about it. He nodded to Walter to rattle the risp, knowing he enjoyed it.

Walter had the chance to rattle a few more risps that morning, for they went from one end of Water of Leith village to the other without finding any trace of Alicia Argo. It crossed Murray's mind that if she were in fear of her life, as George had suggested, she might have moved there under an assumed name, but that would not have helped his search. He made a mental note to ask George for some kind of physical description of the woman if he could not find her today, for he felt increasingly helpless here. At least if Walter had not lost George's letter, he would have had an address to go on.

But presumably if she were living under another name, he went on in his head, she would have told her husband how to address his letters to her, and Argo would have told George (he hoped) and George would have told him, so the likelihood of an assumed name was faint. Heartened, he stopped and bought Walter a bun, fresh from one of the local bakers. Watching him bite into it, he bought another for himself.

'I think we have exhausted the Water of Leith, Walter,' he announced as they chewed, 'even though it somehow seemed more likely. The next thing to try is the Dean village.'

'Where's that, then, sir?'

'Upstream, and on the other side of the river. Come, we can cross at the bottom of Bell's Brae.'

They crossed the busy footbridge, the longest and sturdiest of the three or four that spanned the river, and wound between the buildings on the opposite bank, finding their way, mostly by dint of heading upwards at any opportunity, on to the Dean Path. Here they were on the old lands of the Nisbets of Dean, at least until the Town Council worked out how to expand the New Town north-west beyond the Water of Leith. The path led up away from the baxters' mills as the clattering faded, and through a leafy woodland noisy instead with birds, until they emerged at the top of the hill on a narrow street between small, thatched houses, with a few lanes drawing off to each side.

'This,' said Murray, 'is Dean Village. Rather different from the Water of Leith. How Willie Jack could confuse them ...' His words petered out as he told himself again not to be irritable.

Here the streets were not quite so busy: the main occupation of the inhabitants centred around Craigleith Quarry, and in the middle of the day the men would mostly be at work. A few lads played in the street, though they stopped to examine Walter as he passed, sniggering when he turned to stare at them. They looked unlikely to be helpful, and Murray turned his attention instead to two men who were lounging outside the small inn, propped on the lepping-on stane. One had a short, jutting chin that seemed to be looking for a fight all on its own, while the other was loose-lipped – loose-toothed, too, to judge by how many seemed to be missing. The first man lacked a leg, and the second had something wrong with his hand, but that was not unusual in a quarrying community.

'Hi, Johnnie!' said the loose-lipped one to his companion as they approached. 'Here's a gentleman come to see you!' He nudged him heavily.

'Good morning,' said Murray, pretending not to have noticed.

'Can either of you tell me where a Mrs. Argo lives? She would be new to the place.'

Loose-lips' mouth sagged a little, then drew up into an aimless smile. Johnnie knocked his one foot on the stone he was sitting on, and frowned in thought.

'Argo?' he repeated. 'I dinna think so.'

'Well, do you know anyone who might have taken in a new lodger recently? Someone who lets out furnished rooms, perhaps?'

Johnnie shrugged.

'I suppose up the road there's a couple places. Up yonder.' He jerked his head further north. Loose-lips grinned wetly.

'A couple places, aye,' he agreed. 'That'll be where she is. If she's anywhere, ken,' he added helpfully.

'No strangers staying at the inn?' asked Murray, nodding at the building behind them. It did not look inviting, but if Alicia Argo had felt her life might be in danger who knew where she might take refuge?

'Naw,' said Loose-lips. 'No chance she's there.'

It was oddly phrased, Murray thought, but he let it pass. Loose-lips did not look particularly bright. Johnnie, on the other hand, had his wits about him.

'We'd show you the way, sir, but with my leg … It's not long lost, sir, and I havena my wooden leg yet.'

'Well, you've been very helpful,' said Murray, handing over the expected coins. 'I'll try further up.'

With Walter pattering behind, stoically ignoring the local lads, Murray walked the length of the village street and was about to try the farthest door, planning to work his way back, when from the lane by its side two women appeared, by their appearance a mother and daughter. In serviceable brown, they made Murray think of two large geese coming to see off an intruder.

'Good day to you, sir, and who is it you might be seeking?' asked the mother at once, not standing on ceremony. Her voice was sharp by nature, it appeared: she softened it here with a polite smile. Happy to be offered help without asking, Murray smiled back

'I'm seeking a Mrs. Argo,' he explained. 'She would be new to the village.'

'Oh yes?' The mother was not going to give up any information too easily. 'And you would be …?'

'I am Murray of Letho, in Fife.'

'You're a long way from home, then, sir. And if we knew where Mrs. Argo was, why would you be wanting to know?' They stood side by side like a stone wall in brown muslin.

'Her husband is an officer in Brussels with my brother, and he has not heard from her for a while. He asked me to find her if I could and see that she was well and safe.'

'He'd be a friend of your brother's, then, sir?' asked the daughter, just as sharp but without the smile.

'A fellow officer. I believe they are indeed friendly.' The daughter's heavy face twitched in disapproval, as if she had heard that story before. They stood in silence for a moment, perhaps communing spiritually with each other, though they both kept their pale eyes on Murray. He tried not to flinch: the effect was quite frightening. The daughter, he noticed, was not actually as fat as the mother, but something about her appearance and the way she had walked towards him suggested she thought she was, or expected to be.

'The men down by the inn thought that she might have taken lodgings at this end of the village,' he tried eventually, wilting under their scrutiny.

'Johnnie Norrie and Ebb?' the daughter said dismissively. 'What would they know?'

'So there's no one of that name here?' Murray persisted. The daughter's eyes slid round glassily and glanced at her mother.

'You could try Matt Chisholm,' said the mother in a non-committal tone. 'It's the big house over there. He takes in a few.'

'That's very helpful, thank you,' said Murray, glancing over at the house they had indicated before turning back to the women. He surprised a little smirk on the daughter's face, which he did not like. 'Good day to you.'

He bowed slightly and guided Walter over to the big house.

The house was indeed big by Dean Village standards, but not otherwise enormous. Having seen a number of lodging houses that day already, Murray reckoned that it had perhaps six rooms to let, arranged over two floors. It was slated, which also distinguished it amongst its rounded thatched neighbours, and was well-kept, with a small, swept yard in front and windows wiped of all the quarry dust which seemed to settle everywhere else. At a nod from Murray, Walter stepped forward like a royal page and rattled the risp. After a moment, the door opened and a thin man peered out, not unwelcoming.

'Oh!' he said, taking in Murray's appearance. 'What can I do for you, sir?'

'I'm looking for a Mrs. Argo, wife of an army officer,' said Murray for what seemed like the fiftieth time that day. 'I heard there was a chance she lodged here?' Even as he said it, he glanced up and saw that the words 'Combe's Court' were cut into the stone of the lintel. It jogged his memory, and suddenly he could see in his mind's eye his brother George's letter. 'Combe's Court, Dean village'. He had definitely found it. 'Are you by any chance Matt Chisholm?'

'That's me,' said the thin man. 'The best lodgings in Dean or Water of Leith, that's the place.' He drew himself up, tugging down his waistcoat. Keepers of furnished lodgings must not get out much, Murray thought: this man, too, had a pale complexion.

'And Mrs. Argo? Does she stay here?'

'Mrs. Argo – yes. A fine and discerning woman: it was a pleasure to have her as a lodger.'

'Was?' said Murray. Where had she gone now? Could the woman not stay in one place for more than five minutes?

'Oh, aye, she moved on. She would have left … let me see … about a week ago? She wasna long here, ah, unfortunately. That room up there was hers – do you want to see it? I've no one in it just yet.' He smiled, but there was a look of apprehension in his eyes.

Murray nodded, and Chisholm led them up a generous staircase to a landing with four doors off it. Chisholm opened one and showed them inside. The room had a window each to the front and the side of the house, a wooden floor swept clean, a firwood table, rather stained, a bed frame and two mattresses, and in the corner a curtain cordoned off a triangle for washing, with a jug, basin and chamberpot. Two chairs guarded a small hearth, also clean and bare. The house seemed slightly ashamed of the furnishings, as if it were used to better.

'It's a fine house,' said Murray, turning away. There was nothing to be seen of Alicia Argo in this bare chamber. 'Is it a family one?'

'It was my uncle's, sir. He was a supervisor at the quarry, years ago. Built this place thinking he was going to marry but she turned him down, so here he sat on his own till the day he died, and he left it to me.'

'It's good you have been able to put it to some use,' said Murray politely. 'And certainly it is well kept. Strange that Mrs. Argo should move on so quickly. Did you know her before she came here?'

'I'd never met her before. I had the feeling she knew the village a bit, but she didn't go visiting any friends. She just stayed in her room most of the time, or came and had a gossip with me. Oh, we got on fine, did Mrs. Argo and me.' He fingered his waistcoat buttons and his gaze wandered, perhaps back to gossips with Mrs. Argo.

'When she left, did she say where she was going?'

'No, never a word. As to her leaving,' his mouth twisted, as if wringing out the words, 'it's my opinion she was embarrassed by the boy.'

'The boy?'

'Her son.'

Murray managed to contain his surprise. George had never mentioned a son.

'He lived with her?' he asked.

'Oh, aye, he's maybe ten or twelve? He kept having rammies with the village lads: thought himself maybe a wee bit above them. And if they said ought to him that he took exception to, he never could keep his temper.'

'And Mrs. Argo found that difficult?'

'That's right. She isna someone to flaunt herself about the place. She's a very nice lady. I think she felt he was drawing attention.'

Murray thought for a moment. A son … what difference did that make? It must make some.

'I have to confess I have never met Mrs. Argo,' he said slowly. 'Her husband asked me to make sure she was settled and safe. What is she like?'

'A very – pleasant woman,' said Chisholm, clearly changing his mind on the word partway through. 'A bonny one, too. And very polite – very appreciative of any little thing done for her.' Perhaps unconsciously at this point he gave his hair a little stroke back from his face, as if his appearance suddenly mattered. He looked away out of the window, briefly forgetting that Murray was there. 'I'd have been very happy if she'd stayed on a little longer,' he went on. 'Very happy indeed. But there: there are plenty more, eh?'

'Well, I hope you find a suitable tenant again soon, Mr. Chisholm. You say she is bonny – can you describe her more closely?'

'She's small-made, with a pale face and yellow hair. And dark blue eyes, very deep. A fine-looking woman, all told.'

Murray, armed with this description but with no idea where to look next, took his leave. It was interesting, he thought: she had left the first lodging out of fear for her life, and had left this one much faster, yet seemed to have made no mention of any threats here. Had she not even felt safe enough to confide in anyone here? Or had the threat never existed? Yet she had mentioned it to her husband, and surely she would not have wished to worry him without reason. He sighed. It was difficult to work this out without knowing more of the woman herself: she mentioned her husband, it seemed, but how did she feel about him? Was she glad he was away, giving her the freedom to please herself? Did she miss him? And hadn't George said that the Argos were not long married – where, then, did the son come into it?

Outside in the street, the local boys had gathered again, but this time they ignored Walter.

'You lookin' Mrs. Argo, Mister?' they called.

'I am.' Murray stopped and tried to pick out a ringleader to talk to. 'What do you know of her?' The lads kept moving: it was difficult to focus on one.

'Gey heich-headed!' called one boy.

'Full of herself!' called another.

'Wee lad thought he was too good to go around wi' us!' said the first again. 'Him and his grey breeks!' Clearly the breeches were a sore point, as several of them pranced around just then making much of their legs as the others cackled.

'What's the boy's name?' Murray asked.

'Theodore!' cried one, grandly.

'Oh, aye, Theodore!' Several others took up a chorus. 'Theodore, Theodore, wipe your breeches on the floor! Don't forget to close the door! Theodore, Theodore!' They found this immensely clever and laughed themselves dizzy again.

'And do you know where Theodore has gone?'

'He's gone to Edinburgh,' said the first boy again, as if that were the most pretentious thing Theodore could have done. 'Up till the Old Town. He's away to the Castle to see the sojers.'

'He's no!' cried another, showing the first note of dissension in the ranks. 'He's awa to join his faither!'

'But his father's in Belgium,' said Murray, puzzled. At this, the boys let out a huge crow of laughter between them and skidded off down a side lane, and vanished. The street was suddenly quiet.

'Well, what do you make of that, then, Walter?' Murray asked, on a long outbreath.

'I think they are all very foolish, sir,' said Walter.

'You're probably right. But were they right, too?' He looked up and down the street, dusty and empty. Even Johnnie Norrie and – what had the daughter called him? Ebb? – had disappeared from their perch. What could have brought Alicia Argo here?

'Well, we've gone as far as we can for now,' sighed Murray. 'I think we might as well go back to Prince's Street.'

'Very good, sir,' said Walter, and for just a moment Murray heard Robbins' voice echo in the boy's words. He wished Robbins were here.

They walked back down the street to return to the bridge over the Water of Leith. If, on the way, Murray thought he saw a man in a brown coat and a wide brimmed black hat, lingering in the woodland outside the village, it did not occur to him to think of it as anything more than a coincidence.

Chapter Six

Belgium

I

'Mr. Murray! Oh, Mr. Murray!'

George turned almost without surprise from his perusal of padlocks in the little ironmongers, and bowed to the Misses Fry.

'Good day to you!' he cried as they curtsied in return. 'I was most put out that we had no chance to speak earlier.'

'In the Allée Verte this morning? No, indeed, it was most unfortunate,' agreed Carolina Fry, making a little pout of dissatisfaction. 'But there, we were in our friends' carriage, and not our own, and it did not occur to me to ask them to turn it just to speak to you!'

'Well, not *just* to speak with him, Carolina dear,' corrected Esther with a smile. 'But it would have been quite awkward, Mr. Murray, as Mr. Storey had asked us in order to pay particular attention to Carolina, and so if she had begged him to take her to speak to some other gentleman I daresay he would not have taken it very well, charming though he undoubtedly is.'

'Oh, so you have a beau?' said George, teasing. 'I shall be very jealous, of course.' He was not sure at this stage whether he felt mildly envious or mildly relieved.

'Of course you will!' said Carolina heartily. 'For we seem to be seeing so much of each other these past few days that I doubt not but that in the minds of some we are already an old married couple!'

At this even George was a little taken aback. He had not considered it: after all, it had been Thursday when he had visited the family in their apartment for the first time, and now it was only Saturday. He tried to think back, but it was difficult with both sisters addressing him.

'We had such a jolly time with you in the Allée Verte yesterday morning, and then of course we saw you here at the Petit Theatre last night! Brussels really is an absolutely tiny place.'

'Isn't it?' said George. He had remarked on it himself, enjoying the constant possibility of meeting friends and acquaintances.

'And then of course the two of you ...' began Esther, then stopped, met her sister's eye and giggled. Carolina immediately giggled, too.

'Of course! Yes, didn't we?' She looked sideways at George, very coquettishly under her bonnet. His heart warmed at the sight, yet his head still worried. Where on earth had they met? And what, oh, what, had they done? And how could he possibly have forgotten? He resorted to what he thought of as a manly grin, saying nothing.

'But I am delighted to see you here, too,' Carolina was going on, fortunately, away from the mysterious subject. 'For you can settle an argument between Esther and me. Come, away from this dull ironmongery, for there is a silk merchant just over there, you must have noticed!'

There were in fact six little booths within the Theatre du Parc, amongst which George felt the ironmonger's sat slightly oddly. The other booths held a bookstall, an engraver stocking prints of Brussels which were selling well to the British officers, a jeweller, and a perfumer, and indeed a silk merchant who had some very attractive wares on his stall.

'Look,' Carolina was saying, having conveyed them all over to the silk merchant. 'These tiny silk roses, in the French style: they would be just the thing for a little lace cap I have in mind for going to that dinner next week. I think they are charming, but Esther, my unkind sister!' they giggled at each other 'She says they are much too small, and that as a consequence they will not hide enough of my hair! Did ever you hear such an insult, Mr. Murray? I declare I feel betrayed!' The pair of them giggled again. George examined the roses with some solemnity, taking as long as possible to scrutinise each petal and fold.

'Well, Mr. Murray?' Carolina was growing impatient.

'The flowers are completely charming,' George agreed. Carolina gave a little squeak of triumph. 'Though they are indeed small,' he went on. Esther beamed and nodded. 'Though I should like to know, as an fellow ignorant of these things,' George continued, his face serious, 'why it should be considered such a crime to wear small flowers, and not obscure hair which is, in my no doubt unworthy opinion, of a perfectly delightful colour and style?'

'There!' Carolina crowed, and elbowed her sister in her skinny ribs. 'Mr. Murray says I should not hide my hair! Esther is prodigiously proud of her ringlets,' she added in a loud whisper. 'She is convinced that my hair is much too straight and dull.'

'Not at all, not at all!' George rejoined rapidly. 'Though ringlets, too, have their charms – framing the right face, of course,' he added, with a little bow to Esther which redressed the balance between the sisters fairly well.

'The most unfortunate thing, though,' Carolina went on, with another little sideways pout under her bonnet, 'is that the shopkeeper tells me that the roses are selling frighteningly fast, and neither Esther nor I have brought any purse with us. So I am reduced to gazing at them until some lucky girl buys them, and after that perhaps I shall only see them on someone else's cap, and whether or not it hides her hair is completely immaterial.'

'Tragic, don't you think, Mr. Murray?' added Esther, with an identical pout. George found himself reaching for his pocketbook before he had even realised he was going to.

'Then you must allow me to make you a little loan of the money,' he said.

'Oh, no! I could not! What on earth would people say?' asked Carolina.

'People really need not know,' said George, puzzled. 'It is surely business only between the three of us.' He picked up the little spray of roses and gestured to the shopkeeper, who conveyed to George by means of very simple French the price of the roses. George tried for a moment to ask whether it was just the one spray he was paying for at that price, or the whole shop, but gave it up as a bad job and made over the coins. The little spray – really, a very little spray – was wrapped in tissue and tied with pink string, and handed over to Carolina to carry on one little finger, while George put away his distinctly thinner pocketbook. Each girl took him firmly by the arm and led him away from the silk merchant and along the row of booths towards the exit, though he did feel a little resistance as they passed the jeweller. He gently tugged them on and into the street.

Outside the day was pleasant and fresh. George breathed in the air, and began to appreciate being seen with a pretty girl on each arm, his red coatee bright in the sunshine, his gold lace agleam, cutting a very fine figure. And after all, what were a few shillings which no doubt she would pay him back at the first opportunity?

'Shall we take a turn in the Parc, ladies?' he asked. 'I must depart soon for the men's camp, but I have a little time to spare and would be delighted to spend it with you.'

'In that case perhaps you would simply escort us home, Mr. Murray? It is not far, as you know.'

'I should be honoured.'

It took only a few minutes to reach their apartment building, and George saw them to their door with gallant efficiency. Mrs. Fry appeared behind the maid and greeted him.

'You must come in, Mr. Murray! I declare we have not seen you for so long! Since last night at the theatre, at least!'

'I fear I cannot stay now, madam: duty calls!'

'Then you must join us for dinner this evening. You really must. I know it is a short invitation, but it will be quite informal!'

'Then I should be honoured, madam,' said George with a bow, and left, smiling, for the camp.

When he reached the camp, George was somewhat surprised to find that Argo had already left for the day. He was much less surprised when the post corporal informed him with ill grace that Lieutenant Argo had gone off to haunt the town's post office instead, 'and much good may it do him,' he added, sourly. He received a severe overgoing from George, though principally because George thought much the same thing himself. George settled down at the desk in the next tent to go over the day's paperwork, checking the quartermaster's accounts and pondering the mysteries of military supplies: sometimes he could not manage his own little requirements. It was a good thing Charles was the older brother – much more suited to dealing with the estate at Letho. He was just working his way through an account of buttons used when he was aware of movement at the flap of the tent, and looked up. In a moment he was on his feet.

'Captain Gunn! You are back!'

'We are, indeed,' said the newcomer with a smile in his voice. He was against the light and George could not see him clearly, but there was no denying him, and now he was into the tent himself, along with a large, sharp-looking man and a young lad of around ten or twelve: George was no expert on children and their ages.

'Major Saddler,' George bowed hurriedly to the sharp man. Saddler responded almost as an aside. Gunn and George shook hands warmly.

'This lad is James Graham, a new drummer boy. I'll just show him where to put his kit,' said Gunn, a hand on the boy's shoulder. The boy looked as though he would have liked to shrug it off, and was only just too polite to try.

'Sergeant Lamb is with the boys at present,' George called after him. 'He can take charge of him.'

Gunn left with a nod, and George turned his attention to Saddler.

'Is all in order, Murray?' Saddler asked. He was already behind the desk and skimming through the papers George had been working on.

'Yes, sir. One man's under the surgeon for a broken arm and two have stomach upsets, but it was undercooked meat, sir, not the drink. They're due back tomorrow. All others present and in order, sir. The mails aren't what they could be, but it'll take a while for them to be up to Spanish standards, I daresay.'

'I trust we shan't be here long enough to find out, Murray.'

'No, sir. Any word on Bonaparte?'

'He'll leave Paris next week, they're saying, but who knows? The place will erupt when he leaves, no doubt. But all his supporters are between Paris and here, and all the Bourbons are too far to the south. If we don't have time to gather all the allies here, it might not go our way.' He looked up from the papers, which he had been reading as he talked. 'Buttons?'

'I think they've been giving them to local girls as love tokens,' said George helplessly.

'Then the next soldier who loses one will pay for it,' said Saddler, and it was not clear whether that meant with money, with privileges, or with something more permanent. 'Ah, Gunn.'

'You found the Sergeant, then?' asked George, turning to meet his friend, and saw him for the first time with the light on his face. He stopped, and swallowed.

Gunn was a chubby man, for a soldier: he was not tall and his movements seemed a little clumsy until, as George knew well, he was on a horse or wielding a sword – then he seemed to come into his own, and from chubby he became close-knit, efficient, substantial. His hair was fairish, straight and flat, and his round cheeks were sallow, his expression serious without severity. Well, half of it was: the other half was no longer as it had been. The sword blow George remembered had been a downward one, so it must have been the surgeon's doing that one side of Gunn's face now twisted upwards, from his jaw to the corner of his eye, giving him a cynical look which George felt changed him very much. The sword must also have gone on to strike him on the shoulder, for he hunched that side a little and his uniform did not sit as well as once it had. George realised he was staring, and was about to apologise, when Gunn gave him a half-smile and said,

'A bit of a shock, isn't it? Still, no matter: everything still functions much as it did.'

'Good thing, too,' snapped Saddler. 'We need every good man we can get in this one. I don't see Miller or Wright in the battalion, Murray? Or Easson?'

'Wright lost a leg on the way back from the Peninsula – fell under a gun carriage, sir. Miller and Easson were transferred to the First Battalion: they should be in Canada by now.'

'Shame about Wright and Miller. Easson's no great loss. Where's the new Lieutenant? Argo, isn't it?'

'He's in town this morning – I mentioned we'd had some trouble with the mails, and he's off to talk to the post office people.'

'What like of a man is he? Any use?'

'I think he might be, once he gets going,' George said, having prepared this answer. Saddler sometimes had the effect of making George say things he did not intend – true things, no doubt, but often best unsaid. 'What do you say we all have supper tonight? I shall see him when I go back to town, and arrange ... there's a good little place I know called the St. Pierre, a decent wine or two and some solid food.'

'There's a great deal to be done here,' said Saddler.

'Gunn?'

'I'm not sure ...' said Gunn, with a twisted frown. 'It's been a long journey ...'

'Oh, for old times' sake?' asked George. He had been so looking forward to the camaraderie of his fellow officers. 'And it might be a fine thing to welcome Lieutenant Argo formally to the company.'

'It's true: you could maybe come to a clearer judgement of him over a comfortable jug of wine, sir,' said Gunn gently. Saddler peered more closely at something written in a daily report, and George squinted to try to see what it might be, in case he needed another ready answer. He jumped when Saddler glanced up.

'Yes, right, that sounds like a good idea. Best to get to know the man.' Saddler continued his rapid perusal of the papers. George was pleased.

'And you, Gunn?'

'Oh, well, very well, since I talked the Major into it!'

'Splendid, splendid! I shall have a word at the St. Pierre as soon as I return to the town.'

George was delighted Saddler and Gunn were back, and very happy – not to say relieved - to hand over his papers, but he did hope that Saddler's scrutinising would not make him late for dinner. How difficult it could be to fit in all one's social engagements in the army!

II

Though he stopped to make sure Argo knew where to find the St. Pierre and what time to meet there, George was not late for dinner. General Fry, however, did not seem particularly interested in meeting him, and was not forthcoming in conversation before or over dinner. On the other hand, it would have been a man possessed of courage, determination and a carrying voice that could have made himself heard against the conversation of Mrs. Fry and her two daughters. George suspected that General Fry had long ago given up trying.

'See what Mr. Murray bought me, Papa!' cried Carolina, cupping the precious silk roses in her long fingers. 'I am keeping them to be perfect for the dinner next week, Mr. Murray. They are not to be wasted on mere domestic dinners!'

George was not sure whether or not to be flattered, and decided that it was more straightforward just to smile and nod. The girls fluttered in and out of the room, as did their mother, the only steady characters being the General and Mrs. Fry's mother, who spoke not a word all evening. Eventually the meal was over and the ladies, picking Mrs. Fry's mother up amongst them like a forgotten shawl, vanished into the drawing room calling instructions not to take long, and George was left with the General.

The General poured himself a glass of port, and pushed the decanter silently towards George. George thanked him, and poured a small glass for himself. He looked back up to see the General eyeing him, fiddling as he did so with the top of his own collar. He was clean-shaven, except for what George could only think of as a beard that had slipped: a line of whiskers frilled his neck a couple of inches above his collar. It was strangely fascinating.

'So, you are from Fifeshire, sir?' said the General. His voice was soft: George could not imagine him giving an order.

'That's right, sir. Do you know the county?'

'Not at all.'

'It is a pleasant place, with a prodigious length of coast, and good farmland.'

'I'm delighted to hear it.'

'There is also a house in the New Town of Edinburgh.'

'That is, I am sure, a convenience.'

'Yes, sir.'

There was a silence so long that George felt as if his tongue had glued to the roof of his mouth. The General pulled at his misplaced beard.

'Mr. Murray, are you here to ask me a question?'

'No, sir, I don't believe I am.'

'Good.'

There was another long pause.

'You are with the third battalion of the Royal Scots, are you not? The old Royal Regiment?'

'That's right, sir.'

'Hm,' said the General. 'I hear one of your officers attacked Sir Alexander Gordon a week or so ago. At an inn in the north.'

'I have heard the same story, sir.'

'Do you doubt it?'

George became cautious.

'I do not doubt, sir, that Sir Alexander believes that to have been the case.'

The General stared at him, and fiddled with his collar.

'I don't believe it would be a good idea to place one's faith in anyone opposing Sir Alexander Gordon, Mr. Murray.'

'I don't suppose it would, sir.'

The General stood abruptly.

'Let us join the ladies.'

III

George tried to put his strange conversation with General Fry out of his mind as he made his way to the St. Pierre after dinner. There were distractions enough: the Parc was busy even after dusk, and any number of fashionable equipages were stopping at the classical façade of the Theatre to disgorge silk dresses and best uniforms for the evening's entertainments. The windows and doors splashed light into the street and tantalised the passersby with colour, music and scent. By contrast, the house that George knew the Duke of Wellington inhabited, with a fine view of the Parc, was almost unlit and silent: the Duke, he thought, must still be in Ghent - attended by Sir Alexander Gordon, no doubt. What had Gunn been up to?

Argo was already at the St. Pierre when George arrived, seated at a table on his own with his hands curiously placed on the table in front of him, his cloak expeditiously arranged over the opposite bench to claim it for the rest of the party. George waved and began to make his way over: Argo was always early for appointments. He'd be out on the battlefield, his sword polished and his shako brushed, a week before Bonaparte arrived, thought George: in fact, he might be more useful than the beacon towers. Argo had a jug of wine and four glasses in front of him, but the glasses were unused. Or they were until George sat down, when he seized one, filled it and took a deep gulp.

'Thank you for that, Argo!' he said in satisfaction. 'I'll buy the next jug.'

'Should we order food?' Argo asked, 'or should we wait?'

George looked around. The broad, low room was only about half-full.

'They're not too busy. Let's wait – Saddler and Gunn shouldn't be long.'

'How was your dinner at the Frys'?'

'Oh, very pleasant, very pleasant! The ladies are very charming, and I met the General.'

'And what nature of man is he?'

'He seems a fine man. Quiet, at home – he may be different with his fellow officers.' A second of discomfort passed over George as he thought again of the General's words about Gunn.

Argo sighed through his nose: he had asked his polite questions, and his gaze wandered away from George to rest somewhere on the smoky cream plastered wall opposite. George allowed himself a little roll of the eyes.

'Any word yet from Edinburgh?' he brought himself to ask.

'No …'

'Oh, look!' cried George, loud with relief. 'Here they are!'

He was on his feet before he knew it, and Argo rose uncertainly, looking about. Saddler and Gunn were just leaving their cloaks by the door, and casting about the room for George. The ceiling was low: Saddler made it look much lower.

He led the way across the room as if the other customers did not exist, and Gunn followed in his wake, eyes low, making small placatory gestures at one or two of the customers Saddler had nudged or wobbled. Saddler nodded in acknowledgement of the delighted grin on George's face, and they bowed.

'Murray. Good to see you.'

'Major Saddler. May I present Lieutenant James Argo?'

Argo bowed and the Major nodded, subjecting him to a long assessing look which Argo seemed to feel physically.

'Captain Gunn,' George went on after a moment, 'may I present Lieutenant James Argo?'

'Delighted, sir,' said Gunn, bowing as Argo turned to him in relief. 'I hear you are not long from Edinburgh?'

'Yes, sir,' said Argo. 'That is my home. My wife lives there. I hope,' he added, and George felt like kicking him.

'A wife, eh?' said Saddler, establishing himself at the table.

'Caught so young!' He poured himself a generous glass of wine. 'Your health, sirs.'

Argo gave a weak smile and waited until the others had sat before returning to his seat. He perched as if half-afraid the bench might be snatched from under him.

'You're just back from Edinburgh yourself,' said George to Saddler, feeling Argo's anxiety beside him. 'Any news from the town?'

'Nothing much,' the Major replied. 'Nothing you wouldn't likely have heard by now, if you have correspondents in the town.'

'My brother has just gone back from Fife: I had word from him what? Two days ago?'

'Then you'll likely know all there is to know,' said Saddler shortly.

'Where in Edinburgh were you?' George asked again. He had no clear idea of Saddler's background.

'Oh, here and there.'

That was probably why, George thought. Saddler was not very forthcoming.

Gunn nodded at Argo.

'I'm frae Corstorphine, myself, outside Edinburgh. And you, sir?'

But George was determined not to let Argo get on to the subject of his wife, and spoil the evening.

'And how was your journey?' he broke in, beaming encouragingly at both Saddler and Gunn. Oh, it was fine to have them both back!

'It was a fair passage,' said Saddler, without looking at Gunn. 'The packet from Leith to London was dull enough, but there were plenty of officers aboard at Dover.'

'Did you come from Edinburgh, too?' George asked Gunn. He found himself staring at Gunn's scar again, and made himself meet Gunn's eyes instead.

'No, I joined at London.'

'And how did you find that, then?' George poured himself another glass. Neither Saddler nor Gunn seemed to have touched theirs, and Argo had only drunk half: even at that he was a little pink. George did not know him as much of a drinker. This might not, therefore, he reflected, be much of an evening, by army standards. Gunn was taking his time to answer, but that was not unusual for him.

'London is grand for an invalid,' he said at last, 'and while I was one I found its diversions pleasing enough. I was able to join an excellent reading room which allowed me to take a selection of books to my lodgings. When one is recovered, though, one is expected to rejoice in the social whirl, which for me was something of a trial.'

'Oh! Because …' Argo's first foray into the conversation was unfortunate, as was his accompanying wave at his own face. His pinkness instantly darkened to red.

'My scar? No, not really,' said Gunn calmly. 'There were plenty of wounded officers about. But balls and routs are not my preferred amusements.'

'Damned waste of time,' agreed Saddler, and Gunn nodded. 'Not that it wasn't inevitable anyway, but I for one was delighted to hear the fat little Corsican had escaped from Elba. I was mad with boredom in Scotland.'

George beamed again. He was not sure he agreed with either of them: a fine ball with good music and enough pretty girls to go round, and a decent supper in the middle, was an excellent way to spend an evening, as far as he was concerned. But it was very good to be gossiping away like this, like the old days in Spain, with a battle to look forward to and a company to tend to.

'How are your billets? Comfortable?' Saddler asked. 'The old crone that has ours must be a hundred if she's a day, and not a word of English.'

'We're well enough served,' said George. 'Ours does our breakfast, and it's grand, then we fend for ourselves. I speak a little French,' he added, with well-founded modesty. He emptied his glass, and noticed that Argo's was empty, too. He decided not to refill his own for a moment or two, so that he could avoid filling Argo's, but Saddler reached over and filled both their glasses, then called for another jug and some food. With a flurry of servants such as George had not previously seen at the St. Pierre, bread and roast mutton arrived on the table. Saddler examined his critically, then set to with scientific zeal to clear his plate. George, too, ate as though dinner at the Frys' was a week ago. Argo poked at his food and took another draught of wine. Gunn ate slowly, and George wondered if his scar hurt when he ate. It seemed likely. What else had such a swipe done to him? Could it have caused his strange attack on Sir Alexander? So far, George had seen no difference in his character at all. But he was pleased to have them back: that was nearly an hour now and Argo had had no chance to mention his wretched wife. Poor Argo. Should he ask Gunn about Sir Alexander? Perhaps not. He should probably ask Saddler, but the idea did not appeal. Yet he had told Sir Alexander that he would tell Gunn of the aide-de-camp's visit, and anyway, he owed it to his friend and fellow officer to warn him that Sir Alexander was looking for him. And still he was half-convinced that Sir Alexander must be mistaken, as he studied Gunn out of the corner of his eye. Surely he had the wrong man.

They had concentrated on the food for some time, and George was lost in his own thoughts when Saddler suddenly broke the silence and made him jump.

'You're a bit old for an ensign, Argo, but a bit green for a lieutenant. What's your story?' Saddler demanded, forthright as usual.

'I had a commission in the Edinburgh Volunteers, sir, so I'm hardly inexperienced.' George blinked: the wine must be making Argo bold. 'I know every Dundas manoeuvre off by heart.'

'Ever done them under fire?' Saddler snapped.

Argo at last had the sense to look dismayed.

'No, sir. Not yet.'

'No doubt the opportunity will soon present itself,' said Saddler acidly. 'The civilians are still here in Brussels, I see? The British, I mean. I thought the Duke had told them all to leave?'

'He may have done, but they don't listen,' said George with a grin. 'Many of them are officers' families, and they don't want to leave their husbands and fathers.'

'Rumour has it that Bonaparte is to leave Paris next week,' put in Gunn.

'The Duke should march them all out of the town. They're nothing but distractions,' said Saddler.

'That's true, isn't it, Murray?' said Argo, nudging George.

'Oh, aye?' said Saddler sharply. 'What's been going on?'

'I had dinner this evening with General Fry and his family, that's all,' said George quickly.

'And his daughterses,' added Argo, slightly unsteadily.

'Pretty daughters?' asked Saddler, in the same tone as one might say, 'Enemy spies?'

'Reasonably pretty,' said George, cautiously. He was not pleased to have the Fry girls drawn into the conversation, on several counts. He touched the stem of his wine glass, then returned to his cutlery instead. 'They do a grand apple pie here – last season's apples, of course, but with raisins and such.'

'Then let's have some,' said Saddler decisively. 'And no more talk of pretty daughters. We're here to fight the fat little Corsican, not find ourselves wives and hangers-on.'

'Of course not, of course not,' agreed George heartily, but he could feel himself redden. Gunn came to his rescue.

'I see there's a theatre here. What manner of things do they do? I have a longing to see Molière done in the original French.'

'It's an odd thing,' said George in relief. 'It's called the Petit Theatre, the Little Theatre,' he added the translation with flair. 'They have children playing all the parts, not a child above the age of fourteen, apparently. Damned clever they are, too.'

'I don't believe it,' said Saddler, half an eye on the servant bringing their apple pie. 'It will be dwarves, no doubt, pretending to be children.'

'Why should it not be children, sir?' asked Gunn.

'Children acting?' said Saddler, as if it were argument enough.

'Children are perfectly good at acting,' said Argo suddenly. His face had returned to its usual complexion: he seemed abruptly sober.

'Got them, have you? With this young wife of yours?' asked Saddler.

'I have a stepson,' Argo said. 'A fine lad, Theodore by name. I'm proud to have him. Though he's as good as any grown man at pretending he hasn't done something when you know he has.'

'Does he live with your wife, then?' asked George in surprise.

'Of course he does: he's only eleven.'

'Then when you were worried about your wife … Theodore would be with her?'

'Of course. I was worried about him, too. Didn't I mention it?'

'No, you didn't.'

'I was sure I had …'

'You were worried about your wife, sir?' asked Gunn. 'I hope the concerns were unfounded.'

'I have no idea, sir,' said Argo, at last able to give vent to his feelings. 'She tells me she is in danger of her life, but I cannot find out how.' And he laid his head down on the table and sobbed. The look that Saddler shot George and Gunn over Argo's head was unprintable.

Chapter Seven

Edinburgh

It was with a kind of desperation that Charles Murray viewed that same Saturday morning. He had already written his daily letters to Robbins and to Thalland, the factor: to the latter, he had expatiated on the quality of the red turnip seed from Aberdeenshire currently on sale in Leith, while to the former he had expressed concerns about the leading on the east-facing coping of the roofs at Letho, which had caught the worst of the spring gales head on. He asked Robbins to tell the cook that he had heard the price of cheese was to go up at Cupar Market, and he asked Thalland to mention to the blacksmith that the fixings on the wheel at the Nethermill needed reworking. From his chamber in Willie Jack's flat he could not see Fife, over the hill and across the Forth, but it was in his mind fairly constantly.

So far the mystery, such as it was, of an apparently charming and reportedly decent woman and her son flitting about Edinburgh and its environs in a feckless fashion was not enough to keep him here, though he would like the satisfaction of finding the woman and finishing the task. It was just that, for all he cared for Letho, he was not ready to go home yet.

He had thought his heart had died when Helena Denning died, far away in Delhi. He had thought it did not matter then whom he married, and that in taking Lady Agostinella as his wife he could at least be of use to her, that some good would come of it. But he knew now that hearts do not die so easily, that his affection for his brother, his friends, his home at Letho, was undiminished. It was only for his wife that he could feel no love whatsoever, no matter how he tried: nor could he detect any love in her for him.

The morning was damp and Letitia, Willie Jack's wife, had elected to drape herself across a chaise longue in the parlour and read a novel. Willie Jack himself said he had to go out to see his family's man of business with his brother.

'I'd love to read to you, Mr. Murray,' said Letitia, from her recumbent position, as luscious as any bunch of grapes spilling from a cornucopia. Murray assembled a polite smile on his face, and decided therefore that he ought to go out, too. Walter had settled himself comfortably in a corner of the kitchen, but Murray hauled him out and off they went.

'Where are we going today, sir?' asked Walter without excitement.

'Up to the Castle,' said Murray. 'It'll give us a walk, and give you a fine view of the town, help you to get your bearings, and besides, the people in the Dean Village said Alicia Argo had moved somewhere near the Castle. I don't know if they really knew; I don't know if they were lying, but it's the only clue we have. And at least we have a description of her now.'

He saw Walter give a little nod at the Tron Kirk, recognising it, and was pleased. Turning up the unfamiliar Lawnmarket, though, produced a frown of concentration.

'There's gey many folks up here, sir: where do you want me to go when I lose myself?'

'There's not so many on a Saturday with the lawcourts closed,' said Murray. Walter looked at the Saturday crowds in polite disbelief. 'And,' added Murray, irritated, 'I'll hold your collar.' He twisted a long finger into Walter's collar and pushed him gently forward up the cobbled hill.

The cobbles were not only damp and gritty but also littered with the slippery detritus from the fruit market, and the collar grip saved Walter once or twice from going on his nose. However, the worst of the vegetable hazards passed, and soon they were negotiating the climb past St. Giles' and the lawcourts, with the Council Chambers opposite. Above that were shops again on either side, many long-established, half their wares in the fresh air sheltered by the jutting first storey. Cloth and basketware and leather goods bulked out the doorways, and above the tenements rose tall and stern to the pearly sky. Murray forced himself to slow down as Walter tired towards the top: he knew that with his long legs he often walked too fast for his companions.

Up here there was clear evidence of soldiery: Walter stopped and watched with saucer eyes as a troop of militia exercised on the parade ground to the town side of the castle's ditch, unusually neat, perhaps spurred on by the thought of what was happening in Brussels. The castle itself looked imposing enough even from this, the approachable side: on the rest of its circumference it was an almost impregnable cliff on its steep hill, rising in fortified layers to its summit. Murray had no wish to approach it more closely: he had memories of it which were not particularly pleasant. Walter, however, was still standing in awed silence.

'Have you any notion of going soldiering, then, Walter?' he asked resignedly. Walter shook his shiny head slowly.

'Mr. Robbins says bad things happen to soldiers,' he announced pontifically.

'Quite right, Walter: it is a profession best avoided by any sensible man.' Would his often less-than-sensible brother George come safely through any assault by Bonaparte? He prayed so.

From the north side of the parade ground, where the rough gorse and heather still covered the brutal rock of the hill, there was a grand view of the Nor'Loch, the fragrant remnant of a longer, more wholesome body of water, and beyond it the grid of the New Town with Prince's Street busy in the foreground. Beyond that again was the slate-grey Firth of Forth with Fife misty in the distance: Murray tried not to look at it too longingly.

'So there is Mr. Dundas' flat, down that end,' he pointed out to Walter instead, 'and beyond that is the road we took yesterday to the Water of Leith.' Walter frowned: Murray could not help thinking that the frown was less one of concentration than the hapless expression of someone who held out no hope of ever understanding where he was. 'Up this end,' he went on, 'is Calton Hill. See the buildings on the top? That is an observatory, for looking at the stars.'

'Calton Hill, sir? Is that not where the whale is to be?'

'I believe so, Walter. Can you see how you would get there from Mr. Dundas' flat, should you be permitted to go?'

Walter squinted at the straight line of Prince's Street, following it from the west to where it passed the mighty block of the Register House and into Shakespeare Square at the foot of Calton Hill. He took a long moment before he shook his head at last.

'There's an awful crowd down there, sir. How could any sane

man find his way through all that?'

'But you follow the street, Walter. It's a straight line.'

Walter shook his head again.

'You could never walk a straight line along that, sir. The carts would knock you flat, even if the people moved out of your way.'

Murray had to restrain himself from cuffing Walter's ear: at least the lad knew his own limitations. Daniel, for instance, would have dived into the wonder that was Prince's Street and become joyously lost without ever admitting to it.

He sighed.

'I suppose it is just a matter of practice and custom, Walter,' he said. 'Come, we'll walk back again and see if you can find the turning on to the Bridges yourself.' He shepherded the boy back on to Castle Hill, and they began the long descent back to the Tron.

He had to admit it was busy on the High Street today: the inhabitants were probably ensuring they had enough food and fuel for the Sabbath, tramping up and down with baskets and bundles and ducking in and out of doorways on either side of the street. Ahead, a couple of women in matching brown gowns, topped with undyed woollen shawls, emerged from a close and started down the hill. Murray had a feeling that they looked familiar, and he followed with his eye on them, trying not to lose them in the crowd. Brown gowns … two identical brown gowns, on figures of generous build … that was it! They were the two women who had given him directions in the Dean Village yesterday. Now, he thought, still following, what would two women from the Dean Village be doing in the Old Town? Visiting a friend? Shopping for fruit? But they would have gone past the Tron market. Buying a basket? It could be anything, but it was a bit of a coincidence that the women directing him to the previous lodgings of Alicia Argo yesterday should happen to be near the present lodgings of Alicia Argo today. Wasn't it?

The carriers of a sedan chair tried their luck at breaking across the flow of traffic to cross the High Street, and caused an instant traffic jam. The women were beyond it and in a moment they had disappeared. Murray stopped, catching Walter before he lost him.

'We need to go back,' he said, and turned Walter to face uphill again. Walter stoically began to climb once more, rather like a clockwork toy that had been picked up and turned round before it reached the edge of the table.

Murray kept glancing back as they climbed, trying to work out from which close the women had emerged. They had to go back some distance before he suddenly recognised it: there was a tobacconist on the ground floor of the stair in front, and a large flat board depicting a pipe swung above the close. The scent of snuff caught his nose again, reminding him that he had unconsciously noticed the same smell as they had passed the close going down the hill. He caught Walter's shoulder and propelled him gently towards the narrow gap between the tall buildings.

It was dark in the little alley, but it soon opened into a courtyard that was almost as gloomy as the alley. Walter coughed: the smell was derived chiefly, Murray thought, from the pile of kitchen waste swept into a corner behind some steps, where a straw-coloured dog sat and watched them with an expression of resignation in its brown eyes. Even as they paused there was the scrape of a window being hauled up above them, and a cry of 'Gardy loo!' Murray snatched Walter back against the wall as a finely aimed chute of fluid fell hard into the waste heap, refreshing the smell no end. The dog, which had moved faster than even it had expected, returned to its perch and sat down again. Murray wondered if its sense of smell had been overwhelmed by its surroundings completely, or if it was somehow managing to hold its nose.

An old man, with a jaw like a fortification and eyebrows the size of mice, sat on a flight of steps mashing his toothless lips together vacantly. As far from the midden as possible, a scrawny young mother arranged greyish napkins and shirts on a line, while a boy of about a year kept an assured grip on her skirts and surveyed Murray with a calculating stare that Murray felt probably took in the height of Murray's pockets and the likely profit in picking them. He would have backed him against Walter in any fight.

Apart from the one occupied by the old man and the one beside the midden, several sets of steps wound out of the courtyard, and Murray looked about in the faint hope of a further clue – a nice little tuft of brown cloth, perhaps, on a railing, or fresh footprints in an appropriate size. Nothing appeared, though, and he was about to approach the young mother when one of the city's sergeants emerged from a doorway, replaced his hat on his head, and glanced around. Murray recognised him as a man he had had some dealings with before, and was pleased.

'Sergeant Home?' he called.

The man saw Murray and quickly came down the steps towards them. He was sturdily built but of a height with Murray himself, with sandy hair and a scrubbed look about his rosy face. He bowed, smiling.

'Mr. Murray, sir! A pleasure to see you again.'

'And you, Sergeant! Is this where you are working now? You used to be over in the New Town. I knew I hadn't seen you for a while.'

'That's right, sir. We're sent where we're needed, aye? But what would you be seeking in this place, sir? Would you be lost?' Murray liked the man, and therefore was amused to see his quiet investigation into Murray's motives: Home was not a person who missed anything out of its place.

'I'm not lost myself, but I'm looking for someone I'm having trouble finding. She might not even be here at all.'

'A woman?' Again, Home's pink face was expressionless.

'A woman I have never met, which makes it all the harder. She is named Alicia Argo, and I'm led to believe she is yellow haired, small, with blue eyes. She apparently moved here from the Dean village around a week ago. Do you know anyone who might fit that description? And she would have had a boy with her, a lad of about ten or twelve, her son.'

Home pursed his lips and his gaze wandered beyond Murray: you could almost see him working his way around the tenements he knew in his head, counting off the inhabitants one by one as they failed to match the description. Slowly he spun on his heel, watched with detachment by the straw-coloured dog, and settled at last on the steps next to the midden heap. Up the building his eyes travelled, almost to the top and then, with a little shake of his head, back down a floor or two to a small, closed window on the first floor.

'I believe she might live there,' he said, pointing. 'The lassie there is new, indeed, and though I have seen her only the once, she sounds like a similar body.'

'Is it furnished lodgings, then?' asked Murray, trying to

postpone the moment when he might have to approach the midden more closely.

'Well, it depends what you might mean by furnished,' admitted Home. 'There'd be a mattress, maybe, and a kist, and if you're lucky maybe a table with more than the two legs. Or a chair. Both would be a bit fancy, for round here.'

'She left a decent enough lodging in the Dean. And only a little while before that, she left an even better one in Potterrow,' Murray told him.

'Coming down in the world?' asked Home. 'You see it often enough. Is she a gin drinker?'

'I don't think so. And she didn't flit without paying, in either place: both landlords were sad to see her go, they say.'

'Lost money in some speculation, maybe – or has a husband abandoned her?'

'Quite the opposite. Her husband is an officer with the Royal Scots in Brussels, but very concerned about her welfare. Apparently she told him she was frightened for her life, but if she told him in any more detail than that what was happening, it hasn't reached me. My brother asked me on the husband's behalf to visit and make sure everything was all right.'

'An officer wouldn't be too keen to see his wife in a place like this, I'd have thought,' said Home. 'Do you want me to go up with you? These places are not well-lit: you might not find your way too easily.'

'That would be most welcome,' said Murray with relief. He had not realised how little he had wanted to enter the building on his own – or only with Walter. 'Would you like to lead the way?'

The sergeant nodded smartly and headed up the steps past the midden, apparently unaffected by the smell which grew the richer the closer one came. The door was not locked, and was pulled to when required with a length of rope which had met so many greasy fingers it looked almost polished. The hallway was indeed dark, and they were glad of the open door until a figure appeared from the nearest internal door and suddenly shrieked,

'Get that door shut! Ah'm tryin' to keep out the reek!'

Sergeant Home gave an unexpectedly heavy sigh and turned to address the vision. All Murray could see in the dim light was that it seemed to be wearing more than an ordinary number of shawls, but as his eyes grew used to the dark he could distinguish, gradually, a female, with a loose knot of wiry grey hair on her head to match the thick whiskers around her toothy mouth. Her eyes were not quite as focussed as one would like at this time of day. She made a fairly straight line for the door, though, and slammed it shut, leaving Murray's eyes to begin adapting again.

'Oh, Eppy, I doubt half the reek's coming from within. Have ye no the time to scrub down these stairs?' said Sergeant Home.

'The tenants are supposed to do it,' grumbled Eppy. 'How am I supposed to make them, and me only a wee weak woman that couldna say boo to a goose?'

'I'd no like to be the goose,' Home remarked. 'Eppy, is it not so that you have a new lodger up the stair? Maybe on the first flat? A lassie, it would be.'

'Who wants to know?' said Eppy, suddenly sly. She looked Murray up and down with open calculation.

'I do, Eppy,' said Home firmly. She wobbled a little as she turned back to him.

'A new lodger … That would be her Ladyship, I suppose.'

'Is she in?'

'Och, now, you've no to go and arrest her nor nothing, Sergeant! You canna do that! She's to pay me well for that room, and I only got the week in advance! The Dear help us – you canna judge a'body by their looks these days, and her that respectable-looking and all neat and tidy and there you are, the next minute she's bringing police to my home and strange gentlemen that want who kens what from her and I swear I'm going to give up this trade for it's nothing but worry to a poor old body that has never done a'body any harm in my life but only wanted a decent household and not to be lonely in my old age –'

'Och, be quiet, Eppy: you're never lonely, whether it would be your daughter out there in the yard with her wain or the next fellow to share your bed. Is the lassie upstairs in or no?'

'She's no out, that I ken,' Eppy said sulkily, and pouted at Murray. Murray pushed Walter in front of him to follow Home up the stairs, nodding to the woman on the way past. She retreated to her room, muttering.

The stairs were lit, a little, by some high windows, but one or two of the treads were worn almost away and it was wise to feel for the next step before trusting it. Nevertheless they came safely to the first floor, and paused while Home worked out which door to chap. The little landing was quiet, except for scrabbling from within the scruffy walls. Walter's eyes were wide.

'This one, I think, sir,' said Home after a moment, and knocked. There was no answer. He knocked again. Murray found that he was holding his breath, and breathed out as quietly as he could through his nose. 'She'd have made it to the door by now, sir, if she was coming: they're no exactly big rooms in there. Do you think maybe we should …?' And as he said so, he gently tried the doorhandle. It turned, and the door swung open.

The room was indeed small, though it had two windows, one facing forwards and one back. Home had not exaggerated the quality and quantity of the furniture. There was a table with a stool by it. On the table, beside an upturned tin, were a plate, knife and fork (the first sign of quality) and a spoon, and three surprised rodents, which quickly vanished into a hole in the floor. In a recess which had a thin curtain to divide it from the rest of the room, a low bedframe held a neatly made up mattress with decent sheets and a couple of thick blankets, for which Alicia Argo must have been grateful as one window was broken. A press on the wall had presumably held food, but it was open and empty. Drawn up to the table, as though for a second person to sit on it, was a smallish travelling kist, which two people could carry between them. It had a hasp, but no padlock.

'Not much here, is there?' Murray turned about, but the delights of the room were indeed limited. 'Do you think she's gone out, or flitted?'

'It doesna look as if she's been here in a whiley,' Home observed, poking one of the plates with a dubious finger. 'The bed neatly made, but this mess left, and left a few days, anyway.'

'Left in a hurry? She would hardly abandon decent things like these in a place like this unless she was in a rush.' Murray fingered a blanket. 'Clean, and a good weight. Chamberpot empty,' he added, noting with some amusement that Walter's jaw had dropped. 'More likely to have been their supper than their breakfast, then.' He returned to the table and sniffed at the plate: it smelled of beef, he thought. Cautiously he lifted the upturned tin. Beneath it was another plate, complete with knife and fork, also used. He blinked. 'Odd.'

'There are no clothes lying about, unless they're in the kist – is that the only piece of luggage?'

'I think so,' agreed Murray. 'There's not much of a hiding place for anything else, is there? And I don't think I would trust my belongings to a shared attic here.'

'Well, we'd better look in the kist, in case there's something,' said Home with a sigh. 'I don't much like the look of this, but maybe she's away for a few days with just the clothes she needed.'

'I'd be surprised to find she didn't wash up, though,' said Murray, approaching the kist with Home. He regarded it for a moment, then said, 'Walter, be a good lad and go and stand on the landing, and let us know if anybody is coming. I'd hate her to walk in on us rooting through her possessions.' Walter nodded and went out, and Murray and Home exchanged a significant glance. Home nodded.

'Right, then, sir: let's see, shall we?' He flipped the hasp with one large, capable hand. The lid lifted off with a slight sigh, and then a buzzing noise. Flies billowed out into their faces, and it was a moment before they could bat them away and see clearly into the kist. There, folded tightly into the narrow space, was what Murray had reluctantly half-expected. No clothes were stored there, except those already being worn on a small, tidy figure, with yellow hair tumbling from a white cap. The dark blue eyes he had heard about were gone. The dark blue gown wrapped about her had presumably set them off very prettily.

Murray reached forward with extreme delicacy, and with two long fingers drew back the lace of her chemisette, to reveal a slim neck already darkening with death. On it, though, could still clearly be seen thick black fingermarks.

'Aye,' said Home sadly. 'And you think this'll be the lassie you're searching for? What was the name again?'

'Alicia Argo,' said Murray. There was a little gasp from behind him. He turned, and saw Walter staring into the kist, clutching at his mouth and nose.

'Be sick on the landing!' Murray cried immediately. 'Honestly, why can't you do as you were told? Why didn't you stay out here?'

'Because of her,' Walter pointed, then snatched at his mouth again. There was some frantic swallowing, but to his credit he brought himself under control, and pointed to Eppy who was standing on the landing pressing the wall hard for balance.

'What in the name of the Almighty is going on in there?' she shrieked, her nest of hair wobbling furiously. 'Are you robbing her the now, the pair of you? And what – what is that smell?'

'Your tenant was in after all,' said Murray sourly. 'But here's a question – where, now, is her son?'

Chapter Eight

Belgium

I

'That's grand, son,' pronounced Sergeant Lamb. 'You just keep drumming like that, and the whole company'll march just lovely – as long as every second soldier's a three-legged donkey with a bad hoof. It'll be grand.'

'But – ' retorted the new drummer boy – James Graham, George remembered Gunn had called him. There was a good deal of rebellion in the lad's eyes but he managed to stop himself before he said anything the Sergeant might regret. George turned away and grinned at Gunn: it was true the boy's drumming had been less of a march and more of a cross between a polka and a collapse in a carpenter's shop. He hoped young James would learn drumming as fast as he was learning discretion.

George was at the camp earlier than usual this morning, and had even foregone his ride in the Allée Verte. The foregoing was not quite voluntary, for Saddler, followed by Gunn, had appeared at George's lodging at an hour George had not been sure existed on the Sabbath, and had insisted on waiting while George and Argo, the latter rather green, had completed their rapid toilet. Then all four had ridden in brisk silence out to the camp, which had not improved Argo's colour at all.

Now he could see, along the avenue of the camp, Argo staggering out of the headquarters tent. George nudged Gunn and they quickly abandoned Sergeant Lamb and the drummer boy in training, and made their way to the rescue.

Lieutenant James Argo took a long sip from the flask, and managed to pass it back to George before choking.

'What on earth is that?' he demanded.

'Whisky,' said George. 'The genuine Glenlivet – never even seen a gauger's stick.'

'I've never touched spirits,' said Argo slightly sadly, and coughed again.

'They're good in a crisis,' said George.

Argo's interview with Saddler had just taken place: it seemed to George that that was as good a crisis as any. George and Gunn had been keeping a discreet eye outside the tent, purportedly to keep away the ordinary soldiers, but really to work out how many pieces of Argo they might have to pick up afterwards. It was not Saddler's way to admonish a man when he was under the influence of alcohol, or when the man was: instead, he waited until both were stone cold sober before tackling the problem, as he usually put it: George had other, private terms for the way in which Saddler would take an officer or a man and quietly, icily, flay him. He had not discussed the matter with Gunn, who was, he knew, Saddler's ardent follower, but he did know that on several occasions he and Gunn had wordlessly dealt with the aftermath of such a session.

'He said,' began Argo, 'that the army was no place for wives, either in the battlefield or in your head. How can I not think of poor Alicia? It might be weeks before Bonaparte attacks. It's impossible! Has he no wife?'

'No,' said George. 'At least, if he has we have never heard of her.'

'I should pity any woman married to him,' said Argo, with sudden vehemence, then looked about him quickly in case of eavesdroppers. They were safe: Gunn had been summoned into the tent for daily orders, and George had taken Argo to part of the camp where only the horses stood thoughtfully grazing. The horses would also hide them from Saddler, should he choose to emerge from the company headquarters tent: he would not look favourably on any apparent mollycoddling.

'The thing is,' said George, 'that however much you might have Alicia in mind – and I would strongly recommend that you do try to think of her a bit less during the day – you don't let Major Saddler hear a word about her. If you want to wait till the evening you can talk at me for half an hour non-stop about your poor wife, but nothing in front of Saddler, understand?' He knew he would regret this rash offer, but if it helped Argo escape Saddler's wrath it might be worth it for all concerned.

'Can I, Murray?' Argo turned great hopeful eyes on him. 'That is very good of you. I suspected I might have been boring you just a little about her recently.'

'Not at all, not at all, man! She sounds a delightful person, and an old bachelor like me should have constant reminders by him of what he is missing, or no one would ever marry!' There, off ran his tongue again, he thought: but what else could he say?

'Sir?' Liddell trotted up, panting as his coat flapped around his wobbling stomach. 'Major Saddler wants to see you now in the headquarters tent, sir.'

'Thank you, Liddell,' said George, trying to ignore the way his pulse jumped at the thought. He patted Argo on the shoulder. 'Keep clear of him today if you can, and if you can't, keep quiet. He'll calm down soon: he's too cold to burn for long.'

He straightened his coatee and his shako on the way back through the horse lines, feeling reassured by the neat fit on his shoulders and the shine on his boots. He was not afraid of Saddler, not really. It was more like, er, respect, he thought. Respect and awe.

Saddler was again behind the desk that George had disliked so much when he was in charge: Saddler had no such fear of paperwork. Gunn was seated to one end of the desk, making notes on papers passed to him by Saddler: both nodded a greeting when George entered the tent.

'Murray,' said Saddler, in a temperate tone that reassured George at least temporarily. 'I've been looking over your papers for the last few weeks, and for the most part they seem to be in order. There was the matter of the buttons: I have instructed Sergeant Lamb to tell the men there had better be no more missing buttons or they will be forced to account for them, in several ways. The problems with the postroom you mentioned … a little more supervision of the post corporal would not go amiss, I think, and that will be your continued responsibility. He must send the lists of the mails with the mails, and he cannot do that unless there is a list, and there cannot be a list unless the officers have signed for each of the men's letters. You will henceforth be the officer to sign for them and ensure that the post corporal has all he needs to be able to fulfil his duty. There will be no criticism of the system at our end, whatever might happen centrally. Now, rations. How much oatmeal is to be supplied for each tent each day?'

'Er … a pound or two?' George tried.

'Close, Murray. A pound and a half. Perhaps you would like to explain why the men are being supplied with oatmeal at the rate of eleven pounds each day?'

'Eleven pounds!'

'Yes, for the last three weeks.'

'Eleven pounds …' said George again, trying to picture it. 'I must have … I'm sorry, sir, I must have misread the figure.'

'I believe you must. If you had been here at meal times you might have noticed. I suggest that in the first place, you spend a little time this afternoon finding out what has happened to all that oatmeal, and in the second place, you endeavour to attend more mealtimes in the camp and in general to concentrate rather more on the fact that we are in Belgium to prepare for war with Bonaparte, not to compare social outings, show off our horses on the Allée Verte, and find wives.' George flinched: the prevailing wind had suddenly turned Baltic.

'I'm sorry, sir.' It was best with Saddler, he remembered just in time, not to try lengthy explanations – particularly when anything true would only irritate further, and he was no good at lying.

'Well, make it good,' said Saddler, and sat back in his chair. It sounded as if that was the end of the matter, but George knew that he would be expected to report on the oatmeal by next day. Saddler's frosty eyes contemplated him, as if assessing what level of information he could cope with. 'Now, here is the situation. We are not moving yet, but we need to be prepared to move at short notice, so all must be held in readiness.

'The Duke has plenty of spies in Paris, as you can imagine. We'll hear as soon as there is any sign of the fat Corsican's beginning to move, but nothing has happened yet. We can be fairly sure of two things: he will try to move north through territory which is friendly to him, and he will try to break through between us and the Prussians when he reaches this length. As to his route, there are two strong possibilities: he will come directly from the south, through Charleroi, or he will tend more to the route from the south west, through Mons. There is a third possibility, though less likely, and that is a route through Tournai: the Duke is not discounting that one, but he believes that either of the others is better from Bonaparte's view.'

Gunn nodded intelligently, and George tried to copy him. He had a fairly good map in his head, though, and could picture roughly the roads to Mons and Charleroi. They were both quite close – his heart slipped a little at the thought of battle approaching.

'We could go to meet him, advance as far as the French border, but without the Austrians and Russians – I'm told they're on their way, but don't hold your breath, gentlemen – we don't have the men to cover both possibilities, and if we went as far as the border towards Mons, which the Duke thinks is the more likely because it would put our communications at risk and advantage Bonaparte – if we went towards Mons and the fat man came through Charleroi, it would be too far for us to run back and stop him. We need to wait our time, and make him make the first move.

'Once he's up here, he's bound to try to split us from Blücher's Prussians. We know he likes the tactic: he's done it before. If he succeeds, he'll fight each of us separately and I wouldn't like to bet that he would not beat us. He's missing some of his best generals, one way or another, but he's still Bonaparte and as the Duke says, when Bonaparte is there, every Frenchman loyal to him fights like two. We need to make sure that the Prussians stick with us – no danger of Blücher letting Bonaparte away with anything if the choice is his – and we need to wait till we're sure where the French are going, and above all we need to be ready to jump when the Duke says jump. It's forty-odd miles to Charleroi and a little less to Mons: that's not a distance I want to make the men run at the last minute.'

Saddler stood up and stretched, and buttoned up his waistcoat with precision as if readying himself for a fight at any minute. Gunn stood, too, adjusting his sword. George felt himself straightening in response, his hand on his own sword hilt.

'So,' said Saddler, 'there will be no more theatre visits, no more dinners, no more suppers, no more polite afternoon tea parties with lovely ladies and their families. You are here to work, to organise, to prepare the men and to listen for Wellington's call. Murray, I don't care if your general's daughter is Helen of Troy or Cleopatra: you can lay your trophies before her when Bonaparte is defeated, and not before.'

'Yes, sir. It's nothing serious, anyway, sir. I've just met her a couple of times, and of course, that's the last time I'll even think about her or any other lady for the rest of the campaign, of course, sir.'

Saddler nodded almost as if he believed George, but his focus was on the tent flaps. Gunn and George fell in behind him as he headed out – and the first person they all saw as they emerged from the tent was Carolina Fry.

Saddler stopped abruptly.

'Who is that person?' he snapped.

'Ah,' said George. 'Ah. Um. Miss Fry and Miss Esther Fry, may I present Major Saddler and Captain Gunn? The Misses Fry, sir.'

Gunn bowed and the girls, smiling charmingly, curtseyed. Saddler nodded, forced into unwelcome courtesy, but went no further.

'I'm afraid, ladies, that you must have missed your way. This is an army camp. Mr. Murray will show you back to the road.'

Esther looked dismayed, but Carolina was not to be put off so easily.

'Dear Mr. Murray, always so helpful!' she said at once. 'But we simply must wait for our Papa. We cannot leave without him. Our Papa the General, you know, sir,' she added to Saddler, with only the lightest glance at his major's shoulder lace.

'He's here?' said George sharply. He looked at Saddler: Saddler's face was like a brick, behind which solid façade no doubt he was wrestling with the impossibility of expatiating to a senior officer his feelings on bringing families near a battlefield. George was about at least to move the girls away for everyone's safety, when General Fry himself appeared from the post tent.

'Damned Scottish regiments, can never find what you want. Ah! Murray. Where is your commanding officer?'

'May I present,' said George again, nervously, 'Major Saddler, sir. Major Saddler, General Fry.'

'Is this your headquarters, Saddler?' asked the General. 'I had hoped to see you at church this morning, but was disappointed.'

'We had prayers in camp,' said Saddler shortly. 'The men prefer the Scottish service, of course.' He paused long enough to reassume some control over the situation. 'Will you enter, sir? How can I be of assistance?' He ushered the General before him into the tent and managed to convey with a backward glance that Gunn should follow him, but that George should continue with the order to remove the girls from the camp.

George sighed inwardly. Carolina was watching her father vanish into the tent with Saddler.

'What is the matter with Major Saddler? Is he always so grumphy?' she demanded. Esther nodded.

'I am sure I have never met so ungallant an officer. And poor Captain Gunn so polite despite his injury. Is that a battle scar?'

Her voice was high and clear, and George began to shift them away to the road.

'Yes,' he said, 'it was a very bad sword stroke, but he is much recovered. Please, ladies, do come this way. I'm afraid Major Saddler is very anxious that the company will not be ready for Bonaparte's attack, and he wants us to concentrate on that and not to spend time in, ah, pleasanter pursuits.'

'Is that why we missed you on the Allée Verte this morning, Mr. Murray?' said Carolina sadly. 'When I wore this gown especially for you!'

'Good heavens, did you?' said George, who had too many thoughts in his head at present. 'I mean, I'm very flattered!'

Esther was still in a gown of the fashionable Pomona green, but Carolina had assumed the style that George had mentioned the other day, a red spencer with gilt buttons and navy facings on the cuffs, with a neat tall collar, and a bonnet that definitely echoed the form of a shako. He had to admit it was charming.

'Do you think I would be taken for a soldier, Mr. Murray?' she teased him, twirling.

'I don't think anyone would take you for one of our rough fellows.' George was struggling, but the flirtation was coming more easily now. 'See – there are some cleaning their kit. There is not one of them half as charming as either of you, you have to admit!'

Carolina and Esther surveyed the men outside the closest tent, as if they were on exhibition. Three of the soldiers had their haversacks unfolded flat on the grass and were blackballing their boots and cartridge pouches with an enthusiasm that George suspected had been stimulated by Saddler's return to camp. The fourth was mending a shirt and trying to keep it clear of the greasy blackballs. When they saw the Frys watching them, they slid to their feet and stood to attention.

'Thank you, men,' said George, and was gratified to see a swift glance of approval pass between Carolina and Esther. Then Carolina looked the men up and down.

'I thought the Scottish regiments wore kilts?' she asked. 'Isn't that the name for those thick woolly skirts?' George saw the men, barefoot in their moggans, begin to grin, and hurried the girls along.

'Only some of the Highland regiments are kilted,' he explained. 'Look out for the 42nd., for instance, with their dark tartan, or the 79th. Or the 92nd., they're kilted, too. And very fearsome they look, too,' he added, defending his countrymen against the charge of wearing woolly skirts.

'But why did those men have the bottoms cut out of their hose, then?' demanded Esther. 'For I could see that they had cut them round the ankles.'

'They like to march barefoot inside their boots,' George explained. 'It hardens their feet faster, and they get fewer blisters. The soldier's worst enemy, sore feet,' he added knowledgeably.

'Worse even than Bonaparte?' asked Esther, shocked.

'Bonaparte only happens now and then,' said George with a smile. 'Sore feet, like the poor, are always with us.'

They were close to the road, now, and to an open carriage waiting presumably for the General and his daughters. In it were Mrs. Fry and her mother, the latter so cocooned in shawls that if the carriage had overturned she would most likely have bounced and rolled away unharmed. George approached and bowed.

'Will you come to us for supper tonight, Mr. Murray?' called Mrs. Fry.

'I fear I must decline, madam,' said George. 'My commanding officer wants us to remain much more in the camp for now and oversee the men's preparations.'

'Oh, that is a shame! But you will be coming to that dinner on Thursday, won't you? We shall see you there?'

'I fear not, madam.' In his current mood, Saddler was unlikely even to countenance an accepted invitation.

'What a pity – then you will not see Carolina wearing those pretty silk flowers you presented to her! That seems most unfair!'

'Here is Papa coming now,' announced Esther, before George could respond.

'Come, girls,' said the General, 'we have other calls to make. Up you get, miss,' and he hoisted Carolina unceremonially into the carriage. Esther followed quickly.

'Delighted to see you again, sir,' said George as the General pulled himself up, too, and called to the driver to start.

'Goodbye, Mr. Murray,' said the General, his eye on the road, while his wife and daughters waved farewell. He watched them as far as was polite, then turned back into the camp, unexpectedly relieved to see them go. Was it because their visit would have annoyed Saddler? Yes, he thought, but it was more than that. The Frys were pretty girls, and it was pleasant to have somewhere to visit – when he was allowed to. But he realised that he was going to have to tread a little more carefully: his helpful loan to Carolina to buy the silk flowers was, he felt, being dangerously misinterpreted. It was lovely to be flattered and flirted with, but he did not want to allow himself to be caught at this stage. What would Charles say? Trapped by an officer's daughter, when he himself had happily secured his contessa? If only he could remember, though, what had happened after the Willis' dinner party.

Dinner, he thought: he was hungry. Then he remembered the oatmeal, and swore. There were twenty company tents, and for three weeks he had provided each tent with about ten times the oatmeal they were supposed to receive. That amounted to … well, quite a lot of oatmeal. He stopped and took a glove off: he always found it easier to count on bare fingers. It came out as an excess of forty-five stone of oatmeal, even though he worked it out three times. He sighed heavily, and began to work his way along the tents to find out what had become of it.

II

It was a good hour later when he sat down on a stool outside the headquarters tent and tried to reassemble what he had learned into some kind of report for Saddler. He gazed into the middle distance as he thought: Sergeant Lamb was still trying to beat some sense of rhythm into James Graham, along with a couple of other drummer boys: Gunn was overseeing some gun repairs, a line of the short India Pattern muskets propped in a wooden frame before him, and Saddler seemed to be working with a group of the tallest men practising throwing grenades. George noticed with curiosity that whenever Saddler went to retrieve one of the mock grenades from near Sergeant Lamb, Gunn almost immediately went to meet him, going back to his gunrack when Saddler returned to his grenadier class. But he had to concentrate on his report, and soon forgot Gunn's odd symptom of hero-worship.

III

At five, Saddler reappeared at the headquarters tent.

'Well, Murray: any news of your generous oatmeal ration?'

'Ah, yes, sir, most of it is accounted for.'

'Well,' Saddler sounded almost pleased. 'Let us have your report.'

'Most of the men just had double rations, sir, so that accounts for some of it. Around twenty-five stone is still in sacks in the tents, and I saw to it that it was stored off the ground and away from vermin, sir. Only one of the sacks had attracted rats, and that one has been disposed of.'

'So there's another eighteen stone or so to go!'

'Yes, sir. Around fifteen of that is, um, gone, sir.'

'Sold off?'

'Yes, sir.' George swallowed.

'To whom?'

'Other camps, sir, they said. The local villagers turned up their noses at it.'

'And by whom?'

'Mostly Rettie and Macfarlane, sir. They're the sharp lads.'

'Right, they'll be dealt with. And the last three stone?'

George swallowed again, and fiddled with his swordhilt.

'Well, it appears that's been eaten, too, sir.'

'By our men?'

'Ah, well, yes. Sort of.'

'Sort of?'

'Just by one man, sir. By Liddell, that is. But at least he's our man.'

Saddler stared at him.

'Three stone of oatmeal? Three *stone*?'

'Well, that explains why the man's the size of a house,' put in Gunn. Saddler pushed himself out of his chair.

'I'm going to go and see about supper,' he said, shaking his head in unaccustomed bewilderment. He went out, and Gunn moved almost as if drawn by a string to the tent flap, watching him go. George realised he had been holding his breath, and let it out in a long sigh.

'Three stone? Really, Murray?' Gunn asked, grinning.

'Apparently so! He has his own private pot of cold porage with a lid to it by his bedroll, and any spare minute he's into it, according to his pals.'

Both men laughed, appalled and delighted at the idea.

'Happy to be back, then, Gunn?' asked George when the laughter had eased.

'Heartily relieved, in some ways,' said Gunn with a frank smile. 'I'll have to admit there was a moment when I thought I had fought my last battle – or even breathed my last breath.'

'It didn't look too good from where I was standing, either,' said George with feeling. 'I can't say how pleased I was to have your letter when I was in Bath.'

'But your own injury – you are quite recovered?'

'Oh, fit as a flea! I was exceptionally lucky,' said George. 'And you? I mean, apart from the scar … no, er, lasting effects?' He tried to watch Gunn out of the corner of his eye, but his face had never really been designed for subterfuge. Gunn, in any case, seemed quite relaxed.

'I believe so,' he said. 'A little less strong in my left arm, of course, but I have been practising sword swings and dagger thrusts and all kinds with it: there is a fencing school in Pall Mall that is heartily pleased to see the back of me, I fancy, though their income will be greatly diminished!'

Silence fell between them for a moment, before George blurted out,

'Sir Alexander Gordon was here looking for you. You know, Wellington's aide-de-camp?'

Gunn's face stiffened.

'Oh, was he?' He seemed to swallow, before going on. 'A tall, well set-up gentleman with black hair?'

'That's the one.' George's voice was not working to his satisfaction, either.

'He – did you see him yourself?'

'I did. It would have been …three days ago. It's been busy, you know,' he added fatuously, as if every day brought the Duke's closest circle to visit.

Gunn fingered his scar very tentatively. It was the first time George had seen him the least conscious of it.

'And did he make any comment about why he was looking for me?' Gunn asked at last.

'He said – he said you'd attacked him. At an inn,' George added, as if it might make a difference. Gunn raised his eyebrows. 'I think he was just trying to make sure he had the right man, maybe seeing if you were the kind of man that usually did that kind of thing.' He knew he was gabbling.

'And may I ask what you said?' Gunn's voice was gentle, but there was an edge to it.

'I said you weren't, that I'd never have thought you would ever do such a thing! I can't tell you when I was so astonished to hear something! Only that he had Saddler's name too I would have thought it was some other Gunn – maybe from some other Royal Regiment … a Belgian one, or suchlike …' Gabbling again, he said to himself.

'Well, I thank you for your loyalty, Murray: if it helps, it is an incident that is very unlikely ever to happen again.' He paused, glancing out of the tent while George found himself nodding enthusiastically. 'Listen,' said Gunn, 'you know I firmly believe that Major Saddler is an excellent soldier and officer: his tactical skills are considerable, he thinks only of the wellbeing of his troops, and in a fight there is none braver. You do know that, don't you?'

'Of course: we all know you admire him, don't we?' said George, puzzled. Did Gunn think he was questioning his loyalty to Saddler, or to the company?

'Well –' Gunn glanced out of the tent again, and broke off abruptly. Saddler strode in.

'Ready for some supper, then?' Saddler asked. 'It's all cooked. Come and join the men: there's a little beef, and some small beer, but I think you'll find that your meal consists chiefly of a fine and abundant porage.'

Chapter Nine

Edinburgh

I

'So you can see, my dear George, that I have sent you some truly awful news for your friend. No doubt he will have plenty of questions, and I shall tell you all I know and you may judge for yourself how much and what to tell him from your knowledge of the man. Of course we do not know what she brought with her into this flat: it was not a very respectable stair and there was plenty of evidence of vermin, but her own belongings such as they were were clean and well kept. There were no clothes except for what she was wearing, there was no money, and the only paper in the place was the newspaper under her in the kist which was a Courant of 25th. May: those who know of these things believe that she has not been moved since she was put into the kist so we may assume that she died some time after the 25th., but probably not very long. She had been dead for some time.

'The man George Home, who is from the police office, is a competent fellow whom I have met before. He brought along a woman whom the police office employ in such cases, and she examined the body and though there was some decay she gave it as her opinion that Mrs. Argo had in no way been forced or interfered with, which may be of some comfort to Argo. There were fingermarks on her throat, however: that was the only visible injury.

'There is no sign of the son, Theodore: you did not mention him, but perhaps as he is Argo's stepson he did not think to ask. Apparently he had some ambition to be a soldier, a fact I believe I mentioned to you before. Perhaps he has gone to join his father in Belgium? If he appears, I wish you would let me know: he will be

able, no doubt, to answer many curious questions. But why would he have run to Belgium?

'Of course I shall look further into this matter unless Argo expressly wishes me not to. I cannot look on a body that met death by violence but that I find myself driven to find out how it happened, and in this case I am further plagued by a sense that if I had worked faster, I might have prevented this from happening.

'I plan to return to the close tomorrow and ask some questions. It really is an unsavoury place and if nothing else I want to find out why Alicia Argo sank so low in her accommodations, from a respectable flat in the Potterrow to a shabby house in the Dean to this squalor in only a few weeks. Was she robbed? Was it blackmail? Or was she indeed fleeing for her life, but was unsuccessful?

'Yesterday's Courant reports that there are rumours of a victory over the French, but you know the cautious old Courant: it's all hedged in ifs and buts. If you have had a victory, I shall raise a glass to you tonight: if not, I shall raise a glass anyway to your continued safety in camp. You may imagine us, if you will, home from afternoon service at St. George's (why do the Episcopals have such better music than us?): Willie Jack and me, old married men, and Willie Jack's wife, like a goddess from a Titian painting, casting her liquid gaze from one to another of us in a way any sensible man would flee from. Poor Willie Jack: he always went for the dangerous ones! And now he has his wish, and she is all his ... one hopes.

'Well, dear brother, fight nicely and remember your French, and don't drink spirits before breakfast, and never go to your bed with cold feet, your own or anyone else's. I'm sure the Lady Agostinella would join with me in wishing you every blessing.

'Your elder and better brother,

'Charles.'

II

Walter had attended church stolidly with Murray on Sunday, though Murray thought he had perceived some very fervent prayers: Alicia Argo had been Walter's first corpse, and it was not a good one. Murray still had the impression of the retching stink of decay in his nostrils. On Monday morning Walter's face grew very bland when he realised they were to return to the fragrant close off High Street, but he made no comment, only hunching his shoulders a little in his new coat. Murray's lips twitched in approval. Walter seemed to grow smaller, however, when they finally reached the mouth of the close, and the midden was worse than before. There were already grey clothes on the greasy washing line, and the old man still perched, or perched again, on his step, unaware of them. The straw-coloured dog, though, sat up straight when they appeared, cocked its head on one side, and gave a sharp little bark of welcome. It trotted over to Walter and offered up a grubby head for patting, and Walter, after a moment, complied.

'You seem to have made a new friend, there, Walter,' said Murray. 'Would you rather stay out here with the dog?'

'No, sir – or anyway, will the lassie still be there? The lassie that's – dead?'

'Mrs. Argo to you, Walter. No, I don't think they will have left her in a kist in her flat. Dead bodies, once discovered, have a way of demanding attention.'

'Then I'll come in with you, sir. I mean, the dog is fine, but that midden is a thing all on its own.'

'Then come along.' Murray led the way with a little more confidence than on Saturday.

He knew he was going to have to talk to Alicia's landlady, but as he passed along the dark, stuffy passage to the common stair, no one emerged to challenge him and for now he was quite relieved. He found himself tiptoeing up the stairs and wincing when Walter stumbled on the worn stone and squeaked in surprise.

On the landing, nothing had changed from Saturday except, Murray noticed when he looked carefully, a couple of scuff marks had appeared where either the kist or the coffin had been brought out to descend the stairs. When he tried the door to the flat, it opened easily, and he laid a hand on Walter's shoulder to reassure him before they entered.

The room had been cleared. The table, stool and bedstead, with the thin curtain, were all still there, but the bedclothes, crockery and cutlery were all gone and the wooden press was bare. A rat meandered along the window ledge with an air of disappointment in life, before squeezing itself down a hole in the corner of one window. Most of the smell of decay had dissipated, thanks to the broken window pane, though there was still a faint lingering miasma near the table.

He wandered about the room, thinking, trying to imagine what life had been like here, briefly, for Alicia Argo and her son. Had he gone to any school? Surely not, for they had only been here a few days. Where had Alicia bought food? She would probably have had to venture down the High Street for it. What meal had they been eating when … had the killer been a guest, or had he interrupted their meal? Or – but if the killer was the guest, why had one plate been hidden? Surely even the stupidest killer would not expect any investigators not to look under the upturned tin. And where had Theodore been through all this?

'There's nothing much here, sir,' said Walter, half-relieved, half-disappointed. 'The Dundases' maid wanted to know if there were bloodstains.'

'She was strangled, Walter, so no, no bloodstains.'

'Good. I mean, that's good, sir. I mean, I'm sure they'd be gey hard to wash off.' Walter went to a window in his confusion, and peered down the hole after the rat. Murray continued his pacing. Presumably mother and son had shared the same bedstead, or perhaps the son had wrapped himself in a blanket on the floor. He fingered the curtain at the bed recess: it was thicker than he had thought, though with holes here and there thanks to industrious moths. The mattress on the bedstead was rough and grey and smelled very old, even from some distance above it, the straw rank and flat. He placed a careful foot on the bed and gradually lifted his weight on to it: the contraption looked frail enough, but perhaps the mattress gave it solidity, for there was not a creak or a wobble from it.

'Oh, no!' breathed Walter.

'What's the matter?'

'Oh, no, it's all right, sir. It's just – well, I liked that dog, and now it's making up to a wee lassie.'

Murray went over to look down into the courtyard. The straw-coloured dog was indeed enjoying the attentions of a girl of about Walter's age, fair-haired under her bonnet and neatly presented for this neighbourhood.

'Ah, a fickle thing is a dog,' said Murray. 'Well, actually, no, it isn't usually. She must have something you don't have, Walter.'

'Likely a bone in yon basket,' said Walter darkly.

'Maybe. Well, I don't think there's anything more to be seen here. Let's go and tackle the landlady.'

'Ha!' cried Walter triumphantly.

'What now?' Murray had already moved away from the window.

'The lass keeked up and saw me, and she was away like a lilty! Likely she was there to steal the dog and thought it was mine and I'd be down to face her with the crime.'

'Highly likely,' said Murray drily. 'Well, you've saved the dog for another day. Let's go and see the landlady.'

They closed the door of the flat behind them and returned to the downstairs hall, this time not bothering to tiptoe. Murray cleared his throat loudly, and was about to knock on the door to the landlady's flat when the outside door opened and against the bright daylight they beheld Sergeant Home appearing.

'You back again, sir?' he asked, seemingly not displeased to see them.

'I see the flat's been cleared,' said Murray.

'Has it, now?' The sergeant was mildly surprised. 'That wasna us, I can tell you. We'd enough to get the kist and then the coffin down the stair: nearly upright, she was, and I was that afraid she'd fall out on top of me. Well, well,' he tailed off, perhaps aware of Walter's horrified face.

'I thought I might benefit from a word with the landlady,' Murray went on.

'We might both, if you don't mind sharing,' said Home affably. Murray smiled, and Home chapped the door briskly. It shot open.

'Be quiet, there, you'll wake the bairn!' shrieked the apparition that blocked the doorway. It was Eppy again, her eyes tight closed to concentrate on yelling.

'Eppy, Eppy, if the bairn's asleep at all it'll be you that's waking it,' said Home, and Eppy's eyes snapped open.

'You again?' she said, with a sideways slithering glance at Murray.

'Are you no inviting us in?'

'The bairn's asleep,' she faltered.

'Aye, well, maybe,' said Home. 'You'd better have us in, all the same. A cold draught from this hallway might see the poor babbie off entirely.' He led the way inside the gloomy flat, and Murray and Walter followed, closing the door behind them.

The flat must not have been much bigger than the one above where Alicia had lived: there was one extra room, Murray thought, but in fact it was hard to tell as the entire place seemed to be filled with stuff. Old furniture had been stacked in a random fashion against the walls, a table topped with three stools with a chair balanced across their upturned legs, and two pictures over that again; armchairs piled to the ceiling with a washing bowl on each of their seats; a large kist prickling with mismatched fireirons balanced on a bedstead turned sideways, with a mantel clock on the top. There was more, besides, with carpets rolled and folded, bedlinen stacked and strewn, blankets flowing out of boxes like grey bathwater. Before the fireplace in the midst, like jackdaws in a particularly ancient nest, sat Eppy and her daughter, the girl who had been hanging clothes on Saturday, and the little boy who had held her skirts. In a cradle which Murray reckoned must be two centuries old at least lay a very quiet baby, sound asleep and a slightly unhealthy colour. The room smelled of old wool, unclean children, woodrot and whisky.

'Are you no finished with the flat upstairs yet, then, George Home?' demanded Eppy.

'We've a few more people to talk to around the close,' Home said easily. 'What for would you be in such a hurry? The poor woman was only found there the day before yesterday.'

'Aye, but you said she'd been dead a week. It's no my fault if you didna find her straightaway. I've an honest living to make. Just like you and – and him.' She peered at Murray. 'Well, maybe no him. He's a gentleman. They're no very honest, in my experience.' She flashed Murray what he suspected she had thought would be a winning look.

'What about the boy, Eppy?' he asked, changing the subject. 'What about Mrs. Argo's son?'

'A son? Did she have a son?'

'You ken she did, Ma,' said the daughter wearily. In profile she showed a flattened nose, long-broken. 'Folks will have seen him around the place.'

'Oh, aye, him. The lad with the yellow hair. Dinna tell me

you've found him dead up there as well!'

'We haven't found him at all,' said Murray. 'Has he been seen in the last week or so?'

Mother and daughter exchanged looks, but for all Murray could see they were not conspiring, simply wondering.

'I dinna think so ...' said Eppy. 'I'm about a good deal on business, you ken, and I dinna always see a'body's comings and goings.'

'You mean you're out with the whisky,' said Home bluntly.

'That's no fair! I run a good business here! I already have an offer in on that flat, so if you've finished wi'it I'd be pleased to get in and give it the usual good clean before a new tenant arrives.'

Home snorted.

'A good clean? I doubt you'd ken what one was. And how much of this stuff has come into your hands from your tenants, eh?' he asked, waving at the precarious heaps around the walls.

'This is all honestly come by!' snapped Eppy. 'Or I'm looking after it for a friend,' she added uneasily, 'one or the other.'

'Including these blankets?' Murray asked, poking a heap of material at the top of a sack. Eppy's face turned even more hunted.

'Them's my own: they were the very blankets in my marriage kist. The very best quality of things I had for my marriage –'

'I'd swear these are the blankets from the Argos' flat,' Murray said to Home. He lifted one out, and a jingle came from the sack. He peered inside. 'Cutlery, crockery, bedlinen – the very things we saw in the flat on Saturday, and they're not there today.'

'We'll be taking those, Eppy,' said Sergeant Home, gathering the mouth of the sack in his large sandy hands.

'Why for? She has no use for them!' Eppy was angry now.

'But what about her son? Or her husband? This gentleman is acquainted with Mr. Argo, and these items belong to him.'

'Mr. Argo? Is that the officer she was always on about? He's real?' Eppy's daughter was surprised.

'I thought she was putting on airs,' said Eppy. 'No husband could be as good as she made him out to be.'

'Did she say anything else about herself?' asked Murray quickly, for Home seemed keen to leave with his treasure before Eppy snatched it back.

'Her? She was too high to claik with the likes of us. She nearly never left her flat, nor the boy neither. What they were doing here was a wonder to me. Lost their money somewhere, I'd wager,' said the daughter, with a not unsympathetic sniff.

'And did you see anybody visit her at all? Either around the time she died, or generally?'

'She never had no visitors,' said Eppy, a little disappointedly.

'She had that man,' said the daughter suddenly. 'Do you no remember, Ma? The man that swanked up the stair looking about him as if it would bite, and him not much better, if you ask me. He went up and there was a terrible row!'

'A row?' Home asked, his gaze sharpening on the girl.

'Aye, a row. Shouting and throwing things, all that.'

'And did anybody go up to see if she was all right?'

'And get shouted at myself, and likely things thrown at me, too?' demanded the daughter. 'Go and chase yourself, I have more sense than that.'

'And did you see the man come back down?' asked Murray.

'Oh, aye. I keeked out the door to see was he away, and off he swept, not what you'd call happy.'

'What did he look like?' Home had the same look on his face as Murray could feel on his own: were they near? Would this be the information they needed, so easily?

'A thin man, full of himself. I think his hair was on the dark side, for his jaw was dark, but I never seen him without his hat. He was pale, I'd say, but that could be that he was raist. Some people go pale, the ones that dinna go red.'

'Aye,' said Home. He glanced at Murray: the description was a broad one. 'And when was this?' he asked.

'Och, near a fortnight ago. She'd not long moved in.'

Home and Murray gave a collective sigh.

'So you saw her after he'd left?'

'Oh, aye, she was out next day and came back with some plates. I reckon she'd thrown the old ones at the man and needed new.'

III

'When you can't go forward, Walter, you might as well go back,' Murray had remarked, which was why, an hour later, they were walking to the Water of Leith village on their way to Dean.

They had gone almost half the distance when Walter pointed out that the straw-coloured dog was following them.

They made their way back to Combe's Court, Alicia's former lodging, and rattled the risp at the door. While they waited they looked about: the street of the village was very much as before, except that Ebb and Johnnie Norrie were no longer slouched outside the inn. Murray was slightly surprised: they had seemed like the kind of men to spend their lives there, watching the world go by, or such of it as reached the Dean Village.

'Aye?' The thin landlord, Chisholm, had opened the door behind them. 'Oh, it's you again, sir. Mr. Murray, wasn't it? How can I be of assistance this time? There's been no sign of Mrs. Argo since you were last here.'

'I'm afraid we're the ones with the news of Mrs. Argo,' said Murray, following Chisholm into the dim hallway. 'We found her in the Old Town, up near the Castle. Have you any idea why she might have moved there?'

The landlord looked slightly uneasy, patting his slick hair as if it might otherwise be doing things of which he knew nothing.

'She didna say much to me about it. What does she say to you?'

'Not much, either. I'm afraid Mrs. Argo is dead.'

'Dead?' The landlord blanched, and Murray thought he was going to faint. He reached out to steady his elbow, but the man recovered, though he leaned back on the wall. 'How did that happen? She wasna ill, was she?'

'She was murdered.'

'Murdered!' The colour left his cheeks again, making the speckles of his unshaven chin stand out black. 'Murdered! Who would do such a thing? Was it her son? I told you he'd a temper. Would he have lashed out, do you think?'

'We don't know. Her son is missing.'

'Then maybe that's it, then. Oh, my. Murdered!' He pushed his way past Murray and into a small parlour at the back of the hall. Murray followed and found him sitting on a hard chair, clutching its seat. 'Forgive me, Mr. Murray, it's a terrible shock!'

It certainly seemed to be, or Chisholm should have had a career on the stage. Though a killer might be as shocked at the news that his hidden victim had been discovered, Murray supposed. He had drawn breath to ask a further question when there was a gentle tap at the door of the parlour, and he looked round. A little woman was there, poised almost on tiptoe, head on one side, looking anxiously at Chisholm.

'Mr. Chisholm?' she said, in a voice as delicate as her appearance. 'Is something the matter, Mr. Chisholm? Have you had bad news?'

'Oh, Miss Smillie! It's – everything is quite all right, Miss Smillie. No need for you to concern yourself.' Chisholm had pulled himself to his feet and was ushering the little woman out of the room again, but Murray raised a hand.

'Miss Smillie? Forgive me – my name is Murray of Letho. Do you –'

'Mr. Murray of Letho? How charming!' Miss Smillie returned to the room and curtseyed in a little billow of lace. Murray bowed quickly, noting that closer to, she was much older than she dressed.

'Do you live here, Miss Smillie?'

'Oh, yes! Mr. Chisholm is kind enough to let me the rooms across the hallway.'

'Have you been here for long?'

'Oh, several years, Mr. Murray! It is a very healthy setting and the people in the village are most interesting.'

'I'm glad to hear that, Miss Smillie. Were you acquainted with Mrs. Argo and her son who left here lately?'

'Oh, I was indeed!' A sharp little look snapped out of her expression of gentility and found Mr. Chisholm, who ignored it. 'A very nice girl, and young Theodore – well, noisy of course, as boys will be! But well-behaved on the whole. Are you acquainted with Mrs. Argo, Mr. Murray?'

'We did not meet,' said Murray carefully. 'Do you know where she moved to after leaving here?'

'I have no idea. She was not here for long, that is true. I had the impression that she was anxious about something: she never really settled. Of course, she may have been worried about her poor husband – he is an officer in the Royal Regiment, you know. She is prodigiously proud of him: she told me that he was much, much nicer than her first husband, you know!'

'Her first husband?'

'Oh, yes, Theodore's father. She confided in me that he had been a most objectionable man, though of course she was far too delicate to go into details. A master baker, I believe she said. He died several years ago.'

'And she didn't mention any other source of anxiety?'

'Not to me,' said Miss Smillie. Another little look was shot at Mr. Chisholm.

'Or to you, Mr. Chisholm?' Murray chose to take the hint.

'To me? No. She never said anything to me.' Chisholm toed the chair he had sat in. 'Nothing at all,' he added, with the faintest hint of bitterness. Miss Smillie's mouth twitched.

'So presumably,' Murray went on after a moment, 'you were unaware of Mrs. Argo's death?'

'What!' squeaked Miss Smillie. 'Dead? No, you must be mistaken.'

'We think not,' said Murray. 'But we cannot find Theodore. Have you seen him since Mrs. Argo left?'

Miss Smillie shook her head, pursing her little lips into a rosebud.

'Oh, poor Mrs. Argo!' she cried. 'How did she die? Was it – an infection?' She gave a little shudder, but Murray was sure that there was a light in her eyes: she was not altogether sorry to hear that Mrs. Argo was dead.

'I'm sorry to say that she was murdered, up near the Castle.'

'Murdered!' Miss Smillie sank on to the seat Chisholm had vacated, and clutched for his hand. Chisholm winced. 'But who would have done such a thing? And poor Theodore – are you sure he is safe, if his mother is dead?'

'We don't know who killed her, and we don't know if Theodore is safe,' said Murray bluntly. 'If you can tell me anything that might help, I should be grateful. Mr. Chisholm here, for example, believes that Theodore killed her in a fit of temper and has run away.'

'Oh, no, no. I don't think that would be the case,' said Miss Smillie, faintly, though her grip on Chisholm's hand was still strong. 'No, poor Theodore does have a temper, it is true, but he is devoted to his mother. If anything … well, he did have fights with the other boys here. What if he had started a fight and poor Mrs. Argo had somehow got in the way? Whoever he had provoked might have killed both of them. Oh, poor Theodore! Poor Mrs. Argo! Mr. Chisholm, I am quite overcome!'

She burst into tears, maintaining her firm hold on Chisholm's hand. Chisholm's face was a picture of horror, but Murray had no mercy.

'I am sorry to have upset you both. Please excuse me,' he said abruptly, and bowed his farewell. In the hall he collected Walter, and outside on the street the straw-coloured dog waited. Walter had a satisfied look on his face: Murray was not sure what the boy was going to do with a dog in Willie Jack's servants' quarters.

He paused for a moment, wondering what to do next. Alicia Argo had moved swiftly through the Dean Village and off to the High Street: she did not seem to have made friends to any extent or confided much. He decided that he would be much more likely to find out more about her in Potterrow, where she had lived for longer.

'You here again, then?' demanded a voice behind him. He turned, to find himself facing the mother and daughter he had met here before, the ones he had seen on the High Street when he had been looking for Alicia's new flat. The mother's chin was tilted up at him, challenging. The daughter was looking past him with scientific interest at Walter and the dog, as if they were the first of their kind she had seen.

'I know I have had the pleasure of meeting you before,' Murray said, 'but I have not heard your name, madam.'

'You can call me Mrs. Brown,' said the woman. 'And this is Miss Brown.'

'Delighted,' said Murray, with a quick bow. 'My name is Murray of Letho. I seem to remember you were kind enough to direct me to the home of Alicia Argo, who was lodging with Mr. Chisholm here. Do you know her well?'

'I don't think we said we knew her at all,' said the woman calling herself Mrs. Brown. 'We thought it the most likely place for a stranger to be staying, that was all. So you found her, then?'

'She had moved on,' said Murray. 'So you know nothing of her?'

'Not at all,' said Miss Brown, her voice as sharp as her mother's. 'Why? What are you seeking?' Like her mother, she tried to soften the blade of her voice with a crisp smile.

'I was looking for her, but I have found her, I'm afraid.'

'Afraid?'

'She is dead.'

'That's unfortunate,' Mrs. Brown nodded. 'Summer's a dangerous time.'

'She was murdered.'

'Even more unfortunate, then,' said Miss Brown. 'The Old Town can be a dangerous place.'

'And her son is missing,' added Murray.

'Missing? That's very strange. Not killed, too, then?' asked Mrs. Brown.

'Not that I'm aware of.'

'But you don't know where he is?'

'No. I'm concerned about him, I must admit. Mr. Chisholm thinks he might have murdered his mother and run away. Miss Smillie – you may not know her, but she lodges here too – she believes that the boy may have been killed in a fight and his mother was also killed because of her involvement with him. What do you think?'

'I know nothing of boys,' said Miss Brown with contempt.

'But I wouldn't like to see any harm come to the child,' said her mother. 'Indeed, I am more anxious for him than you would believe. It's awful to think of the poor child maybe wandering the town, frightened and alone, knowing his mother was murdered. Oh! my heart hurts at the thought!' She patted her solid bodice where she might be presumed to have a heart.

'Your humanity does you great credit,' said Murray smoothly.

'I hope you will be hunting for the poor child?' asked Mrs. Brown, with an undulation like a kind of sob.

'I am doing so,' Murray agreed.

'Then you will be able to reassure us if you find him?' she said. 'Please – I shall not be able to rest in my bed until I know he is safe.'

'Of course.'

'And should we see him – should he appear here, perhaps, seeking the safety of the last place he felt he had a true home – is there a place we can contact you and let you know?'

'I am staying at the flat of Mr. William John Dundas, at the west end of Prince's Street. I look forward to hearing from you. Yes, Walter?'

'Sir, I forgot. It was just when you said Mr. Dundas' name

there. He said to me this morning to say to you they were going to a – a – a supper party tonight, and you're invited too.'

'A supper party? Did he say where?' Murray pulled out his watch, dismayed.

'Um …'

'You are very busy, and we are detaining you,' said Mrs. Brown, with an anxious look. 'We hope you will be able to bring us good news very soon, Mr. Murray.' When he glanced back at them, they had vanished, like a pair of very unlikely spirits. He frowned after them, and then at Walter.

'We had better go, then,' he said.

'They were helpful, sir, weren't they?' Walter asked cautiously. The dog thought for a moment, then trotted after them.

'They seemed to be,' said Murray absently. 'Yes, on the surface. But I'm afraid I was unconvinced by Mrs. Brown's anxiety. And I'd like to know how they deny all knowledge of Mrs. Argo and her son, but knew that she had moved to the Old Town. And worst of all, it seems to me that despite myself, I have given them more information than they have given me. Come on: we'll be late.'

Chapter Ten

Edinburgh

I

The hosts of the supper party, Mr. and Mrs. Findlay, had been somewhat over-ambitious with their guest list, and by the time Murray arrived, late, with Willie Jack and Letitia, the small rooms of their flat were packed and sweaty. As an Old Town flat, though, it served as a pleasing contrast to the one in which Alicia Argo had spent her last days: there were warm carpets on the floors, drawings and sconces with good wax candles on the walls, which were in places cream-washed and in places neatly panelled, and comfortable chairs and sophas. Some dozen prosperous merchants and their wives filled the available space like the stuffing in an overfilled cushion, and the bright fires which had no doubt made the first few guests feel welcome were now stifling.

Murray was annoyed at having to be here at all, when he could be in Potterrow trying to find out who might have wanted to kill Alicia Argo, and if he had to be here he hated being late. But he could hardly refuse to accompany his hosts, and if Letitia's nutbrown gown had needed adjusting at the last minute, apparently, there was little he could do to help it. Walter had been left at the Dundas' flat and told not to go out and lose himself: he was disconsolate, anyway, as the straw-coloured dog had abandoned them in Water of Leith village and vanished into the crowd, refusing to return. Murray had had to put up with Walter's miserable silence all the way back to Prince's Street and had to resist shaking him.

In the Old Town, they shed their cloaks quickly in the hallway, and Letitia thereby revealed that her nutbrown gown was adorned with a neckline of startling depth. Murray felt himself blinking and swallowing, before looking sternly away, his head full of rich images of harvest. Willie Jack, apparently oblivious, took his wife proudly on his arm and led her into the parlour to try to squeeze into the last few inches of spare space. Murray, looking about him rather than ahead at Mrs. Dundas, followed.

Letitia seemed to know everyone, and Murray belatedly realised that she was probably from a merchant's family herself: Willie Jack would have been a good match for her. She introduced Murray to their host and hostess, the Findlays, a watchmaker and his wife ('No, no, you're not late at all! It's only he has to have everything run exactly to time, don't you, dear?'), then turned as her name was called from near the door.

'Letitia! Tisha dearie, is that you?'

'Uncle!' Letitia led Willie Jack and Murray over to a tiny man perched on a chair a little too large for him. He bounced up to embrace his niece.

'Uncle Brewster, may I present Charles Murray of Letho, a friend of Willie Jack's, who is staying with us?'

Charles bowed, feeling ten feet tall as the little man bowed in return and nearly vanished around his knees.

'Delighted to meet you, sir. Have you known Willie Jack long?'

'Oh, years and years, sir. We met at school.'

'Then you'll know he's a fine fellow. Tisha was lucky to get him, weren't you, you rascal! Have you taken him off to meet your parents yet?' he finished with a warning frown. Murray's ears twitched – had Willie Jack entered into an irregular marriage, without her parents' consent?

'We are off to visit them very soon, Uncle, but you know my sister Julia is there at present, and she must take that little dog with her everywhere, and poor Willie Jack comes out in a rash if it is in the same room as him.'

'Oh, aye? Look, Susan dear, here's Tisha!'

A middle-aged woman a head taller than him pulled herself backwards out of an adjacent conversation and turned to greet her niece.

'Letitia, dear! Have you forgotten your chemisette? You'll catch your death of cold!' Mrs. Brewster was well wrapped up herself, but Murray felt she had a good point. He would have gone back to Prince's Street to fetch the chemisette himself, if he had believed it existed.

'Aunt Brewster, Mr. Murray,' said Letitia, paying her no attention.

'Oh, aye? Grand, grand. Letitia, I have a spare shawl here. Would you not wrap it round yourself?'

'Aunt, it is very warm. You would not want me to faint?' Anyone looking less as if they were going to faint would be hard to find, Murray thought: Letitia was as rosy and bright as a fresh-picked apple, her eyes sparkling like autumn sunlight on brown glass. He turned away, about to try to make conversation with Mrs. Brewster, but then a chirrup of music came from somewhere in the crowd and he spun towards it. In the midst of the room, adding, no doubt, to its congestion, was a piano, and someone had begun to play it, and to play it very competently. For a lovely moment, only the music filled his head, easing out all thoughts of Letitia or Alicia Argo or her son. He found himself making his way towards it, slipping through the crowd, letting the sweet cadences soothe him, ignoring the guests who talked over the music. He reached the centre of the room to find a plain little girl of around thirteen, the daughter of the house, just reaching the end of the piece. She finished it to perfection to the last note, then leapt down and ran off, and the music trickled out of his mind and stopped again. He almost swore.

The press of people and his momentum towards the piano swept him on beyond it where a servant managed to reach him to hand him a glass of negus. The quality was good, and the quantity was generous: he only felt that a cold drink would have been more welcome. He sipped it, closing his eyes, and when he opened them Letitia was in front of him, smiling.

'Mr. Murray! You are alone, it seems.'

'Well, you seem to know many of the people here,' said Murray quickly. 'Why not introduce me?'

'Oh!' She glanced round in surprise, and chose the first people her eyes lighted on. 'Well, these are the Sangsters. Charles Murray of Letho,' she announced to them like a prize, 'Mr. and Mrs. Sangster. Mr. Sangster is a master baker.'

Mr. Sangster could have been a master baker or a street scaffie, but he was deep in conversation with someone else and only broke off to nod in Murray's direction. Mrs. Sangster, bony-faced under a well-trimmed bonnet, gave an apologetic smile with her curtsey.

'Mr. Murray of Letho?' she repeated pleasantly. 'Where's that, then?'

'In Fife, ma'am, near Cupar.' She was very densely powdered, he noticed: given her husband's trade, he could not shake the idea that she was coated in flour. 'Do you live in Edinburgh, then?'

'In Water of Leith,' she corrected.

'Of course: the bakers' capital.' They smiled. 'A strange coincidence – I had not been there for years and yet in the last week I have been through it four times. Walking to Dean village.'

'Oh, aye? What took you there? There is nothing much in the Dean but rock and dust.'

'I was seeking the wife of a friend, but unsuccessfully, as it turns out.' A pleasant social occasion was not really the time to introduce murder victims into the conversation.

'Unfortunate. And is that what brings you to Edinburgh, or are you enjoying the end of the season?'

'That, and visiting my friends the Dundases. I was at school with Mrs. Dundas' husband.'

'I see. Very pleasant. And I suppose you are a bachelor, then, to come visiting and see how married life is?' There was a twinkle in her eye. Murray tried to smile back.

'No, no, I am a married man myself. My wife stays in Fife: the town does not suit her constitution as the weather grows warmer.' It was a part of the truth, anyway.

'Fortunate, then, that she can escape.' Mrs. Sangster rocked thoughtfully a little on her heels, and sipped her negus with appreciation. Her face had rather more chin and nose than was handsome, but her expression was certainly full of character. Brown curls with the merest hint of grey unfurled from beneath her cap lace. 'Is she from the country herself, or from Edinburgh?'

'Neither, ma'am, she is from Naples.'

'A foreigner! Well, that is an adventure! How did you meet?'

'I was acquainted with the family when I stayed in Naples.'

'My! You will be telling me next you have a sister in Kamchatka and a brother in Brazil!'

Murray laughed. She was easy to talk to.

'Not at all! I have no sister, and my brother is in Belgium with the army, or was a week ago.'

'An officer, I take it?'

'That's right. It was his friend's wife I was seeking.'

'I see. What regiment are they with, these valiant officers?'

'The Royal Scots – you know, the Royal Regiment as it was.'

They were interrupted as Mrs. Findlay, the hostess, squeezed past them to the window.

'I must open this, if you can stand the draught a moment or two, Mrs. Sangster. The heat is extraordinary!'

'Too many guests, Mrs. Findlay: your suppers are too popular,' said Mrs. Sangster. She said it with humour, but Murray thought he surprised a harder look in her eye. Mrs. Findlay gave an anxious chuckle and opened the window.

'I must leave you,' said Mrs. Sangster to Murray, 'if you'll excuse me – I cannot take a draught on my neck, or I shall seize up for a week.' She made her way determinedly through the crowd, as if a rock had suddenly taken it into its head to move upstream. Almost as if it followed on, a ragged cheer rose from the street outside.

'Good heavens, what is that racket?' asked Letitia's aunt, who was nearby. Mrs. Findlay peered out of the window.

'Some stooshie going on down the street,' she sighed. 'The drawback of living in the High Street, I'm afraid. I'll have to close this again.'

'That's good: Letitia's liable to catch a chill in that gown,' said her aunt grimly.

'I beg your pardon,' Mr. Sangster turned and finally gave Murray his full attention. 'Charles Munro, was it?'

'Murray, sir.'

'Of where was it?'

'Letho, in Fife.'

Sangster thoughtfully ran his fingers over waistcoat buttons that could have done with a little less strain.

'I had an older man in mind for that name and estate,' he said.

'My father, sir, had the same name. He died some years ago.'

'Did he, indeed? A house on … Queen Street, comes to mind?'

'That would be the very man, sir. Were you acquainted with him?'

'I believe that one of our customers supplied his household with bread.'

'Of course: in that case I'm sure the bread was excellent: my father enjoyed good food.'

'I am sorry to hear of his passing, then.'

Murray nodded in acknowledgement.

'And you're his only son, then, are you?' Sangster looked him up and down, as if to say that if Charles Murray senior had had any choice in the matter, Murray would not have been his heir. Murray tried to smile.

'No, I have a younger brother.'

'Married?' The vast expanse of Sangster's white waistcoat put Murray in mind of flour sacks, on which his rosy, white-haired head sat like a dumpling, a little wider around the chin than around the brow. He shook off the image.

'He is not married, no, sir.'

'I meant you – are you married?'

'Yes, I am.' Sangster must have a daughter to find a match for, he thought: both Sangster and Mrs. Sangster had enquired after his marital state.

'Sons?'

'I beg your pardon?'

'Have you sons?'

'We have not yet been blessed with children, sir, no.'

'Then you'd best get on with it. If you died, then your brother would inherit, and he's not even married. You need to consider your estate, Mr. Murray. Think of your lineage. It's like a business: businesses need sons, healthy, intelligent, loyal sons.'

'I'm not sure one can guarantee intelligence and loyalty – or even sons,' Murray laughed, but Sangster was serious.

'You must see to it. Wife healthy?'

He was not sure, and felt angry at the question.

'Of course, sir.'

'You look healthy enough yourself. Sons, Mr. Murray, that's what you need.'

II

As the evening progressed, Murray emptied several more glasses of negus until he felt slightly sick with the heat and the sweet spiciness of it. By the time he had been there a couple of hours, he felt as if he had been interrogated by everyone in the room on his marital state, and many of them had offered advice on how to run Letho as a sound business, whether Murray wanted the advice or not. He had left the supper table early, and had clenched his fists so many times that he had marked his palms with ridges, and had had to stop himself a couple of times before he broke his glass. Wherever he went he could hear Letitia's throaty laughter, and no one reappeared to play the lovely piano.

By the time the party was over, and Letitia had agreed to leave, he was ready to burst out of the windows. He forced himself to replace his hat, cloak and gloves with meticulous patience, to smile and thank his hostess, to follow Letitia and Willie Jack at a decent pace down the curling stone stair. Out in the street, he breathed in the mild June air with relief, feeling the sweat blissfully icy on his brow. He dropped behind the Dundases, removed his hat and ran his fingers hard through his hair, wriggling and jiggling his shoulders in the discreet dimness of the street.

'Oh, aye, what's going on here?' came Willie Jack's voice. Murray became aware of shouting from further down High Street, shouting that did not sound like friendly drunken banter, or indeed anyone calling for help. He remembered Mrs. Findlay's remarks when she had closed the window earlier.

'I think it's a fight,' he remarked. 'Better cross the road.'

'I'm not frightened,' said Letitia, and Murray believed her.

'It's not a question of whether or not you're frightened, my love,' said Willie Jack, guiding her with unexpected firmness to the opposite side of the street. 'It's a question of potential danger just from being nearby.'

As if to make his point, there was a sudden sound of smashing glass, followed by an ominous cheer. Murray and the Dundases paused, tucked into the head of a close, trying not to draw attention to themselves. Not far down the street there was a crowd of around twenty people – mostly men, Murray thought, though it was hard to be sure about that or the numbers in the variable light of the street, a mixture of candles at windows, starlight and the odd hurrying link boy. The focus of their attention was a lit window, one floor up, at which two figures were leaning out, waving glasses and apparently taunting the crowd. Murray assumed they were drunk: even in the dark this did not look like a crowd it was wise to taunt.

'Can you think of a better way around?' asked Willie Jack quietly.

'Slip back up the hill and down the West Bow to the Grassmarket,' Murray replied. 'It's not too bad this time of night, if you avoid the taverns, and you might get a chair there. If not, back up quick to Greyfriars and home from there.'

'Then I think we had better go that way, don't you?'

The crowd surged a little towards them and they drew back into the close. Murray peered round the corner, ignoring Letitia's complaint that she had stepped in something foul.

The crowd had grown again and was becoming more focussed, less mobile. The men at the window seemed to quieten them for a moment, but whatever they said it started a dissatisfied rumble through the mob. Even from the close head Murray could feel the wave of hostility. Then a clear voice cut through, old and sensible.

'Right, now, lads, go on away home to your beds. And you twa up yonder: you've had more than enough, that's plain. Shut that windy and put out your lights and awa to bed wi' you and all.'

There was a moment of silence, a long second when it almost seemed that sense would prevail. Then a low, carrying voice from the shadows straight across the street hissed out:

'It's the City Watch, lads! Gie 'em laldy!'

There was a great shout from the mob. Murray turned and shoved Willie Jack and Letitia further back into the close.

'They're stoning the Watch!' he cried, as a chunk of rock bounced off the close entrance near them. Almost immediately a cheer went up: Murray peeked round the corner in time to see the two officers of the City Watch in their red coats making a rapid and strategic retreat down the High Street. The crowd smelled victory: the cheer was followed by laughter, and for a moment it looked again as if the crowd might disperse of their own accord. Several of them were as drunk as the men at the window, but by no means all of them had drink taken: Murray could see a pale man, almost opposite him, wearing a wide-brimmed hat and balancing some kind of sack on his back. He had taken care to stand out of any direct light, but a section of white-washed wall beside him reflected a dim glow into his face. It was stone cold, observing the scene with a chilly absence of emotion.

'Could we go now, do you think?' whispered Willie Jack from behind Murray.

'Wait: there's something happening.'

The men at the window had ducked down at the stone-throwing, but now they reappeared, and one opened the window as wide as he could while the other levered something heavy on to the sill. It was a mighty chamberpot.

'Take that, ye scoundrels!' the man cried unsteadily, before upturning the pot on the crowd. Whether he meant it to or not, the pot slipped from his grasp, and fell suddenly with a great crash. Two men dropped to the ground, and one did not rise. The crowd found its rage again, and surged towards the building.

'Police!' came a shout from down the hill. 'Police!' Murray thought he knew the voice: he squinted through the dark, to see the sturdy figure of George Home at the head of a band of men from the police office. He walked with authority towards the mob, lit intermittently by a fellow with a lantern.

'Pollis!' came a hiss. Murray glanced back: the pale man in the shadows was smiling, calculating. He shifted the sack on his back, and raised his carrying voice again. 'Go for them, lads! Go for the pollis! They're nae better nor the Watch!'

'Good lord!' cried Willie Jack, holding Letitia back safely behind him. 'They're attacking the police!'

'Get Letitia away up past the Castle,' said Murray, 'and take these.' He swung off his cloak and gave it and his hat to Willie Jack.

'Where are you going? Willie Jack sounded distraught.

'To help,' said Murray, and with two long strides he was in the midst of the fight.

The first few punches felt wonderful. His gloved hands connected with a jaw, then with a nose or two, with satisfying results. He managed to push through to Home before someone tried to arrest him.

'Here to help,' he gasped, 'if I can.'

'Many thanks, sir,' said Home, twisting a man's arm behind his back in mid-punch and handing him back to another police officer.

The fighting was too close for stone throwing now, and some of the men had found sticks from somewhere. Murray reeled as a plank made contact with his cheekbone, and the night spun green for a moment. He jabbed the man in the stomach and he dropped the plank on his own toes, leaping back with a squeak of pain. Murray wheeled away and almost hit a policeman in his hurry. They ducked round each other in search of more of the mob, but the wild moment had passed: four or five men lay on the ground, and the police officers had another half dozen or so manacled, beginning to move them off to the police office. Murray looked about for Home: where was he? An officer was leaning against a wall, looking dazed, dabbing blood from the corner of his mouth with his cuff, but it was not Home. Quickly Murray crouched to examine the figures on the ground. The first might have been dead: the second was groaning and clutching his leg, sprawled in the stinking shards of the chamberpot. The third, out cold, was Home.

'Sergeant Home is injured!' Murray called. 'Quickly!' He turned to see if anyone was responding, and had just seen that two officers were running to him when he noticed a sharp smell of burning. Overhead he heard a crackle, then a roar.

'What the – ?' He leapt up, scanning the building above them. The window where the drunken men had stood spat flame. 'Fire!' he bellowed. 'Fire!'

The Old Town's reaction was instant. Too many times had fires destroyed huge swipes of the tight-packed tenements: in minutes bucket chains had formed to the local wells, and in half an hour the fire was all but out. Murray crouched in the midst of the chaos. He had hauled Home aside by his armpits, then torn off his split and filthy gloves, hurling them aside to pull off his coat and fold it under Home's head. The light was uncertain, fading from firelight to candlelight and lamplight again, but even at its best Home's sandy face looked grey. Murray rubbed his hands, rubbed his face, trying to bring life into him, and was relieved to feel a pulse still in Home's rough neck.

Two officers, white with exhaustion, came with a stretcher and lifted Home away, dodging smouldering detritus being flung from the burned-out flat. Murray pushed himself upright against the wall of the tenement, watching them go. They vanished from sight, and he looked about him, tasting blood and wiping it absently from his mouth and nose. Beside him was the entry into the court where Alicia had spent her last days: there was the tobacconist's sign. He jumped at the sudden familiarity of it.

But if that was the court, with its midden and its straw-coloured dog, then … he stared up at the open window where the drunk men had leaned out not long before. He knew the window, now he came to look at it. It was Alicia Argo's.

Chapter Eleven

Edinburgh

I

'Well, I'm sorry, sir, but I've just lost it, and that's a fact.'

Murray could not decide if Walter was genuinely contrite or not. He was used to servants who either managed without making quite so many mistakes, or if they did so, made excuses. For Walter, it seemed that losing things, including himself, was just a fact of life against which it was useless to struggle. Somehow that took the energy out of being angry with him, too. Murray rubbed his scalp, and winced at the pain in his face.

'Go through again what happened, and maybe you'll remember where you put it.'

'The maid answered the door about half past eight, sir, and she called me to talk to the messenger. He said he had come from – someone you talked to last night, sir, with a message for you, and he handed it over. So I took it – I think – and then what?' His brow furrowed with concentration under his thick chestnut fringe. Murray gave him a moment, then tried prompting him.

'Did you bring it in here?'

'No, sir, for you were still asleep.'

'Into the parlour?'

'I don't think I would have done that, sir. It was a message for you, not for anybody else.'

'Well, good. What about the kitchen, then? Maybe you went back there with the maid?'

'Maybe …' But Walter was still frowning, unconvinced.

'Well, go and look,' snapped Murray.

'Sir,' said Walter, 'what happened your face?'

'I walked into a plank,' said Murray shortly, and Walter, finally sensing his mood, left to search the kitchen.

Murray peered into the mirror by the window. He had a superb bruise on his cheekbone, a black eye, and a split lip, and there was some evidence that his nose had bled a little in the night. When he had returned to the flat, feeling more the worse for wear with every step from the Old Town to the New, Willie Jack and Letitia had already retired for the night and he had done his best to wipe off the worst of the muck and blood with cold water from the jug in his room. Now he tried again with hot water and soap, before dressing and presenting himself for breakfast in the parlour.

'Well, thank heavens you're back safely!' said Willie Jack, hearing him but attending to a dish of kidneys on the sideboard. 'We were afraid you would be knifed in a gutter!' Then he turned, and nearly dropped his plate. 'Oh, my!'

Letitia looked up, and gasped.

'I must apologise for my appearance,' Murray said, trying a painful smile. 'It is a good deal worse than my actual injuries would justify.'

'But what happened? Did you fight?' asked Letitia, her eyes bright.

'The police sergeant was an acquaintance of mine: I offered help, and unfortunately met with an enthusiastic member of the famous Edinburgh mob with a plank. The sergeant was considerably less lucky. The last I saw him, his men were carrying him off in a swoon to the police office. Then there was a fire in a tenement, and when that was out I came home.'

'What a night!' cried Letitia. 'And we returned home without further incident.' There was something in her voice which Murray could only describe as wistfulness. Willie Jack was more concerned.

'I thought the Edinburgh mob was a thing of the past – gone with Captain Porteous,' he said. 'It's absolutely shocking. What on earth do you think they were up to?'

'Oh, don't keep poor Mr. Murray talking,' said Letitia, rising from the table. 'Can't you see it hurts his poor face? I shall fetch some of my salve.' She left the room in a swirl of skirts, and Willie Jack looked anxiously at Murray's injuries.

'It's really not that bad,' Murray reassured him, though it was true that talking hurt. He felt reluctant to see what eating did, though he was hungry.

'I should have stayed ...'

'Not at all: you had Mrs. Dundas to look after. Anyway, if the mob was that way inclined, there was no point in you being injured, too.' Willie Jack managed to combine relief with concern in his face, and sniffed in confusion. Letitia returned with a stoneware pot and a white cloth.

'Sit down, Mr. Murray, please: how on earth can a little person like me hope to reach your face all the way up there?' She smiled, and Murray found himself sitting.

'I'm sure I can manage on my own,' he protested, but not to much effect. In a moment she was bent over him, gently smoothing the sweet-smelling salve over his cuts and bruises. He closed his eyes, partly to avoid looking too closely at her, and partly to inhale the scent of rosemary and sharp ginger and comfrey. 'Your own receipt?' he asked, keeping his eyes firmly closed though they leapt to a picture of Letitia brushing through burgeoning herb beds.

'A family one,' she said.

'It's her mother's. She sends it by the box,' added Willie Jack. 'I don't know what she thinks we do here in Edinburgh.'

'It's very soothing,' Murray said, thinking of the lovely salves his old housekeeper used to make in the stillroom at Letho. His wife kept the house now: he did not think she stooped to salve-making. Letitia touched his split lip, and he jumped back.

'Oh! Sorry,' she said. 'That must be particularly painful.'

'Yes,' he agreed, and moved away firmly. 'I don't think it needs salve, though: lips heal quickly.'

'Now, what about some breakfast?' said Willie Jack with unusual briskness. 'You must be starving.'

Both Dundases settled to the table again, and Murray helped himself to meat and bread from the sideboard.

'An interesting evening last night,' he remarked, wanting to move away from the fight in the street. 'Your aunt and uncle are charming people.'

'Oh, they're all right,' said Letitia, sipping her hot chocolate. 'They're really my parents' circle. What did you think of the Sangsters? They're prodigiously rich.'

'He was very keen that I should have as many sons as possible,' said Murray, trying to make a joke of it. 'He didn't want Letho to leave the family, which was kind of him.'

'Ah, well, he would say that, wouldn't he?' Willie Jack looked ominously at Letitia, and she nodded.

'He had two sons,' she explained, 'and I suppose thought he was secure, but one died and the other is estranged from him.'

'Oh, that's unfortunate.' Murray felt more sympathetically towards the old baker. 'Did the dead son reach maturity? Was there any chance of a grandson?'

'Oh, I'm not sure,' said Letitia. 'He was certainly in his manhood. I remember seeing him oh! ten years ago, perhaps, when I was a girl. Maybe less. He was very like his father in looks, you know, very solid looking, rather stern and determined. I didn't take to him.' She smiled at Willie Jack, who put out a hand to touch hers.

'What are your plans for today?' he asked Murray after a moment.

'I must visit Potterrow again. This poor woman, George's friend's wife – no one at her last two lodgings knew much about her. I hope that as she stayed for longer at Potterrow I might have better luck there, for it is nigh impossible to know who might have killed her if I don't know more about her life, her friends, and if possible her enemies.'

'Will you take young Walter with you?' asked Willie Jack with a grin.

'I probably shall.'

'Our maid is growing very attached to him – I think she sees him as a long-lost son.'

'That would be Walter,' Murray agreed. 'If nothing else, he'd be long-lost. By the way, have you seen a message for me? Walter took it in from a messenger this morning but he can't remember where he put it.'

But neither Willie Jack nor Letitia had seen the message, either.

II

Potterrow was not significantly different in the sunshine. Again Murray paused as he entered it, making a final decision on how to proceed. He turned right, one hand on Walter's shoulder, and went to number 47, which number, he noted, had been painted very precisely above the low doorway. He knocked again, almost afraid to damage the polished door.

Little Bob Campbell appeared promptly and, recognising him, ushered him inside straightaway.

'We're in the parlour, Mr. Murray, sir. That is, my good friend Mrs. Brotherstone and I are having a dish of tea and a clishmaclash together. Would you be so good as to join us? Mrs. Brotherstone makes a very fine black bun, and it was that we were having with our tea.'

He led the way into the parlour, Murray feeling enormous behind him. Mrs. Brotherstone, happy to direct gentlemen in the street but less familiar with them socially, stood in a fluster as Murray entered and Walter disappeared towards the back of the house, instructed to find the kitchen. Murray waved her back into her seat.

'Mrs. Brotherstone, please, no,' he said. 'I am very glad to find you here together.' He folded himself into a delicate little rosewood chair, and prayed it would hold him: Mrs. Brotherstone, he noted, had found a sturdier armchair to support her comfortable shape. Mr. Campbell hurried back into the room with an extra teacup and saucer, and a plate for the black bun.

'There we are - not what you're used to, I'm sure, but Mrs. Brotherstone and I are fond of a good cup of tea when we have the time.'

'It's perfect,' said Murray. 'Thank you.' He was aware of both of them eyeing his bruises, but neither dared ask about them.

'I daresay,' said Mr. Campbell, bouncing a hand back over his hair, 'that you are here again about Mrs. Argo?'

'I am. Have you heard any news of her? Or her whereabouts?'

'We have not, Mr. Murray. To be honest, Mr. Murray,' he said, 'with respect, of course, your visit here before made me very anxious. I told you, I think, that Mrs. Argo had said she was moving because some unpleasant people had been threatening her. Well, you were not the only person to ask about her, though I was most careful not to tell anybody anything. I really was.' He took his napkin into both hands and pulled it straight, then crumpled it together in a way that Murray felt sure he would regret later.

'Well, as it happened,' said Murray, 'my brother wrote again after I visited you, to tell me that Lieutenant Argo had received a letter from Mrs. Argo and it told him that she had moved, and what her new address was. I was able, therefore, to follow the trail a little further.'

'Oh! Then you know all about the Dean Village?' blurted out Mrs. Brotherstone, and Mr. Campbell glared at her. Mrs. Brotherstone blushed heavily.

'I do, I think: but she had moved on from there, too, by the time I reached it.'

'Afeart again?' asked Mr. Campbell with what seemed to be genuine concern.

'I think so. She left the Dean for a close off the High Street.'

'The High Street? But if she was coming back into town she should have come back to us! We would have looked after her, wouldn't we, Mrs. Brotherstone?'

'Indeed we would, Mr. Campbell, for the safest place for anyone is amongst their friends.'

'Mrs. Argo had friends here, then, did she?'

'Well, apart from us … well, there's Bessie Cordiner,' said Mrs. Brotherstone. 'They were often about together.'

Mr. Campbell nodded.

'That'd be right. And then the Lieutenant, he was friendly enough with young Mr. Malcolm up the stair. He's a medical student, studying at the College, you ken?'

'And does Bessie Cordiner live here, too?'

'Not in this stair, but nearby. She's the daughter of the shoemaker across the street. A nice enough lassie,' said Mr. Campbell. Mrs. Brotherstone turned up her nose.

'Sly, I'd call her. Nice enough if she thinks she's getting something.'

'Well, I suppose.'

'Oh, aye, she is! And her mother was the same.'

'Well, I'll bow to your superior knowledge of the fair sex, Mrs. Brotherstone,' said Mr. Campbell, and Mrs. Brotherstone gave a little chuckle. Murray cleared his throat.

'Mrs. Argo's son – Theodore, is it not? You didn't mention him the last time I was here.'

'Did I not? That was not deliberate, I think,' said Mr. Campbell precisely.

'Did he have any particular friends around here?'

'I don't know that he did. He played in the street with the other lads, though his favourite games, he told me, were to do with being soldiers. He was determined to join the army like his father.'

'Do you mean Lieutenant Argo, or his real father?'

'Ah! No, I mean the Lieutenant. I have no notion that her first husband was a soldier, you ken.'

'So Theodore and his stepfather were on good terms?'

'Oh aye, oh aye!' said Mrs. Brotherstone. 'It was lovely to see! The Lieutenant treats Theodore like his own son, and Theodore just adores him. They are a very close family. I'd say they were as happy as could be here: it fair amazed me when Mr. Campbell said there was any threat to them. I always – I never thought she had been happy in her first marriage, that was the impression she aye gave, though she was never one for going into the details. She aye said how lucky she was now, better than in the past.'

'And you haven't seen her back here since she left?'

They both looked at one another, thinking.

'No,' said Mr. Campbell, and Mrs. Brotherstone agreed.

'And Theodore?'

'He'd hardly be here without his mother,' said Mrs. Brotherstone, slightly shocked.

'But even so – no sign of him?'

They both shook their heads.

'So have you seen her, Mr. Murray? Did you follow her to the High Street? Is she all right, or has she moved on again, poor soul?' asked Mr. Campbell. Murray took a deep breath.

'I did find her, I'm afraid. She was in a flat off the High Street, up near the Castle end. I'm afraid she was dead.'

Both Mr. Campbell and Mrs. Brotherstone gasped, and Mr. Campbell turned even whiter than usual.

'Do you mean murdered? You do, don't you?' he whispered, while Mrs. Brotherstone rounded the table to rub his wrists. 'Poor Mrs. Argo! Oh, dear! She was quite right to be feart, then!'

'It seems so,' said Murray. He paused only briefly. 'Now, you said that someone else had asked about her after my visit. Can you remember who that was?'

Mr. Campbell took another moment, and a full cup of tea, to pull himself together.

'Oh, dear, oh, dear,' he murmured. 'Poor Mrs. Argo. Such a lovely, clean, tidy tenant. And her poor, poor husband. Such a thing when you're off fighting. Oh, oh, I feel responsible! What if he thought she was safe here and I would look after her?'

Murray doubted that Lieutenant Argo was as misguided as that. Mr. Campbell did not look the protective sort.

'This person that called to look for her: was it a man or a woman?'

'Oh, a man, aye.'

'It couldn't …' Murray hesitated. 'Are you sure her first husband is dead?'

Mr. Campbell looked shocked.

'Oh, aye, surely! They were properly married, her and the Lieutenant, in this very room, by the minister from the West Kirk. I was here myself. No, he was dead, no doubt. But that's not to say I liked the look of this fellow, either. I mean, she always said her second husband was better than her first, and I had the idea – Mrs. Brotherstone kens I had – that he was cruel to her. And while I'm sure as can be that this was not her first husband, I'd have said he could be cruel, too, when he wanted to be.' Mr. Campbell gave a little shiver.

'What did he look like?' Murray had always been a patient man, but he felt his patience had worn very thin in the last while. He wished there was a salve for that.

'He was gey pale.' Coming from the indoor-reared Mr. Campbell, that was a remark indeed. 'Tall – no so tall as you, sir – well enough built without being fat nor thin, and he wore a brown coat – very nice cut, I thought, did you no think so, Mrs. Brotherstone? I thought it was a very nice coat. And he had a hat with a wide brim, hardly ever jooked out from underneath it, to tell you the truth, so I'd be hard put to ken him without it.'

'And he was definitely here looking for Alicia Argo?'

'Alicia Argo indeed, he had both names. But I never told him anything to his benefit: said she'd gone, I knew not where. I even told him I was glad to see the back of her! I dinna much like telling untruths, Mr. Murray, but there was something about this man that made me feel I would swear black was white if it would stop him doing whatever it was he was up to, for it could be nothing good.'

'And yet,' said Mrs. Brotherstone with a sniff, 'he must have got her in the end.'

They put their heads together over the tea table and had a hearty sob, while Murray tried to restrain himself from tapping impatiently on the sparkling white cloth.

Eventually the sobs subsided, and he felt he could reasonably interrupt again.

'So you believe that that man was the murderer, then? There is no one else who springs to mind who might have found some benefit in her death? I've been told, for example, that Theodore had a sharp temper, and that either he might have been involved in some argument in which she came to be killed by accident, or that he killed her.'

'No! Surely he must deny that!' Mrs. Brotherstone was horrified.

'He might well, were he around to do so,' said Murray. 'But nothing has been seen of Theodore since his mother's body was found.'

'He's missing? Then how can you be sure he's not been killed, too? Oh, the poor boy!' Mr. Campbell was off again, his sodden handkerchief uselessly dabbed at his streaming eyes until Murray gave up and offered him one of his own. Mr. Campbell paused in awe of the fine linen for a second before blowing his nose loudly on it.

'We can't be sure, in fact,' said Murray. 'He was not in her flat, that is all we can say. He could be dead or fled, and if fled he could be in fear of his life, or guilty, or something in between. He could have been taken captive by whoever killed his mother. I have no idea. But if you see him, please can you tell me? If you trust me, that is, or you can tell Sergeant George Home at the police office in the High Street.' He hoped Home was fit to be told.

'I cannot think of anyone else that would have wanted to harm Mrs. Argo,' said Mrs. Brotherstone, who had evidently been giving it some consideration. 'She was a gey friendly body, gey kindly, a good wife and mother, the kind men would sooner protect than not. I'm sure she would have done anything for anybody, and most of all for the Lieutenant or Theodore. I've never heard it said that she owed money, or gave a body an unkind word, or was in anybody's way. Whatever that man wanted of her, he must be the one that tracked her down and killed her.'

III

'Oh, aye, me and her was great friends,' said Bessie Cordiner, with a bright smile. It had been easy to find her at Mrs. Brotherstone's direction, over at the very shoemaker's where Murray had asked directions on his previous visit. Bessie was a cheery young woman, with pretty red hair and the taste to dress to set it off. Her tears over Alicia Argo had been brief, cancelled out by just a little excitement at the thought of a tragedy.

'How long had you known her?' Murray asked. They were in the kitchen of her father's house, with the door open to the shop so that, presumably, her father could overhear any cries for help from his daughter, interviewed by a strange gentleman.

'Only a couple of years,' said Bessie, thinking back. 'Mr. Argo, he lived here before that. Then he married her and brought her back here.'

'Was he an officer then?'

'No, he was a – what was he, Father?'

'A gunsmith, to his trade,' her father called back, proving that he was alert. 'He was his father's apprentice, but then his father died and left him a wee bit money, and he bought his commission with that.'

'He'd always wanted to be a soldier,' Bessie went on. 'He looked awful grand in his regimentals! Just lovely. That's not why, though: he just wanted to see a bit of the world and I suppose he kenned enough about guns and all.'

'I see. So he married Alicia ...'

'Aye, even though she had that boy from her first husband.'

'And that was when you first came to know her?'

'Aye, that'd be right. There aren't so many girls of my age round here, so it was nice to have her, even though she was that wee bit older. We'd have a wee gossip three, maybe four times a week. Told each other all our secrets!'

'Then no doubt you know all about her first marriage,' Murray encouraged her.

'Oh, aye. That wasna such a happy one, I'm thinking. No wonder she latched on to Mr. Argo. He was a bit of a catch, I'd say! Fine looking and a bit of money. She did well there, I always said.'

'But her first marriage, that was less successful?'

Bessie thought a bit, and looked a little sheepish.

'Well, now, you can't expect me to give up all our girls' secrets, sir, can you?' she simpered. Murray realised that whatever girls' secrets Bessie had given up to Alicia Argo, the compliment had not been returned.

'Did you see her or Theodore after they left their lodging?'

'No, I didn't even see them leave. I'd have been pleased to help them pack up their things. She had some lovely things.'

Murray thought back to the bare flat off High Street. Where had the lovely things gone, then?

'Did she mention being frightened of anyone? Of anyone threatening her?'

Bessie thought again.

'I'm not sure she did. I can't imagine her being frightened. I mean, she had everything she could wish for, did she no? She had the wee lad she loved, the handsome, lovely husband, all the nice clothes and the furniture and whatever, plates and things. She had this lovely table, I think it was a wedding present. It had wee flowers painted on the top. It was just lovely. Oh, she had fine things, all right! She had no cause to be afeart of anything!'

Murray shook his head, wondering at her. He was fairly sure this had not been an intimate friendship, and even if it had been so he was going to learn very little. He rose and bowed, and Bessie gave a pretty blush and a giggle. It was possible that the friendship with Alicia Argo was more to her with Alicia dead than with Alicia alive.

IV

Back at Mr. Campbell's lodging-house, the medical student, Mr. Malcolm, had returned from his day's classes and was at home. Mr. Campbell, still tearful, led Murray upstairs to meet him.

'You are friends with Lieutenant James Argo, I believe?' Murray started.

'Oh, aye, that's so. But he's not here: he's off with the regiment just now.'

'I know: my brother is in the same regiment. Argo has been very concerned about the safety of his wife, and asked my brother to ask me to find her for him.'

'Well, she's moved away,' said Malcolm, as if anybody should know that.

'Yes, I know. Unfortunately she has been found dead in a close off the High Street.'

'Dead?' Malcolm looked interested for the first time, and rubbed a bony finger up and down his large nose. He had inkstains on his hands and what looked disturbingly like blood on his waistcoat. He eyed Murray's injuries with a calculating air.

'I'm afraid so. I gather you were quite friendly with the couple?'

'Aye, I visited with them a few times. Argo lived here before he married. We've both been here three years or so.'

'Did you know anything of Mrs. Argo from before her marriage to the Lieutenant?'

'Well, she was a widow, with a son. Beyond that …'

'So would you know of any reason why she would have been killed?'

'She was killed?'

'Strangled.'

'I see.' Mr. Malcolm took the news calmly. 'Well, it does not entirely surprise me. She was the kind of woman who did not choose her friends particularly wisely. Too kind for her own good, I sometimes observed.'

'Did you? Have you anyone particular in mind?'

'That foolish woman across the street, for one: all she wanted was everything the Argos had, probably including Argo himself. But off Mrs. Argo would go for her gossips, and like as not give her little presents, you know the sort of small tat that women seem to value.'

'And men?'

'No one in particular. Argo himself is as decent as you could meet. But she was the kind of woman that men always feel protective towards. Some women would use that – Lord, I've seen a few! But Mrs. Argo hadn't the brains for that kind of scheming. Not an intelligent woman, I've always thought.'

Well, Murray thought, if he had wanted a scientific analysis of

Alicia, this was probably as close as he was going to get. A thought struck him.

'If you are here, then did Argo not write to ask you if his wife was well?'

'He may have done: I don't bother much with letters,' said Malcolm dismissively, and gestured to a small pile of scruffy papers set as kindling in his little hearth. Even from there Murray could see that one or two pieces had unbroken seals on them. Murray wondered why he went to the trouble of paying for them.

'Have you seen either Mrs. Argo or Theodore since they left?' he asked at last.

'I don't believe so,' said Malcolm after a moment. 'I'm not sure I would notice the boy if I were not expecting to see him.'

'Of course. What was his surname again?'

Malcolm's brow furrowed, eyes down as he retrieved a lost fact.

'Sangster, I believe. That was her first husband, of course. Sangster.'

Chapter Twelve

Belgium

I

George had to admit that the company, which he had considered to be on a war-like footing, was a different body of men since Major Saddler had returned.

It irked him very slightly – but only very slightly, for George was not a competitive man – to say, too, that the company was also, after a few days of settling down, happier than it had been under his temporary command. He thought he had handled the men rather well, allowing them their few liberties, but it turned out that what many of them preferred was a sense of purpose and pride in their achievements that was not too easily earned. He pondered on this a little as he walked with Gunn along the line of tents: no more were there lazy parties outside brewing tea and mending their kit, for every daylight hour was spent drilling and practising, bringing the men to a peak of fitness that George almost envied, though to be truthful he and Gunn had been run off their feet, too.

'*Think you not that the powers we bear with us Will cut their passage through the force of France?*' Gunn remarked with a smile as they walked past a dozen soldiers trotting on the spot. By the dust at their feet they had been there for some time.

'Shakespeare?' hazarded George, from experience.

'We've all been through this before,' said Gunn. 'If in doubt, fight France.'

'Well, Napoleon,' said George, not quite understanding the allusion. Gunn grinned, and clapped him on the shoulder.

Further along Sergeant Lamb was working again with the drummer boys, though this time it was more a question of teaching them what they needed to be quick messengers in the case of need. This morning's class seemed to be a lecture on how to recognise different regiments and ranks, a good idea if you didn't want a message delivered to a French officer through sheer ignorance. George saw Gunn eyeing young James who, once the drum had been taken away from him, seemed to be doing well: though he was the newest recruit, he had all the answers down pat. George wondered what Gunn's interest was in James. Had they simply formed a bond in their journey from England, or was there something more? Perhaps Gunn just saw a young lad with a future – though not, sadly, in percussion.

'Where is James from?' he asked Gunn casually.

'Ah, well, I'm … I'm not sure.' Gunn fingered his scar, looking far away at the horse lines.

'You're not sure? Where did you find him, then?'

'Well, it's an odd thing,' said Gunn. 'You know I was in London. The lad came to me, said he'd been sent by some old soldier.' He drew breath, and then continued more readily. 'He's Scottish, of course, as you can tell: he'd come to London to seek his fortune and met an old Scots soldier and the soldier happened to know that I was in town. Of course there were many Scots officers in town, I think I just happened to be the nearest. Anyway, the lad was keen to learn the army trade, and so I had him signed up and brought him with me. With so many soldiers away to America, we can do with all the recruits we can get, I should think.'

'Certainly,' said George easily. The story made sense: it was just surprising that Gunn did not know more of the boy, for he had a kindly way with new people and soon found out their families and histories. Was the boy hiding something? If so, he was not alone in the army. A man could hide amongst his fellows easily enough if he had a mind to.

A soldier ran up from the direction of the company headquarters tent, and saluted George with a precision unknown a fortnight ago.

'Major Saddler's compliments, sir, and will you attend him immediately?'

'Of course.' George sighed. No doubt he had another minor mistake to explain in the company accounts: Saddler was following up every farthing. George felt they both had better things to do, but would never have dared say so.

But for once, Major Saddler had no bone to pick with George.

'I want this taken to the Duke forthwith,' he said, handing a letter to George.

'The Duke of Wellington?' George swallowed.

'No, the Duke of Wamphray. Of course, the Duke of Wellington. He found I had spent some time in Mons a few years ago and he wanted a report. There it is.'

'Yes, sir.'

'Well, go along, then!'

George told off one of the men in the horselines to saddle his horse for him – the black one – for he found his hands were shaking just a little with nerves. He had never reported to Wellington directly before. He mounted and rode off, going over in his mind whatever he had heard of speaking to the great man: be precise, be definite, be brief. Wellington preferred someone who gave firm facts straightaway, even if they corrected them afterwards, to someone who prevaricated and meandered. That was fine, then. George was sure he could be decisive. Thereafter he practised saying his own name for some distance, just to be sure he could say it without stumbling. It was not as easy as he had supposed.

Of course he never actually came to the point of having to say his name to Wellington, anyway. He saw the man, seated at his desk in an inner room, instantly recognisable from his cartoons, if nothing else, and his heart beat faster. Then it doubled again as an aide-de-camp greeted him and took the letter from his hand.

'Ah, George Murray, wasn't it?' said the lofty officer, and George bowed to Sir Alexander Gordon.

'Sir.'

'From the Royal Scots. Any word from your friend Gunn yet?'

'He has arrived at the camp, your honour,' stuttered George. 'I told him of your honour's visit.' Once again the tall officer made George feel about as elegant as a farrowing sow – and even that rustic simile would not normally occur to him.

'Then I expect to see him call on me to provide me with an explanation of his extraordinary behaviour,' said Sir Alexander. 'As time goes on, I find I feel less the insult and more the bewilderment.'

'Of course I shall tell him again, your honour,' said George.

'Very well: this is from Major Saddler, is it not? The man who pulled Gunn away.'

'I believe so – that is to say, it is from Major Saddler, sir.'

'I shall see that His Grace receives it at once. Good day to you, sir.'

George bowed again, confused his sword with the furniture, and left in a muddle.

He was a much happier man, he told himself, when he did not have to apply his mind to puzzles like these. To be truthful, though he liked his little bit of Edinburgh society and smart officers and pretty ladies, he was also a happier man when he did not have to deal with the upper echelons of command. It was an important moment for George. He had always assumed that he would climb from Lieutenant to Captain to Major and beyond as the opportunity and money permitted. Now he was not so sure that he would be happy with a rank much higher than where he was now. Had he done a good job with the company in the Major's absence? Well, up to a point, but the skills which Saddler was now applying to it were not skills that came naturally to George. He did not like to be harsh with the men, and yet it seemed that that was what they both needed and wanted. He was quite happy to be told by Saddler what the state of the war was, and what strategies were to be applied, as long as he was not expected to contribute much in the way of strategising himself. Well, he thought to himself as he rode slowly back to the company's camp. I shall not be a soldier forever, then. I wonder what I shall do next?

II

He was toying with various unlikely ideas, when he heard his name called. He stopped his horse and looked about. Not far away, in a dangerous-looking high wheeled gig, were Carolina and Esther Fry. If they were not so slim, they would not both have fitted in beside the smart looking young officer in charge of the horses: as it was, both dressed in that Pomona green he now recognised, they looked almost like one girl with two heads, a notion he wisely decided he should keep to himself. He rode over cautiously: the horses looked as if their nerves were out on wires.

'A fine set-up!' he called, keeping his own horse clear in case the gig horses bolted.

'Dear Mr. Murray!' Carolina cried. 'May I present Lieutenant Crosby, of the 33rd. – Father's regiment, you know? Mr. Crosby, Lieutenant Murray of the Royal Scots.'

The two officers bowed to the best of their ability. Crosby was handsome, George supposed, in a cheap, glossy sort of way.

'You're a brave man to bring a gig out here,' he remarked, trying not to sound too much as if he meant 'mad'. 'The roads weren't up to much to start with, and now with every soldier in Europe up and down them I wonder you have a wheel left!'

'It's true one cannot get up the speed out here that one can in the Allée Verte,' said Crosby with a superior smile. 'But that just gives fellows more time to admire it, eh?'

'Just be careful you don't lose your passengers on a bump, though!' George kept smiling back, though he was genuinely anxious. The gig's wheels were so fine he expected them to splinter under the weight of the axle.

'Oh, we're well jammed in, Mr. Murray!' said Esther. 'Indeed, I fear I might need a shoehorn before I should ever leave this gig again!'

'I don't suppose you often see an equipage like this in North Britain,' said Crosby carelessly, managing to make George detest him more with every minute. 'If the roads here are bad, no doubt you must be restricted to carts and donkeys in Edinburgh.'

'Oh, we manage well enough, I thank you,' George replied. 'Though of course two such charming young ladies would be hard to find anywhere.' Carolina and Esther inevitably giggled. Esther had managed to spread a parasol behind her and it lent them both a greenish, unhealthy hue.

'Well, we mustn't keep you,' said Crosby, with a dismissive glance at George's muddy horse. 'Clearly you have some kind of business to be doing. And I must deliver these young ladies to their father, as requested.' He made it sound like some royal command, and George could not resist flinging back, as they started off,

'Yes, I'm just back from seeing the Duke, you know!' But the gig made its own rattling progress, and he doubted they had heard.

Back at the camp he reported quickly to Saddler, and went to find Gunn. He was overseeing gun drill, watching a small body of men with their powder flasks, twists and rods. Saddler had followed George out of the tent and taken himself off on a quick tour of inspection, as was his habit, and Gunn's eyes drifted to watch him.

'Nearly supper time,' said George, and Gunn jumped.

'Aye, I suppose.' He glanced at the sky, then his gaze dropped and swung until he found Saddler again. Saddler was talking to the drummer boys, apparently testing them on what they had been learning. Gunn's gaze sharpened.

'Do you think we could get away for some food, or will Saddler ask us to eat here again?' George asked.

'What?' Gunn spun round and stared at George as if seeing him for the first time. Then he looked back at Saddler. 'Look, Murray, can you do me a favour?'

'Certainly. What is it?' asked George.

'In the battle – when it comes – if I can't keep an eye on James, will you?'

'On James? The drummer boy?'

'That's the one. Will you watch him for me?'

George stared at him.

'Well, of course,' was all he could think to say.

III

Edinburgh

If anything, Murray's bruises looked even worse on Wednesday, though his head felt slightly better, and his hands, which he had had a little difficulty slipping into gloves the previous day, had recovered from the exertions of punching jaws and noses. He had belatedly come to feel rather ashamed of himself, not so much for going to the aid of the police, but for enjoying it so much. He felt he deserved to ache with every bite he ate, but at the same time he thought he might just do it again, should the situation arise.

He stared into the mirror, wrinkling his nose, trying to ease his stiff skin. At least his lip was healing: he had no wish for Letitia to have the excuse to touch it with salve again. Did he look respectable enough to call on acquaintances to break the news of the death of a daughter-in-law? That was debatable, but he very much wanted to confirm that Theodore Sangster was the grandson of the couple he had met on Monday evening and if he was, to find out whether the boy had fled to them. He had an aversion to the theory that Theodore had killed his mother, but the boy stood a good chance of knowing something about her death, and besides, it would be a prodigious weight off his mind to be able to tell George that Argo's stepson, at least, was safe.

Letitia was vague about where the Sangsters lived in Water of Leith, but was quite sure that Murray would have no difficulty finding them as simply everybody in the village would know the Sangsters' house. Walter seemed almost eager to go back to Water of Leith though he still was not sure which direction to set out in: his hope was that the straw-coloured dog, hound of his dreams, which he had last seen in the village, might reappear. Murray was less optimistic.

'The dog abandoned you, Walter. I don't see why it should suddenly find you appealing again. Though you could look on it as a small triumph – at least it left of its own accord and you didn't lose it.'

Walter pursed his lips: the missing letter had still not turned up, nor had he remembered who had sent it.

There was no sign of the dog on the steep riverside streets, but Letitia had been right: the first person Murray asked was able to direct them to the Sangsters' house. It was old, part of a terrace perched on the hillside, with tiny windows set deep in pale rendered walls. Murray had the impression of a guarded look, something not ready to be openly expressed, a narrow front door like a mouth primly shut.

It opened readily enough to his rattle, however, and a manservant greeted them with courtesy, then hesitated. The reason soon became clear.

'Mr. Murray!' came a voice from just behind the man. Mr. Sangster had evidently been crossing the hall just as the door was opened, and the manservant, confident now, bowed and admitted them.

'Mr. Sangster, I am glad to find you at home,' said Murray, giving his hat and gloves to the manservant. 'I have a question to ask, and then perhaps some unpleasant news, I regret to say.'

'That sounds very curious,' said Sangster. 'Lauder, will you fetch some tea for Mr. Murray? We'll have it in the parlour – is it all right if my wife is there, Mr. Murray?'

'I imagine so,' said Murray carefully. Mrs. Sangster had not seemed to be the type of woman it was easy to upset.

'Very good, sir,' said the man. His dark eyes quickly took Murray in from head to foot, as if grading him. Then he gave the tiniest of nods, and marched Walter off to the servants' apartments at the back of the house. For a wild moment Murray almost grabbed Walter back. There was something about Lauder that made one think he was not a safe person to be near. Ridiculous, Murray thought to himself, though he had felt himself move, his hand twitching to seize Walter's shoulder.

'Mr. Murray, please come in,' Mr. Sangster was saying, and Murray pulled himself back. Sangster led the way upstairs into a cosy parlour, filled comfortably with a mixture of old and modern furniture, a family room built up over decades. At the bow window Mrs. Sangster was seated in an upright armchair, with a box of threads on the windowsill, a sewing table at her side. Before her, squatting on a low stool, was a maid, tongue caught in her teeth as she focussed on a stitch. It made a domestic picture that called to Murray's mind Dutch paintings he had seen: there was something about the clear late morning light on the whitewashed walls and dark wood, the maid's fair hair escaping from her cap, the distinctive profile of Mrs. Sangster as she supervised the maid's work.

'My dear, Mr. Murray – you remember?'

'Of course!' Mrs. Sangster stepped around the maid and curtseyed to Murray's bow. 'To what do we owe the honour?' she asked.

'Mr. Murray has some news for us – perhaps not good news, he thinks.'

The maid went still, Murray noticed. If she could genuinely have pricked her ears, he thought she would. Perhaps Mrs. Sangster noticed, too, for she touched the girl on the shoulder.

'That's enough for now, Jemima: see if you can make that seam straight, and bring it back to me later.'

The girl gathered up her needlework and made a somewhat lopsided curtsey before leaving the room remarkably slowly. Mrs.

Sangster drummed her fingers sharply on the arm of her chair, and the girl scurried for the door.

'It's quite astonishing how few girls know their needlework nowadays. I blame their mothers, myself,' she remarked as the door closed. In a moment it had reopened, and Lauder entered with the tea tray. He arranged it beside Mrs. Sangster, peacefully attentive to his work without a glance at Murray, but Murray still felt that curious … competence, was the word that sprang to mind, though competence in what was anybody's guess. The fancy came to him that if he asked Lauder for a knife, he would have one to hand.

'Now, Mr. Murray, what is your business?' asked Mr. Sangster the moment the door was once again shut.

'As I said, I must ask a question first. I gather, if you will forgive me, that one of your sons, who was married, is now dead?'

'That is so,' said Sangster, with a look at his wife.

'Then the question I must ask is this: was his wife's name Alicia?'

'It was,' said Mrs. Sangster clearly. 'Alicia Baxter, to her own name. Her father had owned a bakery here in Water of Leith but the business was not what it had been. Nevertheless, it was a good match.'

'Do you know what came of Alicia after your son died?'

'Regrettably we lost touch, Mr. Murray. She was young, and though of course she was part of our family, she had ideas of going her own way. I believe there may have been a second marriage.' Mr. Sangster had said nothing, but was paying close attention.

'Her own family?'

'All dead, which of course is why we would have taken her in, willingly. But no, youth must have its day. I hope she may return one day and be family with us again.'

Murray cleared his throat.

'Then I regret to say that I think I do indeed have bad news for you. Alicia – Argo is her name now – is dead.'

'Dead? Surely not!' The cry came from both husband and wife, who exchanged shocked looks. 'Was it the typhus? Some accident?'

'I'm afraid not,' said Murray, as gently as possible. 'She was killed. Murdered.'

'Oh!' Mrs. Sangster sat hard back in her chair, and her husband hurried over to assist her to some tea. 'Oh, good heavens! What on earth could have happened?'

'That is not clear, as yet. The police are of course trying to trace the killer, but they have no particular person in mind. She was found … she had been dead some days.'

'And no one knew?' demanded Mrs. Sangster.

'Apparently not. Her husband is with the army in the Low Countries. Which brings me to the principal reason for my visit, though I think you have already answered my question. You'll know, no doubt, that she had a son – your grandson. Have you seen him recently?'

'Theodore? No, we have not seen him – for some time,' said Sangster himself this time. 'Then you are not saying that he was murdered, too?'

'They think not, but he is not to be found,' said Murray. 'When I discovered your existence, I had hoped that perhaps he would have fled to you, but I can see this is not so.'

'I only wish he had,' said Sangster, with feeling. 'Poor boy: if he saw his mother murdered, and feared for his own life – but where could he be?'

'How did she die, then?' asked Mrs. Sangster suddenly.

'It seems she was, er, throttled,' said Murray cautiously. It was not normally information he would expect a woman to request, but Mrs. Sangster seemed resilient enough. She nodded, frowning.

'In the street?'

'In her flat, in a close off the High Street.'

'And was she robbed?'

'That's not clear. There was hardly anything in her flat, but it seems she brought little to the flat with her. The last few weeks of her life are indeed a mystery, for she changed flats twice, and told people that she was in fear for her life.'

'Oh, well, as to that Alicia always had a lively imagination, didn't she, Willie?' Mrs. Sangster gave her husband a look that Murray found hard to interpret.

'I'd hate to speak ill of her, but she was that wee bit flighty, it's true. She was the kind who was always imagining things, draughts down her back or faces at windows or strange noises in the night. Not that there was any harm in the lass: not enough to do with her time, that was most likely it. And I believe she sometimes read novels.'

'Aye, I heard that and all,' agreed Mrs. Sangster. 'Weak-minded women should never be let near a novel.'

'Well,' said Murray, seeing that the shock of his news was wearing off swiftly, 'I must trespass no further on your time. May I return, though, and ask more of her family at some point? Should we think it has a bearing on the crime.'

'Of course,' said Mr. Sangster, standing. 'Though why a gentleman like yourself should concern yourself with such a matter I cannot tell. Ring for Lauder, my dear, and I'll see Mr. Murray to the door.'

'I am sorry to have disturbed you,' Murray continued as they made their way back to the hall. Sangster glanced behind him, then unexpectedly drew Murray close.

'As I said, I have no idea why you should be involved in this, but Mr. Murray, if you find my grandson please bring him back to me! I had only the two sons, but thought that enough for any man. Then one died and the other: well, he's a wastrel, would throw the business aside for any whim of his own. He's run away to the army and for all I ken he's dead. For all I care, either. So that grandson, that Theodore, he's precious to me. I'd – I'd pay you.'

'There's no need for that, Mr. Sangster,' said Murray hastily: he had no love for commissions. 'I assure you I'll do all I can to find Theodore and make sure he's safe.'

'And bring him to me,' insisted Sangster. 'Bring him here. He needs to be back with his family.'

'I'll do what I can, Mr. Sangster. Ah, Walter: time to go.'

Chapter Thirteen

Edinburgh

Somewhere in Murray's mind there had lingered the conviction that Theodore Sangster had found a place of safety with friends, and when he had realised that the Sangsters were his grandparents he had convinced himself that he would find Theodore there, secure and cared for. If Theodore had been, though, of course Alicia's body would have been discovered sooner and the killer would have been identified and caught. Now that Murray knew they had not even heard of Alicia's death, he was suddenly much more worried than before. His best hope was that Theodore had done the most extreme thing and had somehow set off for the Low Countries to find his father – his stepfather – but that seemed unlikely, and was certainly not something he could assume. He would have to instigate a search for the boy in earnest, not only for the boy's sake but also for the sake of his anxious grandparents. But where was he to start? If Theodore knew of his mother's death, he must be hiding either because he was guilty or because he was afraid – perhaps he was not even deliberately hiding but had simply fled, in shock, and was still running. Did he know who the killer was? If so, he was in danger, if he was not already dead or being held captive. If he did not know of his mother's death, where had he gone? There were too many questions, too many possibilities for a boy of ten or twelve in a city like Edinburgh, with nearly two weeks' start. He decided that the best thing to do would be to consult with Sergeant Home, if the good man was recovered from Monday's bruising, and see what they could do together. Accordingly on Thursday morning he set out with Walter in tow for the High Street and its police office.

Walter for once managed to turn the right way on Prince's Street and Murray felt charitably disposed towards him.

'What were the Sangster kitchens like, then, Walter?' he asked amiably as they walked. Walter's eyebrows disappeared into his hair as he considered.

'Old-fashioned-like, I suppose,' he conceded. 'And gey poky. And hot.'

'A large household?'

'There's the maid,' said Walter, pausing to arrange his fingers, 'then there's the manservant, and a cook, and a scullery maid.'

'Just for the two of them? That's quite a few,' Murray remarked. The Sangsters were indeed comfortably off. 'What did you think of – Lauder, wasn't it? The manservant?'

'I didna like him,' said Walter firmly. 'He had his eye on Jemima – that's the maid. She wasna having none of it, though.'

'Good for her!' Murray laughed.

'Aye, you say that, but if you saw Mr. Lauder's face when she shifted away frae his wandering hands, you wouldna laugh.' Walter was ominous, and Murray remembered the chill he had felt himself when he met Lauder.

'You think he is dangerous?'

'I dinna like the man at all. I was that glad when the bell went for us to go. Except that that left Jemima there with him.' He sighed. 'She's a grand lass.'

'You got on well?'

'Oh, aye. We couldna talk much for that Lauder was derning to catch every word, but you could tell for all that. She's the kind of lass you'd trust with your dog. If I had a dog,' he added, expressionless. Murray swallowed a laugh and turned on to the North Bridge, then reached out a long arm to pull Walter after him as Walter, his mind on the charming Jemima, went to walk on past the junction.

The police office on the High Street was a low-ceilinged building, the ground floor of one of the tenements that lined the street. Murray, whose memories of the old City Guard were still fairly fresh, was pleased once again by the air of comparative efficiency and smartness about the office. He looked about for Sergeant Home, but, not seeing him, approached the clerk who sat on a high stool at a tall desk, designed, no doubt, to intimidate smaller members of the criminal classes. The clerk glanced down then straight across in surprise at Murray's face.

'I'm looking for Sergeant Home,' Murray said politely, presenting his card. The clerk's face shadowed immediately.

'He's no here, sir. He's dead.'

'Dead?' Images from Monday night careered suddenly across Murray's mind.

'He was hurt in a rammie on Monday night, and he never came round.' The clerk seemed genuinely distressed, even as he enjoyed being the bearer of bad tidings. Murray touched the corner of the desk with one hand, as if to reassure himself that he was really there. He shook his head.

'He died of his injuries on Monday? When?'

'Tuesday morn. And not one of us but misses him.'

'When is the funeral? Did he have family?'

'It's the morra, sir, at the Canongate Kirk. No, he had no family: he used to say we were all his family, sir.' The clerk gave a sharp sniff.

'He was a good man,' said Murray sincerely. For a moment he could think of nothing else to say. Could he have done anything more on Monday night? Had he caused more harm by moving him, as he thought, out of harm's way? Too late now, anyway, he told himself sternly. He cleared his throat. 'Is there anyone here who could tell me more about what happened on Monday night? And who now might be in charge of any investigation into the death of Alicia Argo?'

'Oh, that'd be Mr. Clyne, sir. Sergeant Clyne, now. Let me fetch him.' The clerk slipped down off his stool and darted into an inner office, and a moment later reappeared. 'You can just go in, sir.'

Murray found that the inner office was dark and small, but neatly laid out. Sergeant Clyne had, like George Home, a look of sturdy reliability to him, though by contrast to Home's reddish fair complexion Clyne's hair was black and thick. Home's bulk had been muscle, where Clyne's ran more to fat. He stood and bowed very properly when Murray entered.

'You're Mr. Murray?' he said. 'Mr. Home spoke of you last week. He said you were with him when he found Alicia Argo's body up yon close, in the flat.'

'That's right: her husband is an officer in my brother's regiment, and had asked me to look for her. Sergeant Home helped me to find her flat, but when we went in – well, you know what we found.'

'Aye, aye. Yon's an unchancy place, I doubt.'

'That flat certainly is,' said Murray with emphasis, then raised his eyebrows when Clyne looked puzzled. 'You do realise that the flat that Alicia Argo's body was found in was the same one that was burned on Monday night?'

'Was it? Was it now?'

'Didn't Sergeant Home say where the body was found?'

'Not to the very flat, Mr. Murray. The same flat, eh? You're sure?'

Murray reflected.

'It was a confusing night. I think I'd like to take another look to be absolutely sure.'

'You were there on Monday, then, sir?' Clyne gave Murray a justifiably suspicious look.

'I was, though that had nothing to do with Alicia Argo. The friends with whom I am staying are acquainted with a family further up the High Street, and we had been at supper there. Mr. and Mrs. Findlay is the name. We came out to walk back to Prince's Street, and found the disturbance in full swing.'

'And you stayed?' Clyne's tone implied that a gentleman with any sense would have been long gone. He was right, too.

'I saw Sergeant Home and offered some assistance.'

'I see.' Clyne picked up a steel pen with which he had been filling in some kind of register, and carefully picked his nails with it. 'So the fire was in Alicia Argo's old flat, you think.'

'Yes.'

'The fellows we saw there, they were new tenants. We knew nothing of them when the call came that some limmers had flung stones at the City Watch: it was only after that we began to find out a few things, ken.'

'That seems reasonable.'

Clyne completed his nails to his satisfaction, and tapped his teeth with the pen, leaning back in his chair. It creaked in alarm and he froze.

'I think you and I should take a wee wander over there and just make sure it's the same flat in truth.' He pushed back warily from the desk, and they both rose to go. Outside in the main office they collected Walter, standing composedly in the corner, and made for the street.

'I don't suppose you have any notion who Alicia Argo's family are?' Clyne asked as they made their way through the market crowds and the midday lawyers.

'Her husband is in Belgium, as I said before to Home. Her parents-in-law by her first marriage are in Water of Leith, but they had lost touch. She had no family of her own. I don't know if Argo has, but if they live nearby he would probably have asked them to look for her, not me.'

'I only ask,' said Clyne, pushing his hat up on his forehead, 'because she's going to need burying very soon.'

'Of course … are we absolutely sure it's her?'

'What?'

'Just … before she's buried. I only had a description, and I don't know if Sergeant Home had seen her before.'

'Well, we canna wait for her husband,' said Clyne reasonably, stopping to wipe his face on his handkerchief.

'No. Maybe some of her old neighbours?'

'In that place? Eppy would tell you she had Queen Charlotte staying if you paid her the right money – or gave her the right bottle.'

'No, I was thinking of her neighbours from where she lived before. A Mrs. Brotherstone in the Potterrow would probably help you, or Mr. Malcolm, a medical student lodging with Mr. Campbell in Potterrow. Either of them would be able to identify her.'

'Brotherstone … Malcolm …' Clyne muttered the names, apparently memorising them.

'And then, if no one else comes forward, I suppose I should see to the burial myself,' said Murray, partly thinking out loud. Clyne shot him another suspicious glance. 'Of course, if we could find her son, that would help.'

'Her son? Surely that would be her family, then.'

'Well, yes, but he's only ten or twelve.'

'So where is he, then?'

'We don't know. He's missing.'

Clyne blinked.

'A woman murdered, a boy missing, and two men killed in a

fire. This is not looking good, sir.'

'I agree.'

Clyne removed his glove to chew a fingernail thoughtfully, then looked up.

'Well, here's the close,' he said, 'and there's the windae where the fire was, as you can see. What do you think, sir?'

Murray examined it in the daylight. There was no doubt: his night time impression was correct.

'That's the flat all right. No glass and the frame all blackened – how bad was the fire inside?'

'Come and see for yourself, sir.' Clyne led the way down the filthy alley into the courtyard, where for once no washing hung out. The old man still sat on the steps, though, and the straw-coloured dog lounged by the midden. Walter gave an unexpected squawk and ran ahead to greet it. The dog seemed equally pleased to see him.

'See, what seems to me,' said Clyne, as if he had been thinking intensely about it, 'is that if Mrs. Argo was found here, and then there was the fire, then maybe that's not a complete chance, do you think?'

'I think you could be right,' said Murray. 'But what could it be? Was someone trying to hide something? Or destroy it?'

'A fair question, sir. Come on up and see for yourself what the place is like.'

Murray followed Clyne up the steps and into the dark hallway once again, leaving Walter with a nod that said he could stay outside with the dog. The way that Clyne walked along the hall, softly even with his weight, confirmed that he had met Eppy there already. They reached the flat without interruption, but there things were different from before: the door of the flat was broken and fallen, and the stench of the landing was overlaid with a heavy smell of smoke and burning, cold now that the fire was long out, but with a damp aftertaste from the efficient bucket chain that somehow made it so much worse. Beyond the door, the room was almost unrecognisable from the way they had seen it before.

'The door is broken?' Murray queried. 'Does that mean the rescuers needed to break it down?'

'No, it was already ranforced. They found the two men already dead, one by the window and one near the door.'

Murray peered into the darkened flat, bewildered. He had not been looking up at the window when the fire started, he thought: there had been the fight, in all its intensity, and during that he had no idea what the two men had been doing. He stepped, long-legged and careful, into the flat, and Clyne followed, trying to tread where the floor was strongest. Some of the floorboards had been burned almost through.

'Heaps of rags near the door,' Murray observed.

'We ken no reason why they would have had them.'

'What line of work were they in?'

'Dinna ken. Word was they had recently come into some money, and moved here on the strength of it. The stramash started when some fellows they owed money to turned up at the door looking for it back, and they refused to pay, having spent, I reckon, the most part of it on whisky. The fellows we managed to talk to – that'd be the ones too badly injured to run away – they said that the lads had owed money here, there and everywhere, and these ones thought this was their big chance to get it back, see.'

'I can understand they might have been frustrated.'

'There was word one of them had been hurt in some accident, a whiles ago. He was missing a leg. Maybe an employer felt guilty and paid out some money?'

'Maybe so.' It happened, sometimes. 'So they had money, and they refused to meet their obligations. A crowd gathered, and a fight broke out. There was a man at the back of the crowd urging people on, by the way: he was the one that suggested they attack the Watch, and then later that they fight the police. I didn't see him fighting, himself, though.'

'Oh aye?' Clyne turned with interest away from the table. 'What like of a man was that?'

'It was hard to see him, for he had a wide-brimmed hat and kept it low. But he was very pale of complexion. I'm not sure if I would know him again. Sorry.'

'Well, it's something to know there's a lad about doing such a thing,' Clyne conceded.

'Well, there was a fight, and someone was provoking it. I don't know where he went. Then in the midst of the fight – no, the fight was tailing off, really, and Sergeant Home had fallen – I smelled smoke, and heard the fire.'

'It would have been lit a bitty before that, then.'

'I should think so. These rags – do you think that was where the fire started?'

'I think it might be.'

'So what were the men up here doing while the fight was going on? Watching? Drinking? Trying to make a discreet exit?' Murray paced around the room as he had before: more violent deaths in this flat, and he could not get to grips with any of them. He hated the feeling of helplessness.

'Did you think the room was gey brightly lit, behind them?' Clyne asked, stopping by the scorched table.

'Brightly lit? Oh, do you mean did they have a good number of candles?' Murray thought, picturing the scene. 'No, I don't think so. I'd have said there was one, or maybe two if they were dull ones, just near them at the window. Look, here's a stick.' He pointed to a low pewter candlestick on the window ledge, the candle in it only a sprawling mess of tallow.

'And here's another.' Clyne pointed to the table. 'Did they bring one over to see what was going on?'

'They had a window, big enough to get through, and they were only a storey up. I grant they might have found it hard to get to the other window, the one that looks on to the yard, if the fire was fierce, but this street one would have been fine. Why did they go to the door?'

'Trying to put the fire out?'

'Maybe. Confused with drink, perhaps. And whisky would fuel it well. Here's the remains of the keg.' He kicked a heap of charred wood, and the metal bands rattled. It had not been a large keg, and by the looks of it had probably been empty before it burned.

'I thought I heared voices,' came a familiar voice from the door. 'Can youse no leave a body alone? I'm trying to run an honest business here and between corpuses and fires and drunken stooshies what hope does a body have?'

'Good morning, Eppy,' said Murray politely. 'I don't think you'll be able to let this flat out for a bit.'

'Exactly.' She wiped her nose extravagantly with the heel of her hand. 'Never mind the burning – though all that bit of the floor'll need new wood and all - what about the smell? The mannie across the landing is complaining, and he's never at home. You wouldn't mind so much if it was just the burned wood smell, but that reek of old fat – that's disgusting!'

Murray sniffed. There was indeed a reek in the air. He prowled a little: the smell was definitely stronger near the door, where the rags were. He poked a heap with his foot. The rags where they had not burned were crisp with grease.

'What a thing to keep in your house. Why did they have these rags, Eppy?'

'I dinna ken. If I'd kent they were keeping stinking rags in the flat they'd have been out on their ears, rent or no rent.'

'Do you think,' said Clyne slowly, 'that someone might have thrown them in here to get the fire going?'

Murray looked at him.

'So you do think the fire was set deliberately?'

Eppy's dozy eyes opened wide.

'Here, no talk like that round here! It's bad enough it's an accident. At this rate I'll never be able to let this flat again!' She stayed at the door, eyeing the burned floorboards with lop-sided anxiety.

'So we're back to asking why – was it to kill the men, or was there something someone was trying to hide?' Murray looked about the room, burned at one end and blackened throughout, but otherwise much as it had been left when Eppy and her daughter had removed the remains of Alicia's possessions. The two new lodgers had not brought much but the keg of whisky and a couple of cups, by the look of it. The wall press was hanging open and empty. The same mattress sagged on the bed. Clyne caught Murray's eye and took out a pocket knife.

'Here, no!' cried Eppy again as he sliced into the mattress. Murray wondered if he had had another career before joining the police office, for Clyne gutted the mattress with brisk efficiency, spilling out straw that had not seen a field for some years, if the smell was anything to go by. Murray picked up the cover in gloved fingers and flicked it inside out, examining the cloth from one end to the other. Clyne stirred through the straw. There was nothing. Murray dropped the cloth.

'There really is nothing here, is there?' he said resignedly. Around the room the drab plasterwork, already greyish before the fire had done its work, stared back at him, hiding nothing. The floorboards were bare, and showed no sign of having been tampered with except where they had been burned. He returned to the door and kicked at the rags. There seemed nothing distinctive about them, except for a dark brown pattern on some of them. He peered more closely. 'Sergeant, I think there might be something here after all.'

Sergeant Clyne came closer and stared down at the rags, as Murray crouched and turned them over with one gloved hand.

'Blood?' he asked.

'I think so.' Murray sprang up and with eyes more adjusted now he examined the floorboards. 'Look, here – and here. Does it look to you as if something bloody was dragged across here?'

'It does indeed, sir. Now, is this what you mean – someone came in and hurt the men, killed them, maybe, then dragged them over to the rags so that they'd be nearest to the fire?'

'And then they set fire to the greased rags and left, yes.'

Sergeant Clyne's face was solemn.

'So what does that mean, then?'

'It seems to mean that the men were the issue. If the fire was deliberate, it must have been intended for them, not for the flat. Someone wanted them dead, and then wanted their deaths thought an accident. Eppy, where did these men come from, do you know?'

Eppy's face contorted, as if she was about to cry, but no tears came and Murray realised that somewhere behind the film of drink she was in fact thinking. Suddenly her features sagged, and she shook her head.

'I canna recall,' she said. 'It was a wee place outside the town.'

'And their names?'

'Oh, that'd be easier. The one with the yin leg, that was Johnnie Norrie. The other – I dinna ken if I ever heard tell of his surname, for it was always Johnnie did all the talking. His Christian name, though, that was Ebb. Ebenezer,' she amplified, helpfully.

'Johnnie Norrie and Ebb ...' Murray now felt his own face wrinkle with the effort of thought. He had met so many new people in the last week or so, but those names were familiar. Johnnie Norrie and Ebb: he closed his eyes, and suddenly he was back in Dean Village talking to the mother and daughter in their stern brown gowns. 'Johnnie Norrie and Ebb,' said the daughter. 'What would they know?' And Norrie had one leg. It was the two men he had asked directions of in Dean Village, outside the inn. He opened his eyes in surprise. Eppy was still talking, her new mood of co-operation holding.

'The old man who lives across the way, he's Norrie's uncle or something like that. That was how they heard the place was empty. They were in a hurry and I thought I might have trouble finding lodgers, with the corpus and all being found here.'

'That's very useful, thank you, Eppy. Tell me, though: have you seen anything yet of young Theodore around here?'

'The yellow-haired lad? I havena. Would he have killed his mother, do you think, and fled?'

'If you hear any word of him, let me know. There'll be a reward in it for you, if the information's good,' said Murray, handing her his card with Willie Jack's address on the back. He had better start spreading word of a reward: he had to find Theodore. Eppy peered at the card, both ways up and both ways round, then nodded with a disturbingly canny expression and secreted the card in her bodice. Murray managed to conceal a shudder, as she turned with an unsteady jiggle perhaps intended to be flirtatious, and stumbled down the stairs.

'Those names meant something to you, then?' asked Clyne, still unsure of Murray. Murray nodded.

'One of the addresses I was given for Alicia Argo was in the Dean village. They were outside the inn there and I asked them for directions. I wouldn't swear that they knew the Argos, but it's not a big village, even though Alicia only stayed there a little while. It's another coincidence, and I'm not sure I'm happy with any of them. Alicia is killed, and two men who may have known her unexpectedly come into money. Is that connected? They move into her old flat, and it appears a relative lives nearby. Is that chance? She is killed, and then it seems that they are, too. Is that connected?'

'I dinna ken, sir,' Clyne murmured.

'And then – you probably don't know this – Alicia moved house twice in the weeks before she died. She was living in some comfort in Potterrow, then moved without notice to the Dean Village and hardly stayed there a minute before she moved up here. Somewhere she lost or left her furniture and better belongings. She told her husband of the move to the Dean, maybe of the second move, too, though I haven't heard that yet. In that letter, she told him she was in fear of her life, but usefully did not say why or from whom. She told her landlord in Potterrow as well, but after that she seems to have kept quiet about threats. There's some indication she might have been a little fanciful, and maybe these threats were imagined, but I don't think they were: I think Alicia was genuinely in fear of her life.'

'But how can you be sure, sir?'

'Well, Sergeant,' said Murray patiently, 'because she's dead.'

Chapter Fourteen

Edinburgh

I

'Armstrong?' asked Murray.

Walter considered for a moment, then shook his head.

'Thomson?'

'No, sir.'

Walter's capacity for not finding a letter in a small flat was, Murray had decided, unsurpassable. He needed to be entered for some kind of competition, if such a thing existed. High class gamblers could make fortunes on him. With the letter still missing, Murray was now trying to see if he could guess who had sent it.

'Douglas? Simpson? Sangster?' It was unlikely, and Walter shook his head again. 'Not Blair?' Murray added, suddenly hopeful.

'Is that the old gentleman that comes to Letho?' Murray nodded enthusiastically, but Walter shook his head again. 'No, sir.'

'Oh. Argo?' It would make sense, if Argo had been allowed to come back to Edinburgh, that he should have tried to find Murray.

'No, sir.' Walter looked a little reproachful: Mr. Murray must think him stupid.

'Findlay?' tried Murray. It was the only name, apart from Sangster, that he could remember from Monday night's supper party.

'No, sir.'

'Scoggie?' An old acquaintance from Fife. Walter looked scornful this time.

'I'd have remembered a name like that, sir.'

'I'm thrilled to hear you'd remember something, Walter,' said Murray drily. How he wished Robbins had been able to come with him.

In the parlour, Letitia was perusing the *Courant*. Murray said good morning, though in truth there was not much of the morning left, and took a seat at a table near the window. Willie Jack's new married status ensured that the table was furnished with paper and ink, and he took out his best steel pen which Walter had not yet managed to lose.

He had spent too much of the previous night with his head whirling, spinning through every possible answer, he thought, to the questions surrounding Alicia Argo's death. For a while, at that moment at four in the morning when vague ideas take on solid shape, Walter's missing letter had seemed to him certain to hold the key to the whole mystery, but what good was that if it could not be found?

Instead he had decided to arrange his thoughts more systematically, in the hope – probably vain, in his current state of fatigue – that some pattern might begin to consider the faint possibility of emerging from the utter confusion of the last two weeks. But where should he start? With Alicia Argo's death, or with the odd events leading up to it? The death made no sense without the prologue, but then it made very little more sense with it. He sighed, and wrote at the top of the page:

'Around the middle of May, Alicia Argo and Theodore moved from Potterrow to the Dean Village. She claimed to be in fear for her life.

'Maybe a week later, Alicia Argo and Theodore moved from the Dean Village to the High Street. Somewhere between this and the first move, they became detached from most of their belongings.

'Towards the end of May (after the 25th.): Alicia Argo was strangled and left in a kist in her flat. Her son vanished.

'Third of June: Sergeant Home and I found her.'

He stared at this for a moment. It was certainly the bare bones, but only the very barest.

'Pomona green, eh?' said Letitia suddenly, flattening the newspaper on the tea table and turning towards him with a wriggle of her shoulders. 'Mr. Murray, how do you think I should suit Pomona green?'

A vision of her came to his mind instantly, dressed in the colour of the most luscious apples. He shook his head to clear it.

'A little acidic, perhaps?' he ventured. She frowned at him in mock annoyance.

'Listen: *Promenade dress: Round dress of Pomona green poplin, trimmed in a style of uncommon novelty and taste. The body is made in a peculiarly becoming manner, the back plain at the top, is drawn in with a slight fullness at the bottom of the waist, which displays the shape to the utmost advantage.* Doesn't that sound divine?'

'I'm afraid it sounds almost incomprehensible to me,' he admitted, though the visions of shapes displayed to the utmost advantage still played flirtatiously in his mind. She smiled at him as if she knew exactly what was happening, and turned away, humming, to tear out the notes from the newspaper.

'I must take these fashions to my dressmaker. I simply must have something smart to wear when we go to my family. We'll be going soon, you know: no need for you to rush, though, for the cook is away to her daughter's confinement so it certainly won't be today or tomorrow.' She smiled at him again, her lips extraordinarily full and moist. He made himself turn back to his notes.

'It's very kind, but I'm sure I shall find somewhere when you are ready to leave.'

'I'm quite sure you would be welcomed anywhere,' she said, and it seemed to him that her voice was unnecessarily low and breathy. He swallowed, torn between the good manners of looking over at her, and the knowledge that it would be a dire mistake. He held his breath, and let it out in a gasp as the door opened.

'Come, now, my dearest, don't tell me you're not ready to go!' Willie Jack bounced into the room with a look of indulgence. 'I knew you would still be sitting here chattering away with Murray. We're expected there in ten minutes, you know that! Murray, are you sure you won't come?'

'I'm sorry, Willie Jack: please make my apologies. I must sort out this matter of Mrs. Argo's death as soon as I can.' It was true, though he was also delighted not to be going out again with Willie

Jack and his wife. He stood as they left the room together, off for an afternoon's picnic on Arthur's Seat. The door closed behind them and he breathed a hearty sigh of relief.

'Around the middle of May, Alicia Argo and Theodore moved from Potterrow to the Dean Village. She claimed to be in fear for her life.' He read it again, then added: 'She didn't say what she feared, but she did tell her husband and her landlord, Mr. Campbell, that she was afraid. Did she take her belongings with her?' He made a note to ask Mr. Campbell. 'Her friends in the area include Mr. Campbell (not the throttling type, and I suspect Alicia could have fought him off), Mrs. Brotherstone (capable of anything necessary, but seems an unlikely killer), Miss Cordiner (possible, if she thought she had a chance at Lieutenant Argo and Alicia's belongings) and Mr. Malcolm (quite capable of killing, possibly making notes as he goes, but probably not interested enough in her as a human to bother).

'She tells Mr. Campbell where she is going, but he claims to have told no one. Nevertheless he seems to have told Mrs. Brotherstone. Someone apart from me came looking for her there.' He paused while he tried to remember Mr. Campbell's brief description of the man. 'Tallish, pale, in a brown coat and a wide-brimmed hat.' Now, there's a thing, he thought to himself, and reread the description he had just written down. It was not that there was anything particularly uncommon about it, but it did call a memory to his mind. The man who had urged the crowd on to attack the police and the City Watch had had very much the same appearance. 'Hmm,' he said aloud, and tapped the paper with his pen. Then he added:

'She seems to have been happy in Potterrow, and regarded as a good tenant, neat and clean, and envied by Bessie Cordiner who said she had "lovely things". Where are they?

'Everyone seems to be under the impression that she was happy in her marriage, that her present husband was better than her late husband, and that Theodore was also fond of his stepfather and vice versa. No one has seen Theodore since they left.'

He tried to think of anything else he had learned in Potterrow, and reflected for another moment on the man in the wide-brimmed hat. Would he know him if he saw him again? The light had not been good, and the wide-brimmed hat had cast an extra shadow of its own. But his voice? Maybe …

He read the next piece of what he had written earlier.

'Maybe a week later, Alicia Argo and Theodore moved from the Dean Village to the High Street. Somewhere between this and the first move, they became detached from most of their belongings.'

'Dean Village,' he added, 'is Combe's Court, a fine house but not as prosperous as once it might have been. The landlord here is Chisholm, and there is a neighbour, Miss Smillie. Chisholm seemed very upset at the news of Alicia's death, but immediately thought that Theodore would have been to blame. Miss Smillie disagreed, though she said that Theodore had a temper. Alicia does not seem to have told him that she was afraid. Here, too, she left the impression that her second marriage was much happier than her first.' He thought back, picturing the parlour and Miss Smillie's hand clutching Mr. Chisholm. 'Miss Smillie is an older person, but seems intent on winning Mr. Chisholm. This does not seem to be something Mr. Chisholm appreciates: in fact, I think he may have had his eye on Mrs. Argo.

'Also in Dean Village were Johnnie Norrie and Ebb, and Mrs. and Miss Brown,' he added slowly. 'Mrs. Brown and her daughter claim to know nothing of the Argos, but let it slip that they knew she had moved to the Old Town. There is more to them than they are telling.' He left them at that for now, and moved on to the two quarrymen. 'Johnnie Norrie and Ebb also claimed to know nothing about the Argos, but did point me in the right direction. One of them is related to the old man in the High Street close. They later came into money, source unknown, took Alicia's old flat, and started a riot by refusing to pay their debts. The flat was set on fire, and they died.' Again, the bare bones. He frowned. 'Did they send Alicia to the flat? If not, did they know she was there? Where did the money come from? Did they tell someone where she had gone, or did they somehow come upon her missing belongings and sell them?' He paused, and then added, 'Did they kill her?'

His gaze rose unconsciously and he found himself staring through the window, across the busy ebb and flow of Prince's Street and up to the Castle. It stood out stark against a pearl-grey sky, glaring a little around the edges.

'Possible murderers,' he wrote at the top of a new sheet.

'Theodore: suggested by Chisholm at Dean. Denied by Miss Smillie there, and by neighbours at Potterrow. Missing. I'm not sure a ten year old boy could strangle his mother ...' He tried to picture it, but as before he could not convince himself that Theodore was a killer. To strike out, even at someone one loved, in a moment of rage: that was not unlikely, but to throttle someone he reportedly cared for, that he could not see. He drummed his fingers for a second.

'Johnnie Norrie and Ebb: they seem to have gained from her death and they knew where she had moved to. Again, perhaps throttling is unlikely. Difficult to interview them now. If they killed her, who killed them? Theodore?' He found he was writing more now, giving himself thinking time as the pen dipped and filled, slid over the paper and ran out again. It was comparatively easy to think of a boy setting fire to a flat. But he had seen no boy in the mob on the High Street: if it had been intended to be a distraction, how could Theodore have caused it? 'Or,' he began again, suddenly excited, 'someone paid them to kill her, then killed them because they knew too much.' Would that fit? Someone who did not want to be seen near Alicia, because they would immediately be suspect, but could dispose of their agents afterwards? Would Johnnie Norrie and Ebb kill for money? How could he find out? Who might be able to tell him more about them? Well, he only knew of two people who might know, though where he could find them was another question.

'Mrs. or Miss Brown,' he wrote next. Certainly they knew more than they were saying, and he had seen them in the High Street the day they had found Alicia's body. But would they have come back if they knew she was already dead? Or were they looking for Theodore? What, indeed, were they up to? If he found them and asked them about Johnnie Norrie and Ebb, what could they or would they tell him? He made a note to try to find them, probably in Dean Village. How could he persuade them to talk?

'The stranger seen visiting her a few days before her death. She argued with him. Could he have gone back and killed her?' He tried to remember Eppy's daughter's vague description. 'A thin man, full of himself ... maybe with dark hair ... pale.' Hum. Was this the same man as the pale man that urged on the mob? The same one that had been looking for Alicia at Potterrow? True enough, it was not a detailed description, but it was a start. But who was he?

Murray did not feel he was getting anywhere. He leaned back in his chair, staring out at the street. Who could he be? Was it someone he had met, or heard of? Perhaps he should look at the whole thing from the other side: what kind of person would have a reason to kill Alicia? She was not particularly wealthy, but Bessie Cordiner had been envious of her 'lovely things': did anyone envy them enough to kill her? Had she attracted the attention of some man who did not take her rejection well? The only person he had come across so far who seemed likely to fit that category was Chisholm at Dean Village, but perhaps there were others. Another possibility: she was killed because she was Lieutenant Argo's wife. Perhaps Argo had made enemies and they had killed her to punish him? Perhaps some random drunkard had lurched into her flat and done the deed. He was clutching at straws.

The door opened gently, and he jumped, half-picturing Letitia coming back. Instead it was Walter.

'Sir ...' he began. 'I was wondering ...'

'Yes, Walter?'

'Do I get any days off, at all?'

'If you did, what would you do with them?'

'Well, there's that whale, sir. But also, that Jemima down at Mr. Sangster's house, she said she had an afternoon off today, and she asked me when mine was.'

Murray was amused that 'that whale' and 'that Jemima' seemed to have equal appeal. Perhaps it was indeed time to let Walter out on his own, though the temptation to tie a thread to the back of his collar was quite strong.

'Have you found the letter yet?'

'Oh, no sir. I dinna think there's much point looking now. It's one of those things that'll just turn up when it's ready,' Walter replied, quite sure of himself. All at once Murray was cross with him again.

'Oh, go and see Jemima, then, Walter, if you're sure you can find your way. Be back here by sundown. And if anyone mentions anything about Theodore Sangster, be sure to remember it and tell me: we know so little about him.'

'Thank you, sir,' said Walter, though he was already halfway out of the room. In a moment, Murray heard the flat door slam. He wondered if he would ever see Walter again.

Theodore, presumably, could find his way around Edinburgh, so where had he gone?

He stood up to stretch his legs, and wandered around the room, poking the *Courant* on the table with one long finger. He turned the page from which Letitia had ripped the fashion descriptions, and idly scanned down through the news, then read the *Courant*'s account of Monday night's riot on the High Street. George Home received an honourable mention. Murray sighed: he had attended the funeral yesterday, almost alone amidst a crowd of police officers, some in tears, at the police office and then at the Canongate kirkyard down the hill. Much brandy had been drunk, and Sergeant Clyne, after reluctantly confirming that further examination had found stab wounds on the bodies of Johnnie Norrie and Ebb, had turned philosophical on the subject of finding the fire-setters or Alicia Argo's killer.

'See, if we dinna have anybody seeing anybody ... seeing anybody at the place, at the right time at the place, then we canna be sure of anybody being the man who did it.' He had nodded solemnly, rather more than he had intended, and his nodding head had sunk quietly on to his full chest. A few minutes later he had had to be roused to take his place amongst the bearers, all of whom were almost too glazed to walk in a straight line in the same direction. Murray had seen them through the interment, and then wandered back to Willie Jack's flat, thoroughly miserable.

He twitched the paper away and sat back down again by the window. He drew a third piece of paper towards him, and pondered the question of Theodore.

'Own freewill', he wrote on the left of the page, and 'under duress' on the right, then started to add possibilities. Under the second column he began bleakly with 'Dead', then wrote 'taken captive by murderer'. Under the first there were more possibilities. 'On run, guilty. On run, frightened of killer as can identify. On run, frightened, but did not see killer. Chasing killer. Lost for some other reason: had row with mother and ran away; looking for something; looking for someone.'

No body had yet been found. Where could he be? If he were on the run, was there someone or somewhere he would run to, some place of safety? No one had mentioned anything, and his own family had not seen him. His stepfather's family? Did he have any, and where were they?

He pictured the High Street flat as it had been when he and Home had found the body. That dish, hidden under the box … that was interesting. He closed his eyes, screwing up his face in thought. Why would anyone hide a dish under a box? Well, how did this fit: Alicia and Theodore are sitting at a meal at the table. There's a knock at the door. For some reason, they realise there's a threat – Alicia's fear for her life coming to visit. Theodore runs to hide on the bed behind the curtain, and Alicia drops the box over the second plate, nowhere else to hide it, and goes to open the door. The killer comes in and kills her, and hides her body, and leaves. Theodore emerges and runs away.

He liked it. It did not tell him where Theodore was, but it seemed to show where he was not: he was probably not dead or captured, and he was probably in hiding because he not only saw who killed his mother, but recognised or knew the name of the killer. And Alicia too knew who her killer was, and had persuaded Theodore not to do anything to protect her if anything went wrong – so was Alicia protecting Theodore? Was it really Theodore who had been threatened? If that was so, then Theodore running to his stepfather in the Low Countries seemed much more likely, or to some agreed safe place. Well, that felt like progress.

He sat back, feeling more satisfied, and looked up at the Castle again. He could see one or two redcoats high on the battlements, and could nearly smell the wool as he realised it was raining. He wondered how soon Willie Jack and Letitia would be back, and whether Walter was lost yet. The rain smeared the windows, blurring the street scene below. Another column of soldiers marched their way smartly through the carters and pedestrians, the sergeant shouting at a carter who tried to cut across them. Murray smiled, and wondered what his brother George was up to.

II

Belgium

George was in a quandary.

George was a simple soul, and he was not accustomed to

quandaries. In his experience, anything too complicated to be sorted out at once would either sort itself out eventually, or someone cleverer than he was would sort it out for him. Just recently, however, his quandaries seemed to be multiplying: he had no idea how to deal with any of them, and the people he usually relied on to make quandaries go away were all intimately involved in producing them in the first place. There was Captain Gunn's strange attack on Sir Alexander Gordon, for example: what should he do about that? Should he tell Gunn again that Sir Alexander wanted to see him, and probably therefore involve him in a duel? Duels, as George well knew, could turn out nasty for all involved, which was why they had been outlawed amongst the civilian population. Only the army, where they had the capacity to be much nastier, still allowed them. Then there was Gunn's mysterious request to George that he look after James Graham, the new and chronically unmusical drummer boy. Should he try to find out why? What was the link between the officer and the boy? George was deeply curious, but also suffered a distinct dread of finding out what he might not want to know. Then there was a particularly distressing quandary, for he had received his brother Charles' letter telling him that Argo's wife was dead, and dead by violence, and he had found no way yet to tell Argo this awful news. Edinburgh felt a long way away at present, with everything focussed here, but no doubt Argo would fall apart, and that would do good to no one.

Lastly, his latest quandary – and therefore perhaps the most distressing, for George was quite good at putting things to the back of his mind – had arrived that morning in the apparently innocent shape of an invitation to dinner. The invitation had come from the Frys. Major Saddler had expressly forbidden his officers from attending any social events before Bonaparte made his appearance. General Fry outranked Major Saddler, but then he was not George's commanding officer. Should he go to Major Saddler and plead a special case? But on the other hand, did he really want to go to dinner at the Frys? Why had he been invited? Was General Fry testing him for the role of future son-in-law? And if so, was it a role that George wanted? Should he in fact be grateful for a cast-iron excuse to turn down the invitation? But then, was it really cast-iron? Would the Frys be offended that he should turn it down, when most other officers in Brussels were happily attending all kinds of parties and balls and routs?

George turned these thoughts over in his mind in rotation as he worked at the camp with the soldiers. The dinner quandary was becoming urgent, as he had out of good manners to reply soon: the dinner was only next Thursday. Tonight, however, it would be supper in camp, and already he could smell the beef stewing over camp fires outside each tent. Major Saddler had wisely stockpiled firewood under a sheet of canvas, so while one or two of their neighbours were still struggling to light their fires in the thick drizzle, their company were sitting smug under the flaps of their tents warming their damp boots. George did admire Major Saddler. A low level Wellington, that was what he was, as concerned for the baggage train as for the cavalry. That was the kind of thing that won wars.

With the uncanny ability that he was known for, Major Saddler turned up at that very moment.

'Murray, ah. Glad to find you here. Go round the tents, would you, and make sure the men have tightened their ropes? They'll slacken fast in this rain.'

'Yes, sir.' George set off. It was a matter of moments to trot down the line of tents: the men were not too keen to shift outside, but they knew that if they did not they would find themselves in an intimate embrace with their tent canvas in the morning. He glanced back and saw Major Saddler heading for the beacon tower they had raised before his return: it too had guy lines which would need attention. It was dusk now, and the top of the beacon tower had disappeared into the murky sky: the campfires had a cheerful air. George reached the end of his row, and turned to see if he could see Gunn or Argo, to find out when supper was expected. Instead he saw a dim shape which resolved itself, on closer inspection, into James the drummer boy, dawdling across the grass towards his tent.

'Hello, there,' he said, reminded suddenly of one of his quandaries. 'Where are you off to?'

'Going back for my supper, sir,' said James, not quite stopping.

'Then where have you been?' George was keen to keep him in conversation.

'I've been on a message to the Colonel, sir,' said James.

'Of course.' James may have had little skill with a drum, but he had emerged as one of the fastest runners in the company, and therefore very useful for messages. He bounced on his toes now, waiting to be dismissed.

'You and Captain Gunn travelled here together, didn't you?' he asked, not sure where else to start.

'That's right, sir.'

'Where did you meet him, then? How did you come to join up with us?' Gunn had already told him, of course, but George's brother Charles had said to him several times that one person's version was only that, *one* person's version. He did not quite see the point, himself, but it gave him something to ask.

'In London, sir. My mother's housekeeper where Captain Gunn was staying, so she asked him if he would take me back when he was going. Time I was doing a man's job, she said, and here I am.'

George blinked. This was not quite what Captain Gunn had told him. Perhaps Charles was right: it was a good idea to listen to more than one version. But in this case did it matter? There could have been an old soldier as well, and Gunn might not have realised that the boy he was taking on was the housekeeper's son.

'So you're from London, then?' he asked, as James tried to leave.

'That's right, sir.'

'Then it's a strange thing that you have a Scots accent, don't you think?'

James flashed him an odd look.

'Oh, that's a fault of mine!' he said quickly. 'I pick up the voices of the people around me. I canna help it. It's like mud on my shoes, it just sticks. Sir.'

'Well, you sound like a Scotsman born and bred,' George told him with a smile, 'and certainly, Captain Gunn seems to be impressed with you. You must have done well on your journey here.'

'It was just a journey, sir,' said James.

'I daresay you've never been so far from home, though?'

'I daresay, sir. Captain Gunn made it quite straightforward, though, sir.'

'Even when you had to leave an inn rather suddenly?' George found himself asking. 'Someone mentioned something about an argument? With Sir Alexander Gordon?'

For a moment James said nothing. George kicked himself for his timing: it was almost impossible to see his expression in the dusk.

'I ken nothing of that, sir. Such things are no business of a drummer boy. I go where I'm tellt and do as I'm bid, and ask no questions.'

'But you must have seen –' began George. He broke off at a yell from someone nearby.

'Sir!' cried James. 'Watch - !'

George glanced up at the darkened sky. Too late, he realised what was happening. The beacon tower had slipped its guy line, and was toppling towards them. George gave James an almighty shove, and slipped on the mud, as the tower broke and tumbled around him. He saw sparks in the darkness, and then nothing.

Chapter Fifteen

Edinburgh

I

Sunday again, thought Murray, and no progress whatsoever.

He flopped over in bed, face still aching, noting that the light in the room was as dull as yesterday. It would be a wet walk to church, no doubt, and then a sombre sit in damp clothes, while the beadle ran around trying to decide whether to light the stove, cold since Easter, and dry everyone off, or leave it to stop the close day feeling any heavier. Anyone would think that wet weather in June was a phenomenon scarcely heard of in Edinburgh: Willie Jack and Letitia had come back from their abandoned picnic yesterday with a sense of outrage, and Walter, returned by dusk in quiet triumph, had been pressed to work helping the maid take mud off the Dundases' clothes and boots.

Murray heard movement in the house now and had dragged himself into a reluctant sitting position by the time Walter appeared with his hot water. This time last week they had only just found Alicia's body: this time last week he had assumed, stupidly, that Theodore was safe and well, and this time last week Sergeant Home had been alive and hale. On many levels that was a shame: he had a feeling that Sergeant Clyne was less sympathetic to his interest in the investigation – and indeed less interested in its outcome.

Walter was standing attentively with towels, and Murray, dripping, took one.

'You've recovered from yesterday's adventures, then, Walter?'

'Yes, sir. We went a walk up into the Old Town, and looked at the sojers at the Castle. Then we came back down and went to see if the dog was there, and he was, and he followed us around the stalls in the Lawnmarket. Jemima had pennies for buns and so did I, so that was our dinner. I told her a bit about the country because she's a town lass herself, and she told me a bit about the town. Then she brought me back here and went off home.'

'And where's the dog?' Murray asked, suddenly suspicious.

'In the kitchen,' said Walter blandly. 'See, she said if it followed her back to the Sangsters it'd likely be whipped, and it did want to follow her, and I didn't think you were the kind to whip a dog, sir, nor indeed a servant, howsoever cross you might be,' he added, just making sure.

'Oh, Walter!'

II

'Well, it would have been all right anyway,' said Willie Jack with a sniff. 'I quite like dogs, really.'

'It could have done with a bath,' Murray remarked, still apologetic.

'I think that was the problem,' said Letitia. 'The maid tried to give it a bath in the yard, and it ran off.'

'After Jemima, I daresay. Walter is desperately disappointed, of course, but he should never have brought it into your home without permission.'

'Oh, never mind,' said Willie Jack. 'I hope the maid won't be long with that tea: I'm in need of reviving after that sermon.'

As if conjured up solely by this wish, the maid suddenly appeared at the door. She was not carrying the tea tray, though, but a letter, which she presented to Letitia. Letitia flicked it open impatiently.

'Oh! That's nice. Dearest, the Sangsters have asked us to their house this afternoon to make up for that dreadful picnic yesterday: everyone is to go.'

'Well, that's something,' said Willie Jack, brightening at once.

'You are included, Mr. Murray!' Letitia added, leaping up. 'And I must change my gown. How I wish I had that Pomona green this instant! It would be perfect.'

'What on earth is Pomona green?' Willie Jack asked as she

flowed from the room. 'Oh, it doesn't matter: I'm sure she'll look splendid in it! You will come with us, won't you, Murray?'

'I'd be delighted,' said Murray. If there was a limit to what one could do on the Sabbath, then the chance to find out more about Alicia's first husband's family and friends was not to be ignored. Maybe there was a chance that Theodore had taken refuge with one of them.

It took longer than expected to arrive at the Sangsters. Inevitably it was some time before Letitia was dressed again to her own satisfaction, and then there was the matter of how to travel to Water of Leith village. Particularly as the sky was still threatening, it was clearly impossible to walk (according to Letitia), so Willie Jack spent some considerable time on Prince's Street and its environs trying to find a cab driver who was willing to work on the Sabbath and prepared to stray as far from his own hearth as the Water of Leith. There were murmurings about friends who chose not to live within the environs of civilisation, and yet thought they could invite guests on wet days. When at last a cab was secured and they had travelled all the way to the village – which Letitia thought took hours and Murray felt had taken seconds, used as he was recently to walking there – the driver refused to take his vehicle into the steep, narrow streets, and they had to descend in a heap and walk the rest of the way. Still Letitia managed to arrive looking like a budding fruit tree in a fresh spring shower – or so Murray thought until he realised what he was thinking, and pulled himself together.

The advantage of having taken so long was that by the time they assembled with the others who had abandoned yesterday's picnic, the weather had actually improved again. There were thirty or forty of them, including children, and in the little rooms of the Sangsters' old-fashioned house there seemed to be a good deal more, so that it was a mighty relief when Mrs. Sangster announced, managing some clarity in her speech even though she was invisibly crowded somewhere near the fireplace, that they would all adjourn to the garden and try another picnic there. Murray wondered what size the garden could be in the serried streets of the Water of Leith, and he had plenty of time to wonder. The house, narrow as it was at the front, extended backwards into a real rabbit warren, taking in parts of adjacent properties. He followed Willie Jack, who was following Letitia, who was following someone else, down ungenerously proportioned passages and round tight corners, sometimes in daylight, sometimes in candlelight, sometimes in darkness altogether, until finally they emerged with a shock into a walled and cobbled yard. The stream of guests continued to troop across to a short flight of steps which led to a little gate in the wall, and once through that, Murray's question was answered.

The garden was old, and cleverly cut into terraces up the steep hill on to which the house backed. Little paths and steps led between the terraces, some of which had been made wide enough to plant a reasonable lawn, while others had only stone benches and flower beds. Facing north, it must have presented its challenges to the gardener, but on a June day when the sun was just beginning to warm the stone and dry the grass, it was unexpectedly delightful.

Tables and chairs had already been laid out on different levels, and the party quickly sorted itself out and prepared itself for food and conversation. Willie Jack and Letitia found themselves a pair of seats at a table for four, and another couple immediately joined them, leaving Murray adrift. Not quite sure enough of himself in this unfamiliar company, he meandered away, realising that for the most part the guests were all those who had been at the Findlays' supper party last Monday, where he had first met the Sangsters. None of them seemed particularly interested in talking to him: his novelty had worn off, he supposed, and he had little in common with any of them. He was beginning to regret coming with the Dundases at all when he heard his name called, and found that the Findlays themselves had remembered him and were gesturing him to join them at their little table. With them was their daughter, the pianist, and a young couple Murray vaguely remembered having met on Monday. They glanced up and greeted him politely but without enthusiasm and continued their own conversation. The Findlays, on the other hand, were very friendly.

'Mr. Murray! How lovely to see you again so soon! Are you still staying with the Dundases?'

'That's right, Mrs. Findlay. They are very kind to put up with me, for they intend to go to the country soon.'

Mrs. Findlay beamed: she was not a noticeably pretty woman, but she had a face full of good humour.

'I doubt they'll be away for a while yet!'

'Thank you again for the delightful evening on Monday. I shall remember with pleasure for some time your daughter's playing.'

'There, a compliment, Anna dear!' The girl beamed like her mother, and tucked into a plate of bread and butter with relish.

'I hope the noise from the street did not disturb you too much in the end,' Murray added.

'Oh, wasn't it dreadful? Did you hear a police sergeant was killed later that evening? And there was a fire in one of the flats, too: it would be very nice to leave the Old Town altogether, but then the New Town is a long way for my husband when he is to travel around his shops.'

'I believe a number of people find Newington very convenient,' Murray said. Edinburgh was spreading out in all directions now, he felt. 'I hope none of your friends was directly affected by the fire or the mob?'

'Oh, the fire was in a close that is really not very nice, Mr. Murray. We have no acquaintances there, thank goodness.'

'Is that not the close that Theodore lived in, Mamma?' asked her daughter suddenly. Her mother looked confused.

'Do you know, I believe it is? He was a very nice boy, Mr. Murray, but his mother died and he had to move away.'

Murray nearly choked on his bread. He swallowed quickly. Lauder, Sangster's manservant, hovered anxiously and filled Murray's glass.

'That's a shame. Did he have to move far?' He waved Lauder off gratefully, but the man still made his skin crawl.

'Do you know, Mr. Murray, we have no idea! He simply vanished. And his mother ...' Mrs. Findlay eyed her daughter, who immediately pretended to see something fascinating further up the garden, 'well, Mr. Murray, she was murdered, they say! So we have really no idea what happened to poor Theodore.'

'Good heavens!' said Murray obligingly. 'I suppose there's no chance he did the deed and is fleeing justice?' He gave the question just a hint of dark facetiousness, just in case the Findlays had been particularly attached to Theodore.

'Oh, no, Mr. Murray, Theodore was a very nice boy indeed. His mother – well, I only met her once, for the children were playing in the close and she came to fetch him – his mother seemed very genteel. I did wonder what she was doing living in a close like that, but then, who knows in this day and age? And her husband was an officer in the army, so he was not there to protect them. It was all very sad.'

'What an interesting mystery,' said Murray. 'You must tell me if poor Theodore ever turns up: I should like very much to hear if he has anything to add to such a fascinating story.'

'Oh, I shall, Mr. Murray, I shall!' Mrs. Findlay's eager face was filled with delight at the possibility of providing such intriguing gossip.

'I must say, turning the subject,' Murray pressed on while the wind seemed to be in his favour, 'I find our host and hostess a charming couple. I only met them for the first time at your home last Monday. He is a baker, I believe?'

'Ah, well,' Mrs. Findlay was clearly getting into her stride. 'He is indeed, and as to charm, take care not to be too charmed, Mr. Murray.' She had lowered her voice now and looked about her for possible eavesdroppers. Lauder and Jemima, who were still serving drinks and food, were out of earshot. 'You would find him less charming, I believe, if you were the owner of a small but profitable bakery in the city.'

'Is that so?' asked Murray, raising his eyebrows to invite further confidences, but it was Mr. Findlay who joined in.

'It's all too true, Mr. Murray,' he confirmed. 'We know of at least two bakers who have been – well, forced is not too strong a word – out of business in less than clear circumstances, and somehow Sangster has been there both times with the best offer on the table. I'd say, my dear,' he added to his wife, 'that you probably shouldn't say such things, for there is no proof in either case. It could simply be that he is a very fortunate businessman, always to have the right money for the right business at the right moment.'

'Mrs. Findlay!' came a cry from behind Murray. He turned to find a couple who clearly knew the Findlays well, and he excused himself and stood so that they could sit down together. He bowed to Mrs. Findlay and found himself wandering again.

He walked slowly up the terraces, trying to seem as if he were looking for someone specific rather than just feeling lost. At various levels tables were filled with middle-aged women talking animatedly, young couples discreetly holding hands, elderly deaf relatives staring helplessly at conversations, waiting for someone to make the effort to speak loudly to them, children itching to break free and play. One child was not to have that opportunity, of course: Jemima, the maid, had a frown of concentration on her face and was collecting empty glasses on a tray. Murray saw her approach the top of a set of steps with ferocious care, counting under her breath, but as she reached the last step Lauder, the manservant, appeared behind her, gathered a handful of skirt around her bottom and gave a playful pinch. Only by a miracle did Jemima save the glasses from crashing to the ground, and she turned on Lauder with a look fit to set fire to him. Murray found himself gasping at Lauder's expression as Jemima left him on the step: in Lauder's face there was a look of deep hatred that sent chills down Murray's spine. Murray looked away quickly, and his gaze happened to fall on Mrs. Sangster, who was seated nearby. She had clearly seen the whole incident, and on her face, surprising Murray again with its appearance, was a little smile he could only describe as nasty.

He found himself a quiet stone bench at the top of the garden and took a substantial mouthful of wine. People were not always what they seemed, he thought: Mrs. Sangster had appeared very charming, but then the Findlays had things to say about trusting the charms of Mr. Sangster. Perhaps they were a couple with more in common than one supposed. On the other hand, the expression he had just seen on Lauder's face only confirmed his instinct that Lauder was at least unpleasant and possibly dangerous. He was glad he was not Jemima: he could see why Walter was worried about her.

'Mr. Murray, isn't it?'

He looked up, and looked again, for the man addressing him was around his own level though he was seated and the man was standing up. It was Letitia's uncle.

'Ah, Mr. Brewster!' Murray rose and bowed, and moved along the bench to allow Brewster to join him. 'How are you, sir?'

'Och, tolerably well, tolerably well. Did I get your name right? My head's a sieve when it comes to names. Now, ask me what I paid for a boll of cloth two years ago past Thursday and I could tell you to the farthing, but I'd forget your name again the next minute.'

'Well, you were right with mine this time,' Murray reassured him, laughing with him.

'My niece and Mr. Dundas are still in town, then, are they? Well, there's a surprise,' said Brewster, settling down comfortably on the cold stone. 'There's no drive in her, and I doubt, forgive me for saying so for I ken he's your friend, that there's much drive in Mr. Dundas either.'

'I fear you're right there,' Murray admitted.

'Ah, well, I suppose with his money they'll do all right. You ken her father's well enough off, too, and no doubt when they go to the family there'll be plenty of gifts given and that'll keep them going a bit. My sister's husband will no see them starve, anyway, as long as they go to see him.'

'Well, Willie Jack wouldn't allow her to starve either,' said Murray, belatedly defending his friend. 'He's all right when he needs to be. And he's clearly devoted to her,' he added, though it occurred to him to wonder whether that devotion was mutual.

'Aye, well, I suppose,' said Brewster again, without rancour, and swung his little legs out from the bench, thoughtfully contemplating his boots. 'What are you up to in the town yourself, then? for I hear tell you've a fine estate in Fife.'

'I have,' said Murray, 'and no doubt I should be there, though my factor is reliable. Ah, I have a brother in the army who has called me back to town on an errand for him, which has turned out more complicated than either of us suspected.'

He wondered whether or not to leave it at that, but then thought of Theodore. There was a chance he had taken shelter with some of these people, his grandparents' friends, and he would never know if he did not ask. He drew breath, but Brewster was already keen to hear more.

'And what nature of an errand would that be, if you don't mind me asking?' And Murray explained about the search for Alicia, then the discovery that Theodore was missing, and then the link with the Sangsters. Brewster's little face stretched in astonishment.

'And you've said that you'll do what you can to find the killer? And the son?' he asked in disbelief. 'How in the name of all that's good and holy are you ever to manage that?'

'Well, that's a very good question,' Murray agreed reluctantly.

'I'm spreading the word as much as I can about Theodore – and of course the Sangsters are very eager to find him and take care of him, and I'm sure they'll have a whole network of friends who can help there. But they could tell me very little about Mrs. Argo. I'm in communication with her old neighbours, for her new ones scarcely knew her. And of course the trail is over a week old, now. I should be asking questions in Potterrow and the Dean Village, not sitting here drinking wine. But I did hope that someone here might have seen Theodore or be protecting him.'

'I'll ask around: they might be more willing to tell an old gossip like me than a stranger like you, Mr. Murray, particularly if they think the lad's in danger. I'll see what I can find out, and send you word if I hear anything.'

'I'd be more than grateful,' said Murray. 'It's not the first time I've had cause to ask questions about a death that happened a while before, but there was rarely so thin a field of suspects.'

'Is that a fact?' Brewster regarded him curiously for a moment. 'You'll have to tell me your stories some time. Did the Sangsters tell you themselves they were both eager to have the lad safe back?'

'Yes - or rather no, now I come to think of it, it was Mr. Sangster. He followed me out into the hall and asked me to help find Theodore.'

Brewster was nodding.

'Aye, aye, that's very likely. For Mrs. Sangster always favoured her other son, the one that's fallen out with the father, and never the one that's dead. And the day those two agree on anything – well, I'd watch out for blue moons and earth cracks, and the like.'

'They don't get on?' Murray stared down the steep garden to where Mrs. Sangster busied herself with her guests, and Mr. Sangster sat regaling a few cronies with some tale or other.

'In much the same way as Wellington and Bonaparte don't get on. And no doubt if your brother's in the army, he'll tell you not to be around when the twa meet.'

'No doubt,' said Murray quietly. Several thoughts had begun to buzz around in his mind, and Brewster seemed to recognise this. He hopped down from the bench, and nodded his head.

'I'd better get claiking then, if I'm going to be any help to you.' He skipped off down the steps, faster than his age would seem to allow.

'Thank you!' Murray called belatedly. He sat a moment longer. But there was little point in perching here like a poor imitation of a Greek god on Olympus: even they had had to stoop to earth a few times to find out what was going on. He stood with a sigh and began to make his way back down the garden.

Brewster was probably right that the guests were more likely to talk to him than to Murray, but Murray still felt he had to try. Rather than asking about Theodore, though, he elected to try to find out more about the Sangsters' late son, Alicia's first husband and Theodore's father. It was still not easy: it seemed that the Sangsters' social life had grown since John Sangster's death, and not before. They all knew of him and of his wife, but had not, it seemed, met her.

'I had the impression,' said Mrs. Findlay, 'that the family were not too pleased about the marriage.'

'She was the daughter of a baker – Baxter, his name was,' said her husband. 'That was one of the poor unfortunates we told you about. I knew of him for his wife had just bought him a watch of me, for his fiftieth birthday, if I remember right. Not long after, I was looking for her to meet the bill and I heard they'd gone under, something to do with rumours of pieces of rat found in the bread.'

'That would do it,' agreed Mrs. Findlay, turning up her nose.

'Baxter was found in the Water of Leith: he had probably thrown himself in somewhere near here, but they found him down by the harbour. His wife died of shock. The girl was left orphaned and John Sangster married her, I think that was the story.'

'And of course Sangster himself took over the business,' added Mrs. Findlay, with a significant look at Murray.

'Well, he'd hardly have made his son marry the girl for the business,' said Mr. Findlay, but Mrs. Findlay simply met Murray's eye, and gave a little shrug.

Letitia knew a little more.

'The second son, what's his name? Peter, maybe? Very dashing! Oh, my dear, if he'd asked me to marry him I shouldn't have dared say no! Where did I leave my shawl, Willie Jack, dear?'

'But he didn't ask you?' Willie Jack queried, clearly surprised.

'Well, no,' admitted Letitia. 'He and John, the older brother, they never got on. John was all for going into the family business, but that wasn't Peter's idea at all. When John died, Peter and his father had such a row! It was the talk of the town for weeks, Mr. Murray. Off Peter went, and there's poor Mr. Sangster without anyone to take over the business from him. Mrs. Sangster, I always heard, sided with Peter, and I'm not sure that I wouldn't have, too. John was a cold character, I think.'

'Yet he swept Alicia off?' prompted Murray.

'Well, who knows? Even cold characters sometimes flare up in the most unexpected ways,' she said, meeting Murray's eye in a very disconcerting manner.

'I'll see if I can find that shawl,' Murray said hurriedly, and continued down the garden.

He reached the yard without encountering either the shawl or anyone else who seemed to be useful to talk to. It was indeed turning slightly chilly as the evening wore on: warm food had been brought out to the guests, but with sunset approaching some more direct action would be required. Murray was not very keen on staying if the guests were all to be squashed back into the house again: he liked the fresh air, and the garden, despite the oddness of the occasion, charmed him. Besides, there would be no hope of having anything like a discreet conversation if they were all crushed into the house. If it would help persuade people to stay outside, he would happily find Letitia's shawl.

He wondered where she might have left it, and decided that the most likely place was in the drawing room where the guests had first assembled – either that, or she had dropped it on the way out into the garden. He entered the house.

He had forgotten what a complete maze it was inside. The changing lights and the hurrying guests had meant that he had not taken much note of his route, and he was lost within seconds. Which way could it possibly be? In these old houses, there was not even any clear delineation of servants' quarters and family rooms, and he assumed the kitchens were at the back, too. He had to get past them and through to the front, but knowing that was much simpler than doing it. The house seemed completely free of any straight lines or clear passages, and he blundered about in semi-darkness, wondering when he might meet someone who could direct him.

At last he came to a dead end, with two doors facing him, both closed firmly. He could not recollect coming through either of them. He tried the one to his right first. The handle turned, and the door opened into another passage.

'Well, I think it's heading in roughly the right direction,' he muttered to himself, and went in, closing the door behind him.

The walls in this part of the house were panelled: before the doorway they had been unpainted, and now they were white. He wondered if this had any significance whatsoever, but doubted it. The passage was candle-lit, and inclined slightly upwards.

'Upwards … maybe not so good. Is it taking me back again?' he pondered aloud. A door appeared on his right, and he tried it. Again, it opened.

Inside, there was a little room, with a high window in one wall, too high to see out to get his bearings. Here the white panelling continued, and in the dim light from the window Murray could make out that he was in some kind of coat room. From the quality of the coats, he thought it might be for the servants, but he wanted to make sure: after all, if a servant had found Letitia's shawl, they might have hung it up in here for safe-keeping.

He turned back into the passage and carefully lifted one of the candles off its sconce, carrying it into the little room. He raised it for a better look. On the hook next to him was a man's brown coat, and over it, on a separate hook, hung a wide-brimmed, dark hat.

'Oh,' said Murray.

Of course it could mean nothing. How many men in Edinburgh had brown coats, and with them chose to wear a wide-brimmed black hat? A very practical attire, particularly for the servant class, for it would wear well and not show much in the way of dirt. There were plenty of brown coats and wide-brimmed black hats around.

Nevertheless he found himself quickly perching the candle on a sconce in the room, and inserting his long fingers into the pockets of the coat. One pocket was empty, except for a clean handkerchief. In the other, his fingertips met a cold, hard shape. He pulled it out swiftly. It was a tinderbox.

And why not? he asked himself. Why should a manservant not carry a tinderbox in the pocket of his coat? Who knew when he would ever have to strike a light?

But in his mind's eye he saw the brown-coated, dark-hatted man in the High Street last Monday night, and the flames leaping from the flat where Alicia had died, where Johnnie Norrie and Ebb had died.

There was a sound in the passage outside. The door he had left shut had opened, and footsteps were heading towards the coat room. He stuffed the tinderbox back, nipped the candle out, seized it, and spun around. Behind him was another door. He opened it, and flung himself inside.

He was just in time. The coat room door opened, and someone came in. He could hear someone sniff, as if they had caught the whiff of candle smoke. He could hear it quite clearly, for though he thought the second door might offer an escape, it turned out that he was crouching, very awkwardly, on the floor of a narrow press, built into the wall. The door opened outwards: he did not dare touch it in case it swung open, but there was hardly room for him beneath the lowest shelf in the press, and the space was already partly taken up by boots.

He held his breath. Someone trod softly on the stone floor in the coat room.

He was going to look thoroughly ridiculous if someone opened the door of the press. A panicky laugh rose in his throat, and he nearly choked.

His ears strained to catch any sound. There was a light scuffling, as if someone, like him, was going through the pockets of the coat on the hook. The door of the press was open a crack. He prayed the room was too dark for the person outside to notice that the press was fuller than usual. If they saw Murray ... but he could not resist glancing quickly up. It was Lauder.

Lauder was indeed feeling inside the pockets of the brown coat. In a moment he produced the tinderbox that Murray had held only moments before. Murray tried hard not to look at his face: he was sure that if he did so, Lauder would somehow sense it. What was it about this man? Murray had not felt so baselessly frightened since he was a boy.

Lauder paused. What was he doing? He seemed to be listening. Murray continued to hold his breath, though he was starting to feel dizzy. He breathed out as gently as he could, and silently inhaled again. Still Lauder had not moved. Murray thought he would burst.

Suddenly Lauder turned on his heel, scraping on the stone floor, and left the coat room, closing the door carelessly behind him. Murray heard his footsteps return down the passage, heard the far door close too. For a long moment he remained motionless. Then he rolled quietly out of the press, and rubbed his stiff knees as he sat on the floor. He left it five minutes before he returned to the passage himself, set the candle, relit, back in the sconce, and found his way back to the garden, without Letitia's shawl. He felt as if he had aged ten years.

Outside, Lauder was lighting lanterns around the garden. He glanced at Murray as he passed on his way back to the Dundases, and Murray tried to hide his shiver.

The evening wore on without any particular purpose or drive, as Uncle Brewster no doubt noticed. Murray sat in the dusk watching the other guests, sipping wine but too unsettled to allow himself to relax. The Sangsters circulated separately amongst their guests but he managed to remain mostly unnoticed, until at last Letitia came upon him and tugged him to his feet.

'Time to go, Willie Jack says,' she declared cheerfully. 'Have you been hiding here all along? I wondered where you'd got to.' She led the way back down the garden, confident that he would do nothing but follow.

They had made their farewells and descended the narrow street to the river when Letitia exclaimed,

'Oh, my shawl! I must have left it in the garden this time – I'm such a fool!'

'I'll go,' said her husband indulgently. 'Clearly Murray is simply useless at finding shawls.' He laughed, pleased to be better than Murray for once, and immediately jogged back up the way they had come. Letitia watched him go, then turned to look at the river. The moonlight caught the braided water and made it flicker.

'What an enchanting evening!' she whispered. 'Mr. Murray, I think I'd like to cross this little bridge here. Isn't it delightful?' She took his hand and led him out on to the bridge. It was no more than two or three planks wide with a sketchy handrail, a shortcut for the villagers who would otherwise have to go to the stone bridge further up the river. Murray held back and examined the fragile construction: neither end was easy to see, for there were bushes around the edge of the river here and the bridge looked like nothing sturdier than a thin branch stretching out of one of them in a vain attempt to reach the other side. The handrail, on the upstream side, was low for Murray, though Letitia seemed to find it strong enough to lean back on and stare up at the moon. She had pulled off her bonnet: she glanced back at him and reached out her hand again.

'Come, Mr. Murray. Did you ever see such a fine moon? The light it casts is magical ...' The words came out on a long sigh. The moonlight slid over her dark hair, her pale skin.

'Mrs. Dundas, I'm not certain it's entirely safe,' he said as prosaically as possible, even though he was fairly sure he did not mean the bridge.

'Then you must help me keep my balance,' she said, hand still stretched towards him. She did indeed seem to be unsteady on her feet. He reached out and took her hand, holding it firmly and testing the handrail at the same time. The supports that held it seemed very few and far between. He found he was concentrating on it, rather than look at Letitia. He was heartily glad he had not drunk much wine.

'Mr. Murray,' whispered Letitia, and he found himself reluctantly meeting her gaze. 'Mr. Murray ...'

There was a resounding crack. The bridge lurched, and the handrail seemed to vanish. Letitia shrieked, and in the same instant there was a terrific splash. A second later, and Murray too was in the water, tumbling over the weir.

He was filled with dread. Water, spinning, churning water, flinging its victims through the darkness. Where was Letitia? Could he save her? Could he save himself? He felt sick. He had failed before. Wouldn't he fail again? His mind spun with the water, his clothes heavy, his limbs heavy, his head full of darkness, while the moon laughed above them.

Chapter Sixteen

Belgium

George woke with a splitting headache and a nasty taste of rum in his mouth. Things had not noticeably improved since the last time he had surfaced, his vision bleary and his stomach vigorously stirring, to the realisation that he was mostly still alive. At that first awakening the company sawbones had been there, and he had recollections of being prodded and perused and eventually proclaimed likely to be grand. The harsh rum taste had been there then, too: soldiers thought rum cured everything, even a crack on the head.

Rest, however, was the key memory that he was clutching in his pounding brain. The sawbones had said he needed rest, and with that George was wholeheartedly prepared to agree.

He squinted upwards: he was in a tent, he realised, seeing the pale canvas slope into dim obscurity above him. Early morning? Late evening? Duskish, anyway. He seemed to be lying on a decent camp bed – Gunn's, perhaps? - still in his shirt and breeches. He hoped that someone had polished his boots, and then was suddenly grateful that he could still care.

The camp seemed peaceful, and for a wild moment he wondered if the call to battle had come while he was asleep and they had all marched off to meet Bonaparte without him. Then he heard voices outside, and relaxed again. The voices were close by: he recognised Liddell, the man with his own private porage pot, and after a moment he was fairly sure he had the other voice, too. But what were they saying? They were certainly not aiming to attract attention.

'You said I could have a share!'

'You've had a share, laddie.'

'I've had a mouthful, and not much of one at that,' said Liddell's companion with asperity. 'It wouldn't have filled a hole in my tooth!'

'It was plenty, son.'

'After all I did? I did most of the work and you come off with the prize!'

'You're just thinking of what happened on the day, laddie,' said Liddell soothingly. 'You're not taking into consideration the brain work that had to go on to plan the thing.' Liddell's voice was easy, secure, but his companion was having none of it.

'Brain work? You near got the wrong tent: it was me that pointed it out to you. Then you got the words wrong. And in the end, you couldna have done it without me.'

'Is that what you think, son?' said Liddell, beginning to sound irritated.

'No question. Your running days are long gone: the only way you'd have got it from them is to sit on it, and they'd have needed a block and tackle to shift you.'

'Here! Who do you think you're talking to like that? You're in the army now. I could have you lashed!'

'Not if I had you lashed first! The army? Dinna make me laugh. The best way to use you against the French would be to roll you at them down a steep hill! Now give me my share, or I'll tell Captain Gunn what you made me do, and we'll see who he'll believe!'

'Oh, well, I suppose ...' grumbled Liddell, and there was a scrabbling sound as if heavy hands were searching through full pockets. 'Here you are – and it's a good deal more than is good for you. These foreign foods ...'

'Right, I'm off, before you change your thick head,' said the other, and footsteps scampered away. George grinned. Whatever Liddell had been up to, it seemed that James was more than a match for him. They'd better keep an eye on James, though: he was young to be falling into bad company.

George was slipping gratefully back into unconsciousness again, when an irate yell came from outside the tent. He sat up in alarm, and clutched his head sharply. The voices had been on his left, but the yell had come from outside the front of the tent. George held his head tenderly in one hand, and swung out of the cot, scrabbling the blanket around him. The smell of cooking fires told him at last that it was the evening – he hoped it was only a day since the beacon had hit him. Outside there was no trace of the wrecked beacon – that was Major Saddler's camp for you – but Saddler himself, as George had feared, was in the midst of the camp, not far from the tent. He had James by the ear and in the other hand was waving a long object that George could not clearly distinguish in the dusk. A truncheon?

'What's this?' Saddler hissed.

'I think they call it a wurst, sir,' said James. He was as tense as a bowstring but clearly trying not to wriggle. 'I found it over there.' He pointed to the side of George's tent.

'You found it?' Saddler did not sound convinced.

'Aye, sir. I was taking it to Sergeant Lamb, sir.'

A small crowd, including Sergeant Lamb, had gathered, and Saddler scanned them abruptly.

'Has anyone else found any - straying sausages?' he asked, in a voice that dared them to laugh. There were negative mumblings. 'I thought not. Where did you steal it from, boy?'

'I didn't steal it, sir!'

'Then how do you suggest it got here?'

'Maybe they threw it out? The Germans next door? Sir?' he added belatedly. In the pause that followed, George thought he could hear ice crystals crackling.

'The Germans threw it out?' Saddler repeated, in a voice like a hard frost. 'All the way to the other side of our camp?'

George, with an instant image of a sausage bombardment in his head, stifled a sudden, panicky giggle. If James escaped a lashing it would be a miracle, yet he was not giving up his fellow soldier, Liddell. And where was Liddell?

'Here's an extraordinary thing, Saddler!' came a new voice, and Gunn appeared innocently in the midst of the crowd. 'Those Germans next door must have a poor guard on their quartermaster's stores. I've just found one of the dogs with – what do they call it? A wurst!' And he held out for Saddler's inspection a long German sausage, to all appearances in this light the same as the one Saddler had taken from James. Saddler glared at it, then slowly released James's ear. He examined the wurst in his hand.

'It does look a bit chewed,' he admitted. 'Well, best give them back to the dogs, then. And we might want to tell the Germans that dogs are getting into their stores. We don't want a plague of rats on top of everything else.' He straightened his waistcoat, and turned. 'Ah, Murray. Good to see you up. How are you feeling?'

'A bit better, Major, thank you,' said George, though his head was bubbling with puzzled delight at how James had been so lucky, that Gunn had found a sausage at just the right moment. The crowd, unwilling to press a point, dispersed quietly to their tents, but he thought he could detect some quiet laughter.

'You need to rest a bit longer, by the look of you,' said Saddler. 'I'll go and have a word with the Germans.' He strode off with his usual energy. Gunn, who had handed the sausages to Sergeant Lamb, came over to the tent, and he and George returned inside.

'He's right: lie down, Murray, you still look grey,' Gunn said cheerfully.

'It's the dusk,' said George. 'I feel a lot better. As long as I doesn't move my head. Or laugh. Or frown. Where on earth did you find that sausage? Your timing was perfect!'

'It was – fortuitous, wasn't it?' Gunn turned away.

'You know,' George went on, keeping his voice low, 'James didn't exactly find that sausage.'

'I don't suppose he did,' said Gunn, equally quietly. 'Nor did I – or at least, I suspect I found mine in the same place as James found his – in the capacious pockets of Liddell.'

'How did you know?' George breathed.

'Liddell's father's from Hawick. He's a border reiver born and bred. He can't help himself – and being Liddell, what he steals is mostly edible.'

They laughed quietly.

'Well, young James owes you a favour, anyway,' George said. Gunn grew solemn.

'He'd have been flogged. It wouldn't have been right, for a first offence, and it should have been Lamb to have the say of it, anyway. But I could see how angry Saddler was.' He breathed in sharply through his nose, frowning. 'I admire the Major, no one more. And when he finds a breach of military discipline, he is quite rightly outraged on behalf of the company and the battalion. Sometimes, though … I myself would use a lighter touch. But then I have nothing like his experience.' He frowned again, concerned to find himself in opposition to his commanding officer. A thought struck George and, being George, he had to voice it.

'When you challenged Sir Alexander Gordon – he hadn't insulted Saddler, had he?'

Gunn was astonished.

'Insulted Saddler? Good heavens, no! And if he had, I am sure the Major can look after himself. Yes, perhaps I should go and speak to Sir Alexander ... I wonder where they are now?'

Looking unusually preoccupied, Gunn pushed back the tent flaps and went outside abruptly. George, suddenly weary, sat on the bed, and felt his head. The beacon had not been nearly as well constructed as they had all intended, and only a flying chunk of wood had caught George across the top of his skull, but judging by the lump he had there he was heartily thankful it had not been more. His forehead was tight, as if his skin had been drawn back into his hair.

He wondered if he should rest a little more, or rise and have something to eat. The thought of eating introduced interesting ambiguities in his stomach, and on the whole he thought it best left for a while. Nevertheless he reached for his coat and boots – not polished – and began to render himself fit to meet the world.

He stood and smoothed himself down, and noticed a crackle in the pocket of his breeches. He felt inside and pulled out his brother Charles' letter, folded neatly. Typical Charles! he thought to himself with a grin. Even in his absence, his letters tidied themselves into flat squares, when he himself always just shoved them into his pockets!

On reflection, though, he did think that it was odd. Perhaps it had slipped out when he had fallen, and someone had smoothed it out to put back. He thought about the contents of the letter, and fetched a heavy sigh. How on earth was he to tell Argo about his wife?

He had scarcely seen Argo this past week: Saddler had him running all over the place, and mostly had George himself occupied about the camp. Last night, of course, George had not even gone back to his billet in the town. On the whole, George had to admit that he had not considered missing Argo to be a bad thing, for himself. First there had been the avoidance of Argo's anxiety and post-watching, and then there had been the dread of how much worse it was going to be when Argo found out the truth about his wife. Now, though, George was willing to accept that he could not, in all decency, put the matter off any longer, and he fastened on his sword belt as if about to face the enemy, and strode out of Gunn's tent.

It took him a little while to find Saddler, who had returned from the Germans' camp with a bewildered look on his face.

'I'm looking for Argo, sir,' George explained. 'I'm afraid I have some bad news for him.'

'His wife?' said Saddler quickly, showing that as ever he had all the concerns of the company members at the forefront of his mind. 'Then she's dead?'

'Ah, yes!' said George in surprise.

'Well, he seemed to think she thought her life was in danger,' Saddler explained testily at George's expression. 'You'd better tell him then, and get it over with. You'll probably find him back at your billet: I sent him to talk to the surgeon-general about supplies for our own sawbones. Thankfully you didn't use up valuable dressings yesterday: you had the decency not to break your skin on that beacon.'

'I did my best, sir!' George laughed. It was rare for Saddler to crack a joke, so all the more to be appreciated when it happened.

His horse was in the lines: it did not take long to saddle it, and before darkness was anywhere near solid he had reached the centre of Brussels and was stabling his mount at the usual mews. Saddler was right: Argo was already at home, and just wondering, as it happened, where to go for his supper. George offered to accompany him. The ride had made him think he might manage a little something before bed, and a flagon of wine would make the news he had easier to give, and perhaps easier to take.

They established themselves at a small table at the back of the St. Pierre, and George made sure Argo's glass was full. Argo looked more ready to sleep than to eat and drink.

'What have you been up to, then?' George asked him.

'Oh, back and forth, checking this, telling someone that, asking someone else something else. It was mostly to do with supplies. I think ...' he tailed off sadly, with a yawn, 'I think Saddler's trying to keep me out of the way.'

'Out of the way of what?'

'Well, I thought he just didn't want me around when the fighting started, but now, well, Headquarters from all I've heard thinks Bonaparte's never going to leave Paris. He says we're too strong.'

'Well, we do look pretty impressive,' said George loyally. 'I thought people were saying Major General Soult was already on his way?'

'I suppose even Major Generals can turn round and go back.' Argo sounded thoroughly dejected. 'And there's a rumour that Spain is advancing from down south, supported by Portugal. Bonaparte would have the good sense to know he can't allow himself to be squeezed in the middle.'

'He would, if it happened, but I can't see Spain and Portugal shifting themselves all the way up here just to help us,' said George flatly.

'It's all just rumour, isn't it?' sighed Argo. 'We don't know anything for a fact.'

'Not much. It was different in the Peninsula,' George began, but stopped as Argo heaved another great sigh. 'Am I boring you?' he asked, slightly tart.

Argo gave a twisted smile.

'No, not at all. It's just that I seem to have missed out – as Saddler has pointed out I have no proper experience as a soldier or an officer, and apparently everything was better in the Peninsula!'

'Just different. And it's only that we haven't been here as long, really, which is a good thing. I grew heartily sick of the Peninsula in the end. But it seems so long ago, now, and the army is so different – like you, half the men weren't even signed up then, and so many good fellows are dead, or wounded, or off in North America, which could be worse, who knows?' He tried for a joke, but it fell resoundingly flat. Heavens, Argo could pull him down – and he had brought him here to break even more misery over his head.

'So where did you get to last night, then?' Argo too seemed to feel that they had sunk low enough for now. 'I hope you weren't sneaking off to some party, after all Saddler has said?' He made an effort at a teasing wink, though it did not come naturally to him. Still, George felt he ought to encourage him.

'Oh, I was having a great time! The beacon toppled over at the camp and part of it fell on my head, so I spent the night at the camp, though I can't say I remember much about it!'

'It knocked you out?'

'It did – out cold! I'm fine now, though: just a nasty great bump on my head which sets my shako crooked.' He laughed, then grew serious, for he felt that if he did not say something soon he would eat and drink and go home and still not have told Argo the bad news. 'Listen, though,' he said, 'I had a letter from my brother yesterday.' Well, it had been a couple of days ago, but better not to let Argo know he had been sitting on the news. 'I'm afraid there's very bad news.'

He paused, letting that sink in, and topped up Argo's glass – and his own. Argo said nothing: he seemed to be holding his breath. George took a moment to swallow wine as he stared at the table, trying to find the words.

'I'm afraid he found Mrs. Argo – she was … er… dead.'

Argo made an odd gurgling noise in his throat. His face was paper white.

'Ah … I'm not sure what else to tell you.'

'The boy?' Argo choked out, swallowing hard.

'No sign. My brother's trying to find him.'

'She – she was murdered, wasn't she?' Argo managed. George nodded. 'Just – just tell me all you know,' said Argo, so George pulled out Charles' letter and read most of it word for word, showing Argo that he was concealing nothing. As he read, Argo watched him with eyes that felt like hooks, tears running down his face like water from a bucket. When George broke off they sat in silence for a long time, George fiddling with the letter and staring at the table, unable to meet Argo's eye.

The waiter came and set meat down on the table, glancing at them both with a complete lack of interest. Argo shivered violently, and wiped his face with his hands, then with his handkerchief. He drew a long, unsteady breath.

'Ah … he thinks Theodore might be on his way to join us?'

'That's what he says. I don't know that he knows it – he's just wondering.'

'You said your brother has done things like this before – I mean, looked into … sudden deaths, and things.'

'It's – it has happened that way, yes,' said George more

carefully: he had been going to say something much more flippant. 'I gather he's quite good at it. Do you want him to carry on? Or would you rather he left it in the hands of the police?'

'The police? Well, surely it would be better if they both did it?' said Argo. 'Attacked the question from two sides?'

'There! You're thinking like a soldier!' said George cheerfully.

'I'd like him to carry on,' said Argo firmly. 'I want to find out what happened.'

'Well,' said George, 'is there any way we can help him? For example: your wife said she was in fear for her life, didn't she?'

'And she was right!' exclaimed Argo.

'I know, I know. But are you sure she didn't say who she was frightened of?'

'No! She said nothing of it. She didn't want to worry me!'

Damned silly woman, thought George, but managed not to say it.

'Then what did you think when you read it? Did anyone spring to mind? Even vaguely?' George was quite proud of himself for thinking this way: he would have to tell Charles and show him how intelligent he had been.

'No! Who would want to harm her? She's – she was lovely! And sweet, and kind, and everything she could be!'

'All right, then: I take it she was married before? Whose son is Theodore?'

'He's Theodore Sangster. His father was a master baker, apparently: I didn't know him. He died young, of some kind of consumption, I believe: bad lungs, from the flour. From what Alicia told me, he was not very kind to her, and though his family are still in Edinburgh she had no wish to see them.'

'Would they have wished her harm?'

'I shouldn't think so. She didn't like them, certainly: she said that old Mr. Sangster was completely obsessed with his sons inheriting his business – there's another son, I think, or maybe two – but that Mrs. Sangster was a really unpleasant person. She didn't really want to talk about it any more than that: she simply said that she was just as happy not to see them again.'

'And what about her own family?'

'Her parents were both dead, and she was an only child. I never heard of cousins or other kin. They were bakers, too: that was how she met her first husband, I believe. They all lived in Water of Leith: it's a close community.'

'Your family weren't bakers, then?'

'My father was a gunsmith,' Argo said. 'When you see them all round you every day, you take a fancy to see them in action, you know.'

George smiled, too.

'So you don't think that anyone in her past would have killed her,' he pressed on, 'so what about people you knew while you were married? You lived in Potterrow, didn't you?'

Argo smiled wistfully.

'We were very happy there,' he said. 'We had very pleasant neighbours: I had lived there a little while before I met Alicia. The landlord is a Mr. Campbell: he keeps a very clean house, very respectable. I have to say I had absolutely no concerns about Alicia living there in my absence. There was another lodging house keeper nearby, a Mrs. Brotherstone, and she has been like a mother to both of us. Then there's a medical student – well, I think he is still there, but I wrote to him several times, first out of friendship and then to ask – to ask if Alicia was well, but he has never answered … Then Alicia had a friend across the street, a Miss Cordiner. It was all extremely friendly and sociable. I was particularly pleased that Alicia and Bessie Cordiner were friends, for I had the impression … well, you know how it is. When I announced that Alicia and I were to be married, I thought I saw just a hint of disappointment in Bessie's eyes. Perhaps I flatter myself! And I had never, to my knowledge, given her any reason to hope …' He tailed off, frowning, eyes glazing as he looked back into the past, re-examining long-gone moments.

'Well?' said George eventually, gently as possible.

'I wonder … I have seen, sometimes, Bessie looking at Alicia in a way … it never really struck me at the time, but now … I think I would have called it a hungry look.' He scowled. 'Your brother would think me a monster, if you were to tell him that I suspected a woman of killing my wife.'

'My brother has had to deal with many ghastly women in his life!' George gave a little laugh. 'I shall tell him all you have said, with your permission, and who knows what he might find useful. He's a bookish man, but despite that he has a sensible head on his shoulders,' he allowed generously. 'I think he will be able to find his way through this as well as any man, and maybe with more kindness than the police officers. If this Bessie Cordiner had anything to do with your wife's death, he will find it.'

Chapter Seventeen

Edinburgh

I

Murray was furious.

Annoyed at falling into the river in the first place (something he knew would have caused him more amusement than anger only a few years ago), he was cross with Letitia who, having been dragged over to the bank and pushed out by him insisted on regarding the whole episode as a huge joke, cross with Willie Jack who flapped around rather than helping him pull his abundant wife and her skirts out of the water, and cross again with Letitia who had taken the opportunity to wriggle against him as he shoved her. He was particularly cross with himself, he admitted later, for enjoying that wriggle. But when he stalked back upstream to where the bridge had started, and had found that the ropes holding it had clearly been kicked from their pegs, he was reduced to silent fury.

The one good thing was that Willie Jack had surpassed himself by securing a carriage to take them back to town, a carriage whose driver did not blink twice at the soaked condition of two of his passengers but instead offered them blankets, at no extra cost. It meant that they did not have to go back and beg comfort from the Sangsters, which, to Murray, was a great relief.

They returned to Prince's Street in a condition even wetter than the picnickers the day before, but with Letitia in much better spirits. It took some effort on Willie Jack's part to despatch her to a warm bed, and Murray was happy to encourage her retirement by disappearing to his room himself with a hot toddy, leaving Walter once again to improve his training as a manservant by dealing with Murray's wet and filthy clothes. Sleep did not approach more than tentatively, but the toddy eventually helped, and Sunday, as far as Murray was concerned, was over.

After some time the two women watching in the street outside concluded that that was the case, and set themselves to the long walk home in stony silence.

II

Murray woke, much revived, at eight, and reviewed with a cooler head what he had learned the previous day. The Sangsters did not get on, and perhaps only Mr. Sangster wanted the safe return of his grandson. There had been two sons, John and Peter: John was dead and Peter gone. Mrs. Sangster rather unpleasantly found animosity between her servants amusing. Lauder, the manservant, owned a coat and hat very like those seen on the man in the High Street and on the man who visited Alicia before her death. And somewhere, in the midst of all that, was presumably something someone did not want him to know, for they had followed him and slipped the ropes on the bridge – as a warning or as something more conclusive, he did not know. It was nothing to be angry about, he told himself firmly: if it was the latter it had failed, and for it to be either meant that at last he was making progress.

He breakfasted with Willie Jack, who chatted with some animation until a message arrived for Murray. It was from Mr. Campbell, the lodgings keeper in Potterrow.

'The funeral of Alicia Argo will take place on Tuesday at eleven from this house and to Greyfriars Kirk. Mr. Murray would do us great honour if he could attend, but there is no question of his going to any expense as his kind offer expressed, as we are happy (the last word had been crossed out heavily) content to meet the expenses of burying our old friend ourselves, but would very much like his presence so as not to take offence.' It looked a little as if the last piece had been said by Mrs. Brotherstone at the end of her dictating the note, and had not been intended to be included. He realised what they meant, though, and was determined to go: he would have wished to go in any case. He was very glad that Alicia had not been found to be friendless even with her husband and son away.

'A funeral for the poor woman tomorrow: I shall be out most of the day, no doubt,' he remarked to Willie Jack. 'I hope that causes no inconvenience.'

'Not at all,' said Willie Jack. 'I'm glad you could spend yesterday with us: I feel as if I've hardly seen you.'

'I wish, though, it were because I was making good progress with this matter,' said Murray, despite his earlier optimism.

'Where are you with it?'

'The woman was murdered. The son has vanished. After that, two men who had known her slightly before took over her flat, and they were killed. A man in a brown coat and wide black hat was seen near the flat at the time of their deaths. A man in a brown coat and wide black hat was seen visiting her about a week before she died, or less. Her husband loved her, her neighbours liked her, her first husband's family had nothing to do with her but the father wants his grandson found. His manservant owns a brown coat and a wide black hat.'

'I think you've solved the case, then!' said Willie Jack cheerfully.

'But where's the grandson? What was the reason for the death? Where are all her belongings? Why were the two men killed? And what were the Browns doing in the close where Alicia was living, after she had died?'

'The Browns?'

'I have a feeling it is not their real name. A mother and daughter, built like a couple of Highland cows, who seem to know more than they are prepared to tell.'

'You say Brown – do they, by any chance, dress in brown?' asked Willie Jack.

'Why?'

'Oh, just that there was a couple of women across the street like that earlier. I noticed them because they were staring up at this flat, but then they saw me watching and pretended to be looking at something further down in the street. They were wearing brown dresses and they were – well, solid.'

'That sounds like them. Well, there's another question – what are they up to? I'm nowhere near the end of this yet, and certainly not in a position to go charging off to your friends the Sangsters and accusing their manservant of murder.'

'Well, all right, then,' said Willie Jack with a smile. 'I suppose I'll let you get on. And today? What are your plans?'

'I'm going back to the Dean Village to see if I can talk some more with Chisholm – that was her landlord there, for all of about five minutes. I think there is more he can tell me, though. What about you?'

'Oh, I don't know,' said Willie Jack with his usual energy. 'I might see if I can get some fencing in. You never know when you might have to call on me for protection!'

'Very true, Willie Jack: it is certainly not something I've anticipated up to now,' Murray agreed, and remembered to add a smile.

III

The street of Dean Village was as empty as it had been the last time he had visited. Though Murray found himself glancing down every alley to see if the Browns, mother and daughter, were lurking anywhere, he did not see them. Combe's Court loomed again at the end of the street, and he took a moment this time to survey it from a distance. It was a mysteriously unattractive house: on paper it should have been fine, impressive, even, but in the little street it sat squarely, bulky, with windows of slightly the wrong size and a door that seemed just a little too low. The rendered walls had a greenish tinge, suggesting damp, and the paintwork was past its first brightness. The garden in front, even in June, was dull: the roses had been overpruned to stumps, too frightened to sprout, and not a weed had been permitted to raise its head. Murray could see why Alicia might have moved here if she had really felt unsafe in Potterrow: Combe's Court looked too respectably dull to have anything unsafe about it, unless it was mould.

'Now, Walter,' he murmured.

'Yes, sir?' Walter had been waiting incuriously behind him, watching out not for the Browns but for small boys who might tease him.

'You know what you have to look out for in the servants' hall?'

'It's no much of a hall, sir. It's really just the kitchen, or it was the last time,' he added carefully, in case there had been massive extensions made since their last visit a week ago. 'There's just the yin wee lassie to the place.'

'Well, that will make your job much easier,' said Murray. 'Now, what is it you are looking for?'

'I'm looking for … a black coat and a brown hat, sir.'

'Try again.'

'A brown coat and a black hat?'

'That's the one. Let's see – how could you make it easier to remember?'

'Um … It's the same as Mr. Lauder, sir,'

'Ah, yes. That's right, it is.' His mind flashed back to the cramped cupboard at the Sangsters', and the chill Lauder caused in his spine. 'Keep your eyes open, then, eh?'

'Yes, sir.' Walter hurried after Murray as he strode towards the front door of Combe's Court. 'Please, sir, can I?' he gasped, waving at the risp.

'What? Oh, all right – if it's that exciting for you.'

Walter rattled the risp with enthusiasm, and in a few moments Alicia's old, temporary, landlord appeared. He recognised Murray straightaway this time, and his face assumed an expression reminiscent of a man who had sucked in a wasp and was trying to be polite about it. His damp eyes blinked in the daylight, and he irresistibly touched his hair into its greasy mat on top of his head. With the other hand he grasped the edge of the door, ready to bar the way.

'Mr. Chisholm,' said Murray pleasantly.

'Mr. Murray. How can I help you, this time?'

'I'd like a little further conversation about the late Alicia Argo, if I may?'

Chisholm stared past in him into the street for a moment, as though weighing up his options.

'Better come in, then, I suppose,' he said, and reluctantly released his grip on the door.

In the hallway he turned and stopped, and Murray realised that Chisholm intended to have this conversation where he stood, and not anywhere that implied that he anticipated the conversation being either lengthy or enjoyable. Walter, doing his best to look like a competent and discreet young servant, scuttled past and disappeared towards the kitchens.

'So what is it this time, then?' Chisholm demanded sulkily.

'I thought you might like to know what has been happening in my enquiry into Mrs. Argo's death: you seemed very attached to her. Was I mistaken?'

Chisholm folded his scrawny arms and propped himself against the newel post. The action reinforced how thin he was: the folds of cloth around his elbows and waist were generous. With his heavy jaw, it implied that he had been very ill some time recently, and lost a good deal of weight.

'Ahm …' he began.

'By the way,' said Murray thoughtfully, glancing around him at the several closed doors off the hallway, 'is your delightful tenant Miss Smillie in?'

'No, no she's not,' said Chisholm at once. 'She's away out sketching, or some such.'

'Then we shan't be disturbed, shall we?'

Chisholm regarded him suspiciously, and cast a resentful look at the door presumably of Miss Smillie's room. He sagged a little against the newel post.

'I liked Mrs. Argo,' he mumbled.

'You did? Well, that's good, isn't it?' Murray was encouraging.

'I liked her a lot.'

'You knew she was married, of course.'

'Aye, well: soldiers die, don't they? And sooner than most. She'd been a widow before.'

'That's not to say she wanted to make a habit of it,' said Murray.

'Oh, aye,' said Chisholm, working this out, 'but it meant she might not be averse to marrying again, if she was a widow with Argo.'

'Did you ever meet Argo?'

'Naw. He was away the whole time she was here.'

Murray considered. He wished that he could bring Eppy's daughter down here to take a look at Chisholm: in fact, it would be useful if he could drag all Alicia's old acquaintances around after him in a cart so they could all see each other. He felt sure it would make things move faster.

'So you had Mrs. Argo in mind as a future Mrs. Chisholm.'

'Aye, why not? You have to take your opportunities in this world.'

Murray looked him up and down: he was not sure that Alicia Argo would have considered him to be much of an opportunity, but who knows?

'So did you go and see her after she left here?'

'Naw.' Chisholm's gaze slid to Murray's boots.

'Are you sure?'

'Of course I'm sure. She didna tell me where she was going.'

'That can't have pleased you, when you were considering marrying her.'

Chisholm made a brief dismissive puff with his teeth.

'So you had no idea where she had gone, and you didn't see her.'

'That's right.'

They both jumped as a door slammed, and Walter appeared in the hall with a ponderous air. A very small maid darted behind him, her face a picture of dismay and excitement.

'Well, Walter?'

'Aye, sir, both there. Just like Mr. Lauder, sir.'

'Well done.'

Walter nodded solemnly, and herded the maid back to the kitchen quarters, depriving her of whatever spectacle might have been on offer. Chisholm watched them go unhappily, avoiding Murray's eye. Murray left the moment to lie, before saying quietly,

'Someone saw you, you know: one of her neighbours saw you quite clearly.'

Chisholm sagged, lacking the self-confidence to fight.

'Who was it? This Lauder you said about?'

'Never mind who it was: you went to see her. You'd better tell me all about it, hadn't you? Tell me how you came to know where she was?'

Chisholm sighed, and sat on the stairs, spreading his thin legs out like a disheartened spider.

'I went up to her room one morning a few weeks ago to have a claik with her, and there she was, gone. All her stuff cleared out. I thought first she had flitted, but there was the rent she owed on the table, all in order. I looked but there was no note nor nothing. It was … I was disappointed. I thought she and me had got on well.' He sighed again, and rubbed at his knees as if they hurt. 'Of course the boy had gone too. I asked the lads in the street but they hadn't seen them go or heard aught about it. Then I called to mind that the day before that, I'd seen her talking in the street with a couple of limmers that waste their days in the village – one was injured in a quarry accident, but the other has no excuse – and I wondered if they were bothering her. I was just on the point of going over to send them packing when I realised she was asking them something, and it was all gey friendly. I had no idea what she'd been asking, but now she had gone it made me wonder, so I went and found the same lads and we had a wee chat in the inn. Them two, it's the only way to get anything out of them, is to fill them with drink. In the end it came out that she had asked them if they knew of any accommodation up in the town – I don't know why she asked them, of all people, but she did – and they did, for the uncle of one of them lived in that close and he knew fine there was a room to let. Maybe it was because she wanted somewhere cheap and thought that would be the kind of place they might know about. But if she was tight for money why did she no just tell me? I'd have let her be for the rent for a bittie.' He rubbed his great damp eyes, still not looking at Murray, but undoubtedly seeing Alicia.

'So I went up the town to see her. I asked her if her husband had deserted her, and was that why she'd had to go. She said no and we talked a wee bit, and then I left her.'

'You talked a wee bit,' said Murray gently. 'And then you left her – in what state did you leave her, tell me?'

'She wasna dead, I'll tell you that!' snapped Chisholm. 'Who could do that to a fine woman like that? She was alive and well.' His lips pursed shut as if a string had been drawn through them.

'And you parted on good terms?'

'Aye, aye. Of course we did. We was aye friendly.'

'Not quite what I heard,' said Murray. 'I heard she threw every plate in the place after you.'

Chisholm scowled.

'I suppose your Lauder saw that, too? Damn the man! Yes, we had a wee – dispute. I maybe made it too clear that I'd look after her if she needed it.'

'And how, precisely, did you make that too clear?'

'I tried to kiss her,' Chisholm admitted sulkily. 'She wasna having it.'

'Right – that sounds more like it,' said Murray kindly. 'So she turned you down, after all you'd done to find her.'

'I suppose,' muttered Chisholm.

'Then you went back – when was that?'

'Went back? I never!'

'Didn't you?'

'I was only there the once! If your Lauder says I was there again he's lying!'

'You really never went back to that close to see Alicia Argo?'

'I never did!'

Murray regarded him. Chisholm, sulky before, seemed quite outraged at the thought. And he really had seemed shocked at the news of her death. But he had the brown coat and the black hat: and he seemed to have been the man seen, not by Lauder, as far as Murray knew, but by Eppy's daughter; he was the one who had had the row with Alicia a few days before she died. Clearly there were two men, if not more, around this matter with brown coats and wide-brimmed black hats.

Murray considered: one of the other sitings had been in Potterrow, where a man of the same description had tried to find out Alicia's whereabouts from Mr. Campbell. That was unlikely to have been Chisholm either: at that point Alicia had just moved to the Dean village and Chisholm would just have met her – he would have known perfectly well where she was living. But the riot, the man who had urged the mob on to attack the police officers last Monday night – was that Chisholm? For if it was, then he had likely murdered the two men in the flat, and set the fire that had at first concealed their murders. He had drawn breath to ask another question when the front door opened behind him, and with a flutter of lace and clatter of drawing boxes, Miss Smillie entered the hall. When she saw Murray, she dropped the boxes and hurried forward, pointing her toes, to curtsey, but with a reproachful frown.

'Oh, dear, oh, dear! I am so sorry, Mr. Murray, but I am not at all pleased to see you here! Don't you know that the last time you visited us, you set poor Mr. Chisholm back a whole week? He is scarcely out of his bed now – he collapsed the minute you last left – and here you come no doubt with more bad news!'

'Miss Smillie, I must apologise. I had not realised that Mr. Chisholm was so unwell.'

Chisholm glared at Miss Smillie, but she went on quite unconcerned.

'Oh, yes, he is very delicate, you know! He needs me to look after him quite often! Well, last week after you left he was in a terrible state with what you had said about poor Mrs. Argo, and I simply had to put him to bed and sit with him until he had calmed down.'

The look on Chisholm's face amply demonstrated just how welcome this attention had been, but Murray had a feeling that Chisholm owed Miss Smillie a favour. He thought back quickly.

'That was last Monday, wasn't it, when I called?'

'That's right – a week ago today. I hope most sincerely, Mr. Murray, that you have not caused more harm!'

'Then I must go, and leave you both to revive yourselves,' said Murray politely. 'Perhaps again I can remind you of my request to let me know if you see Theodore, but otherwise allow me to summon my servant and go.'

He did go, with Walter trotting along behind him. Chisholm had not instigated the riot, either: he was quite sure that Chisholm had not even understood the significance of the alibi that Miss Smillie had just provided for him, and nor, he was sure, had she. Chisholm's only appearance in his brown coat and wide-brimmed black hat had been at the close off the High Street, where he had been to find the object of his affections, and to be told by her to leave in no uncertain terms. He had, Murray was sure, done nothing else.

A question occurred to him, and as the door was closing he stepped back and put a hand against it. Chisholm's eyes rolled, but he waited.

'When the men in the inn told you where Mrs. Argo had gone – did you notice anyone else listening?'

'Naw, why would they?' Chisholm pushed the door, then stopped. 'Wait, though: there was a couple of women outside the window, I remember now, blocking the light. They were solid, you ken? In brown gowns.'

'Had you seen them before?'

Chisholm shrugged.

'Don't think so,' he said.

But Murray had.

IV

For the second time in two weeks, Murray dressed in his funeral black the next day and made his way to Potterrow. Walter was a good servant to take to a funeral: he always seemed to look solemn. Murray thought he had rarely seen the boy smile, and yet he seemed happy enough.

Mr. Campbell's lodging house was already sombrely busy by the time they arrived, but Murray was greeted with respectful enthusiasm.

'Mr. Murray, thank you so much for coming,' said Mr. Campbell, bowing. He and Mrs. Brotherstone stood protectively over the black-clothed coffin. 'It was more than good of you to offer to pay for the funeral expenses, but she was dear to us in the while she was here, and we're honoured to do what we can for her.' He patted the coffin softly, a gesture that suddenly endeared him to Murray more than before.

'We thought it might be more proper to have the funeral from my house,' put in Mrs. Brotherstone. 'Not leaving the house of a single gentleman,' she explained, nodding to Mr. Campbell, who nodded back anxiously. 'But then we thought, where would she be most at home? And here she is.'

'Of course – and quite right, I think,' said Murray. He felt very touched that poor Alicia, dying out of reach of her family, should have been taken in like this.

'A closed coffin, of course,' Mr. Campbell went on. 'That Sergeant Clyne was very insistent on her going, and I suppose ...'

'It was only proper, Mr. Campbell,' said Mrs. Brotherstone. 'We couldn't leave her up there in the mortuary like that – not in this weather. And he said that you wanted us to make sure, Mr. Murray, that it really was her. So we did: well, I did,' she clarified, with a glance at Mr. Campbell. He had turned rather green. She moved him a little away from the coffin and made sure that Murray had some brandy, incidentally, it seemed, sliding a glass into Mr. Campbell's hand, too. 'Tell me, now, Mr. Murray: have you any more idea than you did before about who might have done this? Or where poor Theodore is, for we have had neither sight nor sound of him?'

'We put an advertisement in the *Courant*,' said Mr. Campbell, perking up. He reached over to the mantelpiece and lifted a copy of the paper, well folded. 'Here: see?'

Murray took the paper and read.

'The funeral of Mrs. Alicia Argo, wife of Lieutenant James Argo, Royal Scots, will take place on Tuesday, 13th. inst., from the lodging house of Mr. Campbell at Potterrow and to the Greyfriars kirkyard.'

'I paid for the bigger letters,' Mr. Campbell explained, 'for I thought he might well not afford a newspaper, but might chance to see it over someone's shoulder. But there's no sign of him yet.'

'I have put enquiries in progress amongst the merchant families who knew her first husband, as well as his grandparents,' Murray said. 'And the police, of course, know that he is missing. I fear, though, that if he is in hiding he might well not appear, even for his mother's funeral.'

'True, true.' They both sighed, nodding at the wickedness of the world.

'I now know who went to visit her when she was in the High Street – the landlady's daughter heard her argue with someone, and that turns out to be her landlord from the Dean Village, where she lodged after she left here. I don't believe that man had anything to do with her death, however – except that in finding out where she had gone, he might inadvertently have let other people know, too.' He had worried over this last night. He was fairly sure that it was the Browns who had overheard Chisholm's conversation with the men in the inn – and who could they have been but Johnnie Norrie and Ebb? Could the Browns have killed her? But why? What was their connexion with any of this? But he had seen them emerging from the very close the day they had found Alicia's body, though that, of course, was not the day she had died. What were they doing there?

'But how did he find out where she had gone? She was so careful not to tell people here.'

'He found the people who had recommended the flat to her. The odd thing is, they moved into it, with new money, after she died, then someone set fire to the flat and they died, too.'

'Could they have killed her?' asked Mrs. Brotherstone, 'and

then, dear forgive me, could Theodore have killed them in revenge?'

'I was there, and I didn't see any young lads – but it was dark, and that is no proof.' He considered it again. Even though Johnnie Norrie and Ebb were drunk, could a lad really have stabbed them both and set fire to the flat as they lay dying? If only he knew more about Theodore, but only Mrs. Findlay's daughter, the pianist, seemed to have known him at all. He should go back and talk to her again, if her mother allowed it.

He realised that Mr. Campbell was talking to him, and pulled himself together to listen.

'It's no an easy job you've given yourself there, Mr. Murray, but I wouldn't want you to think it's no appreciated. We'll help as well as we can, won't we, Mrs. Brotherstone?' He tentatively patted Murray on the arm, and Murray saw that he must have been looking particularly thoughtful. 'Mr. Murray, I have a wee keg of fine Highland whisky, if you would like a dram: I keep it for special visitors. You look as if you could manage a wee toddy.'

'Do you know, I think it might be the very thing,' said Murray, trying a smile.

'I'll fetch it, Mr. Campbell,' said Mrs. Brotherstone kindly. 'I ken where you have everything, and you can keep with your guests.'

The room was filling gradually as she bustled off: another hour or so and they would be ready to set off for the kirkyard, well fuelled. It was a handsome enough room, a decent house, thought Murray: Alicia's life here must have been a comfortable one. All her fine things … where were they?

'That's something I wish I knew,' he said to Mr. Campbell, as Mrs. Brotherstone hurried back with the toddy. It smelled wonderful. 'Where are all Mrs. Argo's good clothes and so on? She had the bare essentials in her flat in High Street – I'm sure the landlady has lifted some of it, but the flat was bare even when we found – her.'

'Her clothes? Her curtains and so on?' said Mr. Campbell, surprised. 'But they're here, in the attics – didn't I say?'

'Ah, no: I'm sure you didn't!'

'When she left she asked me to hold them for her until she came back. She said she had to travel light, because of the threats, she said. It seemed sensible to me,' said Mr. Campbell reasonably.

'You have that all in your attic?' came a new voice, and Murray turned to find Bessie Cordiner, décolletage heaving, at his elbow. 'All her fine clothes? Her jewellery?' Murray could not help thinking she was just about avoiding licking her lips.

'That's right, dear,' said Mrs. Brotherstone with a wary look.

'But that must be taking up an awful space up there,' said Bessie, breathless. 'I was her best friend: I should really look after it for her. Until Lieutenant Argo comes back for it – and then you can direct him to me.'

'It's really no trouble at all,' said Mr. Campbell, anxious.

'But it would be no trouble for us, either,' Bessie came in quickly. Her fingers slid down the front of her black gown, as if she could already feel the fine cloth of Alicia's clothes. 'I could keep it in my own chamber: that would be better than a dusty old attic.'

Mr. Campbell's frown deepened, not happy with this but not sure how, politely, to refuse. Murray came to the rescue.

'I'm sure that Mr. Campbell is trying not to alarm you, but it really would be much safer for you if Mrs. Argo's belongings were kept here. After all, we still don't know why she was killed: her murderer could be looking for something in those very belongings.'

'Oh, I'm sure Alicia's murderer is far away by now!' said Bessie, but there was an edge of panic in her voice – and in her eyes. Murray looked sideways at her with interest.

'Well, whoever it is they've been around for a while, asking questions. I wonder how they found where Mrs. Argo had gone?'

But Bessie had vanished, scurrying through the gathering mourners, and out of the house.

Chapter Eighteen

I

Edinburgh

Murray strode after Bessie out into the street, and quickly caught up with her. A stern hand on her shoulder spun her round.

'What's wrong, Bessie?'

'Wrong? What should be wrong? It's my best friend's funeral, and you're accusing me of all sorts!' Her big eyes sagged with self-pity.

'Your best friend?' Murray gave a short laugh. 'I don't believe you cared for her at all. Or not as much as you cared for her fine gowns, and her fine husband.'

'That's not true! You're horrible!'

'Don't be childish. Your friend has been murdered. Do you want to find out who did it, and have them brought to justice, or could it be,' he lowered his voice very slightly, 'that you killed her yourself? Jealous of all those fine gowns, or the fine husband? Well?'

Bessie glared at him, squeezing thin tears from her eyes. She sniffed.

'I did not. How could you say such a thing?' But she was more subdued, less defiant.

'You wanted her things, though.'

'Of course I did. And she would never even lend them – she wasn't half as nice as that Mrs. Brotherstone says.'

'Bessie, she was half your size! What good would the loan of one of her gowns be to you?' Murray was not in the mood for delicacy.

'She could have lent me a hair comb, or a brooch. She had

229

plenty. What use is it to her now? Or to that Theodore? Or to Mr. Argo himself?'

'So what did you do? How did you find out where she was?' He hoped that people were not staring at them, out here in their funeral black with neither hat nor bonnet. He wanted this to be uninterrupted.

'She told me, didn't she? She was my best friend. She told me she was moving to the Dean Village, because she thought someone was coming to kill her. Well, that was obviously daft, wasn't it?' She caught Murray's eye, and suddenly looked abashed. 'Well, it seemed daft at the time.'

'And then what?'

Bessie looked down at her black gown, and fiddled with her own fingers.

'A man come round looking her.'

'What like of man?'

'Not a very nice man,' said Bessie, with a shiver that seemed quite genuine. 'He had a white face, and a brown coat and a big black hat.'

'Oh, yes?' said Murray.

'I'm not making it up! He came here and he said he'd been to see Mr. Campbell but Mr. Campbell would tell him nothing but he knew I would tell him. I said how did he know and he said if I didn't,' she sniffed again, and again it seemed more heartfelt than before. 'If I didn't, I wouldn't be safe going out after dark ever again, because he knew fine where I lived and he'd be waiting for me!'

This time she burst into tears, and Murray, reluctantly, handed her his handkerchief.

'If you saw him again, would you know him?'

'I never want to see him again!'

'But if you did?'

'Oh, aye, I'd ken him fine.' She shuddered. 'He was horrible. I hated him.'

'But you told him where Alicia had gone.' He had to make sure.

'Oh, aye. I was too scared not to.'

Murray reflected, while she blew her nose earthily. It could not – or at least it made no sense that it should – be Chisholm. Was it Lauder? But why would Theodore's grandparents be looking for

Alicia? Well, whoever it had been, at least he now knew how they had traced her from Potterrow to the Dean Village. There was every likelihood that having told Chisholm where she had gone, Johnnie Norrie and Ebb could have sold their information for a few drams to any other enquirer who asked, so tracking Alicia and Theodore from the Dean Village to the grubby close off the High Street would not have been difficult. But why? And where was Theodore?

Murray sighed heavily, and abandoning Bessie in the middle of the street he returned to Alicia's funeral.

II

Belgium

George, in Brussels, thought he might as well be at a funeral. General Fry was not what he would consider congenial company.

Obtaining permission to attend the Frys' dinner had been much easier than he had expected: in fact, in the end he had not even had to ask. It transpired to his astonishment that both Major Saddler and Captain Gunn had also been invited – so had Argo, as the last of the company's officers, but his recent bereavement made his attendance inappropriate. About twenty altogether had sat down to dinner, the male guests all being army officers of ranks junior to General Fry, and the female guests for the most part the officers' wives and daughters. Only Saddler, Gunn and George were unattached, and George had confidently expected to be seated beside one of the Fry girls, Carolina or Esther. For some reason, though, he was not: Carolina, wearing the little white silk rosebuds like snowflakes in her hair, was beside Gunn, not far away but not easily accessible. Esther was even further away. By the looks of him Gunn was enjoying Carolina's company, even to the extent of indulging in a little flirtation. Gunn might not have relished large parties, but George had seen him charming ladies before. Was he jealous? He was still not sure.

He found himself between an enormously large officer's wife from Prussia, who of course spoke no English, and Mrs. Fry's elderly mother – the one, George suddenly remembered, who had revealed herself to have her ears stuffed with cotton to ward off her daughter's incessant chatter. He was not sure he had ever known her name. She seemed very tiny as he sat beside her, though he knew that when he had taken her arm to lead her into the dining room it had felt like taking hold of a sturdy piece of horse harness. He wondered what on earth they would talk about: he was sure they would have little in common. He was not left to wonder long.

'You have your eye on young Carolina, don't you?' Grandmother asked as soon as the soup plates were removed. Hers had been scraped clean. Her voice was surprisingly pleasant, light and younger than her years.

'I think,' said George with care, 'that it is too early to say.'

'But you like the look of her, nonetheless.'

George nodded. Carolina was just the kind of girl he liked the look of.

'But I have no dishonourable intentions,' he added. 'I am very far from being assured that Miss Carolina would welcome my attentions, anyway.'

'Hm,' said Grandmother, with some cynicism. 'Miss Carolina would take you quite happily, unless a better offer comes along. Tell me,' she went on, 'how did you first meet?'

George felt himself blush a little.

'Apparently we met after a supper party I had attended. Unfortunately – most regrettably – I had taken a little too much wine, and I have no very clear recollection … I hope I did nothing to offend her.'

'Is that what she says?' demanded Grandmother. 'Did she give you the impression that the pair of you were more intimate than you remembered?'

'Well, yes,' said George dismally, wiping his hands on his breeches. They seemed unaccountably damp. 'As I say, I cannot truly call to mind …'

'Oh, she's done this before, you foolish man!' said Grandmother, still keeping her voice low. 'I thought she might be up to her tricks again. She will hook you in until she decides whether or not she wants you, and then if she doesn't, she will toss you aside like an unsatisfactory tiddler. Don't touch her with a barge pole, young man: you'll find a better woman than my granddaughter, and deserve her better too, no doubt. Pass the nutmeg, if you'll be so kind.'

George did so, his jaw hanging open. He wanted to ask more, but at that moment the general conversation faded a little, just in time for Carolina's voice to carry the length of his ears.

'Oh, Captain Gunn, don't you remember? How ungallant of you! We met only a week ago and had the loveliest conversation!'

George felt himself pale, and stared bleakly down at his plate. Grandmother beside him had heard, too: she cleared her throat, not without sympathy, and to the end of the meal she kept the conversation strictly on the subject of horse breeding and racing, on which matters, it appeared, she was quite the expert. He wished he could take notes.

Shortly after the ladies left the table, a note arrived for Major Saddler and, excusing himself, he read it quickly. Then with a word to the General, he left the room.

'Something's afoot,' remarked Gunn to George.

'I hear the French really are on the move this time,' an officer commented from the other end of the table. There were murmurs, some of disbelief, some of assent.

'Which way are they coming?' asked George, trying to look as if he knew what was happening.

'Wellington says the west. He says Bonaparte will cut round to the west, cut us off from Antwerp, and push us back on Blücher.'

'That's what Wellington would do himself. I'm not sure it's what Bonaparte will do, though,' said Gunn.

'Fighting two armies at once? Even Bonaparte wouldn't do that, surely,' said George, pleased with himself.

'Wellington's just thinking out loud,' said Gunn. 'Bonaparte will cut up the middle, and try to keep us and the Prussians apart. Don't you think, sir?' he added to the Prussian officer beside him.

'He will not avoid Blücher, whatever he does,' said the Prussian soberly. 'Blücher has a hatred of Bonaparte that will not let him rest until Bonaparte is defeated.'

The conversation went on in a lacklustre way for some minutes: they had all talked it out, if not with each other, then with other officers, so many times in the last few weeks. General Fry stared at them in turn as if he thought them all fools. At last he rose.

'Shall we join the ladies, then?'

George made a face to himself. He did not know what he was going to say to Carolina after his conversation with her grandmother. Which of them was to be believed? He had reached the drawing room door with the rest of the officers when there was a scuffle at the front door, and as a servant went to open it, Saddler burst in.

'Orders have been following me around all evening,' he snapped. 'Excuse me, General. Bonaparte's on the move. Gunn, Murray, come with me. The army is going south.'

III

Edinburgh

There was no point, Murray had decided, in accusing Sangsters' manservant of murdering Alicia Argo until he had some more information. He was not even slightly sure of his ground, and going to Sangster to tell him that he vaguely suspected Lauder of murder based on the colour of his coat and a nasty feeling in his spine when he met the man was unlikely to help the process of discovering Alicia's murderer. Instead, he thought he should concentrate on trying to find Theodore. If Theodore was alive and not actually guilty, he almost certainly had good information about his mother's death. If he was dead – and Murray prayed that he was not – even the state of his corpse and where it might be hidden might tell Murray something useful.

He made sure that at Alicia's funeral, in the house and in Greyfriars kirkyard, he circulated amongst as many of the mourners as possible asking about Theodore and leaving multiple copies of his own visiting card in the hope of more information emerging later. He felt he had grown eyes in the back of his hat, for all the way from the Potterrow to the kirkyard he was as alert as he could be, watching for any small boy taking more interest in the funeral than was normal. The only one he saw was Walter, who clearly felt some ownership of the process, having been there at the finding of the body. He stood in the hall as the coffin left through Mr. Campbell's tiny front door, with his usual solemn expression, beside Jemima: the Sangsters had turned up at the last possible minute, and Mrs. Sangster settled herself in to gossip in the parlour while Sangster himself followed the coffin with a grim expression on his floury face. Murray had the impression that Sangster's eyes were as busy about the cortège as Murray's own were. Was he also looking for Theodore?

If they both looked, they looked in vain. Theodore did not appear.

When the funeral was over, Murray began to search in earnest. Over the next few days he wracked his brain to think of ways to find Theodore. Following Mr. Campbell's example, he visited all the newspaper offices and inserted an advertisement into each paper. He exhausted Walter by going to all the police offices he could think of in the city, and leaving as detailed a description as he could of the boy: he had gleaned only a few more details from Mrs. Argo's mourners, but he made sure that if a body turned up of the right kind, he would be told. He tried the coach offices, in every direction. Finally, he walked down to Leith and asked everyone he could find whether a boy of Theodore's description might have boarded a ship or a boat, possibly, but not definitely, heading for Belgium. Everywhere he left his card, or more than one, praying that one small piece of pasteboard might eventually meet someone who would connect the enquiry with a small boy, and bring him news.

Thursday morning dawned bright and cheerful, the morning air too cool yet to carry the stench of the Nor'Loch over the street to the flat. The *Courant* was delivered while Murray and the Dundases were at breakfast, and Murray asked if he might see it to confirm that they had placed his advertisement prominently. He was pleased to see they had.

'Any news?' asked Willie Jack, though he seemed more interested in his plate of eggs.

'Let's see … Bonaparte was still in Paris on the 9th., for what that's worth. They're expecting Wellington to have moved on the 13th. to go to meet him. That was the day before yesterday, wasn't it? Hm.' He reflected on George for a moment, hoping he was safe. 'Prince Alexander Berthier has fallen from a palace window in Brussels.'

'Oh, aye?' remarked Willie Jack, cynically.

'Who might he be?' asked Letitia, trying to read the social notices on the back of the paper at the same time.

'He was one of Bonaparte's generals, I think, but deserted him. Did he jump or was he pushed, though?' asked Willie Jack, not expecting an answer.

'Oh, Bonaparte!' grumbled Letitia. 'Isn't there anything about Edinburgh in there?'

'The first strawberries have arrived,' Murray told her.

'Oh, delightful! You must buy me some,' she said, giving him a smile that would have melted Bonaparte's artillery. He looked firmly back at the paper.

'Complaints about the scavengers ... Oh, here's something terribly exciting: the Wonderful Nottinghamshire Hog will be exhibited on the Mound.'

'A hog? What's wonderful about that?'

'No idea. The fact that he's come all the way from Nottinghamshire? Perhaps he drove himself in a coach and four.'

'A hog *and* a whale!' breathed Walter later, glimpsing the paper before they went out.

'And so few pennies to go around,' Murray reminded him.

'Yes, sir ...'

'If we're not doing anything else on Sunday, Walter, you may go to see your whale after morning service.'

Walter did not smile, but managed to exude a deep content that was almost as good. Murray gave a nod of satisfaction: he did not smile much these days, either.

This morning he had decided to return to the unwholesome High Street close and see what more could be found out about Theodore there. It looked unpromising. The sun, warming as it rose, coaxed new odours from the midden. There was no sign of the straw-coloured dog, but a pig had appeared, snuffling breathily through the rubbish, flapping the hens, and the old man who was apparently Johnnie Norrie's uncle sat as usual on the edge of the sunlight. Murray stepped carefully over to him.

'Good day to you.'

The man's gaze did not move, nor did any twitch of his face or hands show that he had heard at all.

'You're Johnnie Norrie's uncle, are you not?'

The man's milky eyes swivelled around and then, inaccurately, wandered in the direction of Murray's face. He mashed his mouth for a moment, heavy jaw levering up and down.

'You're no wi' them weemin, are ye?' he managed, his breath redolent of some long-consumed ale and tobacco. Murray tried not to choke.

'Which women?' he asked. 'Eppy and her daughter?'

There was more lip movement, as if the man had to warm up before speech was possible.

'Naw, no Eppy nor the lass. They weemin in the brown. They wouldna leave me be, wi' all their questions. Can a body no sit in peace?'

'Aye, indeed,' Murray agreed, with sympathy. 'Were you here the night of the fire?'

Tears easily flooded his old eyes.

'Aye, aye. But no out here. I was up my stair. I ha' a flat of my own, ken,' he added proudly.

'So you saw nothing?'

'No' a thing at all.' The man's sorrow was genuine. 'I'd be glad enough if I could tell the pollis a'thing about what happened, but I canna at all. I canna at all,' he added, sadly.

'The women in brown – what were they asking you?'

'They weemin? They wanted to know about that lassie that died, ken?'

'Aye,' agreed Murray. 'What did they want to know?'

'They wanted to know where she lived. They said they was friends of hers. I didna like the look of them: they looked like the kind of bodies would come in and clean your flat wi'out asking, and tell you what to eat.'

'I know what you mean. So did you tell them anything?'

'I did not. I tellt you, I didna like them. Anyway, Johnnie says I wasna to tell a'body where she was.'

'Did he say why?'

'Naw, he didna. Johnnie thought I was stupid, like, ken?'

'Did he, indeed? I think he was wrong there.' Murray was delighted not to have made the same mistake.

'Aye, aye!' agreed the old man, with a creaking laugh.

'Did you know the lassie's son? A young lad, ten or twelve.'

'Oh, aye, aye, I did. He'd play out here a few days. A decent wee lad, no harm in him.'

'Have you seen him since the police came and took the lassie's body away?'

'Naw, I havena. I dinna see so good these days,' he added sadly.

'If you do see him, will you let me know? I want to make sure he's safe.'

'That's what those weemin in the brown said, an' all,' said the old man, his face darkening again.

'In that case,' said Murray, 'give him the choice himself. Here's my card: if you see the lad, give it to him and he can decide.'

The man thought for a moment.

'Aye, aye. That'd do no harm to the lad. But I havena seen him. I'm feart they got him too: killed him like the way they killed the lassie.'

'And who do you think 'they' are?'

The man did not hesitate.

'The weemin,' he said definitely. 'The weemin in the brown.'

IV

Murray could hear Eppy screaming at her daughter even as he left the close: it seemed unappealing to try to speak with her again today. Instead he paused at the mouth of the close, thought for a moment, then turned and climbed towards the Castle. In a few strides he had reached the stair where the Findlays had held their crowded supper party over a week ago. He knocked.

Mrs. Findlay seemed delighted to stop her household duties to sit and have a cup of tea with him. The parlour was as neat and decent as he remembered, and he hoped that he had not carried in with him any of the miasma of the close down the street. When he explained what he wanted, she was perfectly happy to help, and left him for a moment, returning with her daughter Anna.

'Mr. Brewster was asking the very same thing on Sunday, you know: I'm delighted that people are looking for poor Theodore. I had no idea that that poor girl was John Sangster's widow, the very woman we were telling you of.'

'But Anna actually played with Theodore: didn't you?' Murray asked the girl, who had taken the opportunity to grab a slice of teacake and stuff it into her mouth. They had to wait a moment while she chewed, pink in the face.

'I'm no sure I played with him,' she said at last, with only a small spray of crumbs.

'Anna! That's terrible!' said her mother, flapping a napkin around her.

'We were sort of friends,' Anna went on, unconcerned. 'I liked him. Most of the boys round here are a bit wild. He was happy to talk, not just to try and stuff feathers down the back of your neck or empty a cludgie over your head.'

'I can see he might have had some appeal,' agreed Murray drily. 'What did you talk about? What were his interests?'

'He wanted to be a soldier like his stepfather, only he always called him his father,' said Anna.

'They got on well, then?'

'Very well, I'd say,' said Anna, sensibly. 'All of them. He was kind to his mother, too, doing messages for her and such. She was anxious about him, I think, but he didn't push against that like most boys – he'd say 'Oh, she'll be worried about me, I'd better get home.'

'A decent lad, as you say. So how did you spend your time together?'

'We sometimes watched the soldiers at the Castle – as I say, he was determined he was off into uniform as soon as he was old enough for his mother to let him. And we'd go out for walks with his dog. He was gey fond of his dog.'

'His dog?' This was news to Murray. 'What kind of dog?'

'Oh, I'd be hard put to tell you! It wasna big, and it wasna small, and it was friendly like.'

'That's a start! What colour was it?'

'Yellowish – well, I suppose you'd say it was straw-coloured.'

V

Belgium

The previous night, the company, trailing their baggage train behind them, had marched south according to orders, not entirely sure where they were going or what they could expect when they arrived. They had been given a place to camp south of Brussels and waited, as only soldiers know how to do. Card games were resumed, carvings were brought out of knapsacks and whittled, arguments came and went like a quiet tide. The women, not settled enough for much domesticity, took out mending and one or two lit fires. Even when word came that battle had been engaged somewhere ahead of them, the officers were set more on their mettle than the men, twitching at their horses' reins, trying to peer along the road to the south, anxiously awaiting despatches. The day passed painfully slowly, in a state of uncertain tension: in the distance they could hear guns, and some dwelt fretfully on family left behind in Brussels, while others itched to be in on the action.

At dusk, a few groups of men began to trickle back towards their lines, and carts brought the wounded, and worse. A bedraggled officer walked his horse past the lines: George recognised the uniform of the 42nd. Regiment, and hoped for information from a fellow Scot.

'Hey there! Any news?'

The man turned towards him, clearly grateful for the excuse to stop for a moment. George held out his whisky flask and the man seized it with enthusiasm, pouring spirit past his prominent front teeth and handing the flask back with a grin.

'That was most welcome!'

'Any news?'

'Just come from Quatre Bras – a crossroads, you know, on the road to Charleroi. We were crushed by Ney and hopelessly outnumbered. Not good, sir, not good. But Ney moved along like a tortoise – I nearly felt like going up to the man and telling him to get move on! Then praise the Lord, Wellington turned up. Still it was cannonade, sharpshooters like bees, and a cavalry charge, then the same again, over and over. Any more of that whisky, sir?'

'Here – your need is greater than mine,' said George, generously.

'I don't know where Wellington was keeping his reinforcements but they kept coming, like minor miracles. I think the Netherlanders had a panic: there was one point when they seemed to be everywhere, but heading in entirely the wrong direction.'

'Wellington's right not to trust them, then – that's interesting. If not entirely reassuring,' George remarked. The young officer grinned.

'Well, there aren't so many of them now. I swear I saw Wellington leap the entire 92nd. Regiment at one point to avoid them – I think his horse sprouted wings! But the bloody Dutchmen ran into a supply train as well and we've lost a good deal of food: I passed them on my way back, broken carts and stuff all over the road. Silly boys – which is all they are, really. But it didn't stop us – we were hiding in the crops and you should have seen the French stop when we appeared! I think they'd never seen the like. They'll not be invading Fife any time soon,' he added proudly. He took another long swallow of whisky, and went on with the glint in his eye of an enthusiast. 'Well, around five o'clock things were a touch hot and I thought the 28th were going under, but Picton rallied them tremendously. We were just about holding them when more Brunswickers turned up looking like a great funeral procession with their black and their death's heads, and the Guards were with them, late as ever, in time to tidy up the woods nearby and make sure there were no lingering Frenchies. Ney just seemed to lose heart then, and though a few of our cavalry appeared there was really nothing much left for them to do.'

'So it was a victory, then?' asked George with delight, mixed with a mild disappointment that he had missed the action. The young officer considered for an uncomfortable moment, sucking on his large teeth.

'I'd put it down as a draw, if I was honest,' he said at last.

'And the Prussians? Did they join in?'

'I heard tell they were fighting Grouchy somewhere nearby. No idea how it went, though.' He contemplated his horse, and gave it an absent rub on the shoulder. 'And I'd better get on, for this old fellow needs a stable, and I need a new horse. To whom am I indebted? For I'd say you're a Fifer like me.'

'George Murray, of the Royal Scots,' said George, with a bow.

'Robert Scoggie, at your service, sir. I hope we meet again under happier circumstances.'

George watched him leave, easing his horse up the hill to the Brussels road. A draw? Then there would still be a chance to fight Bonaparte. He hoped they were up to it.

Chapter Nineteen

Edinburgh

I

The thought of putting his feet back into his boots on Friday morning was a painful one, but he just about managed it. He felt slightly guilty when he noticed how carefully Walter was also walking, seeing how he steered his way to the softest parts of the carpets. But when Murray enquired of the maid, there had been no responses to his widespread cards and requests, and during the night he had come up with another list of possible places where Theodore might have found himself, or taken refuge.

'Are you on the hunt again?' asked Willie Jack when Murray appeared at the breakfast table. He set down his paper, always preferring human company to written words. There was no sign of Letitia. 'I'd have thought you would have exhausted every possible possibility this week. Surely the boy must have left the town, if you haven't managed to find him by now!'

'I'm worried about him, Willie Jack,' said Murray seriously. 'Yes, maybe he has gone to find his father on the Continent – and I've left word all around the harbour and at the coach offices, but even then he might have left on foot – but if he hasn't, then where could he be? And is he safe? And what does he know about his mother's death?'

'Oh,' said Willie Jack, 'it's all too complicated for me. I don't know how you manage to keep all these ideas in your head at the same time. It's completely impossible.' He gave his attention to his eggs, with a look of mock horror on his face.

'Well, it has to be done,' said Murray, though there was no

reason, he considered, why he should not avail himself of a decent breakfast first.

'Well, if you have any time this afternoon,' said Willie Jack, pausing to blow his nose, 'Letitia and I are going to see how that new place is on Calton Hill – the one that was advertising in the *Courant*. They sell ices and so on. No alcoholic liquors, but I'm told the buns are fine. Care to join us?'

'If I'm done, I might, thanks. Don't count on me, though: I plan to visit every church in the town today, and then I'll go where the inspiration takes me, after that.'

'You'll exhaust yourself,' said Willie Jack sensibly. It was not a method he often used himself. 'Then what use will you be to Theodore or his papa? You said yourself: the boy's probably gone to join his father, and when he arrives George will probably let you know, if he remembers. You said the close they lived in was a rough place, and there was nothing left in her flat. What more likely than that robbers burst in, killed her and stole all her things? Why on earth would anyone else have bothered?'

'But her things weren't there.'

'That's what I mean – the robbers robbed her,' said Willie Jack slowly, as if to a dim child.

'No, I mean I found out that her things were never there. She never took them with her from the Potterrow lodgings.'

'Then is the whole thing just a story? She was robbed in the Potterrow, her landlord there, or landlady, whichever it might be, has taken the things and took her body away to the High Street close where no one would bat an eyelid at a murdered woman? No one but you, of course,' he added, with a sigh. For a brief moment, Murray toyed with this idea: Mr. Campbell and Mrs. Brotherstone in connivance over Alicia's murder. But it seemed ridiculous: how many false trails would they have had to lay for the people in the Dean Village and the neighbours in the close all to contribute their parts of Alicia's story?

'Well,' he said, draining his coffee canister, 'I must make a start, if Walter can face it. I'm off to the High Kirk to start with. Wish me luck!'

'Oh, good luck, good luck,' said Willie Jack with a grumpiness that was only half assumed. 'I hope we'll see you on Calton Hill later. And I hope you find your lad, alive and well. And I hope you can get this matter over with soon, and spend some time enjoying yourself for a change.'

II

The High Kirk of St. Giles rose impressively from the middle of the Lawnmarket, or it would have done, if it had not been surrounded by market stalls, ruins and crowds. Murray had always liked its crown spire, so distinctive amongst the town churches, but he did not often attend church here, preferring Greyfriars and the New Town's St. George's when he was in Edinburgh. It might have been something to do with the High Kirk being so far up the hill.

He was not expecting to find Theodore at the church, but he did hold out hope of finding information. If Theodore had fled, he might have taken shelter in the church, and it was a large building: he might just still be there. If he had fled and not hidden in the church, he might still have applied to the kirk session or the minister for some poor relief, or for help to find a place to hide.

The interior was vast and shadowy, high whale-boned into the darkness above. He was not quite sure where to look for the beadle, but he had a plan: he was going to stand in the middle of the church looking prosperous, and wait for an approach. A church like the High Kirk was always looking for charitable donations – and so were beadles. It worked: he had been there for about a minute and a half when a middle-aged man in a black gown limped hurriedly up to him, and asked if he could help.

He did make a contribution to both the church and the beadle, but it was for the man's time and courtesy only, not for any information. The same thing happened down the spine of the long Castle Hill at the Canongate, though less grandly, and at Mr. Alison's Episcopal Chapel in the Cowgate (it had not occurred to Murray to ask anyone if Alicia had belonged to the established Kirk), then again at Greyfriars Kirk, where Alicia's grave sank quietly in the kirkyard, waiting for a headstone. There, however, the minister, knowing Murray well, had a suggestion.

'What about the poorhouse?' he asked.

So before Murray could return across the North Bridge to interrogate the clergy at the West Kirk or at St. George's, he took

Walter to the poorhouse, not far from Greyfriars in Port Bristo.

'It's the biggest building I've ever seen!' Walter gasped, when he realised that the poorhouse was all one building, and not another tenement.

'We have close to seven hundred here,' said the warden, as thin as his charges, 'and close to two hundred of those are bairns. Are you sure he came here?'

'No,' said Murray, but a small donation encouraged the warden to have a think through his more recent arrivals and reassure Murray that no, none of them was likely to be Theodore.

'He'd have had to be recommended by a minister: if he hadna, I'd have remembered anyway. Try St. Mary's poorhouse, though, sir: he might have got that far. Hey, Rabbie, show this gentleman out the now.'

Murray was ready to go, though Rabbie was slow to do as he was bid, due to his being on crutches. It gave Murray time to think before they reached the gate: he thought first of Johnnie Norrie with his one leg, and then had another idea about where to look for Theodore.

'Infirmary Street next, Walter,' he said, and turned back towards Newington.

The hospital lay off the South Bridge, another mighty building though less conveniently situated, cramped and awkward. Inside it was crowded: the population of Edinburgh had outgrown it even in the fifty years since it was built. Amongst the patients were the old and infirm, the broken and the bulging with abcesses and swellings of various sorts. There were some boys in the men's ward, but none met the description Murray had of Theodore, and all but one had been in the hospital since before Alicia's death. Murray was sure he would have heard, at least from young Anna Findlay, if Theodore had been admitted to hospital. The one that had not been in for so long was only five, and as black-haired as the cows in the Letho fields. The superintendent, however, who had rigorously paraded all the sick children in front of Murray (in return, eventually, for a donation to hospital funds), suggested that Murray should try the orphanage below Shakespeare Square. With a sigh, Murray headed down North Bridge, with Walter trotting behind.

The orphanage was a place Walter did not like at all: the buildings were small, old and decrepit, hustled on either side by grander, modern introductions but never quite enough to improve itself. Murray could sense Walter's tension as they entered the gates, drawing himself away from the orphans as if their condition might be contagious.

The yard was full of children as was to be expected. When Murray and Walter arrived, they were hurtling about the place and shouting as if there was a prize for the loudest: they had just finished a midday meal of broth, and the smell lingered, insidious and greasy. Nevertheless the children looked no worse than many he had seen in the old town, and better than some: Eppy's grandchildren sprang to mind. At least the orphans led a well-regulated life here, and no one forgot to feed them, or spent the money on spirits before food was bought.

The warden greeted Murray with eager chatter, thanked him for his generous donation (Murray thought he would be reduced to writing promissory notes by the end of the day), denied seeing anyone that could be Theodore, and did his best to persuade Murray to take on at least three small children as servants in training. Murray reluctantly declined. Walter stuck very close to him as the gates were opened and closed again behind them: he was not taking the chance of being shut in, at any price.

Then it was down Leith Wynd to St. Mary's poorhouse, if anything more dilapidated than the orphanage, and from there into the refreshing salubriousness of the New Town and its few select churches. At the west end, they finished up with the West Kirk opposite the Dundases' flat, where they had just as much success as anywhere else. Outside in the street again, Murray pulled out his watch, opened it, and sighed. He looked about him.

'Can you think of anywhere else to look, Walter? If it were you, your father away, and your mother dead, where would you go?'

'I'd go to my auntie's,' said Walter at once. Murray realised he must have been dwelling on it, looking for a missing boy the same age as himself. 'She's in the village. And if there was any fearsome body after me, she'd soon give them laldy.' He reflected for a moment. 'If she wasna there, I'd go to my other auntie, but to be honest, she's no so handy wi' her fists. In a fight, I'd be on the side of Auntie Grisel every time, sir.'

'I see,' said Murray. 'I'll bear it in mind. But failing that – and we can't find that Theodore has any living relatives apart from the

Sangsters – where would you go, do you think?'

'That's a hard one,' Walter agreed. 'The kirk, aye – supposing I couldna go to Mr. Robbins, of course, or Mrs. Robbins. But as you say, Theodore didna have them, either.'

'No. Poor Theodore,' said Murray. 'And we've tried all the churches I can think of. He hasn't gone to his grandparents, he hasn't gone to his old neighbours. He hasn't been seen on a coach or a boat. Next I suppose I'll have to try the roads out of Edinburgh one by one and see if anyone has seen him.'

'Not today, though, sir,' said Walter, with a plea in his voice. Murray looked down at him: he looked pale and tired. He patted the boy on the shoulder.

'No, not today. It's time for a rest for both of us. You go on back to the flat, and I'll go and meet the Dundases on Calton Hill.'

The kiosk on Calton Hill was wooden and new, and gave the impression of only ever intending to be temporary. Inside, though, it had been pleasingly adorned with flowers and little tea tables, and the view down over Prince's Street took the eye, glittering prettily in the sunshine. It was hard to miss Letitia, seated abundantly at a table near the door, and he did not know whether to be thrilled or embarrassed when she called him over with her deep, rich voice and every other man in the room eyed him enviously.

'Hello,' he said, taking a seat with his back to the room. 'Where's Willie Jack? Late?'

'No, you are, Mr. Murray! Willie Jack had to go, so I'm afraid you'll have to be my escort for the afternoon. The ices are delicious, by the way.' She took another spoonful from the dish in front of her, and licked her lips. Murray looked quickly at the wall behind her.

'I think I'll have one, then,' he said, as soon as the serving girl arrived. 'It's a warm day.' The girl nodded and fetched an ice from a lead crate on a little table. It was indeed very refreshing, though a little over sugared.

'What have you been up to, then?'

'Oh, still searching,' said Murray. 'No luck, though.'

'And what about the murderer?' Letitia lowered her voice luxuriously. 'Have you found him yet?'

'It might not be a man, you know,' said Murray. 'I've met – well, it's probably not a subject to dwell on, but I have met more than one female murderer.' And one who had done him more damage than any, he thought, bitterly.

'Female murderers? How astonishing! Willie Jack mentioned something of the kind, but I don't think it was something he wanted to talk about,' she added sadly.

'Then perhaps we should change the subject,' said Murray, uncomfortable for himself and his friend. Letitia glanced up at him, and suddenly laid a hand on his arm.

'Oh, I have upset you, Mr. Murray! How could I do such a thing – how unkind and stupid I am!'

'Not at all – you could not have known,' mumbled Murray, acutely aware of her touch. He tried not to look at her, but felt himself drawn like a dog on a lead to stare at her face. She smiled.

'Now, how can I make up for my foolishness?' she asked. Her lips were lush, with just a fleck of ice which he longed to touch away. He took a deep breath, conscious that she saw him do it and was amused. He tried to say something, failed, swallowed, and tried again – and at that moment Walter appeared, in the form of a weary-footed rescuer.

'Mr. Murray, sir, there was a message for you, and Mr. Dundas said to run along with it in case it was urgent.'

'Oh, Walter, your poor feet!' said Murray, unusually well-disposed towards the boy. 'Let me see the message. Mrs. Dundas, will you excuse me? This may indeed be urgent.'

'Of course.' She smiled again and withdrew her hand, slowly. Murray concentrated on opening the note without dropping it.

'Oh!' he said when he read the contents. 'I must indeed go, I'm afraid. Walter will escort you back home, if you wish – Walter, you may go home in any case. I must go down to the harbour.' He rose, and bowed to Letitia. 'Excuse me – this may be the answer.' He hurried out of the kiosk, breathing the fresh air, and almost ran down the hill. In his rush he glimpsed, but did not quite take in, a pair of solid brown figures seated on an old wall near the kiosk. He had news.

III

The news was not what he had hoped. The harbourmaster had seen a young lad going from ship to ship looking for a job as a cabin boy, and had secured him in his office pending Murray's arrival. Murray was delighted that the harbourmaster had remembered to contact him, but the boy turned out to be a shoemaker's apprentice from Portobello whose master was the sort who instructed with a stick. Murray was sympathetic, but the boy had to be sent back, and Theodore was still missing. With some misgivings, therefore, both about the boy and about what might await him at the Dundases', he headed back for Prince's Street, feet aching.

He found that the Dundases had both gone out, to his relief, and that Walter was being cosseted by the maid in the kitchen. He chose not to disturb him, but instead the maid brought him a note herself.

'Young Walter says to tell you at least he didna lose this one,' she said, cautiously, not sure how the guest would take it, but Murray gave a short laugh and let it pass. Walter seemed like a boy unlikely to be bent by servitude.

This time the note was from Mr. Sangster, asking if Murray would do him the honour to attend on him the next day. At least he didn't want to see him this evening, Murray thought with gratitude, easing his feet out of his boots and slipping them, with a scowl, into a bath of mustard. Pain and bliss combined, and for a little while he allowed himself to stop thinking about Theodore and Alicia, and simply to unwind.

IV

Both he and Walter were much refreshed in the morning, though Walter did mention Murray's promise to let him have some time to himself on the Sunday, making sure that Murray had not forgotten. The day was fine again and the Dundases were not up, having returned late the previous night with some hilarity. Murray had already been in bed for a while, and had felt no need to go and greet them.

At the narrow house in the Water of Leith, young Jemima answered the door and gave Walter a slight smile while curtseying unsteadily to Murray.

'We're here to see Mr. Sangster, Jemima,' said Murray, quietly. 'Is he at home?'

'I'll find out, sir,' said Jemima, stepping back to let them in and turning away.

'Wait – can you tell me something? Three weeks ago, that weekend around the 25th. May or thereabouts - what were the family doing?'

'The last Friday of May, sir? I have no notion. I started here on the Monday after that, sir.'

'Oh! I had no idea you were so new. You seem to be settling in well.'

'Mr. Murray! What a lovely surprise!' Mrs. Sangster's voice came from the stairway, and Murray bowed to her.

'Mr. Sangster asked me to call, madam. Is he at home?'

'Oh, he's over at the mill.' She crossed the hall to them, staring at Walter. 'Your devoted servant, isn't he? He seems to go everywhere with you. I wonder who he is? The son of some faithful retainer, perhaps?'

She reached towards Walter as if to pat his head, then stroked his chestnut hair in a way Murray did not much like.

'The grandson, actually,' he said quickly. 'He's very promising. Walter, perhaps you could go and see if that dog was still following us?' But Walter seemed to be glued to the floor, face motionless.

'Jemima, fetch Mr. Lauder,' said Mrs. Sangster after a moment. Jemima skipped off sharply. Mrs. Sangster lifted Walter's chin and stared into his face. Murray was baffled: good manners would have allowed him to tell a man mishandling his maid to back off, but a woman annoying his lad in that woman's house – that was more awkward. 'Perhaps,' said Mrs. Sangster into the silence, 'perhaps you should leave Walter here with me while you go to the mill? It's a messy, noisy place, and he looks so neat and smart!'

Murray saw, as he was sure Mrs. Sangster did too, that Walter seemed to be holding his breath, trying not to move.

'I'm afraid I cannot allow Walter the luxury of waiting here, Mrs. Sangster,' he said, and saw Walter sag a little. 'I need his services much of the time.'

The door to the back hallways, the maze where Murray had lost himself the afternoon of the picnic, opened again, and Lauder appeared like a poisonous snake. Murray was ready for him this time, but he still shivered.

'Lauder, take Mr. Murray – and his boy – over to the mill, please, to meet Mr. Sangster. Apparently he summoned them,' she added, with a note of disapproval, though whether for her husband or the summons it was hard to tell.

'Aye, ma'am,' said Lauder. 'This way, sir.'

Murray laid a proprietorial hand on Walter's shoulder, and pushed him out of the door first.

'You will come back for tea, won't you, Mr. Murray?' called Mrs. Sangster, her rosy face friendly and bright in the little hallway.

'I'd be delighted, madam,' Murray said, bowing, and hoping he might find an excuse not to.

The mill in question, Murray realised as they turned down the street towards the river, was the great modern block on the other side, poised on the edge of the Water of Leith like a brick contemplating a swim. The great stone walls rose unadorned except for multiple windows, and at its base the gently rotating tether of its great wooden wheel bound the building irrevocably to land and water both. He glanced at Lauder. Even in apparent repose, the man's expression gave him pause, but he had to ask.

'Lauder, can you remember back three weeks, the last Friday and Saturday in May?'

'I suppose I can, sir.'

'Can you remember what the family were doing?'

'That Friday and Saturday, sir?'

'And maybe the Sunday, too.'

'Oh, aye.' Lauder nodded. Gentlefolk were allowed to ask strange questions, his shrug seemed to say. 'Well, the master would have been at the mill the Friday and Saturday. I remember he was working late there both nights, for there were men short. The Sabbath they were all at the West Kirk the best part of the day, sir, and back here for a cold dinner.'

'What about Mrs. Sangster?' Murray asked.

'As to the Sabbath, she was with the master and me, sir. As to the Friday and the Saturday, I cannot call to mind.'

'Not at all?'

'Not at all.' Lauder was quite definite, and worryingly incurious. Murray tried to think of anything else to ask, but he was sure Lauder would tell his own stories. They reached the river.

'Ca' canny here, sir,' said Lauder abruptly. 'This wee bridge is a grand shortcut, but the ropes holding it have been known to give way. Even as late as this week, would you believe.' He met Murray's eye with winning frankness, showing every concern for his welfare, and Murray did not believe it at all. Lauder at least knew that Murray had gone into the river on Monday night, even if it was not his own hands that had loosened the ropes – and Murray would not have put that past him, either. Murray made Walter go first so he could keep an eye on him, but they passed over the bridge dry, this time, and in a moment were climbing the cobbles on the other side to the door of the great mill. Sangster, solid as a well-packed flour sack, was just on his way out.

'I thought I saw you over the other side,' he said with a smile and a bow. 'I was just coming to meet you.'

'Lauder was kind enough to show us the way. This is an impressive building, sir! I had seen it some years ago, but had never been this close. It's like a cliff!'

'Oh, would you like to see something of the inside, then, Mr. Murray? I should be proud to show you.'

He led the way back inside. Walter stayed close to Murray, but Lauder unexpectedly followed them in, strolling along behind them as if on a tour of inspection. It made Walter keep all the closer.

Sangster showed them around efficiently. He clearly had a very sound idea of the workings of his kingdom, and was not just a gentrified merchant who consorted only with his customers. Around the mill, the men working at the various processes nodded respectfully to him, though not, Murray thought, with any sense of liking.

'The power of the mill, as you no doubt know,' he explained, 'first of all lifts the heavy sacks of grain all the way up to the top floor. See: the sacks are lifted indoors: in less modern mills they are not so protected from the weather, so we have less wastage in mouldy grain.'

'It's a long way up!' Murray remarked, peering after a sack as it soared upwards to some distant destination.

'We'll follow,' said Sangster, and they creaked up a series of flights of sturdy wooden stairs with open treads. Through the gaps, Murray could see another sack of grain rising, and another. On the top floor, the sacks were being unhooked by two men and hauled across the floor to another pair of hooks around eye height. The wide, high-ceilinged room was airy and well lit, with a great number of windows on each side. Even from the middle of the room Murray could make out a fine view of trees and hills up stream, and buildings across the river, including the roof, he thought, of Sangster's own house. Sangster saw him looking.

'Aye, the tallest building around here,' he said. 'It took some building, I can tell you! There were those who wouldn't credit it, but here it is – a fine legacy,' he added, half to himself. 'Now, this arrangement of hooks pulls the sacks up by their ends and turns them over, so they open down this hopper.' He pointed, just as one of the men tugged the tie off the neck of the sack and the grains fistled their way back down, rattling into the broad-mouthed wooden box that directed them downstairs again.

'The fall from all this height helps, of course: gravity brings the grain down fast,' said Sangster knowledgeably. 'Back down, and we'll see where they go next.'

On the floor below, cordoned off from the stairs by a new wooden partition, were two sets of great mill stones, turning endlessly with a terrific grumble and scrape. Above one set, grain was pouring out of a wooden channel which was presumably the lower half of the one they had seen above, and feeding into the turning stones. They moved slowly, never pausing, while the grain poured and flecks of flour and husk settled in the feather pattern of the stones. Sangster reached out a careful finger and let it rest for a moment on the turning outside edge of a stone.

'You need to be awful canny with these, Mr. Murray. You can see how it would be easy enough to lose a finger in there.'

'Hmm,' said Murray, impressed. He looked around the stones, where massive cogwheels spun solemnly, their gears clicking and clacking. It was like stepping into the pocket watch of a giant. 'All this is run by the millwheel?'

'Aye, that's right. Powerful stuff, water, when you can harness it.'

And more powerful when you cannot, thought Murray, though he tried to shake the memory again.

'So the grain goes in here, and the stones grind – where does the flour come out, then?'

'Down again!' Sangster cried happily, and led them to the stairs. Back on the ground floor, he showed them where the fresh flour poured smoothly out into sacks held by men who were white with it, threequarters composed of flour themselves from eating and breathing it from morning to night.

'It looks fine quality,' said Murray.

'It's the very best,' said Sangster, still having to speak loudly over the noise of the stones upstairs. 'No foreign bodies in here. And we can keep that going day after day, up to an enormous capacity. The daily grind, you might say!' he said, with the air of one who has found a fresh audience for a very old joke. Murray smiled politely.

'Thank you very much for showing me around,' he said, 'but I mustn't take up too much of your time, with you so busy. You wanted to see me, I think?'

Sangster nodded apologetically, and drew Murray back out into the cleaner outside air.

'I'm sorry to summon you like that,' he said, 'but I find it hard to get away from here without – on my own, and I was eager to find out if you had had any word of my grandson.'

'I'm sorry to say I have not,' said Murray, 'though not for want of trying, I think. I have walked most of Edinburgh several times in the last few days, talking to people, leaving word here, there and everywhere. On Monday I plan to ride along some of the roads leading south, to see if anyone saw him on foot or on a cart, perhaps.'

'You think he has left Edinburgh?' Mr. Sangster looked puzzled.

'There is some notion that he might have gone to join his father in the army.'

The puzzled frown deepened, before Sangster said,

'Oh! His stepfather.'

'I beg your pardon, yes. Apparently they were close, and Theodore had some ambition to join the army.'

'Well; well,' said Sangster thoughtfully. 'I could help you there: I have a number of carters who go about the outskirts of the city and to the surrounding villages. Why did I not think of it before? I can send messages with them!'

'That would be very helpful, sir,' said Murray, pleased to be saved another day or two in fruitless searching.

'Come, I'm sure Mrs. Sangster would like to offer you a cup of tea, to fortify you in all your work on our behalf,' Sangster said heartily. He brushed off his floury gloves, and took his hat from a peg inside the door of the mill. They followed him back across the narrow wooden bridge with more confidence, this time, and up the cobbled hill on the other side to the Sangsters' front door. Just as they were disappearing inside, Murray was sure he saw two well upholstered brown behouchies striding further up the hill, away from the house. Perhaps he was going mad, he thought: he was seeing the Browns everywhere.

'Ah, you came back, Mr. Murray! I was sure you would!' cried Mrs. Sangster, as Walter darted off towards the kitchen. Murray could only imagine how he felt, having to choose between Lauder's ferocity and the blandishments of Mrs. Sangster. He himself followed the lady of the house upstairs to the same parlour as before, and Mr. Sangster excused himself for a moment to wash the flour off his face. Murray decided to seize his chance.

'Mrs. Sangster, this may seem an odd question, but do you know what you were doing on the last Friday of May? Or the following couple of days?'

Mrs. Sangster, seating herself at the tea urn, looked up at him with a surprised smile.

'Mr. Murray,' she said sweetly, 'I probably do. Does your wife, the lovely Lady Agostinella, know what you are doing with Mrs. Dundas? Or does Mr. Dundas know what you are doing with his wife?'

Chapter Twenty

Belgium

I

'What are we doing now?' Argo managed to sound like a petulant child, and George drew a deep breath before responding. After all, this was Argo's first campaign, and he might not have had the benefit, as George had, of being forced to read the *Iliad* as a child: for one glorious day in battle, you paid with ten years in tents, slogging back and forth with, usually, no very clear notion of where you were going, or why.

The seventeenth of June had dawned heavily where they were camped outside Quatre Bras, and as far as Pontius Pilate's Bodyguard were concerned, Quatre Bras was still just a name, a name, moreover, of a place where they had not been given the chance to fight. That the French were still nearby you could sense from the alertness of the sentries and, of course, the distant smell of cooking. The French never let a battlefield get in the way of a good breakfast.

'We're waiting to be served,' said George flippantly.

'We're waiting for orders,' Gunn explained at last. 'I gather the battle yesterday was a draw, so Wellington may well want us to finish the Frenchies off this morning. It looks as if we might be on the point of ending all this.' He fingered his scar thoughtfully.

Argo stood beside George and stared off towards the French lines, with a mixture of emotions wandering over his face. To come this far and only to fight at the very end: that would be frustrating. George had been worried that Argo might be too keen to fight, too eager to rush and join his dead wife, but so far he had seen no sign of it. Argo seemed no more doomladen than any young officer facing battle for the first time – and that was quite enough to deal with.

'Aye, gentlemen, I wouldna want to be in Marshal Ney's boots this morn,' remarked Sergeant Lamb, coming up behind them. He pointed his clay pipe in the direction of the French lines. 'The wee man'll no be pleased he didna finish off our lot yesterday.'

'What do you think will happen now?' asked George. Lamb was a veteran of the second battalion, and had fought in Egypt, so he regarded Bonaparte as a boyhood friend of the worst sort.

'Aye, well, I doubt we'll attack just now. It's no a very good position, and I think the Duke has other ideas about where we might be when we attack. You ken what he's like: he was here a year ago laying out the land for this very moment.'

'A year ago!' exclaimed Argo.

'Aye, the Duke's aye prepared.'

'Do you mean he's fortified somewhere ready?' asked Argo. Lamb smiled kindly.

'No, laddie! That would be as good as putting up a sign and saying "Here, Your Emperorness, we'd like to fight here, please!" No, but the Duke'll have his notions, and no doubt they'll be sound ones.' Gunn and George nodded: they too had a deep and abiding faith in Wellington.

'I wonder where the Prussians are?' George asked. 'Fellow I met yesterday said there was no sign of them at the battle.'

'I heard they were engaged over there somewhere – Ligny, or the like,' said Gunn, nodding to the east on their left.

From where they stood, they had a good view of the chaussée pavée, the well-made road that led from Brussels to Charleroi, and a little of the road that crossed it there that linked Nivelles and Namur – George knew the map well, but only now was he painting in the pictures of the places on it. A horseman in the distance hurried from the direction of Namur – and Ligny - towards the crossroads. George peered hard.

'A staff officer … ooh, lovely horse. Tall, dark-haired, I think … Oh, it's Sir Alexander,' he said in dismay, thinking immediately of Gunn, but Sir Alexander had his mind very clearly on more weighty matters than the peculiar behaviour of Royal Scots officers at inns. He disappeared towards the hut, swiftly constructed of branches, where they all knew Wellington had spent the latter part of the night. Gunn, when George glanced at him, was watching intently.

'Something's not quite right, I think,' George said, turning his attention back to Sir Alexander. Argo twitched.

'Aye,' said Lamb, taking a suck on his pipe, 'nae doubt we'll all be killed. Well, I must see to the men.'

Argo, his jaw dropping, watched the sergeant walk away in a plume of blue smoke.

'What does he mean, we'll all be killed?'

George laughed.

'Don't worry, he always says that.'

'I'd think it bad luck if he didn't,' added Gunn. He gave a last hard look in the direction of the French army, and turned back to the company lines. 'I'd better go and see what Saddler needs,' he said. 'No doubt there'll be orders on the way soon.'

'I think I'll go and have a word with my horse,' George announced. 'He's new to this kind of thing. Want to come along, Argo?' George found horses soothing, and he hoped Argo would, too.

The plan did not work as well as George had hoped: Argo was jumpy and ended by making his own horse as nervous as he was himself. George's horse was beginning to catch the fever, and George eventually sent Argo off to Saddler to see if there was any news. To his dismay, Argo came running back almost immediately, waving his arms in a most unsoldierly fashion.

'We're defeated!' he cried. 'Wellington's surrendered!'

'What?' snapped George, glancing round quickly to see who could hear him. Even if it were true, it was not necessarily the kind of thing one wanted to spread around like this. 'Come here and tell me quietly.'

Argo was nearly in tears.

'We're withdrawing to Brussels. We're in retreat – Bonaparte has won!' He gasped, white as a sheet. 'And if Theodore is on his way here, he'll be killed! We've lost, and Bonaparte has won!'

'Right, first,' said George firmly, 'pull yourself together. The men don't need to see you flapping around like a wounded duck. Second, tell me exactly what Saddler told you.'

Argo breathed deeply, quickly, then more slowly as George patted him slightly too hard on the shoulder.

'He says … he says we have orders to pull back towards Brussels.'

'To pull back – those were the words? Right, that's not so bad. As Sergeant Lamb said, this is not a great place to defend. And 'towards', yes? Not 'to'? There we are, then: Wellington is pulling us back up the road towards some place he wants us to fight. Somewhere he would prefer to here,' he emphasised. He was itching to run to Saddler himself and find out exactly what was happening, but forced himself to stand still and set a good example to Argo. 'Now, pass me that brush and let me finish this fellow's mane, and then we'll go and sort things out.'

A few moments later they strolled in the direction of Saddler's headquarters, a folding stool with a small fire in front of it. Saddler looked up from a map as he approached.

'We're pulling back, Murray. I'm told it's some place called Waterloo – that can't be right, it sounds stupid. It's the usual thing, Gunn: garbled orders. I can't see it here. Send back and find out what it's really called. Murray, tell Lamb to get the men ready: the army is to set off in order, and we'll be some of the first, I suspect. Last in, first out as usual. Cooking fires out, gear packed, you know the drill.'

'See?' said George to Argo with what he thought was admirable restraint as they turned away. 'We're not going *to* Brussels – we're going *towards* Brussels. If Theodore's on his way, he'll probably meet us somewhere along the road.' *If* he's on his way, he added to himself. It seemed highly unlikely, but in an army of seventy thousand preparing for battle it was surely no hardship to keep their eyes open for one small ten year old looking for his stepfather. George did not even know what he looked like.

The men, grumbling as only soldiers can, doused their cooking fires as instructed, tied their boots, packed away their blankets, flapped their red coats to air them, rebuckled their leather stocks, straightened their crossbelts, checked their cartridges, fastened their packs, and then sat on them, ready to wait till doomsday or their marching orders, whichever came first. The morning seemed likely to pass slowly: George saddled his horse and then leaned against him, reading a copy of the *Courant* from three weeks before that had been making its way slowly around the Scottish officers. The news in it seemed unreal, a novel without much of a plot. He was just folding it ready to be passed on to the next officer when he heard a shout from Major Saddler.

'Silence, men! Stand to your front. Here's the Duke!'

He dropped the paper and rushed out of the horse lines, straightening his waistcoat as he went. There indeed was Wellington, slipping easily out of the saddle and grinning at Saddler and Gunn who had hurried to meet him. George nipped up behind Argo, ready if needed and desperate to hear what their commander had to say. Then with a kind of horrified curiosity he recognised the aide who had accompanied the Duke and was now dismounting behind him. It was Sir Alexander Gordon.

'All well? Splendid,' they heard. 'You'll be shifting soon. Heard anything from the French, eh? No: I'd almost think Ney was retreating. They're damned quiet this morning. Troops all fresh? Good, good. I say, Saddler, isn't it? Did you read this bit in the paper ...' The Duke waved a copy of a recent gossip sheet at Saddler, the wrong person to ask, as it happened, for Saddler was no enthusiast for gossip. The Duke read out some short passage, and all three men laughed heartily, though Saddler's laughter was a trifle stiff. Gunn seemed to be trying to look anywhere but at Sir Alexander.

'Well, no doubt Picton will have you all organised in no time,' said the Duke, swinging himself back on to his horse. George noticed with envy his beautifully polished Hessian boots, with their little tassels – he wondered if Wellington would take it amiss if he asked him the name of his bootmaker. Then he saw Sir Alexander pause at Wellington's stirrup and say something quietly. The Duke nodded.

'Very well, then: catch up as soon as you can.'

'He's so ... prodigiously easy, isn't he?' Argo was saying. 'It's as if the French weren't there at all!'

'We told you there was nothing to worry about,' said George absently. He was watching Sir Alexander Gordon, who had taken Gunn gently by the arm and walked with him to the edge of the company's area, speaking down into Gunn's ear. They stopped: Gunn broke gently away and turned to face the aide, though he had to look up a little. He seemed to be explaining something complicated: George had the impression that he dearly wanted to point out certain things, or people, but was trying to keep his hands still so as not to be seen to be talking about them. George was on tenterhooks: was Sir Alexander reaching for his sword? No: he was apparently feeling for a handkerchief, with which he rubbed at a small mark on his cuff, but still listened keenly to what Gunn was saying. Gunn's forehead, where the scar allowed it movement, was scrunched into an anxious frown as he came to the end of his tale. There was a fearful moment where neither man seemed to move at all. Then Sir Alexander gave a brisk nod, and pushed his handkerchief back into his pocket. The two officers bowed, and after a second Sir Alexander reached out and shook Gunn's hand. Gunn looked stunned. Then Sir Alexander returned to his horse and trotted quickly away to catch up with the Duke.

'What's going on?' asked Argo, slowly recovering from the excitement of seeing Wellington at close quarters.

'I'm not sure. I'm really not sure at all, but I think it's probably a good thing. Whatever it is. I hope.' A bugle call sounded nearby. 'There's our order, Argo: fetch your horse and let's go. There, we didn't have to wait long, did we?'

'Aye, well, sir,' said a soldier nearby, 'see the problem is, if we get off fast at this end, likely we'll have to wait longer wherever we're going. Where are we going, sir?'

'We're off, at last,' said George with a grin, 'to somewhere that might be, but probably isn't, called Waterloo.'

II

They marched back up the road down which they had hurried the previous day, and the sky loomed heavy over them. The day would have felt close except for a chilly breeze lifting leaves and ruffling the rye fields through which the chaussée pavée cut its swathe.

In the early afternoon the wind suddenly strengthened, and several shakos were bowled across the road. The horses sidled and shied. George looked up: the sky darkened, and a thundercloud seemed all at once simply to come into being overhead. It came so suddenly that they stopped, shocked, the column of men and horses staggering a little.

'What on earth …?' said Gunn, staring upwards. The men fell silent, looking about them: against the muddy sky the rye had turned unnaturally yellow, men's faces dead white, their eyes charcoal. The wind buffeted them from the north west, but to George the sound of it seemed to be coming from the south, behind them. He paused, concentrating. No, the wind was definitely in his face, but behind him there was a whispering, a shuffling, even a murmuring. Then a distinct shout.

'The French are coming!'

George had seized Argo's rein before he had even taken in the statement. Argo flinched.

'Calm, now, yes?' said George quietly. 'You need to be calm for the men.'

'Yes, yes of course,' said Argo quickly.

'Steady, men!' ordered Saddler.

'Move up! Move up!' came the cry from behind. 'Shift up! No room!'

'What on earth?' snapped Saddler. A Hussar slid to a halt near him.

'Not everyone is through Genappe,' he gasped. Genappe: George's mind skipped back to the last small town. Town? A village, one street, a bottleneck. 'Move up and make room, or the French Lancers will have them!'

'March smartly, men,' called Saddler, making it sound like a parade ground exercise. The men, unexcited, added an inch to their strides, shuffling up against the company in front. For a moment all was jumble. Then George thought the sky had fallen in.

There was a terrific crash. A sheet of flame shot across the sky, then another, and with a rumble like the commissariat wagons of heaven rolling over the bridge of the world, the skies opened, and the rain fell.

'The heavens are against us!' cried Argo, or that was what George thought he cried. In a second his ears were full of water, his eyes were pressed closed, his mouth flooded, and he was gasping for breath. With a struggle, he managed to make out Saddler's yells, and stirred up his astonished horse to carry on to the north. Whatever had become of the hussars, they no longer seemed in need of space, for everyone now staggered at the same speed, blown and soaked.

'At least the French are no better off than us in this!' Gunn shouted when the first waterfall had eased very slightly.

'It's a sign!' choked Argo.

'If it is, it's a good one,' said George, trying to wipe his eyes with his saturated handkerchief. 'Lots of our victories in the Peninsula, we had a deluge first. I don't remember seeing one quite like this, though!'

'It's amazing!' said Gunn. 'Do you think Wellington arranged it specially, for an especially great victory?'

'I imagine so!' George gave up and shoved his handkerchief back into his wet pocket. His scarlet coat felt twice its usual weight, but somehow, his heart was lighter. It might not be the fight yet, but it felt like action of a sort. He tried to sing, but the rain would not allow it. Instead, he patted his brown horse – wet to black now – on the neck, and sat back happy in the saddle. After all, there came a point when one simply could not be any wetter, and it was no use trying.

In the late afternoon, someone somewhere ahead called a halt, and the order was passed down the line to make camp. The soldiers near George laughed.

'Camp?' said one. 'No wi'out a boat!'

'Who brought the umbrellas?' called another, mincing round his soaking pack.

'Where are we, any road? Have we arrived?'

'How would you know? I could be outside my ain front door and I wouldna ken it in this rain!'

'Will we light the fires?' called one wit.

'Nah, just have the soup that's falling around you!' said his friend, pulling out a wooden mug to catch the water.

Once off the road, the ground was treacherous bog, though at least they seemed to be up a slope and over a ridge, away from the worst of the water. And even better, thought George, the French were unlikely to attack in this: their skirmishers liked to be firm in their footing. 'Quagmire,' he murmured to himself, liking the word. Quaggy and claggy and mired to the knees. He pulled out his whisky flask and took a draught, then remembered that somewhere in his saddlebags he had a flask of decent red wine. He peered around in the untimely gloom: his men were grouped out of sheer habit much as they would have been if they had pitched tents.

Some were huddled on their packs, hugging themselves, while others were trying to make some shelter from branches. A few had managed to find some dry timbers and had just about started a bonfire: George tried to judge whether they were in the shelter of the ridge they had just passed, or whether they would be giving away their position – should Bonaparte be the least interested in this weather. He decided they were safe enough, and passed his wine flask amongst the men.

'Where's the commie wagons, sir?' asked a private. George could tell even in the present conditions that it was Liddell.

'I gather they're still stuck on the Brussels road. You know that forest we marched through? Where the road was pretty poor?'

'La Forête de Soignes,' swanked a corporal, who wanted to improve himself.

'That's the one – I think. Anyway, something's overturned and everything else is stuck, so share this nicely, lads,' he said, waving the wine flask on.

'Faugh, wipe that, will you?' said the corporal. 'Liddell, you stink! Even after this bath!'

'He should get some soap out and scrub himself down!' called another man.

'It's no him: it's his pack,' reported the corporal, after a little unnecessarily valiant sniffing. 'What in the name of the wee man do you keep in that, Liddell? It smells like …'

'Like wurst,' said George, drawing closer with interest. 'Like German sausage.' Watched by the corporal and several other soldiers, George took Liddell's pack, the man himself standing silent, and opened it. Inside, and instantly soaked, was a spare shirt and a bundle of cleaning equipment. A wooden button stick fell forlornly into a puddle. The smell, though, was quite distinct.

'There, see?' said Liddell, a little unconvincingly. 'Nothing there!'

'Wait,' said George. The wooden laths keeping the knapsack smart were still in place: the only knapsack in the company still straight. It seemed unlikely: much too unlikely. George pried back a board, and behind it, of course, was a fine layer of stolen German sausage lining the knapsack and reeking of garlic.

'There!' said George happily. 'Liddell's brought supplies enough for everyone!'

Liddell's face assumed a hunted look, but George clapped him on the shoulder. 'Share it out, Liddell, and we'll say no more about it, this time. This could be the best-fed company in Picton's brigade tonight!'

III

Despite his satisfaction at finding a use for Liddell at last, George found that the night that followed was very far down the list of the best nights of his life. He found some slight shelter against a rough stone wall and pulled a waxed blanket over himself, then felt guilty and called Argo to come and share it with him. Argo had discovered a pile of dryish straw in a shed, the shed being already occupied by a party of Dutch Belgians in a mood of anti-social misery, and he brought it for them to sit on. This worked well for a while, but by around two in the morning, according to George's repeater watch, the water from the ditch under the wall had soaked up through the straw and made it worse than useless. Argo, no doubt anxious about what might happen the next day, wriggled and sighed, and came near several times to pulling the waxed blanket off them completely. The rain pattered on its shiny surface and dripped resoundingly off its edges, and as the night went on the straw and mud mixture beneath them slurped quietly at every movement. George had developed some skill at sleeping in uncomfortable places and he dozed gently, dreaming of his brother Charles telling him off for going to bed with cold feet.

When dawn dared to show its face, they lifted the edge of the blanket and surveyed their surroundings without joy. It was grey and soaking, calm but still raining, and the only comfort the soldiers around them seemed to be finding was in a low, sustained grumble that worked as steadily through them as a steam engine. Men unwound themselves from blankets and stretched stiff limbs, rubbed eyes, hauled the packs they had used as pillows out of the sucking mud. George sniffed the air, and thought he detected the scent of sweet tea.

'Smell that?' He nudged Argo. Argo stared wordlessly, straining to keep his eyes open. George tugged the blanket off him and rolled it up to replace on his saddle. 'Come on, Argo: you'll be no good stuck there,' he urged, and headed off. Reluctantly Argo pulled himself up by the wall, and followed him. By the road, to their delight, they found an intelligent officer with a large kettle of well-sugared tea, spooning it out into any receptacle for passersby.

'You are a hero, sir,' George remarked, clinging to his cup as much for the warmth it afforded his hands as for the liquid within. 'Your regiment should have a gold tea kettle added to its badge as an honour.'

'The Duke himself made much the same remark,' said the officer, with a grin. They wished each other luck, and George led Argo back to their own lines, passing a couple of officers squatting under a green silk umbrella, smoking cigars. They made a sitting bow to George and Argo, as if they were passing them on the Allée Verte. The Allée Verte, thought George: does that really exist? And only so far away as Brussels?

Sergeant Lamb had discovered a bag of biscuits amongst the horses, no doubt another hiding place used by Liddell, and was sharing them out: there was about one a piece. The men made them last, chewing slowly and examining the day on offer with cynical eyes.

'Do you think we'll fight the day?'

'You'd better ask Bonaparte: I think we're all waiting for himself.'

'Aye, well, I suppose.'

'We'll all die, nae doubt.'

'Aye, I suppose.'

'The Duke's already out and about,' George announced, and the soldiers glanced round at him.

'A course he is,' said one. 'Seen him ourselves already.'

'Of course,' smiled George. 'Well, if we're wet then the French can't be dry.'

'They must be gey wet, then,' remarked a lugubrious soldier, 'for I dinna think I've aye been wetter.'

'Right, lads,' said Sergeant Lamb. 'All finished?'

The men swallowed down the ends of their biscuits and water, wiping mouths on the backs of hands. Sergeant Lamb cleared his throat and nodded to one of the drummer boys – not James – who gave them a note. Then, standing in the drizzle, the men sang.

'I to the hills will lift mine eyes
From whence doth come mine aid?'

The metrical psalm's familiar, awkward rhymes meandered through the air and George, joining in, remembered that it was indeed the Sabbath. What was Charles doing, he wondered, in far away Edinburgh? How would today go – if it went anywhere – and would he and Charles ever meet again?

Chapter Twenty-One

Edinburgh

I

Murray was too shocked to say much through tea. Mr. Sangster returned just as Murray's mouth dropped open, and stayed to consume three cups of tea and several slices of teabread. Mrs. Sangster sat smiling sweetly and making general conversation, while Murray toyed with some crumbs and eventually left the house, followed by a puzzled Walter, an hour or so later. He walked back to Prince's Street in silence.

Murray was horrified at Mrs. Sangster's words. He was furious that Letitia had made advances, angry with himself that he had not repulsed them, and appalled that someone had interpreted them as something more – and that that had been reported to Mrs. Sangster. Was it common gossip? His feet followed the road automatically, his eyes unseeing, as Walter scuttled behind, trying to keep up.

The thought that Agostinella might hear did not bother him too much: she was not inclined to gossip, thinking it beneath her, and though she would be angry – and she could be very angry, in several languages - if she thought Murray was unfaithful to her, it would be nothing to Willie Jack's hurt and betrayal if he suspected his old friend of an intimate relationship with his beloved wife. And if it was common gossip, then Willie Jack would be the first to hear.

A sudden thought came to him, a memory of brown gowned backs heading up the hill from the Sangsters' house. He missed a step, and stopped, staring sightlessly ahead, working back in his mind. There was something about the speed of the women's retreat, their steadfast focus on the road ahead, that even at the time had made him wonder, at some level of his mind, whether they had just left the Sangsters' house.

The thought provoked another memory: he had seen the same brown gowns, he was sure, on Calton Hill when he had fled (he told himself firmly that he had fled, single-mindedly) Letitia's company in the kiosk. From where they were, they could easily have seen into the kiosk, could have seen Letitia's warm hand on his arm, could have seen his own failure to ease politely away. Was that it? Was that what the Browns were up to – spying for Mrs. Sangster? Then he must give them nothing more to spy on: he should leave Willie Jack's house immediately. But where would he go? None of his other friends was in town. And what would Willie Jack say? And what would he say to Willie Jack? I'm sorry, old friend, I have to leave your house because your wife is making advances to me? Trust Willie Jack, he thought bitterly. Trust Willie Jack to find a wife who can't be trusted with his best friend. But that was unfair: Willie Jack had always been drawn to unsuitable women: it was not his fault that, to be brutally honest, Murray was drawn to this one, too.

II

'Ah, there you are!' cried Willie Jack affably as he appeared in the hall of the flat. 'Letitia was just wondering if you would read to us this evening: you do have a nice voice for it, and someone has lent her that new book *Wavey*, is it? that came out last year, and she'll never get it read if someone doesn't read it to her, she says.'

'*Waverley*,' Murray corrected automatically. 'The book's called *Waverley*. I don't think she'd like it. I'm sorry, Willie Jack: I think I've spent too long in the sun today. Please excuse me: I must retire.'

'Oh!' Willie Jack peered with concern at his friend's face. 'You do look a bit peelie wallie, to be honest. Do you want me to get the maid to send in some supper later?'

'Maybe,' said Murray uncertainly: he did not want to starve. 'I don't know, Willie Jack: thanks, but for the moment I just want to lie down.'

'Of course, of course,' said Willie Jack kindly. 'Just ring if you want anything.'

'Of course.' Murray did not like lying to his friend, but he did his best to look frail and tired as he disappeared into his room. Walter disappeared for the kitchen.

With the door firmly closed and, after a moment's thought, locked, Murray tugged off his neckcloth and his coat, and unbuttoned his waistcoat. There was cold water in the jug, and he poured some into the basin, dipping his hands and letting them steep for a moment before wiping them over his face, and through his hair. He sighed, and sat down on the bed.

Saturday, he thought. Tomorrow it would be Sunday again. No letter from George, who was doing who knew what in Belgium. He still had no firm idea who had killed Alicia, and no idea where Theodore was - even less, if that were possible. Mrs. Sangster was threatening him and the delectable Brown ladies were apparently spying on him. His best friend's wife was making advances on him and he would urgently have to find somewhere else to stay.

He flung himself back on the bed, and wished he had gone with his instinct and allowed Willie Jack to send him some food. Willie Jack ... what on earth would happen if Willie Jack heard that he and Letitia ... But why was Mrs. Sangster threatening him? Why would she have had the Browns spy on him? Out of sheer devilment? He remembered the look on Mrs. Sangster's face when she had watched Lauder pinch Jemima, and Jemima's reaction. Was Mrs. Sangster just the kind of woman who enjoyed manipulating her neighbours, finding out their weak points and watching them squirm? Or was there more to it than that?

He lay back and rubbed his long fingers thoughtfully through his damp hair. What was Mrs. Sangster up to? He sat up, searching his memory for all he had heard about her, or noticed. There had been two sons ... she had not been close to her daughter-in-law, who had been the daughter of a business rival destroyed by rumours of bad bread. Sangster had come after him to ask him to look for Theodore – he had not asked him in front of Mrs. Sangster. The Browns knew where Alicia had gone, and he had seen them coming out of the very close where Alicia had lived – though, he reminded himself, by that time Alicia was already dead. The Browns were clearly reporting to Mrs. Sangster.

He frowned harder, as if it would squeeze out the memories. Mr. Brewster, Letitia's little uncle, had said that Mrs. Sangster favoured the other son, the one who had not married Alicia. But what did that prove? Many parents favoured one child over another, however fair they tried to be. The trouble was that he could not quite imagine Mrs. Sangster trying to be fair. Well, supposing she had really hated the first son – John, wasn't it? – and really favoured the second son, Peter. What might happen? John was dead. Was that anything to do with his mother? Had she so deeply wanted Peter to inherit Sangster's business that she had had something to do with John's death? He had no idea how John had died – a fever, was it?

Anyway, that was hardly the point at the moment. The question was, had she killed Alicia, and if so, why?

She must have known where Alicia was, through the Browns. And it made sense – if the man in the brown coat and black hat really was Lauder, then he was clearly obeying Mrs. Sangster's orders. She must have a whole rabble of spies and agents: a female Bonaparte, smiling in her parlour in Water of Leith. Was he being fanciful? But someone had killed Alicia.

But if Mrs. Sangster wanted her other son Peter to inherit – and where was he, in all this? – then what good was it killing Alicia? Murray rubbed his face, concentrating. Why would she have killed Alicia? Murray thought back to the dingy flat off the High Street, the first time he had seen it. There, in his memory, there was still the bed with its heavy mattress and its thick curtain, the table with its dishes – and with the tin upended over the second plate and knife. Alicia had guessed who was knocking at her door, perhaps? Perhaps she had known what the visitor was after, and had quickly hidden the second dish … to hide the fact that there were two of them in the flat. Had Theodore been behind the curtain as his mother was murdered? But more to the point – for Murray was sure he had been, that it had been Theodore's plate and knife under the tin, that his mother had done her best to conceal his presence from her visitor – had she known that the visitor had in fact come to kill, not Alicia, but Theodore? With John Sangster's son out of the way, Peter Sangster, whatever his fight with his father, would have to inherit the business, for whatever the fight, Sangster's obsession with legacy would not allow him to bypass his one remaining son.

It was just about beginning to fit together, he thought. It made sense: if Mrs. Sangster thought he was perhaps drawing close to her – if, indeed, Lauder had in fact seen him hiding in that cupboard (the very thought sent shivers through him) – then it would be to her advantage to find some way to threaten him. He had just made it easy for her by being seen with Letitia. It really did make sense.

But then what was he going to do about it? If he accused her of murder, no doubt she would let Willie Jack and Agostinella know about Letitia. The best thing, he thought, would be to talk to Willie Jack first, then leave the flat. He would move to Mr. Campbell's or Mrs. Brotherstone's, if they had any rooms to spare, and from there he would set about finding proof against Mrs. Sangster. He would continue the hunt for Theodore, too: it was certain, now, that he was in hiding from the murderer, whether or not he knew it was his own grandmother. He would send a note to Potterrow tomorrow, before church – he reminded himself again that he had promised Walter the afternoon off – and then at least he could have his luggage sent there, while he looked for a room if neither of them had one free.

He opened his trunk, and looked around the little room. It would be best to start packing now, and then he could make a quick exit the next day. He might not tell Willie Jack everything, he thought, for everyone's sake. He could say that a murder suspect (probably better not even to name Mrs. Sangster at this point, he thought, for Willie Jack could not have kept a secret in a bucket) a murder suspect was trying to defame him by linking his name with Letitia's, and for the sake of Letitia's reputation (he privately wondered how long she would have that for), he would move out forthwith. That had the virtue of being true, if not strictly the whole truth, and would cushion Willie Jack against any rumours that might start to spread. Murray was not entirely proud of himself, but he told himself firmly that as nothing had actually happened, nor would he allow it to happen, nor did he intend it to happen, it was only fair to protect Willie Jack from suspicion and unhappiness.

He began rounding up his belongings and packing them into the trunk. He laid a cushioning layer of cloak, then went to fetch his writing slope to set on top of it. He lifted the slope carefully off the pretty mahogany table on which it was resting, and a letter was revealed, sitting innocently on the dark wood. He set the writing slope into the trunk, then picked up the letter, assuming it had fallen out of the slope and somehow been pushed under it. The letter was addressed to him, and the seal was unbroken: across the top of the wrapper, the sender had written 'By Hand'. It was Walter's missing note.

'Oh, Walter!' Murray muttered, and slipped his finger under the seal. The note, to his surprise, was from Letitia's uncle, Mr. Brewster. Murray frowned: when this note had arrived, they had only just met at the Findlays' supper party. He read Brewster's spiky writing quickly.

'*Dear Sir,*' it began. '*I hope you will not take this amiss, but it is written in Friendship and with a view to protecting both you and your Friend from Hurt and Damage. To come straight to the Point, it is my sorry Duty to warn you that my niece Letitia is a most convinced Flirt, and that if you wish to guard yourself against her incorrigible ways make sure never to be left Alone with her. She would bring your Marriage to ruins without thinking it any Great Matter. Your Friend Mr. Dundas I fear is lost to her, but at least my wife and I can prevent, if you will, you yourself being the Cause of his Distress. I should recommend that you find yourself alternative Accommodation as soon as possible.*

'*If you are the Gentleman I believe you to be, you will no doubt act on this advice, which is most reluctantly given in the Circumstances, and we shall of course say no more about it.*

'*Believe me, I remain*
'*Yours most respectfully,*
'*J. Brewster.*'

'A case of locking the door after the horse has bolted,' murmured Murray to himself, and folded the letter up carefully. He locked it in his writing slope, and began to pack the rest of his belongings over it in the trunk. Brewster must think him a poor sort of fellow not to have taken his advice.

When he had packed as much as he could, he lay back on the bed again, thinking. How could he entrap Mrs. Sangster? Or find evidence enough to convince Sergeant Clyne that she was guilty? He closed his eyes, and considered, and dozed, and eventually fell asleep.

He awoke to find his room in darkness, and his stomach

rumbling fit to be heard in the Old Town. He listened carefully for a moment, then pressed the repeater on his watch. It gave the last quarter as half past midnight: he was surprised. The household must all have retired by now, but he did want some food. He rose quietly, unlocked his door and slipped into the hall. All was dark, and there was not a sound to be heard.

The kitchen quarters were of course at the back of the flat, and after a moment Murray's eyes adjusted to what little light there was: the full moon cast a slice of white glare through the parlour door. He found the passage he wanted, and padded along it, moving almost silently. At the end of the passage he turned the doorhandle slowly, and found himself in the kitchen itself. The table was central, the range opposite, and a closed door on either side of it. One was almost certainly the pantry. He tossed a coin in his mind, and headed for the one on the left.

He opened it and at first thought the hinges had creaked, but instead it was the maid: he had intruded into her box bed.

'I do apologise,' he said quickly in a low voice. 'I was looking for a little food. I felt under the weather earlier, but now I have woken hungry.'

'Just a moment, sir, and I'll see what there is,' said the maid, equally quietly. She scrambled out of the bed, wrapping a shawl around her shoulders, and took him to the other door. It was of course the little pantry.

'What's going on? Sir, is that you?' Walter's voice came mysteriously from beneath the kitchen table, quarters for visiting manservants.

'Don't worry, Walter, I'm just fetching some food.' He had not thought to waken the whole household. 'By the way, Walter, I found that note you lost.'

'Oh, aye, sir?'

'It was under my writing slope.'

'Oh, aye, of course. That would have been where I put it for safety, sir,' said Walter, with sleepy satisfaction. Murray rolled his eyes.

The maid handed him a plate containing two slices of ham, a sturdy segment of pie, a large piece of bread with butter, a boiled egg and an apple.

'Princely,' he said. 'Thank you.'

She curtsied and disappeared back into her boxbed, no larger a hole than one might find on a ship. Murray called a quiet goodnight to Walter, and returned to the passageway with his prize. He was famished.

He balanced the plate through the dark hallway, but nearly dropped it when he heard a breathy laugh behind him. He spun round.

'What's this?' whispered Letitia. 'Are you thieving from the pantry like a boy?'

'I – no. I missed supper earlier because I did not feel well …'

'Of course. I'm only teasing you, Mr. Murray!' She was pale in a peach silk dressing gown, full and flowing. 'But I did miss you at supper, Mr. Murray. I was hoping we could have a word.'

'Well, I hardly think now is the time,' said Murray, raising his voice to a more normal level. She glided forward, close to him, and he felt the touch of her finger on his lips.

'It isn't the place,' she said softly, 'but I'm quite sure it's the time.'

He backed quickly away from her, but found that he had backed through the open doorway of the parlour. The windows were unshuttered, and the moonlight flooded in, bathing her in silver-white light. She closed the door without taking her eyes off him.

'Mr. Murray – Charles – I'm sure you know as well as I do what I mean to say,' she began, her low voice like warm caramel. 'Though you may agree with me, anyway, that sometimes words are wasted at moments like this.'

She moved so fast towards him that he hardly had a chance to move beyond an instinctive shifting of the plate of food. He held it protectively out to one side, while she pressed against him and he tried – he swore he was trying – to move away. At that precise moment, the parlour door opened.

'Charles! What is going on?'

Willie Jack had a candle, and it illuminated to perfection his horrified face.

'I know what it looks like, Willie Jack, but it really isn't,' said Murray in hurried desperation. 'I mean, why would I have brought a plate of ham?'

'I have no idea.' Willie Jack drew himself up to his full height, and managed, even though he was in his nightgown, to assume an air of some dignity. 'Charles, I never thought I should have to say this to you, of all people, but I must ask you to leave my house this instant!'

'I quite agree,' said Murray. 'I'll just fetch Walter and my coat.'

'And I'll take that,' said Willie Jack with authority, snatching the plate of food as Murray squeezed past him. In a very few moments, Murray and Walter, the latter wrapped in a cloak, found themselves out in Prince's Street in the moonlight.

'Um …' said Walter, not unreasonably.

'Maybe not now, Walter. It's complicated. Come on, let's see if we can find somewhere to stay.'

Fortune's Tontine Hotel, now that the season was over, had several rooms free, to their relief, and a truckle bed for Walter at the foot of Murray's half tester. Now that the season was over, however, their kitchens did not stay open late. A disgruntled servant brought a pewter plate containing a piece of bread baked several days ago and a slice of cheese of a slightly greater vintage, and a tankard of flat beer. Murray was happy enough to make do. Walter, wrapped in his cloak, was sound asleep before Murray had blown out the candle.

In the morning, Murray sent Walter back along Prince's Street to fetch their luggage, so that by the time they were heading out for church neither of them looked as though they had spent the night in a strange hotel at short notice. Walter reported that the maid had told him that she had had a very disturbed night, what with a great row between the master and the mistress, and his eyebrows seemed to ask Murray again what had happened, but Murray chose to ignore them. Instead he breakfasted well, reminded Walter that he was to meet Jemima that afternoon – not that Walter needed reminding – and after some thought decided to go to the West Kirk, not a church he often attended, for morning service.

The West Kirk was an old church on an old site, but the respectable burghers of the New Town were beginning to find it appealing even as the gentry used St. George's, the new grand church in Charlotte Square. The burghers were gathering in force that morning, which was a particularly fine one: rain made a glistening threat along the horizon, but the sun ignored it and carried on warming the streets and brightening the colours of the ladies in their Sunday best. Several were already wearing what Murray took to be Pomona green, a bilious shade that immediately reminded him of Letitia. He had thanked the Lord on several occasions through last night that Willie Jack had come in when he did, and at the same prayed that eventually he might be able to heal the gash that had split them. He would think about that when he had the chance, but for now he had his eyes open for other acquaintances.

A couple of hundred people made their way into the church and Murray paid a beadle to allow him access to one of the public pews, along with Walter. Walter sat beside him like a mushroom, looking about him at yet another new building, then gave a little jump and a wriggle.

'There's Jemima, sir, with that Mr. Lauder and the Sangsters.'

'So she is,' said Murray, pleased. Walter had done his work for him. The Sangsters sat in one of the front pews, for which presumably they had paid an annual subscription: they were treated with great respect as they swept up the aisle arm in arm, followed by their servants. They did not appear to see Murray, and of course they stayed facing the front throughout the service. Murray tried to listen to the sermon but his mind wandered a little, still trying to find a way of catching Mrs. Sangster, still replaying last night's events, still running through possible ways to explain things to Willie Jack. Willie Jack had his faults, but he was still a good friend, and life brought precious few of those.

The service ended, and the slow egress of so many people began. Murray, being at the back, managed to slip out fairly quickly, but then they had to wait for Jemima. It was some time before the Sangsters appeared, and as if by sorcery Mrs. Sangster instantly saw Murray and made her way over to him.

'Mr. Murray! How lovely to see you again. I suppose this must be by far the most convenient church for you staying as you are with dear Mrs. Dundas. How lovely she is, isn't she?'

Murray bowed.

'I understand she is generally considered so,' he agreed politely. Mr. Sangster wore a look it was hard to interpret: weariness, custom, dread all seemed mingled as he avoided looking at the wife he had on his arm. Oh my, thought Murray, the women we end up marrying.

'Now, Jemima.' Mrs. Sangster turned to her maid, and adjusted the girl's bonnet strings. Jemima winced. 'Back by dusk, yes?'

'Yes, ma'am,' agreed Jemima. Nevertheless she stood until the Sangsters had made their farewells and departed in their carriage with Lauder. 'Didn't want him to see us heading off together,' she said to Walter.

'Fair enough,' said Walter.

'Here,' said Murray, for Walter had had a hard few days for a lad. 'There's money for an ice each if the kiosk is open. You're off to Calton Hill, aren't you?'

'We're going to see the whale,' Walter agreed, taking the money with quiet pleasure.

'Back, as Mrs. Sangster says, by dusk. That means if you're sticking together (and I wish you would, Walter, you know how awful your sense of direction is) then you will be back early enough to allow Jemima to get back to Water of Leith by dusk. Off you go: enjoy yourselves.'

The two bowed and curtseyed, and he watched them disappearing into the Sunday crowds on Prince's Street. After a moment, he realised that something was moving in the same direction, trying to catch them up. It was a small straw-coloured dog. Murray smiled. Walter would be happy.

He returned, following them at some distance, to Fortune's Hotel, ordered some food, and wrote a note to Mr. Campbell in the Potterrow. Then he debated whether to pay a hotel servant to take it, or whether to wait for Walter's return.

'Oh, I'll send it by a hotel servant,' he said to himself. 'After all, Walter won't be home till dusk.'

But dusk came, and deepened, and there was no sign of Walter.

Chapter Twenty-Two

Belgium

If George's watch was right, then it was at nine o'clock that the order came for the baggage to be moved to the rear. The men stood motionless for a moment, watching it go, all at once more tense, for everyone knew that that was a sure sign that Wellington meant them to join battle today. Sergeant Lamb, the old hand, had them busy straightaway, cleaning their guns with quick test shots, smartening themselves up and checking they had everything they needed.

'Oh, my, look at our belts!' cried one soldier. 'They're blood-red already, and never a shot fired!'

It was true: yesterday's rain had leached the red from their tunics into their white leather belts and stained them a horrid scarlet. One or two soldiers looked unnerved, but the rest laughed, Sergeant Lamb with them.

'I'll no ask you to blanco them just now, lads,' he said kindly. 'But the minute we're back to camp I want those belts snow white, right?'

The men grinned, and the unnerved ones brightened. George laughed too, as he polished the damp off his sword. He had Argo scrubbing his own sword to keep him occupied: the rain was easing gradually and the day looked set to be tolerable after all. Now that they could see more clearly where they were, it appeared that Wellington had chosen his battlefield very much in accordance with his own tastes: they were on a ridge, with the unlikely sounding village of Waterloo behind them. Before them, to the south, the land fell away in gentle waves, fields of rye and corn bisected still by that chaussée pavée of which they had seen so much in the last few days. George could see farm buildings, substantial ones, down on their left, and the map told him that that was La Haye Sainte: another unlikely name, though, he thought, for when was a hedge ever holy? To the right the cornfields rolled away, interspersed with trees, a pretty view for a battlefield.

Picton's division, of which they were a part, was near the middle of the ridge, which did not reassure Argo at all.

'Surely all their attack will come straight at us?' he demanded. Already the French army was marching in solid columns into place on the slopes opposite, and he had been sizing them up nervously since the first man appeared, as if he was going to have to fight them all individually.

'You never know. It all depends. Bonaparte could try to break our centre, right enough, or he could try to pick off the ends. Or he could go for the weak parts,' he added, nodding at a brigade of Dutch-Belgians in their blue coats with orange facings.

'Why are they weak? They look very splendid,' said Argo, puzzled.

'Oh, yes, very splendid, out there on the front of the ridge,' said George. 'Very valiant of them to stand out there and draw any fire while the rest of us tuck ourselves down sensibly behind the ridge here. Modern warfare, Argo: that's what Wellington likes. Shame no one's told the Dutch-Belgians.'

'Form squares,' came Saddler's order in the distance. The men, who had been lined up, formed as tidily on the awkward ground as they would have done in barracks, and Saddler permitted them a satisfied nod before they lay down in their places. Those towards the front of the squares could see, as George and Argo could, the ever-increasing numbers of the French amassing now on the slopes in front of them. The sight was a splendid one: there were blocks of red, green, white, and blue uniforms, headgear even in tigerskin, flecked with facings in all the colours of the rainbow. Nor did Bonaparte limit himself to mere visual spectacle: drums pounded and trumpets blared and there were frequent, heartfelt cries of 'Vive l'Empereur!'.

'*Can this cockpit hold The vasty fields of France?*' asked Gunn, nodding at them as he passed. George gave him a look.

'Are the cuirassiers' breastplates really impregnable?' breathed Argo, as if afraid of being overheard by the enemy.

'Apparently not: I heard that some of them were pierced with gunshots at Quatre Bras,' said George, surprised himself at the news. He, too, was increasingly fascinated by the manoeuvres below. 'My word, I believe this is more soldiers than I ever saw in one place before. Those are the Dragoons, of course, with the tigerskin things. Hussars … I don't know how they ever remember who's who, there are so many different ones. Oh, and those ones in the big bearskins, those are the Old Guard Grenadiers – fearfully tall. I think they must breed them specially on farms.'

'There must be more of them than of us, surely,' said Argo plaintively. George considered.

'Maybe some more. Lots more guns, I think, nearly twice as many. Ah, well, as Lamb says, we'll all die!'

'I'm not going to,' said Argo suddenly.

'What?'

'I'm not going to die. I'm going to get through today, whatever it brings, and I'm going to find Theodore and go back to Edinburgh and – and – well, I haven't thought beyond that. But I'm not going to die.'

'Very well,' said George, taken aback. 'I'll see you this evening, then, and we'll raise a glass to that!'

They shook hands firmly. Argo had a new light in his eyes, and it was a good and determined one. At last, George thought that any Frenchman who came across Argo today might just be out of luck.

There was a ripple of movement behind them: the infantry were interspersed with artillery, while the cavalry behind them, further down the hill towards the village, waited impatiently. Several officers on horseback rode amongst them: it was Picton, come for a final inspection of his brigade, and with him a dignified looking man and a lad of around fifteen with a pleasant face.

'That's the Duke of Richmond,' said Gunn, hurrying up. 'Is all ready here? They'll be along in a moment.'

'Isn't he supposed to be helping to guard Brussels?' asked George. 'Yes, we're in order.'

'He couldn't resist, apparently. It seems to run in the family: that's his son, and he's wounded: he took a musket ball in his chest last year at Orthez, and it's still there.'

'Well, they're a great addition to the division,' said George, unimpressed.

'Oh, the lad's off to act as aide to the Prince of Orange over there,' Gunn waved. 'What are those guns next to you? Why aren't they manned?'

'Not sure,' said George. The artillery pieces had been sitting in splendid isolation all the time he had seen them, and he had not thought to ask why.

'Oh, Lord,' said Gunn, 'here they come!'

Saddler rode up with Sir Thomas Picton who, though renowned for his foul temper, was clearly more irritable than usual today. He remained silent while inspecting the company's squares, then saw the stray artillery next to them.

'Whose are those damned guns?'

'No idea, sir,' said Saddler quickly. 'They were there last night.'

'Well, they're not bloody mine. Where are the damned artillery men?'

'Never saw them, sir.' George had never seen Saddler quite so prompt and submissive.

'Well, find them,' said Picton abruptly. 'No bloody good without artillery men. Taking up useful space. Get rid – I want them gone forthwith, hear me?'

'Yes, sir, of course.'

'Otherwise you seem to be ready. Good work.'

Picton rode back to join the Duke of Richmond and disappeared to inspect the rest of the division, and Saddler noticeably relaxed.

'Thank goodness that's done,' he said to Gunn with a rare smile. 'If it's a choice between facing him and facing the French, I'd take the French any day. But he knows what he's doing. Now, I was going to have a word with the drummer boys … that new one needs to be watched, I think. He could be up to anything.'

Gunn opened his mouth to reply, but at that moment a spotty young ensign rode up, looking all of about twelve and constructed entirely from anxiety and an overlarge stock. He caught his foot in the stirrup but otherwise managed to slide off his horse with some dignity.

'Who is the officer in charge, please?'

'This is Major Saddler,' said Gunn, 'Third Battalion, Royal Scots.'

The boy nodded, and gave a bow towards Saddler as Gunn hurried off.

'Sir Colville Acton's respects, sir, and could he have his guns back?'

'His guns? What are his guns to me? And who is he, anyway?'

'He's the staff officer overseeing the placement of – well, those guns over there.'

He pointed over to the abandoned artillery pieces next to the company square. At his appearance, a few tentative gunners had emerged from behind the guns, watching him anxiously: it was nowhere near enough men to crew the guns.

'Don't tell me that's all the men you have?' snapped Saddler.

'Well, that's it, sir. The crews are in place, but the guns aren't.'

'Then take them away. I have no use for guns if there are no men to fire them.'

'I can't take them away, sir, not on my own. You see –'

'Don't tell me,' said Saddler, with ice in his voice. 'The horses are in place, but the guns aren't?'

'That's very close to the case, sir, yes. Well, actually – yes, that's the case. The horses and the men are over yonder, with Halkett's brigade. And the guns, as you see …' the poor ensign tailed off, quaking at Saddler's wrath but determined to defend his senior officer.

'Those bloody idiots! Why are the horses over there? How are we supposed to shift those guns?'

'Sir Colville sent them to find forage, sir.'

'I don't care if he's sent them off to find the lost land of Avalon, ensign, they're no damned use to us if they're not here, fed or not fed, are they, any more than they're of use to Halkett? Tell me, has Sir Colville ever actually seen a battlefield before outside his nursery? Murray, Wellington will need to know about this. Go and find him and report. Delegation, it would seem, has its limits.' He spun away with a final glare at the ensign. George tried to look sympathetic, as a private ran for his horse.

'You like Sir Colville, then, do you?'

'Not always, to be honest, sir,' said the ensign bravely. 'But then, he is my father.'

'Ah,' said George, not quite sure how to console him for that, but fortunately his horse arrived, excited to be off and doing. 'Well, good luck! I hope you get men and horses and guns together, in one place or another!'

The ensign rode off, head slumped. George flung himself up

into the saddle and paused: did Saddler really want him to ride off and tell Wellington? Did Wellington really need to know? And where had Wellington gone, anyway? As far as he knew, he had last been seen heading west.

'Oh, well,' he said aloud. 'See you later, Argo.' He gathered the reins and was about to ride off when Gunn returned, pushing James the drummer boy before him. He put out a hand to George's reins.

'Here, take him with you, would you? He's not much use as a drummer boy, but he can run. He could take a message back for you if you needed it.'

'Well …' said George. 'Is this Saddler's idea?'

'Ah … not exactly,' Gunn admitted. 'But it'll be fine. Just take him, would you, Murray?' Gunn looked up, and George almost thought he was pleading with him. James, by contrast, looked thoroughly displeased.

'Of course,' said George at last.

'You'd better take him up behind you. He's not much of a rider, but he's all right if you're walking.'

'Well, that's useful in a battlefield,' muttered George as Gunn gave James a leg up on to the back of his saddle. 'You'd better hold on tight, young lad, and no nonsense!'

James grunted into the back of his coat, and George waved to Gunn as he rode off.

He hoped Wellington had not doubled back already and passed the company's position to go back east, but everyone he asked as he rode west told him they had seen Wellington heading the same direction. He picked his way between infantry and cavalry, keeping to the back of the ridge, amazed at the speckled diversity of the army Wellington had amassed here – and the reserves were still on their way. Brunswickers, Dutch-Belgians, every corner of the British army, not quite as colourful as the French across the valley but somehow much more various. If the Prussians, the Russians and the Austrians all arrived, it would be the strangest army in Europe.

As he progressed further along the ridge, the answer to his directions was gradually more focussed.

'The Duke's down at Hougoumont,' they said, and now that he was far enough west he could see over the undulating cornfields and trees to a small chateau down in the valley which he remembered from the map. He pointed it out to James.

'That's big enough to be a village,' said James. 'Are you sure it's just the one house?'

'Well, it's a chateau,' George explained, comparing it in his mind to Letho. It was probably around the same size, but more compact: the pale brick buildings with their dark slate roofs, including what looked like farm buildings, a large house and even a chapel, were arranged in a square with linking walls enclosing some kind of courtyard. Outside these walls were woods, gardens and orchard, a charming prospect even with the addition of soldiers. As George neared the buildings, he could see firstly that the soldiers inside included foot guards, and secondly that to their left, towards the south, a worryingly large number of French soldiers was approaching steadily, and breaking to enter the woods.

'That's not a particularly good sign,' said George.

'Will we make it to the chateau before they do?' asked James, a slight tremor in his voice. George opened his mouth to reply when the earth shook and their ears jabbed with pain. Before them and behind them grass sprang from the ground and spattered around them.

'The guns have started!' George shouted. A mist spread and settled around them, and a second later it thickened to blackness with a roar as the Allied guns replied.

'Are they aiming right at us?' cried James, clutching George's waist as they broke into a gallop. 'I'm not good at galloping,' he added, 'but that's just fine!'

'Think of it as practice,' George yelled back. 'We'll do trotting tomorrow.'

'If we're spared!'

They reached the orchard, and were quickly admitted at the gate which slammed behind them. As if with another pair of eyes, George noticed the little apples forming on the trees, promising a good crop, while the last of the blossom lay in a quagmire beneath the branches soaked by yesterday's downpour. Panting, James jumped down from the horse and George dismounted.

'Get moving,' snapped a Guards officer. 'Don't you know the French are coming?'

A shell spurted earth right beside an apple tree near them: it toppled, and fell. The officer hurried them over to the inner gate that led to the courtyard. He was a youngish man, with the sandy hair and thoughtful, faraway look of the Highlander.

'Well, have you news?' he demanded.

'Looking for Wellington,' said George briefly.

'He's gone. He was here earlier.'

'Then we'd better get on.'

'Look – no, they're here!' the Guard cried, hearing a signal from high up in the chateau buildings. 'Right, men, fire when ready! Make sure you have a good target!' He ran back towards the orchard gates, and George saw that the inner walls of the orchard were lined with red coated Guards, black Hanoverians and green Nassauers – they were with the Prince of Orange's Corps. Rough loopholes had been knocked through the orchard's brick walls: the men were lined up two to a loophole, firing and loading in turn, though the walls seemed perilously thin, meant to warm the ripening fruit, not to keep out regiments of French veterans. It was not long before there was a breach in the walls and the bluecoats began to stumble in, then to trickle, then to pour. The retreat was sounded, urgently, and in what seemed like only a moment since they had arrived and stood, gaping, George and James were being hurried back, with the horse, into the chateau's courtyard.

Inside the chaos resolved itself swiftly. The great gate was barred and the walls and windows bristled with guns. George pulled his horse to a stable block and tied him loosely into an open stall, not sure when he might need him next. James darted away and George caught him by the ear.

'Where are you off to?' he asked.

'Going to make myself useful wherever I can,' said James. 'The way I see it is we're all in this one together.' He ran up to an impressive sergeant and George could already hear him looking for orders, and a moment later he had vanished into some building carrying a box of cartridges. George nodded sharply, and reported in like manner to the Guards officer they had met in the orchard.

'You still here? Right: I've lost an officer up over there: go and help there.' He waved at a two storey building, some kind of store, near the gate. It was no wonder he had lost an officer there: the French skirmishers had it as their main target as the riflemen up there constantly shot at the French veterans attacking the gate.

George trotted up the stairs and felt very small and plain amongst the splendid Guards.

In a short time, the French had other worries. The heavens seemed to be raining shrapnel from somewhere to the south, the shards whizzing right over their heads and beating back the attackers below. Someone behind the chateau had brought howitzers into play, and with extraordinary delicacy.

'There, that should do them!' remarked a Guard, watching more boldly from the window aperture as the French backed off. Soon they had the gate open and with a cry outside of 'Up, Guards, and at them!' the Guards belted out with their fellows and chased the last of the French out of the orchard. Within an hour, George found himself overseeing a repair squad patching holes in the orchard wall, where James darted back and forth with buckets of mud, dung and straw to help glue the bricks back in place. George hoped he was not going to be carried away with the glamour of army life.

'You still here?' said the Guard officer when he saw George directing the laying of the final line of bricks.

'Looking for an apprenticeship after all this is over,' George joked, wiping the mud from his hands.

'I'll sponsor you,' said the officer, with a grin. 'I'm Macdonnell, by the way.'

'Murray,' said George. They bowed, but as Macdonnell rose he looked past George and exclaimed,

'Oh, not again!'

'They've reinforcements!' cried a Hanoverian, running past to defend the mended orchard gate.

'Have they nothing better to do?'

'I doubt they've mistaken us for Brussels,' George called back, as he swept James back into the courtyard and leapt up the stairs to his old perch in the store by the courtyard gate. The French reinforcements were keen, and the fresh mud holding the walls together was still soft: the walls crumbled and all George's good work was wasted in a few minutes. The Guards in the store settled themselves again amongst the dusty sacks and took aim, firing on the French below while simultaneously cursing the howitzer battery which seemed to have gone home. Then,

'Bloody hell, he's enormous!' cried a massive Guard, and George had to look. A French subaltern built like the side of a house emerged from the mobs in the orchard, and, driven on by the yells of his comrades, put a fist through one panel of the great gate that George and his Guards were trying to defend.

'Vive l'Enfonceur!' cried the French. 'Vive l'Empereur!'

'They're getting in!' cried the same Guard.

'Stand firm: keep firing!' said George, but he had to watch as a handful of French soldiers burst into the courtyard below. In seconds the fight had turned nasty. Swords flashed, but so did knives, and fists were flying with no regard to rules. Every moment a few more Frenchmen pushed through the broken gate, and George could see it swaying and giving way. Then a cry went up:

'Close the gate!'

The officer he had spoken to before shoved through the fray knocking men to either side. A sergeant joined him, and as they pressed their backs against the creaking gate three more officers dusted off their opponents and broke away from the fight to help.

'They'll never do it,' George muttered to himself.

'That's Macdonnell,' said the nearest guard, glancing down. 'Want to bet on it?'

George watched in awe. The French were pressing on the outside of the gate, but the five huge men strained, inching back, boots pressed hard into the cobbles, necks bulging. The gate was closing. Outside the French battered, free to run at the narrow opening, free to poke through gaps with knives and bayonets, and one officer snatched his hand away with a cry, but he did not lose his place, and still the gate was closing. Five inches … four … three … Macdonnell urged them on, cursing their attackers. Two inches … one … The gate closed. With a cry of triumph, Macdonnell spun away and seized up a great beam lying nearby, barricading the gate firmly. If the French outside could not get in, the French inside had nowhere to retreat. They were lost.

George turned away, knowing that that fight was won. The French hammered on outside, and still from their little store the Guards fired down on them.

'Where are those damned howitzers when you need them?' demanded Macdonnell, shrinking the little store the moment he ran in. 'All well here?'

'Could do with more cartridges soon, sir,' said George smartly.

'I'll see what I can do. Damn it, more reinforcements! The man's obsessed!'

'Is it Bonaparte, sir?' asked a Guard, with hope in his eyes.

'In a way, yes: it's his little brother Jerome. If I had a little brother frittering away my army over here when they should be further down the line, I know what I'd say to him,' said Macdonnell as he disappeared back down the stairs. A few minutes later, James appeared, hauling a box of cartridges.

'There's more downstairs, too,' he said, puffed. 'I'll bring them just now.'

'Good man,' said George. James returned more slowly with the next wooden crate. 'That should keep us going.'

'I dinna ken where he gets it all from,' said James. 'That Macdonnell's magic. Did you see him and yon fellows close the gate? They were amazing! I'm off to join the Guards after this!'

'Good lad!' called one of them. 'Though you'll needs grow a bit.'

'I'll do my best,' grinned James, and peeked out of a window under a guard's elbow. 'My, they just keep coming, don't they?'

'That they do.'

'Ah, but look,' said George, whose gaze had lifted from the French at the gate. 'We do, too.'

And at the ruined wall of the orchard, already engaging the enemy, shone the red coats of more Guards.

'Reinforcements! But how many?' said the Guard nearest.

'Not many: three or four companies, I'd say,' said Macdonnell, appearing again unexpectedly behind them. 'No doubt Wellington thinks that's all we'll need. Let's make that the case, then, gentlemen! Up, Guards, and at them!'

Chapter Twenty-Three

Edinburgh

By seven o'clock, the time at which Murray had reckoned Walter should be home in order that Jemima could also be home by dusk, Murray was mildly irritated. He had been to an afternoon service, walked about in the New Town, taken a look at the outside of his house in Queen Street to see that it was still standing, stretched his legs about the parkland opposite, and contemplated, as though from here it was a distant academic problem, how to entrap Mrs. Sangster and how to make up with Willie Jack. Every now and then he paused, and gazed out over the Forth to the misty low hills of Fife beyond. Where would he rather be, now? Usually when he was in Edinburgh he wanted to be at home at Letho. A week ago he was happier here. Now he had no idea.

By eight o'clock, when dusk was already threatening even on a long Scottish summer evening, there was still no sign of Walter and Jemima. Murray began to be more than irritated, and wandered around his hotel room making muttering noises concerning Walter's abysmal sense of direction, before he made himself summon dinner.

By nine o'clock he was no longer angry, and was beginning to blame himself for trusting Walter out even with Jemima. Where on earth were they? Had Walter decided to walk Jemima back to the Water of Leith before coming back to Fortune's? Since he almost had to pass the hotel's front door on his way from Calton Hill to the Water of Leith, Murray tentatively hoped he could not be that stupid, but for his own peace of mind he allowed himself to believe it for another quarter of an hour. Then he abandoned the book he had been pretending to read, pulled on his coat, gloves and hat, picked up his stick, and headed out to Calton Hill. It was a swordstick: the thought did not make him any happier.

The hill rose sharply out of the buildings, it seemed, just beyond the east end of Prince's Street, after the downhill turn to Leith. It was an area that was not very desirable after dark: there were the cheap tenements of St. James' Square, the orphanage they had visited, the new Bridewell tall and stern at the base of the hill, the Shakespeare Theatre and the people it attracted, but nearby was the glowing white palace of the Register House and the edge of the New Town, a gentle stone-flick away. Once past the buildings, it became clearer that the hill was bordered with tree-lined ravines to the west and north, through which paths meandered to the bare top of the hill where, as he was trying not to recall, he had sat eating ices with Letitia Dundas, only two days ago. It was a popular spot for walks: even as Murray climbed the nearest path, he met gaggles of schoolboys scrambling back down for bedtime, clutching Sabbath-defying tissue paper kites and balloons, some more shredded than others. Slower to descend were late-lingering courting couples, taking advantage of the shadowy woodland to wander in blissfully mutual self-absorption. A few families carried what looked like the remains of picnics and the occasional sleeping child, refreshed by the hill air for another week in the smoky town. Of Walter and Jemima there was no sign.

The path Murray had chosen was rougher and broader than usual and he took a moment to look about him not at the passing people but at the trees. A number had been cut down on each side of the track, and there were deep wheel ruts, not brand new, running up the hill. He frowned, and then remembered what Walter and Jemima had been intending to see up here: this must be the track up which the canny organisers had brought the dead whale. He remembered it was to be at the old Lancastrian school, and followed the tracks to its gate. A light breeze that had freshened the evening air dropped away, and he quickly realised that even if he had not noticed the tracks, he would probably have traced the whale's whereabouts fairly quickly. He was not sure how long it had been dead, but he knew it had been in Edinburgh for a couple of weeks, and it had not leapt fresh from the Forth then. There was smoke rising in little feathers from various points inside the school walls, and after he had dismissed the horrible notion that they were cooking rotten whale meat to offer as a sideline to visitors, he realised that of course they were burning brown paper to counteract the smell. It was not working.

The gate was still open when Murray reached it, and the doorman, who had rags over his face, mumbled something about the admission price. Murray guessed what he had said and paid, then asked,

'Have you seen a young lad and lass here this afternoon? The boy has hair the colour of a hazelnut, and the girl is very fair.' He kept his purse out as an incentive, while the man pondered.

'We've had a gey lot of people up here the day.' The rags moved as though he was sucking in his lips thoughtfully. 'They'd be about so high?' he asked, waving a hand at around the height of Walter's head.

'That's right.'

'She would have had a blue shawl?' Murray thought for a second.

'Yes, yes she had.'

'There was a dog with them, gey excited about the smell. A yellowish thing, thin.' The man did not give the impression of being a dog lover.

'That's them. When were they here?

'The middle of the day, I reckon. Just when the reek was at its best. It didna bother them, they went in anyway, but the boy put the dog on a piece of string to keep it back. I think it would have near ate the whale, otherwise.'

'Did they stay long?' Murray asked, pleased to have found a trace so quickly. It gave him hope.

'Aye, they were whiles in there.' He nodded to the tent in the centre of the schoolyard. It bulged ominously in several directions. 'Then I think they took a wee dander round before they came back out again.'

'Where did they go then, did you see?'

'I did not,' said the man, reaching the end of his usefulness. 'It had turned busy then, see, so I saw them go out past, like, for I had my eye on that dog, but I canna say where they went after.' He eyed the open purse discreetly. Murray co-operated.

'This is some job you have,' he remarked, nodding to the tent.

'Oh, aye,' said the man lugubriously. 'It's grand. As long as a'body kens it's no me making that reek.'

Murray turned his back on the gate, and looked about,

wondering what would have attracted Walter and Jemima next. He had given them money for ices, if the ice kiosk was open. He went to see if it was.

The staff at the kiosk were winding down for the evening, though candles had been lit on the tables to help the last few ice-eaters finish off. Despite giving Walter money, Murray was a little surprised to find the kiosk open on a Sunday, but he supposed the proprietors' determined refusal to sell intoxicating liquors may have had something to do with it. He found an intelligent-looking serving woman, and asked again if she had seen two children answering the descriptions he gave her. She had to think for a moment: it had been a warm day, and they had clearly been busy.

'With a yellowy dog?' she asked after a minute or two. Murray blessed the straw-coloured stray.

'That's the one,' he said eagerly.

'Aye, I mind now. A pretty wee thing, the lass – very fair. And the wee lad very serious.'

'Definitely them,' said Murray. This was going well.

'Aye, they had an ice each,' she admitted. 'I think the dog got the most of one, too. It would have been the back of three when they went, I reckon. They'd been to see that stinking fish over yonder, and they were talking of going to see the Nottinghamshire Hog next on the Mound, but I told them it's closed on the Sabbath.'

'Oh. Of course.' That was over six hours ago, now. It was not going that well. 'And have you by chance seen them since?'

She shook her head.

'Naw, I dinna think so. Mind, we've been that busy, they could easy have walked by and I wouldna have seen them. They're no your bairns, are they, sir?' She was suddenly anxious.

'The boy's my servant,' said Murray. 'He hasn't come home.'

'Och, they'll be off playing – you ken what bairns are like. Dinna fret, sir: they seemed a sensible pair, all the same.' She was kind, now she could see he was worried, and not angry: he thought she would have patted him on the arm if they had been a little closer in rank. He thanked her, and wandered out of the kiosk, avoiding looking at the table where he had sat with Letitia. Where should he go now? The ravine around the hill was steep: could one of them have fallen, and the other tried a rescue?

He decided to make a couple of circuits of the hill, at different levels, and began above the tree line. From there he could see most of the hill top as he circled, even into the great fortified square of the observatory compound, and a good way into the loose woodland down the steep slope. The light was definitely failing now: trees deceived with crooked branches, and the dusk changed distances and faded the colours around him. He made himself walk slowly, studying the ground about him, but eventually he came back to the ices kiosk again, and took a path that led down to a lower, broader circuit. He set off again.

This time he was fighting his way through dim undergrowth: he was very glad he had brought his stick. Every now and then he came to a point where he crossed one of the paths climbing the hill, and could take a moment to look around. He called out, too, now and again, for he could not see far. Perhaps they were not here at all: perhaps they had gone straight to the Water of Leith, or were playing by the Nor'Loch, or looking at the soldiers at the Castle again. But they could have fallen here and been hurt. He bashed on through low-hanging branches and gorsebushes. What if he couldn't find the lad? A vision of Auntie Grisell in the village, handy with her fists, sprang to mind, and he almost laughed. He stumbled out on to another path, and walked straight into someone.

'Here! Get off!' said a woman's voice, much more annoyed than injured or, indeed, frightened.

'My apologies, madam,' said Murray hurriedly, disentangling himself from the edges of a carpet-like shawl. He stepped back and peered at the woman. A broad, pale face stared back at him, and despite the poor light he instantly knew the colour of her gown.

'Miss Brown,' he said, with the hint of a bow.

'Ah, Mr. Murray.' Miss Brown did not trouble herself to curtsey. She looked less hostile than worried, though.

'Is something the matter?' Murray asked. He did not like the fact that Walter was missing and she was here, though she did not seem to have Walter, either.

'Nothing you need concern yourself about,' she said shortly, but she was looking off to either side, peering into the woodland as if she could slice trees out of her way with a glare.

'Have you lost Mrs. Brown?'

'Mrs. – oh, aye. Mother. No, I havena.'

'Have you by any chance, then, lost two young children?'

She met his eye at last, and as the moon rose he found himself on the end of a long, intense stare.

'And if I have?' she asked at last.

'I'm looking for my servant Walter and his friend. Have you seen them?'

She seemed as rigid as a rock, and he could see she was gritting her teeth as she stared past him. Then all at once her shoulders sagged.

'Aye, I have. And aye, I'm looking for them. They gave me the slip, the wee fleggers. I didna think they kenned I was following them, but they must have doubled back that way round the hill, and I was expecting them to come out this way.' She scowled mightily: three cheers for Walter, Murray thought, though it was more than likely he had simply gone the wrong way. 'Howsomever,' Miss Brown continued, 'if they have gone that way, they'll meet my mother in the end.'

'Why?' Murray asked abruptly.

'Why what? She thought they might go on round, I said they wouldna. She was right, as usual,' she added sourly.

'No, I mean why are you doing this? Why are you trying to catch them?'

'Och, I dinna ken.' Miss Brown sounded as though she had pretty much reached the end of her tether. 'It's herself that wants them. Who kens why? I dinna much like bairns, but I wouldn't give one of my own to her.'

'To your mother?'

'Naw! To Mrs. Sangster.'

'But ...'

'Whatever Mrs. Sangster wants, Mrs. Sangster gets, aye? So when she tells us to get the bairns, we get the bairns and take them to her. And when she says run up the hill and see if that lassie's in some minging close off the High Street, that's what we do. And when she says find out what yon Mr. Murray's up till, that speaks so nice and looks at you like he'd as soon run you through with a cavalry sabre, you go and you stand for hours outside his pal's flat, till half the carters have made you propositions you'd likely have made more money out of if they'd paid a fair price – which of course they don't – so you can tell Mrs. Sangster Oh, aye, he jooked out the windae at a quarter past four, thank you, ma'am. So that's where we are with that,' she ended flatly, slapping her mouth shut.

'But why do you do it? Does she pay well?'

'She disna pay at all,' Miss Brown was in a talkative mood. 'She has other ways of making us do a'thing she wants.'

'Other ways?'

'Oh, aye. Though how she ever found out about my faither, that's the puzzle. I thought the only ones kent that was Ma and me. Of course if she went to the sheriff no doubt we'd swing, but there's times I think it might no be a bad thing, compared with all that she's had us doing, in all weathers, too.'

Murray's head was spinning slightly.

'So she makes you do things for her because she found out that you – killed your father?' he asked carefully.

'Well, it was an accident. Sort of. And I never tellt you a'thing about it,' she added hurriedly, leaning closer. He caught a whiff of something very like whisky, and realised why she was suddenly so chatty.

'Of course not,' he said quickly, thinking that whatever she might feel like confiding, she was quite capable of pulling out a knife from her stocky person and inserting it in his stomach. He backed away very slightly. 'Shall we go and look for your mother, then, and see if she knows where the bairns are?'

She did then put a fat hand inside her shawl and fidget about, until he wondered what was going to come out. It was a small bottle, which she uncorked and worked at for a moment. She did not offer him any, for which he was duly grateful.

'Ah … what did you say again?' she asked at last.

'Shall we go and look for your mother?'

'Mother? Aye, aye, that would be best. We'll look for Mother. Come on, then.'

She pulled herself together and reinserted the whisky bottle into some inner recess he preferred not to imagine, and led the way on around the hill, finding some approximate path through the trees which she clearly knew better than he did. He struggled a little to keep up, but the way was fairly clear, and in a short while they found themselves on another of the uphill paths, half moonlit. On the path, desolate, sat a straw-coloured dog. Beside the dog, by the gate leading out of the woodland, was Mrs. Brown. She gaped at Murray arriving with her daughter, then grinned.

'Are you looking your bairns?' she asked with a nasty note in her voice.

'What do you know of them?' he asked sternly. She laughed.

'Has she been talking?' She nodded at her daughter, who stood exuding surliness. 'There's no sense listening to her – she's fou, can you no tell?'

'Leaving that aside, where are Jemima and Walter?' Murray asked again. Mrs. Brown aimed a kick at the dog. It shuffled aside, just fast enough, well-practised.

'Ah, you're too late. She's away with them.'

'Who is? Where did she go?'

'Mrs. Sangster, of course. She's away with them in her fine carriage these twenty minutes or more.'

'But why? Why does she want them? And why bother when Jemima would have been home soon anyway?' None of it made sense.

'Why does she want them?' Mrs. Brown cackled at his stupidity. 'I'd have thought you'd ken well enough, Mr. Murray.'

'Humour me,' he said grimly.

'It's obvious. She wanted her grandson.'

'And she thinks I'll look faster if she takes my servant?'

Mrs. Brown crowed again.

'Did they no send you to school? She wanted her grandson – and now she's got him!'

Chapter Twenty-Four

Belgium

Hougoumont was holding: George had no very clear idea about what might be happening elsewhere on the battlefield, but by what he would have liked to be dinner time, in the middle of the afternoon, Hougoumont was still firmly in the hands of the Nassauers, the Hanoverians, the Coldstream Guards and Lieutenant Colonel James Macdonnell.

The air had been filled all day with the sounds and smells of explosions of all kinds, Bonaparte's various delicacies in the form of shells and grapeshot and shrapnel, smoke and spiced gunpowder, that no one could have put their finger on the precise one, or more than one, that started it. All anyone knew was that by the time they realised there was a problem, the fire at Hougoumont had taken hold.

Coughing and blundering, George and his Guards stumbled down the stairs, finding their own little building was on fire. The courtyard below was in chaos: the gates were holding, but within the walls everything seemed to be burning. The house was blazing. The barns, where the wounded had been laid for safety throughout the day, were on fire. Most terribly, the stables were alight, and the screams of the horses split the air. George's eyes streamed with the smoke, and with sorrow. His horse had never been moved out of there.

Where was James?

Men were running back and forth, pulling water from the well in leather buckets, trying to douse flames. The fire was too well established.

Where could they shelter? Grapeshot was still rattling over the courtyard. Outside the French were tiring, but at least they had somewhere to hide. Inside, they heard, the only building not burning was the chapel. George and his Guards ran.

Inside they found more men sheltering, and Macdonnell himself reading a tiny strip of parchment.

'It's from Wellington,' he explained briefly to an aide. He glanced up as George approached. 'I don't know how you Royal Scots do it,' he added. George nodded politely, not sure he understood. Macdonnell went on. 'He says we're to hold on as long as possible, but only as long as lives aren't being endangered by falling timbers. One of your officers brought this in ten minutes ago,' he explained, waving the parchment strip at George. 'How?' George realised it was a rhetorical question.

'Surely our lives would be more endangered outside with the French?' asked another officer, rubbing at his sleeve which was burned and tattered. Underneath it his skin was one large blister.

'What he means is he's not expecting us to hold Hougoumont any longer than we can,' Macdonnell explained patiently. 'How we get out is our concern. There are ways, if a messenger can get in. And I think we could hack our way through a good few of them before we were finished.'

There was a minor cheer from the men in the chapel, but clearly none of them was looking forward to the experience.

'Where's James?' George asked.

'James?'

'The lad I brought with me. A drummer boy from our regiment.'

'There was a drummer boy in the barn,' said someone. George's heart sank, and he ran back out of the chapel.

It seemed much further back to the courtyard than it had been to run from there to the chapel, round and between and through the chateau's various buildings. When he reached it, the barn was too hot to go near. The flames, fuelled by all the timber intended to keep the harvest dry, roared sky high, and even as he watched the roof sagged and fell in on itself with a great crashing sigh. Men who had been trying to put it out stood back, horrified, among a few walking wounded who had managed to flee the flames in time.

'I'm looking for a drummer boy – I'm told he was in there.'

'That'd be him,' said a soldier. 'I don't know whose luck he has today, but there he is.' He pointed to a small, waif-like figure, black with soot, who stood gazing at the fire in a daze.

'James!' cried George and ran over. He seized the boy by the shoulder.

'Quoi?' murmured the boy. George wiped at his filthy face. His hair was apparently properly black, not just sooty. It was not James.

'That's a French lad who got left behind when the gates were closed,' said the soldier, coming over. 'Was it him you were looking for?'

'No, no, mine's a Scot. Royal Scots,' he added. 'Have you seen him?'

'What's a Royal Scot doing here? It's all Guards here,' said the soldier, clearly not taking in George's own uniform.

'Oh, if you see him tell him I'm looking for him,' said George, and hurried off without remembering to say who he was. He doubted the soldier had noticed.

Where would James be? He ran on, not sure where he was running. A bullet, pinging from somewhere, whined narrowly past him and he threw himself into a corner, forcing himself to think. What had James been doing all afternoon? He had, as far as George knew, been ferrying cartridges around the chateau to various firing points. Well, that meant he could be anywhere: most of the firing points had been concentrated near the vulnerable gate, but they were scattered all around the buildings within the walls. Could he have run outside? That was too complicated to consider. Anyway, why would he have run outside?

Why would he have run outside? The words chimed in George's head. Why would he have run … Why would he have run to Belgium? Who? Why would who have run …?

Pressed into the corner, he straightened and drew from his pocket Charles' letter telling him that Alicia Argo was dead. He had read it many times, mostly out of sheer boredom. It was a wonder it was still approximately in one piece. He quickly found the passage he wanted.

'There is no sign of the son, Theodore: you did not mention him, but perhaps as he is Argo's stepson he did not think to ask. Apparently he had some ambition to be a soldier, a fact I believe I mentioned to you before. Perhaps he has gone to join his father in Belgium? If he appears, I wish you would let me know: he will be able, no doubt, to answer many curious questions. But why would he have run to Belgium?'

To join his father, of course, as Charles had said. Even with a war on, he had run to join the person he trusted, his stepfather. But even though he had made it to the right company, he had never quite made contact with Argo – why? Because Saddler, making sure Argo was out of his way, had spent the last weeks sending Argo on every possible errand and keeping him away from the camp where Theodore – for James must be the missing Theodore - was being trained and looking for him. How could he have been so stupid? Now George was talking to himself. He knew about Theodore, and he knew about James. Why had he never thought to put the two together? Now, how was this to be resolved? Argo was determined not to die and to find Theodore. He had promised to meet George that evening. All George had to do was to make sure that Theodore – James – was fit to come with him and meet Argo, too. Well, then, where was he?

George concentrated more than he ever had in his life before. Each time that James had come with a box of cartridges, he had appeared round the corner into the courtyard from the direction of the chateau. If he himself had been Macdonnell, that was where he would have kept the ammunition: it was most sheltered from attack, and there was probably a cellar or something to stop a direct shell setting the lot on fire. Perfect: now he had to get there.

The corner where he was sheltering suddenly felt very safe, and it took a bit of talking to himself for him to leave it, at a run, scuttling back between the buildings towards the chateau's nearest low door. The upper floors were alight, with thin flames licking around the windows. He wondered briefly who had lived here, and where they were now: fled to Antwerp, he hoped, or at least to Brussels. He took a breath and slipped inside. Where should he start? There was not much choice: the stairs were already on fire, and only the ground floor stone-flagged rooms seemed even slightly safe. He ran to the nearest door, felt it quickly with the back of his hand – cool – and snatched it open. He was in luck. It was the cellar door. There was a torch lit on the stairs, and he was about to run down to see what was there when he tripped on something and nearly fell head first. He saved himself and crouched to see what it was. It was James.

Smoke, he thought, lifting the boy swiftly and running back into the comparatively fresh air outside. He sat James against a wall and slapped his face back and forth. There was no response. He felt James' throat above the tight stock: there was a pulse, of sorts. He unbuckled the stock, trying to do it gently, and glanced down as it fell from his hands. Blood. James' coat was dark with blood, and it all centred on a wound in his stomach.

George leapt up, took a step, floundered and crouched down again. There was a fleeting pain in his buttock, but he paid it no attention.

'Right,' he said. 'Right. Got to find … got to stop him bleeding.' He whipped off his silk sash and folded it into a wad, slid it inside James' coat and buttoned it tight over him, holding it in place. 'Got to … got to get to Argo.'

If this seemed rational to George, then the next thing that happened made very little sense at all. He heard a light clipping of hooves, and looked up to see his horse, fully saddled and bridled, walking casually round the corner.

Later he could not say how he had left Hougoumont: there must have been a way, for Wellington's parchment message had entered it. The horse he knew he had left fully saddled, and loosely tied, so that part he could imagine. He had a memory, which he could not properly place, of a garden filled with jasmine and honeysuckle, and an orchard now battered and fruitless. But how he found himself with James across his lap riding around the back of the lines in the late afternoon – that was simply one of the mysteries of battle.

It was not that the ridge felt any safer than Hougoumont had: it was just as smoky, stinking with gunpowder, blood and sweat, churned with mud. George was sure he was half-deaf already, for the thunder of French and Allied guns was almost continuous. He hoped the whole scene made sense to Wellington, for it made damned all to him.

Along the ridge the infantry were still, amazingly, in squares, facing French light infantry that pounded again and again up the hill towards them. How the cavalry even made it, George could not tell: the Allied artillery fired and fired at them until the very last minute, and even as the gun shook with the last shell through it, the crew scurried off with one gun wheel into the nearest square that closed around them. Reeling from the grape and canister shot, the cavalry still staggered up the hill until they were less than thirty yards from the squares. George, sure he was to be overwhelmed, broke his way into the back of a square and held James close against him as he stood by his horse. A thunder of musket fire burst from the square at the advancing cavalry.

'Prepare to receive cavalry!' shouted a lieutenant in the centre, and the front rank knelt at once, gunbutts to the ground and bayonets up. Two ranks of musketmen fired from behind them, and a swathe of French horses and men tottered and fell backwards, down the hill.

'I like a good cavalry charge,' remarked the lieutenant to George conversationally. 'It's a rest from the bombardment.' George stared at him blankly. 'Oh, there go our cavalry again: as long as they remember to come back this time!' the lieutenant went on. 'Right, men, reform. Pull the wounded in. Reload.'

Half a dozen wounded men were hauled through the ranks and deposited as carefully as circumstances would allow in the centre of the square. Here blood mingled with the mud and the ground was slippery. As George thanked the lieutenant and prepared to leave, one man was dragged past him, slashed by a sabre from ear to ear in a manic, bloody grin. He glanced up: the lieutenant was smiling, too. The whole place, he decided, was mad.

The fog did not help: in some places it was in shreds as if a savage hand had ripped it apart, in others it settled like a huge, comfortable blanket that slipped every now and again, revealing horrors beyond. More than once George saw Wellington at the gallop, his blue cloak flying, low black cockaded hat at an angle. A swell of enthusiasm rose from the troops as he passed, though he quietened all attempts to cheer him. Once he saw him sweep after a deserting company and talk them back, by magic, presumably. Magic: he glanced down at James. The boy was horribly pale.

At last he found himself back where Picton's division had started, in front of half familiar trees behind the ridge. There seemed to be casualties – and where were the cavalry, the Scots Greys? – as he found his way to where a surgeon was working hard apparently operating on several officers of a regiment George did not even recognise. He slid off his horse, reckoned he could trust the animal not to run away if not tethered, after today, and taking James in his arms he pushed his way inside.

'Officers only, sir,' said an orderly, trying to stop him at the mouth of the tent.

'Well, I'm an officer,' said George in a sudden surge of unaccustomed authority, 'and this boy's been my right arm all day. Now let me in.'

The orderly backed off as George angled his way into the tent. The only free bed was bloody and rumpled, but it was a space, and George laid James down tenderly. In a moment the surgeon came over, wiping a filthy saw on his apron and pushing his hair back from his forehead with the other, reddened hand.

'A knife or a sword to the stomach,' said George crisply.

'Knife, I believe,' said the surgeon, lifting the soaked sash from James' wound. He unbuttoned James' breeches and slid them down to give himself more room to work. George glanced down.

Well, he thought, laughing aloud, there was irrefutable proof.

This was not Theodore.

James was a girl.

The room blackened round him and he fainted.

Jasmine and honeysuckle, he thought: a summer's day in the gardens of Hougoumont. There was a sweetish scent in the air, but it was not quite jasmine and honeysuckle: he was no gardener, but he felt fairly sure about that. Nor was he lying on soft grass, as he had thought, but on a board with a sheet over it, his head on a thin bundle of rags designed for a pillow. There was a grey blanket over him, he saw, as he dragged his eyes open. Why, though, was he lying on his stomach? He never slept on his stomach. Damn it, rum again, he thought, licking his dry lips. Who had been feeding him rum this time?

He tried to turn over to sit up, but for some reason found it very difficult. Then a grey hooded orderly entered his limited field of vision, and tapped him on the shoulder.

'Awake, sir?' he asked. 'Don't try to move: you won't enjoy it.'

'Have I been wounded?' George asked in surprise.

'Oh, yes, sir, don't you remember?'

'Well, no, truthfully. I remember …' Or did he? It seemed very odd. He turned his head, and saw that young James was lying on an adjacent bed of approximately equal luxury, but on his back. He was apparently asleep, and still very pale.

'James!' he called. The orderly came round the bed to return to sight.

'Did you see him stir, sir?'

'No.'

'Oh. Oh, well. He's sleeping, see, and maybe that's for the best.'

'Did I see … I mean, is it true – that he's … er …'

'That he's in fact a she? Yes, sir, it is. You calling him – her – James made me wonder if you'd remembered, so it was best to go on saying 'he'. But yes, sir, she's a girl.'

George lay for a moment, wondering.

'And orderly?' he said at last. 'How am I wounded?'

'Oh, sir, you've been shot. A pistol shot, so lucky for that: the damage isn't great, but we had to dig the bullet out.'

'But where? I can't feel it.'

'You will soon, sir. You've been shot in the a… - in the behind, sir.' The orderly, coughing slightly, left abruptly, and George was alone but for James, or whatever her name was. He watched her for a moment. She breathed gently, nothing in her pale face to indicate the mischief and bravery she had shown in fairly equal measure. A knife wound, though: for the first time it occurred to him to wonder about that. No French, that he knew of, had made it into Hougoumont after the hand-to-hand fight in the courtyard, and James had been running round perfectly well long after that. Who could have stabbed him? Her? Who? He felt sleep tugging at him again. But he must not sleep: he must consider this important question. What was it again? Oh, yes: James. James was Theodore. He had to tell Argo. But no, there was some reason why James was not Theodore – what was it again? And gradually, George slept.

When he woke again it was dark outside the tent, but someone had lit candles and the place had a cosy look. Across from him, James the girl still slept, but her face had a little more colour, he thought: or perhaps it was the candlelight. Outside, he could hear a raised voice, one that he thought was familiar. Who was it? What was it saying, anyway?

'No, it's an officer I'm looking for. A Royal Scot.'

'Name, sir? We have a Royal Scot here, I think.' George half-lifted his head from the pillow, ears pricked.

'Saddler. Major Saddler. Have you seen him?'

'I don't think that's the name, sir, but you're welcome to go in and look,' said the orderly, and a moment later Gunn strode into the tent.

'Murray!' he cried. 'You're alive!'

'So I'm told,' said George with a grin.

'The last we heard you had made it to Hougoumont, but there weren't that many that came out on their feet. I'm heartily glad to see you – but where's – oh!'

And Gunn knelt suddenly by James' bed, grasping her hand as if by that alone he could revive her. George looked at his face, as he stared down at the girl, and felt stupider than ever.

'She's your daughter!'

'What?' Gunn reeled back on his heels. 'So you know? How did you –'

'Well, I found out when we came here that he was a she, to start with. Then you were very protective of her. And, well, just looking at the two of you now: there's a real likeness, when you know where to look.'

'Aye. Well. Well, yes, she is, the minx.' He stroked her fair hair for a second, cautiously, as if she might break. 'Was she in the fire? We heard about the fire.'

'Yes and no. She wasn't burned at all. I found her during the fire, but she'd been stabbed.'

'In the fight? We heard about a fight, too.'

'There's no story left for me to tell!' complained George. 'No, not in the fight. I don't know how or who did it. The French were all out of the place by the time I found her. She was a valiant lad during the day, you know: she carried cartridges all over the chateau where they were most needed, running around under fire like the best of them.'

'But then who could have done this?'

'I have no idea. I'm sorry, Gunn: if I'd known … I should have looked after her better.'

'I'm sure you did your best, Murray. She's not one to allow herself to be looked after much.' He touched her hair again, minutely, then seemed to remember why he was there. 'We've lost Saddler,' he said, still holding James' hand.

'He's dead?'

'No – well, we don't know. We've lost nearly half the battalion, you know.'

'Half! Oh my.' George fell silent. 'But the battle? When I last saw anything it was about four o'clock: the French were running cavalry charges up at the infantry on the ridge. Someone said the cavalry had gone? Is the battle over?'

'It is, it is,' said Gunn, 'and Bonaparte is defeated – or he's running, anyway. It won't be long now. Damned Imperial Guard refuse to surrender: you simply have to kill them. But we'll finish him off, no doubt. But Saddler – he's vanished. I don't remember seeing him from about the time of the first volleys from the French – that would be the back of eleven this morning. I thought he must have fallen and of course I took command, half expecting to have him come up behind me at any moment, but he hasn't.' Gunn ran his fingers back through his thin hair, worried and perplexed. 'I've walked the ridge a dozen times looking for his body, but there's nothing: I think I must have turned over every dead redcoat between here and Nivelles, and sadly there are plenty of them. They say the Duke's devastated at the losses. But I can't find Saddler: it's as if he's been snatched up to heaven.'

'Or down the other way,' murmured George, but he well knew how much Gunn respected Saddler, and the man was clearly upset. Then Gunn jumped up at the sound of familiar words outside.

'I fink there's a couple more bleedin' Royal Scots in 'ere – we'll stick him with them. He really is a bleedin' Royal Scot,' he added, with the solemnly grim humour of the private soldier at work. Two of them angled into the little shelter with a stretcher between them …

'Where did you find him?' Gunn demanded.

'Bloody Hougoumont,' said the soldier, keen to keep his profanities relevant.

'No,' said Gunn, 'that can't be right.'

'Bloody is,' said the soldier. 'Walked back with them myself.'

'What's wrong with him?' asked George.

'Reckon he's had a chestful of smoke, then a beam fell on him. Found him in the barn, but the end of it, like: middle was – well, no rescues in the middle, put it that way.'

George shivered, remembering the dancing flames and the roof falling in. Perhaps that was what had hit Saddler. But what had he been doing there?

'Oh, he was there, for certain,' came another voice, lightly accented. A Nassauer, his green coat shredded and his leg dangling, glanced in to their part of the tent. 'I saw him myself. He fought so bravely in the courtyard: his sword was knocked from him, but he had a knife out and did oh! much damage to the French. So cold, that one!' he added, and lurched on, called forward to have his wounds attended to.

The orderlies laid Saddler on a board on George's other side, tidying a swinging arm into position, and left to go about their business. George watched him for a moment. Had Saddler come after him to tell him something? It seemed highly unlikely, but then it did not seem like Saddler at all to desert his command in the middle of a battle. A sound came from the other side, and he turned his head back awkwardly. Gunn's gentle rubbing of James' hand seemed to be having an effect: the girl was stirring. In a moment she opened her eyes.

'Captain?' she said quietly. Something in his face must have told her her trick had been seen through. 'Father?' she added. Gunn smiled.

'You've been hurt, Jane,' he said softly. George closed his eyes, lacking the energy to turn his head away in discretion. 'You were at Hougoumont –'

'So I was! That was a day out, I can tell you!'

'So I've heard!' Gunn laughed. 'But you were hurt. You have a stab wound in your stomach. Murray brought you out and you're being looked after.'

'A stab wound? Oh …' She paled again, and looked beyond Gunn's shoulder. 'I thought I'd dodged him, but then it went awful cold. And I saw the blood. Why did he do it?'

'Who, sweetheart?' asked Gunn, as George shuddered. 'Who was it? A Frenchman, I suppose?'

'No, silly. It was Major Saddler.'

George's eyes shot open.

'Saddler?' He could not help himself.

'He's been watching me for ages,' Jane explained. 'Father thought he'd rumbled me, but it can't have been that, can it? I mean, a lashing, maybe, but he stabbed me!' She sounded more outraged than anything. 'And it bloody hurts!'

'That's enough of that kind of language, now you're a girl again,' said her father severely. 'I can see I have a great deal to do with you.'

'Ach, go chase yourself, Father,' said his daughter without hostility. 'I can manage myself.' Her eyes were closing again, but George could clearly see now how much more colour there was in her cheeks, and the mischievous smile on her face was quite familiar.

Gunn stood, slowly, staring down at her, his expression changing from stern fondness as she closed her eyes to something very different. George watched him, but somehow could not find a word to say, not even a foolish one. Gunn stood very still for a long moment, only the slightest twitch of his fingers showing that somewhere in his mind, a long conversation was happening. Then he turned, and walked around the end of George's bed where George could not see him. George moved his head, trying to be as silent as Gunn. On his other side, Saddler lay, stirring slightly, his face sooty and a rough bandage around his forehead. George watched as Gunn lifted a clean bandage from the folding table between the beds, and laid it, very carefully, over Saddler's mouth and nose. He looked down at the Major.

'You were a fine soldier, sir. I would have followed you into any battle. *I served who best was worthy, best to be served.*'

Then he laid his hands across the bandage, and pressed hard. George twisted his head into his ragged pillow, scrunching his eyes shut. He heard, very slightly, thumping, flailing, grunting – and then nothing. When he opened his eyes, Gunn, tears pouring down his face like yesterday's downpour, was refolding the bandage and replacing it on the table. Saddler was dead.

Chapter Twenty-Five

Edinburgh

Murray ran back towards Prince's Street. He was thoroughly confused, but of one thing he was absolutely sure: he had to get Walter back from Mrs. Sangster.

Dark city streets were not meant for running on. He jogged with his head down, trying to see what obstacles loomed ahead, slithering on unseen hazards on the cobbles. A horse would definitely be better. He pelted on, calculating the quickest place to find an available horse. There was a stable behind Fortune's, he remembered, with livery horses handy for hotel guests. The horses would be reasonably good, too. He kept going.

Well, at least now he knew what the Browns had been up to, and that they were definitely working for Mrs. Sangster. If he could make them admit that Mrs. Sangster had blackmailed them into killing Alicia, that would be perfect. But somehow he doubted that Mrs. Brown would be prepared to confess to killing someone for Mrs. Sangster because Mrs. Sangster knew she had killed her husband. Miss Brown might talk after a dram or two, but Mrs. Brown looked as if she had a stronger head.

Prince's Street: he was past the end of North Bridge, past the Register House: not far now to Fortune's. And the road was better. He picked up speed.

And evidently they had been supposed to catch Theodore, too, and bring him to his grandmother. They had failed in the flat, because Alicia had managed to convince them that Theodore was not there, with her quick thinking over hiding the other plate. That must have been what they were doing when he saw them at the close later, the day he found Alicia's body. They were back looking for Theodore. That was why they had been following him ever since, he supposed, waiting to see if he would lead them to the boy. Then somehow they had got it into their heads that Walter was Theodore. And that could not be a good thing for Walter.

He skidded up the lane that led to the stables, smelling the warm straw and dung, and was relieved to see that there were lights inside. He hammered on the gate. In a few minutes, though it seemed like an hour, he had his foot in the stirrup and was off.

What if they had not gone to the Water of Leith? The thought sprang into his mind, even as his hands and knees were learning this new horse and it was learning him. They trotted along Prince's Street, and he itched to go faster. The Water of Leith was the only place he could think of, so he had to try there first. The street was at least clear at this time of night – but no, he had thought too soon. Ahead was a jumble of carriages, queuing to decant their fine-looking owners at some grand flat. Could the horse squeeze through? He quickly decided that it was impossible, and turned through a gap down to the muddy Nor'Loch. Here at least there was no social restraint on speed, though respect for his horse's fetlocks was another matter. In a moment they were at the walls of the West Kirk burying ground, back on the street and round the corner. Now he really could fly, if only the horse would co-operate.

The horse, he knew instantly, would. The novelty alone was lending wings to her feet. This was not the daily lot of the hired nag: this was adventure, and he could feel the excitement flowing from her as she reached and leapt so that it was only seconds later that they skittered on the moonlit cobbles outside the Sangsters' low front door and he slid out of the saddle to knock. The horse, he was convinced, was grinning from ear to ear.

In a moment, he heard the lock clack and the door opened. Mr. Sangster himself pulled it back, then squinted as he saw someone he was not expecting outside.

'Mr. Murray? Is that you? What on earth brings you here at this time of the night? Has something happened?'

'Is your wife in, sir? Is Mrs. Sangster in?'

'Of course she is,' said Sangster, more bewildered than angry. 'Where else would she be?'

'And your maid, Jemima,' Murray hurried on. 'Is she back from her afternoon off?'

'She … ah … I wouldn't know that. Lauder!' he called, but Lauder must have been coming to answer the door anyway, for he appeared instantly at the door to the back of the house.

'Sir?'

'The maid – what's her name? Is she back yet? Surely she is: the sun's set long ago.'

'She's not, sir. She was told to be back by dusk.'

'That won't please Mrs. Sangster,' Sangster commented. 'Where is the mistress, Lauder? Is she in the parlour or has she retired?'

'I'll go and look, sir,' said the servant. In the dim hallway, lit only by a couple of candles, Murray could not see his face, but that did not make him any more comfortable.

'Come in, Mr. Murray, come in,' said Sangster. 'You look as if you've had a bit of a ride. Come in and have a brandy.' He still looked puzzled, but his hospitality – and perhaps discretion - forbade him to discuss Murray's business in the street.

'My horse, sir – ' said Murray. The horse had a fresh, alert look as if she had never had such an exciting day in her life. For an instant Murray almost envied her.

'Oh, that's so. When Lauder comes back I'll get him to rouse the coachman, and we'll find a stable for your horse.' He eyed the mare uncertainly, as if he had not seen a horse up close before. The mare tossed her head, dismissing him. Murray liked her more.

'Ah, here's Lauder. Well, where is she, Lauder?'

'The mistress is not in the parlour, nor in her chamber, sir. In fact, I couldna tell you where she is at all.'

'She's not in the house?'

'No, sir.'

'Then the garden, maybe?'

'The back door's long locked, sir.'

'Even with the maid still out?'

'The maid can chap, sir,' said Lauder sourly. And you were making her suffer for being late, thought Murray.

'Well,' said Sangster, astonished. 'Where can she be? She didn't tell you she was going anywhere, did she?'

'No, sir.' A look passed between master and man: it was a look of mutual sympathy, Murray thought, two men suffering at the hands of the same woman. Murray wondered if, when it came to it, Sangster would try to protect his wife from Murray's accusations. Perhaps not.

'Can you think of anywhere else she would go at this time of night, sir?' he asked, trying to instil in them the same urgency he felt himself. Could he have inadvertently overtaken them, reached the village first? 'Friends? Some open space? Somewhere with room for a carriage?' Had Walter struggled, he wondered, as Mrs. Sangster and Mrs. Brown had pushed him into the carriage? Had he tried to protect Jemima? Had they tricked him in some way? Had he realised that he was in danger? He was not sure he had treated Walter as well as he could have in his short period of service with him. Did Walter even think Murray might be trying to help now?

'Where else would she go, Lauder – can you think?' Sangster asked. 'She has no relations about the place: they're down in the Borders.' Murray flinched at the thought of a midnight ride to the Borders. 'Friends … well, she has acquaintances, of course. But a friend she would go to at this time of night? I canna call anyone to mind.'

'Nor I, sir,' Lauder agreed dutifully. The horse twitched: some noise had distracted her. Then Lauder's head went up, too, like a fox with a scent.

'That's the mill, sir.'

'The mill? What – Oh, devil take it, you're right! The lever must have slipped – but how?'

Already the two men were running down to the bridge. Murray tied the mare's reins to the risp, and sprinted after them. He caught them at the bridge, and the three of them teetered across as fast as they could. Murray realised what the mare had heard. The great millwheel had been spinning as always, but the machinery inside, the cogs and shafts that would never normally shift on the Sabbath, they were now churning too. He tried to get a look at the massive mill as he crossed the river. In a window about halfway up he thought, by the uncertain moonlight, he could see movement. Was there even a candle? But a candle in a flour mill was not a sensible thing.

The door to the mill was shut, and Sangster put out a hand immediately to open it, but Murray held him back.

'Wait,' he said in a low voice. 'Whoever is in there –'

'But there's no one in there!' objected Sangster, clearly thinking he was daft. 'The lever has slipped, that's all!'

'Hush, please, sir,' said Murray quickly. 'There is almost certainly someone in there, and I believe that my servant and your maid are amongst them.'

'The maid?' Lauder snapped. 'She'll pay if she is. What does she think –'

'Please!' said Murray, more loudly than he would have liked. 'We mustn't give them any warning that we are here. Please.'

Lauder watched Sangster. Sangster frowned and pursed his lips, then said,

'Oh, very well, have it your way. But we need to get that machinery closed down.'

'Of course. Now, lead the way.'

'Allow me, sir,' said Lauder, and Sangster nodded. Murray might not like the manservant but it was clear that Sangster was well used to trusting him. Lauder turned the handle silently, and gave the door a gentle push. It opened without a sound.

Inside the noise of the machinery was almost as great as it had been the previous day, but no workers seemed to be about and only a last trickle of flour emerged from the chute that delivered it downstairs. The bitter taste of it filled the air. They looked about carefully. The lever to disengage the millwheel was on this floor, but Murray waved them away from it, pointing upstairs. Sangster scowled but shrugged, and they made their quiet way to the wooden stairs, Lauder still leading the way protectively. Sangster followed, and Murray brought up the rear. At least the noise of the machinery masked any creaks from the steps.

There was a candle on the next floor. It sat on the edge of a motionless millstone, one set aside for removal, worn out. It cast an odd light from its low position, outlining the doorway through the wooden partition that led to the chamber where Murray had seen grain pouring into the crushing machinery. The three men, Sangster shocked at the candle, crept up the remaining stairs and tiptoed round to get a look in the doorway before whoever was inside would see them. This time, Sangster went first.

He poked his head round the doorpost, said loudly,

'Oh! It's only you,' and strode inside. There was a little gasp, just audible over the grinding stones, and Murray and Lauder followed fast.

'Well,' said Mrs. Sangster, 'that's no very convenient.'

She was glaring at her husband, her heavy-boned face oddly shaped by low candlelight and high moonlight now blaring through the large windows. She was in the middle of the room, turned towards the newcomers. Between her and the nearest set of turning millstones were Walter and Jemima. Murray saw that they were holding hands – clutching, he thought, would be a better word.

'Mr. Murray!' Walter squeaked. 'I thought you'd come. Mr. Robbins always says –'

'That's enough,' snapped Mrs. Sangster, and Walter fell silent.

'It's all right, Walter, we'll sort this out,' said Murray, as calmly as he could.

'What are you doing, dear?' asked Sangster, who no longer seemed entirely reassured that it was only his wife in his mill. 'Why are you up here? And why is the machinery running? Did the lever slip?'

'Oh, aye, it slipped,' said his wife, mocking. 'I slipped it. Well, Mr. Murray, you think you're going to sort this out, do you? I can't say I'm that pleased to see you. If the three of you would just go away now for a few minutes, I'm showing these bairns how the mill works.'

'I'm not sure they're interested in the mill,' said Murray, trying to sound calm, 'though I admit they seem to have your full attention. Best answer your husband truthfully, Mrs. Sangster. What are you doing here?'

She glanced from one to the other of them, looking for a weak point. Some movement she made behind her back made Jemima and Walter back closer to the grindstones. She must have a knife, Murray thought.

'I imagine you've already told my husband who this young man is,' she said, pointing with her free hand to Walter.

'He's my servant,' said Murray. 'His name is Walter Fenwick, and he's the grandson of my father's old butler. He was born in Letho, in Fife, on my estate.'

'Well, I'm sure there is such a person,' said Mrs. Sangster with a little laugh, 'but this isn't him, is it? You've been hiding him right under our noses, sending him to walk out with Jemima, trailing him after you when you come to the house. It isn't Walter Fenwick standing there, is it? It's my own grandson, Theodore Sangster.'

Murray had expected this, but Mr. Sangster had not – and nor had Walter. Even as Mr. Sangster cried out, 'Theodore!' and Lauder's jaw dropped, Walter's eyes and mouth widened like pools.

'I'm no Theodore!' he stated firmly. 'I might have been looking him that long I'd near pretend to be him so as not to walk to another church seeking him, but I'm no him.'

'Theodore?' Mr. Sangster had taken a step towards the children, his hand out. But Mrs. Sangster did have a knife, and now she flourished it, taking a step so that she was between Sangster and Walter.

'You have him well schooled, Mr. Murray,' she said. 'How much did my husband pay you to hide him?'

'I did not!' said Sangster. 'I was seeking him, it's true, and I asked Mr. Murray to let me know when he found him. I knew you wouldn't care for him,' he added, pathetically accusing.

'So you were holding on to him for the highest bid? Well, I have him now,' said Mrs. Sangster. She inched nearer the children, making them edge further towards the millstones. Murray gasped, involuntarily putting out a hand. Mrs. Sangster turned the knife towards him so it caught the light. 'And Theodore, keen to find out all about his grandfather's precious business, is going to go much too near to the millstones and meet with a dreadful accident. Isn't that right?'

'But why?' Murray demanded, desperate to stop her. 'Your own grandson?'

'Aye, the son of that pathetic, cold elder son of mine. There was aye a nasty streak in him. Who knows what his son has picked up, between him and that drip of a mother? But if he's out of the way, Sangster, my dear husband, will have to leave all his business to Peter, won't you, dear? He can't thole Peter, but he can thole even less the thought of all this leaving the family.'

'But Theodore!' cried Sangster, and he had barely taken his eyes off Walter. He inched towards the boy. Walter's face was flour-white, baffled. Mrs. Sangster saw her husband move and again edged between him and the children. If she only moved a pace or two further, Murray thought he could slip round the other way. But the machinery was churning: where she was, she would only have to step back to sweep Walter into the relentless stones.

'Aye,' she said, as if they would not notice the way she was angling herself for better purchase. 'Peter thought the lad had gone to Belgium, thought he'd found him. He's in the army, you know, my son: an officer in the Royal Scots. He knows your brother well, Mr. Murray – or he did.'

A chill ran down Murray's spine. What had happened to George?

In that instant, he was nearly bowled over. For a second, he could not work out what had happened. Then he saw Lauder had broken past him, past Mrs. Sangster's knife, and snatched Walter over to the side of the room. Jemima, still gripping his hand, was flung after. Lauder stopped between his master and mistress, trying to push the knife back with his bare hand, while Sangster cowered behind him. The children, for a moment unnoticed, ran to Murray. He pressed them behind his back, and thought it was nearly time to leave. He glanced towards the door, but was spotted at once.

'Get back here!' cried Mrs. Sangster.

'Aye, you can't go now!' added her husband. 'Theodore! I've been looking everywhere for you! You must stay, and I can teach you all about the mill and the flour and the business ...'

There came a sharp sigh from behind Murray's left elbow. He turned. Jemima stepped forward, with a look of exasperation on her face. She patted Walter on the arm.

'He's not Theodore,' she said firmly.

'Aye, right,' said Mrs. Sangster rudely.

'He's not, you stupid old woman,' said Jemima. 'I'm Theodore.'

The silence that followed was abruptly broken by Walter's sudden, hearty laughter.

'You're Theodore?' he choked, when he could. Everyone stared at him. 'I thought you were grand company for a girl.'

'Walter ...' Murray seized him by the elbow and whispered in his ear. Walter took on his solemn, responsible look again and trotted to the stairs. Murray made sure with a look that no one followed. At least one of them would leave this safe.

'Right,' he said, trying to assume some control. He blinked at

Jemima. The revelation had explained a good deal. There was a clunking sound from downstairs, and with a last sighing rasp the machinery slowed to a halt. They could hear the patter of Walter's feet on the wooden floor and the plashing waterwheel outside. 'Let's get this sorted out.'

'Lauder, you'd better get after that boy,' muttered Sangster.

'Don't even think about it,' said Murray, and drew the sword from his swordstick. Jemima / Theodore made an appreciative 'Ooh!'. Lauder, more to the point, backed off. 'Right,' he repeated. 'Theodore – it's really you?'

'Aye, sir. And if Mr. Lauder pinches my behouchie once more, I'll cut his hand off with a blunt knife,' he added with some venom. Lauder had the decency to look a little abashed.

'It never occurred ...' Mrs. Sangster stared at Theodore. 'You were a useless maid, though.'

'That's how you got me cheap, wasn't it?' Theodore, now he was free to talk, was not holding back.

'Right, well, let's talk about your working conditions later,' said Murray, who had other things on his mind. 'Were you in the flat when your mother was murdered?'

Theodore's fair face darkened.

'I was. And I did nothing.'

'Can you tell me something more about it?' Murray asked gently. Theodore gave a little nod, as if telling himself to be strong.

'We were having our supper. It was the Friday evening. She was expecting a visit: we'd left the Potterrow after my father went into the army because she said my grandmother had found out where we were living, and my father was no longer there to protect us. She always said my grandmother had killed my father, but I don't know. I didn't quite believe her then, but now ...' He eyed Mrs. Sangster with a look that did not belong on a child's face. 'We liked Mr. Campbell – he's the landlord – but he wouldna be much use in a stramash.'

'I know what you mean,' agreed Murray. The other three were motionless, colourless pen-and-ink drawings in the moonlight, but he did not take his eyes off them.

'We left most of our stuff there, and went to the Dean Village. She wanted to be near the Water of Leith, because she had some hopes she might be able to argue the case with my grandfather. She said he wanted to bring me back into the family, but from all she's said about my real father's family – and all I've seen since – I've no wish to be in it. She said he wanted to take me away from her. I don't know why she thought she could argue with him over it: she was a gentle person, my mother, but she wasna very strong: she thought other people were much nicer than they really were, usually.'

For some reason a vision of Bessie Cordiner, jealous and greedy, popped into Murray's mind. He nodded.

'So we went to the Dean. We werena there long. The landlord took a fancy to her and she had a lot of trouble with him. So we moved again – we hadna much to move so it was easy for the two of us just to go – and I think she'd changed her mind about arguing with *him*' – he nodded a dismissive head at his grandfather – 'for she'd had word from him again and he wasn't giving in, so she found a place in the Old Town thinking he wouldna look for us up there. My, that place reeked! But she said it wouldna be for long, either, and when my father came back from the army then we could all be together again in our old flat and be safe. Then that man Chisholm – he was our landlord, the one that fancied her.'

'We've met,' said Murray.

'He came looking for her, and she knew we weren't safe there, either, for if he could find us then *he* could, too. She was gey cross,' he added, rather proudly.

There was a mumbled objection from Sangster.

'You'd have been safe with me,' he said, but Theodore cast him a look of disgust.

'So what happened that evening?' Murray drew him back.

'We were having our supper. Ma looked out the window to the yard, and she leapt up and said this was it, we had to get me hidden. I ran and hid under the bed behind the bed curtain that was there, and she hid my dishes and all, and then there was a knock on the door, and in they came. Well, that curtain was thick, and I couldna hear properly, but they had an argument and then everything went very quiet, and it – it all just happened so fast …'

Theodore's shoulders shook in his thin dress. Murray put his free left hand on the boy's shoulder, and gave him a moment to recover. The other three stood transfixed: he would almost have sworn they had not taken a breath between them.

Theodore by contrast drew a long breath, swallowed hard, and swallowed again before he could restart.

'I came out and I found her … I wanted to do something. I couldn't think what. I knew if they found me I'd not get the chance to do anything, so I thought I'd disguise myself. I took what I could of our things because the old woman downstairs would rob you as you stood talking to her, and I came down here and offered myself as a maid at my grandparents' house. I was biding my time.'

'So …' Murray was impressed at the boy's courage. 'So do you know who actually killed your mother?'

'No.'

'Oh.'

There was a small collective sigh from the three witnesses, and Mr. Sangster took out a handkerchief and wiped his white face.

'I ken who it wasna, though,' said Theodore, and the three tensed again. 'It wasna *her*.'

'It wasn't your grandmother? Mrs. Sangster?' Murray tried to hide his surprise.

'It was a man, you could tell by the voice, even though I couldna hear it properly. But it was one of the other two, definitely. I know fine, because I saw the boots. And my grandfather wears those boots, but Mr. Lauder there, he wears his old ones.'

There was a long pause. It was as if all of them knew there was no point in any protest or defence: whatever was to happen would happen, rolling on as inexorably as the millwheel. Lauder took the opportunity to slip the knife away from Mrs. Sangster, and she made no objection, propping herself against the silent stones.

'Well, gentlemen,' said Murray at last. 'Does either of you have anything to say?'

'What should we say?' Sangster asked in a small voice. 'Poor Alicia. She never deserved that.'

'Where were you on that Friday night?' Murray persisted. 'Lauder? You first.'

'I was in the house, sir. And I can say definitely that Mr. Sangster was at home the whole evening. There's no possibility that he killed anyone.' He finished firmly, looking somewhere past Murray's ear. He was so completely sure of himself that Murray was positive he was lying.

'And you, Mr. Sangster?' Here we go, he thought to himself: they'll each defend the other and we'll get nowhere. Sangster gave a little frown, and wiped at his lips with his handkerchief.

'I was indeed at home that evening. I spent the whole evening at home. But as to Lauder here, I'm afraid I couldn't say for certain if he was in all evening or no. In fact,' he added, as if he had suddenly remembered, 'now I come to think of it, I'm sure I heard him go out at some point. He was out for a while, too.'

'What?' said Lauder, and his voice was like blades being sharpened.

'Well, I can't help it, Lauder. You were definitely out. You can't expect me to lie for you now, can you?' Sangster's expression was sanctimoniously kind: he was only, he implied, doing this for Lauder's own good. He did not meet Lauder's eye, and that might have been a mistake.

'You only know I was out because you were with me!' hissed Lauder. Murray knew that hiss: in an instant he was back with the mob on High Street.

'Now, now, you've already said I was at home all evening!'

'You know you weren't! You want me to take the blame, after all I've done for you?'

'Lauder, calm down,' said Sangster, in a voice that made Murray want to punch him, never mind Lauder.

'You want me to take the blame. You – you know I've only done what you've ordered. And what's this for – is this because you think I let you down? Is this just because whatever else I've done, I wouldn't kill a woman for you? Is that it? So you had to dirty your own hands, and now you're going to betray me!'

Murray was holding his breath. Sangster looked horrified, eyes darting back and forth, reminding himself who was listening.

'You can't say that! I'm a respectable merchant, not some scum that kills poor drunkards and sets their flat on fire!'

'On your orders!' Lauder licked his lips: he was fiddling with something in his pocket. 'And only because I'd had to pay them to find out where Alicia Argo was, and you thought they'd talk as easily to the next man! I enjoyed working for you, when you weren't such a selfish old fool,' he added, ominous and low. Then he did punch Sangster, in the ribs.

Or so Murray thought: but Sangster gave a cry, and a gurgle, and sank to the floor. Lauder pulled the knife away and ran for the door. Murray stuck a foot out, but Lauder leapt it neatly, and reached the top of the stairs. And that was where he stopped, for a police officer of enormous size was already looking him in the face from two steps down. Murray went to lean over the railing, and saw a small shape at the foot of the stairs.

'Found your way back, Walter? Well done.'

'Thank you, sir. Is – is Theodore all right?'

Murray glanced back into the room. Mrs. Sangster was on her knees beside her husband: whether she was tending to him or making sure he was dead, Murray neither knew nor cared. Theodore was watching his grandparents in complete disgust.

'I think so. Shall we bring him home with us for now?'

'Aye, sir. I'll give him the lend of some proper clothes, though.'

'Probably best.'

Epilogue

Edinburgh

It was the following Saturday when Murray, returning to Fortune's Hotel from a pleasant afternoon's walk with the boys and the straw-coloured dog, saw a familiar figure lurking outside the hotel entrance. He sent the boys ahead, and waited to see what would happen.

Willie Jack recognised Walter, looked about, and saw Murray. He waved, removed his hat, stuck it back on his head, and hurried up to meet him.

'Charles, um,' he began, and bowed. Murray returned the bow. He fingered his swordstick: he hoped that Willie Jack was not going to do something silly like calling him out. Willie Jack could not shoot for toffee.

'Willie Jack,' he acknowledged. 'I hope you are well.'

'Oh, aye, aye. Just about to leave for the country, you know, any day now.'

'Good. Much healthier than the town.'

'Aye, so they say. Hm. Ah ...'

'Did you need to talk to me?' Murray could not quite bring himself to apologise first: after all, Letitia had been the one doing most of the advances-making.

'Ah, yes, I suppose so. Look, I had a chat with Letitia's Uncle Brewster, do you remember him? Nice fellow, very short.' He waved a hand around waist level, indicating Uncle Brewster's limitations.

'Oh, yes, indeed,' said Murray.

'He said ... well, he explained ... well, he said that Letitia's always been a bit ... uncontrolled ...'

'Mm,' was all Murray could venture.

'And that you wouldn't be the first man she's, er ...'

'Cornered in a dark parlour?' said Murray drily.

'Something like that. I think stables have featured before, a couple of times.' He tailed away sadly. Murray tried not to think of Letitia and haylofts. He mostly succeeded. Poor Willie Jack.

'Anyway, if you want to move back, any time,' Willie Jack continued, with an eager expression.

'I think probably best not, Willie Jack. Anyway, you're off to the country soon and I must get back to Letho, once I can arrange where Theodore is going.'

'Oh, yes. I heard about the Sangsters. An odd bunch, wouldn't you say?'

'I would. But Willie Jack, let's be friends again, eh?' He held out his hand. Willie Jack took it without hesitation.

'That would please me prodigiously,' he said, and added wryly, 'You always said I was rotten at picking women, didn't you?' He laughed, but it lacked humour, and Murray did not do more than smile. After all, he had picked pretty badly himself, in the end. 'Oh, I forgot to say – I have to go, but there was someone called to see you yesterday. An officer.'

'Not George?'

'No, not George. I can't remember his name. I told him where you were, though: I daresay he'll turn up.'

Inside the hotel the landlord greeted Murray and told him the boys had gone out to the stableyard (which was where he himself preferred dogs to be, he added pointedly), and that Murray had a visitor in one of the parlours on the ground floor. An officer, he said. Murray hurried to the parlour. George's name had not appeared in the *Courant*'s casualty lists, but if something had happened to him before Wellington's mighty battle last Sunday – well, who knew?

The officer who stood when he entered the parlour was slim and well-favoured, and in the uniform of a lieutenant in the Royal Scots. His arm was in a sling, but everything else appeared sound, at a glance.

'Mr. Charles Murray? George Murray's brother?' the officer asked. Dread filled Murray's heart.

'That's so. Do you have news of him?'

'I have news from him, sir: I have brought you a letter, and I am to say that he hopes to see you soon.'

Murray's heart gave a bounce, then settled. He took the letter, and gestured to the officer to sit down.

'Whom do I have the honour of thanking, then?' he said.

'I'm James Argo, sir: and if there's any thanking, I should be thanking you. I believe you have been very busy on my account, and the men at the police office have told me a great deal about my late wife's appalling family. But tell me, sir, where is Theodore?'

But at that moment the parlour door burst open, and the boys ran in. Murray sighed: Walter would take some training when Theodore had gone.

'Father!' cried Theodore, and the next few minutes were lost in hugs and handshakings and a general relieved delight. Murray grinned, and toyed with George's letter, trying to be patient. At last Argo saw him.

'Sir, Murray – that is George Murray, of course – asked me to tell you to read that straightaway, so that if you have any questions you can ask me. But he's all right, sir, really.'

Murray tore open the wrapper and read. The letter was lengthy, by George's standards, though the writing was worse than usual.

'That's because he can't sit up yet,' said Argo, with a slightly suppressed chortle. Murray raised his eyebrows, and read on.

George casually mentioned being struck on the head by the falling beacon, then gave a rambling account of his own part in the fighting. Murray had heard of Hougoumont, having pored over the accounts in the papers: he shivered when George mentioned the fire. There was a great deal about a drummer boy which was confused, to say the least, and then about his senior officer, Saddler, of whom he had heard George speak before. The last bit left him gasping: Saddler had tried to kill the drummer boy, who turned out to be a girl, and the daughter of Captain Gunn, who had then killed Saddler. Saddler had also, it was thought, shot George in the buttock. There was some story, too, of how Saddler had previously taken an interest in Gunn's daughter in an inn, to the extent that Gunn had challenged one of Wellington's aides to distract Saddler – a Sir Alexander Gordon, who Murray remembered had died after the battle. It was all very confused, as George's letters often were. But what followed was even more extraordinary.

'Of course we had to go through Saddler's papers and try to find out who his people were, for he never mentioned any family. That was how we found out that he was actually a Peter Sangster, not Saddler at all. There was a letter from his mother in Edinburgh, and do you know it actually mentioned you? And me? Extraordinary. It turns out that Saddler thought that James the drummer boy was his nephew Theodore, in point of fact Argo's stepson that you've been seeking! Well: that explains everything. Or I daresay it does to you, and one day you'll explain it all to me again, and I still won't understand it.'

'Oh, my dear George,' murmured Murray.

'Anyway,' George went on, *'all healing up nicely and soon I might be able to get my breeches back on and eventually even sit on a horse. And then I think I'll leave this soldiering life, and find something else to do. Gunn's keen to carry on, though: now he has a wife as well as a daughter to support. The daughter's mother was some strumpet and died in her cups, leaving young Miss Jane alone. Then there was this Miss Carolina Fry, you see, who kept following us around, and as it turned out she had set her cap at Gunn. She's a clever little thing, but if you ask me, it's James – Jane, that is, who'll run the house. It's a shame she was found out: the army could do with boys like her, the sergeants of the future.'*

All very confusing, thought Murray. Jane and Carolina and who knew who else in the complications of George's life. He looked about him: Walter met his eye and tried to look dutiful under his fringe, while Theodore and Lieutenant Argo were talking nineteen to the dozen at each other and the straw-coloured dog sat between them as if it could not choose which was best. He grinned. It was not an entirely happy ending, but it would do. Tomorrow he would have to return to Fife, he supposed, but for now … He rang the bell, and ordered dinner for all of them. Tomorrow could wait.

About the Author

Lexie Conyngham lives in North-East Scotland and has been writing stories since she knew people did. The sequel to *Death of an Officer's Lady* is *Out of a Dark Reflection*. Follow her professional procrastination at www.murrayofletho.blogspot.com.

Out of a Dark Reflection:
Letho, Fife, 1816: Murray and his guests all have good reasons for not attending Edinburgh's winter season, even down to the new maid. But then an old woman is found dead in the village, and murmurings of witchcraft are abroad. Suddenly everyone seems to have secrets – but who would kill to keep theirs?

The Murray of Letho series:

Death in a Scarlet Gown
Knowledge of Sins Past
Service of the Heir
An Abandoned Woman
Fellowship with Demons
The Tender Herb: A Murder in Mughal India
Death of an Officer's Lady

Made in the USA
Coppell, TX
07 November 2020

40917195R00181